13 HARDCORE DIRTY STORIES

LACEY HARPER

13 HARDCORE DIRTY STORIES

LACEY HARPER

A collection of thirteen filthy erotic stories including...

Punished by the Vampire
Adrian seduces Holly into an erotic show she will never forget, one that might have deadly consequences.

Punished at the Casino
Busted by casino security for cheating at blackjack, Kat is faced with an impossible choice: a lifetime in prison, or one night with two guards. Ravaged, sweaty, and thoroughly busted, she allows the men to use every hole imaginable.

Punishing the Billionaire Heiress
Heiress Brittany is used to getting her way, but her bodyguards are sick of her princess attitude. They decide to teach her a lesson. Fast, rough, and double teamed!

Double Stuffed: Spring Break
An innocent Japanese co-ed isn't sure she can take a big

black cock. And if that isn't bad enough, two more guys show up to help triple team every last hole.

Punishing Bridezilla
When Bridezilla Blair throws a wedding cake topper at the staff, they decide to teach her a lesson in humility. In a secret dungeon, the young, innocent bride is taken unprotected in every position imaginable. But, the rough, sweaty, demanding action won't be complete until her fiancé finishes the lesson.

Taken Hard by 5 Billionaires
Five dirty-hot internet billionaires stuff a sexy real estate agent in every room of the house. She might not make the sale, but she'll be more than satisfied.

Wild and Wasted: Spring Break
Sorority princess Ruby's Spring Break is out of control. A lesbian lover and a pack of wild frat guys are ready to show her how filthy she can get.

Maid for Punishment
When Krista's boss handcuffs her to his bed, she knows she's in trouble. The maid endures a long, hard punishment session and gets a lesson in everything she never knew she needed.

Double Teaming Audrey
No hole's off limits for this naughty sorority escort. Two hot CEOs want to do dirty, filthy things to her and by the time they're done, she might not be able to walk away.

Brittany's Ménage

Sorority escort Brittany can't wait to sixty-nine her friend and suck on her sweet little clit. After she's done making her come harder than she's ever come in her life, she's going to give their pro-football client the roughest, filthiest ride of his life.

Candy
Sorority escort Candy picks up a total stranger while driving on the highway. The next thing she knows, she's in a storage unit with a cock in her mouth. Could life get any better?

Delia's Dungeon
Sorority escort Delia likes to be spanked until her ass cheeks burn and tears fill her eyes. Her client is taking her to a private club tonight to put her on display. She's wet just thinking about it.

Training Temptation
Caught in a web of deceit, Caroline must run the race of her life to save her family home. Her reputation as the high society owner of the #1 stable for Ponygirls in the world is on the line. And, there's only one man who can help her win.

Sign up for Lacey's email newsletter

13 Hardcore Dirty Stories

Copyright© 2018 Lacey Harper
All rights reserved.

No part of this book may be reproduced in any form or by any electronic or mechanical means including information storage and retrieval systems, without permission in writing from the author. The only exception is by a reviewer, who may quote short excerpts in a review.

This book is a work of fiction. Names, characters, places, and incidents either are products of the author's imagination or are used fictitiously. Any resemblance to actual persons, living or dead, events, or locales is entirely coincidental.

❦ Created with Vellum

PUNISHED AT THE CASINO

Kat squirmed in the worn faux leather seat as she added to her already towering stack of casino chips. The dampness between her legs made her bare pussy lips glide across each other. The friction increased her excitement to the point where she didn't know what aroused her more, stealing from the casino or allowing the ancient blackjack dealer to stare down the front of her carefully selected scarlet dress.

"Hit." She tapped a painted nail against the well faded felt.

The dealer peeled off another card. As expected, a five. Her crappy sixteen turned into a twenty-one. Nice score.

The dealer shook his head. "Nice hit against a dealer six."

She leaned forward to rest her breasts on the lip of the table. "I had a feeling about that one."

His gaze dropped to her chest. "You seem to have a lot of feelings."

"I have all kinds." She winked.

A cocktail waitress well past her prime set a dirty martini on the felt. Kat slipped her a green chip.

The old woman's lips twitched into a hint of a smile as the tip clanged into a jar on the tray. "Thanks honey. When I was your age, it rained green. Not so much these days."

Kat intentionally chose an older off strip casino. Security wasn't as tight as some of the newer, flashier casinos, and the senior citizen dealers were too busy staring at her coed body to pay attention to how much money she took off the tables.

She turned to the dealer and set a stack of chips worth five thousand into the betting circle. "I'd like a BJ."

"What?" The dealer's eyes flashed with the type of lust usually reserved for younger men.

She plucked the olive-stacked toothpick from the drink and licked the length of it. "I like big stacks."

Across the table, her partner in crime rolled his eyes. Part of the game involved flirting with the dealers, but she intentionally did it to excess. She liked to watch Ben squirm. Their agreement involved money but never sex. To get involved with a fellow crook invited danger and she needed to avoid that at all costs. Her twin sister's life depended on the money she stole from the casino.

The dealer's gnarled hand patted the felt. "Hit or stay?"

She adjusted her special glasses and checked the next card in the deck. A luminous green mark on the corner indicated a face card. She couldn't hit even though she only had a thirteen.

"Stay."

"Against a dealer ten?" The dealer coughed into his hand then opened both palms to show the cameras.

"That's what I said."

Ben waved a hand over his cards. "I'll stay too."

The dealer grunted and turned over a sixteen. He added

the next card to the total and busted. "If I didn't know better, I'd say you were pros."

Kat tried not to smile as he counted out another five thousand in chips. "I don't even know that guy."

Ben shot her a disarming smile. "But you'd like to."

He reminded her of a young James Dean. So sexy, but with a thief's heart. Too bad. In another time and place maybe they could have shared something.

Kat counted the stack. Twenty thousand dollars. She'd never tried to take this much before, but her sister's medical bills were past due. The relentless collection agencies called Molly several times a day which made recovering from chemo even harder.

Kat glanced at Ben. He set a red chip on the edge of his napkin. She ignored the signal to stop.

Ben yawned and shot her a pointed look. "It's getting late. One more hand and I'm calling it done."

She ignored his glare. One more hand and she'd have all the money she needed to get the medical bills paid.

She shoved a stack of orange chips into the betting circle.

The dealer didn't hesitate to yell over his shoulder. "Checks play."

A tingle of warning whispered up her spine. Her heart raced as the pit boss stalked to the table. Built like a line backer, the man looked ready to kill.

He glared at her. "Go ahead."

An ace landed in front of the pillar of orange chips. The dealer placed a card in front of Ben and one face down in front of himself.

She glanced at the deck. The glasses already told her she'd walk out a winner. She didn't flinch as a king landed on the ace to give her a blackjack.

The pit boss' face pinched as he studied her. She tried to play it cool, as if winning this much money happened to her every day.

The dealer matched her stack then set another stack half as high next to it. She did a quick calculation. The mountain of orange chips equaled fifty thousand dollars. Exactly the amount she needed.

"Goodnight gentlemen." She scooped the chips into her purse then slid off the chair.

She hurried toward the cashier's cage. After this, she'd never have to step into a smelly, smoky casino again. She'd never have to endure the leers from the employees. Never have to worry about being caught and arrested. She could almost taste freedom.

The woman at the cage whispered into a telephone. She glanced at Kat and turned away. What was that all about?

Kat stacked the chips into neat piles of ten while she waited for the woman to turn around. A tinge of guilt snaked around her heart. She hated stealing the money, but she had no choice. How else would she raise this much money in such a short amount of time?

The woman finally turned and stared at the piles. "That's a lot of chips."

Something felt off about the woman. Kat's voice quivered. "I'd like to cash them in."

The cashier smirked. "I bet you would."

Suddenly, a rough hand clutched her left arm. "What the—"

"Let's go honey. We need to have a little chat."

Kat yanked but couldn't free herself. "Let go of me. I was just leaving."

"No. You weren't."

The man half dragged her to a door next to the cage. He punched a code into the keypad and the door clicked open.

"Where the hell are you taking me?"

He didn't respond. A long empty hallway stretched before them. She scrambled to keep up with his long strides.

At the end of the hall, he turned left and continued down another corridor. After a maze of turns, she doubted she'd ever be able to find her way back to the casino floor.

He stopped in front of another door and keyed in a code. The door cracked open. He tugged her into a large barren room. A single light bulb hung over a faded wooden table. Several metal chairs lined the room. Two chairs flanked opposite ends of the table.

"Sit," he commanded.

She didn't have much choice so she perched on the edge of one of the chairs. He wore a security officer's uniform complete with a radio and a pair of shiny handcuffs. A glint of light flashed off the cuffs as if to warn her. The security guard stared her down with gun-metal-grey eyes. A shudder rippled across her chest. She couldn't go to jail.

A pervasive silence filled the room. No sound seeped in from beyond the walls. In the bowels of the enormous casino, they were completely alone.

His gruff voice cut through the quiet. "How long did you think you could steal from the casino and get away with it?"

She crossed her arms over her chest. "I don't know what you're talking about."

He snatched the glasses from her face. "It will be easy enough to convict you. These are so obvious, it's a joke."

"Convict me?"

"Of theft. In Nevada it carries a minimum sentence of at least two years. But for fifty thousand, I'm sure the judge will slap on a few more."

"But I didn't steal anything."

"Right. And you're probably a poor innocent virgin too."

Well, he got the poor part right. "Look, I'll leave the money if you'll just let me go."

"It doesn't work that way."

"What are you going to do, break my legs?"

He threw his head back and laughed so hard tears formed in the corners of his eyes. He wiped them away with the back of his hand. "Oh, you're a good one. You seriously think we still break people's legs?"

"That's what they do in the movies."

He grabbed the chair opposite hers, spun it around then straddled it. "On paper, we're one of the biggest corporations in Vegas. The shareholders wouldn't approve of the old school methods for dealing with cheaters. But since we're off strip, we do things a little differently around here. Things shareholders don't need to know about."

"But..." She stammered.

"You have a nice one."

"What?"

"Butt."

She frowned. He couldn't mean—.

"Your ass. You have a nice ass. Nice tits too."

Her lips parted and a puff of air rushed out. "You can't talk to me like that. I want a lawyer."

"I bet you do."

She stabbed the table with a finger. "Right now."

The door swung open and another security guard strolled into the room. His broad shoulders and buzz haircut projected a commanding presence. Ex-military for sure. In any other situation, she'd be dripping wet for someone like him. But terror kept her in line.

The commander's voice rumbled like a desert storm. "Joe, what you got?"

"Thief. Used these glasses in the blackjack pit and took 50K off the tables." The glasses scraped along the wood as he pushed them across the table.

His superior picked up the glasses and studied them. "Wasn't she the one from last weekend?"

"Came back."

The commander smirked. "They always do."

"She thought we were going to break her legs."

A grin spread across the commander's face. "Oh no, honey. Not those sexy legs. We wouldn't dream of it. But you're going to jail for a very long time."

She hunched forward and pressed her face into her hands. A sob exploded from her chest. "Please, I'll do anything. I can't go to jail."

The commander moved to stand behind her. He gathered her flowing hair into his fist and yanked it back. She yelped.

"What do you mean by, anything?" He released his grip.

She rubbed her scalp to take away the sting. "I don't know, but I can't go to jail."

The men exchanged a look.

Joe leaned back in the chair and rested his boots on the table. "So you're willing to do anything?"

"Anything at all." She couldn't go to jail. How could she possibly help her sister if she was behind bars?

"Give us a minute." The commander motioned for Joe to follow him to the far corner of the room.

The walls sucked their whispers into them. She desperately wanted to get out of the situation but the longer they talked, the more anxious she became.

After a couple of minutes, they broke their huddle and returned to the table. They each took a chair.

The commander leaned his elbows on the table. "We've come up with an acceptable solution."

She leaned forward. "And?"

Joe spoke. "Fuck us until sunrise and we'll let you go. No charges, no one needs to know."

"No way." They had to be joking.

The commander's voice became softer. "We're giving you a way out. You seem like a nice girl caught up in a bad situation. You don't want to go to jail, do you?"

"No. But, I can't do things to you guys."

Joe smiled. "You'll be surprised at what you will do to stay out of jail."

She stared at the lines of wood in the table. One night of sex in exchange for spending years in jail? She shook her head. She couldn't believe she was even considering their offer.

The commander stood and motioned to Joe. "We'll give you a minute before you answer. Think about it and we'll be back."

She didn't say a word as they exited the room. She waited thirty seconds then ran to the door. She twisted the doorknob but nothing happened. Apparently the door locked from the outside as well as the inside.

She paced the room. Escape was impossible so she really only had two choices: years in prison, or one night with the guards. She swore she'd never have sex for money. But she wasn't screwing them for cash. One night wouldn't make her a hooker, especially since they weren't going to give her the money.

How terrible could it possibly be? She'd never been with two guys at once, but they seemed nice enough. And hot.

Just watching the commander stalk across the room caused a familiar tingle in her pussy. If he hit on her in a bar, she'd be naked and spread for him within an hour. She squirmed in the chair.

By the time they returned she'd made peace with her choice. After all, what other choice did she really have?

Joe entered the room with a tray of drinking glasses. "Thirsty?"

Her dry lips and parched throat longed for water. "Yes."

The commander walked in and kicked the door closed. He held a pitcher of water and a bottle of booze.

She reached for the water.

The commander grabbed her wrist. "Not until we hear your answer."

A rush of heat blazed across her skin. If she had any doubt about her choice, his firm grip destroyed it.

She blushed and spoke in a more seductive voice than she intended. "I'll do it."

"Do what?"

"Everything you want."

"Everything?" The commander asked.

"I'll fuck you guys. Is that what you wanted to hear?"

The commander poured a glass of water and handed it to her. "It's not going to be bad. We won't hurt you."

Joe stood and walked behind her. He rested his hands on her shoulders then began a slow, sensual massage. "Have a drink. You'll loosen up and get into it."

His hands slid across her collarbone then dipped into the hem of the dress. When his warm fingers cupped her heavy breasts, she trembled. Oh God, if they found out how sensitive her nipples were, she'd do anything they wanted.

The commander poured a glass of amber liquid. "How old are you anyway?"

"Twenty-two."

He handed the drink to her. "At least you're legal. Drink up, sweetie."

She grabbed the glass. Her hand trembled. Liquid sloshed over the sides and dripped onto the table. She tipped back the glass until the alcohol burnt a trail of fire down her throat.

She coughed and handed the empty glass back. "What was that, Pahrump moonshine?"

One of Joe's hands left her breast and brushed the hair away from her neck. "Relax, sweetie. This is going to be a night you'll never forget."

His lips whispered against the little patch of skin behind her ear that made her slouch against the back of the chair. She closed her eyes and surrendered to the exquisite pleasure.

The commander's boots echoed on the concrete. He stopped directly in front of her. "Stand up."

Her eyes fluttered open. She followed his orders and stood with her back to Joe.

The commander hooked his thumbs under the shoulder of her dress then yanked down the fabric. A few of the threads holding the dress together tore apart. The sound of ripping fabric and his controlled violence excited the nerves along her spine.

He descended on her like a wild man. His hands cupped her ass and pulled her tight against his virile body. The bulge between his legs dug into her thigh. He kicked her legs apart and pulled her up so quickly that she acted on instinct and wrapped both legs around his hips.

She gasped.

Still fully clothed, he laid her back on the table. "Get her shoes."

Joe unbuckled the black satin straps and flung the shoes across the room where they clattered against the wall.

The commander gripped the front of her dress and tore it open. The lust in his eyes both scared and aroused her.

His open palms traced the trembling flesh on her belly. Overwhelmed by a cacophony of emotion, she didn't resist as he grabbed her hips and dragged her to the edge of the table.

The tattered remains of the dress tangled around her arms. She struggled free and swiped them off the table.

Joe watched with a gleam in his eye. "Damn Mac, she's fuckin' hot."

The commander grunted.

Mac. She wanted to roll his name around in her mouth. Savor it. Lick the hard edge of each letter.

The air conditioning kicked on sending a chill across her breasts. Her nipples squeezed into taut peaks. Mac bent to lick the hard ridges. The rasp of his tongue against her flesh made her arch into him. The exceptionally sensitive skin warmed to his touch. His fingers replaced his tongue and he pinched until she gasped from the delicious pain.

Her legs splayed open. A slow heat gathered in the folds of her soaked pussy. Wet panties clung to the bare patch. She desperately wanted to remove the last swatch of fabric that kept her from being completely naked, but Mac grabbed her wrists.

"No. No, sweetie." He pulled the pair of sleek handcuffs from his belt and slapped them onto her wrists.

Before she could protest, Mac cuffed her left ankle. He hooked the open side of the cuffs to something under the table. She wiggled her leg but couldn't move more than a couple of inches. He repeated the process with the other ankle.

Bound, she struggled against the cuffs. "Wait. You guys didn't say anything about bondage."

Joe responded. "You said we could do anything."

"And that includes cuffs." Mac finished.

She wriggled against the table. Trapped and completely at their mercy, her breath came in short pants. She glanced from one man to the other. What else did they have in mind?

The scrape of Mac's belt drew her attention. He pulled the leather strap back until the buckle slid free. Her tongue darted out to wet her lips.

He coiled the belt around his huge fist then laid it on the table a few inches from her head. She turned and inhaled the earthy fragrance. The scent of leather curled into her, so primitive, so primal. The essence of sex distilled into a potent aphrodisiac.

Mac's predatory gaze traveled across the flat plane of her stomach to the valley between her thighs. He unbuttoned the shirt and tossed it across her face. Blinded, she waited.

Her breasts yearned for their touch. Her hips arched toward them, ready to be pounded into the table. And her feverish clit begged for their attention.

Across the room where Joe stood, clothes rustled to the floor. Both men approached her. Mac whisked the shirt from her eyes. He stood before her, naked and erect. A dark thatch of hair trailed from his bellybutton to the patch over his cock. A drop of pre-cum glistened in the light.

She took a deep breath, closed her eyes and realized that no matter what happened tonight, it would be the most erotic night of her life.

∽

Joe strolled to the side of the table where her hands were cuffed. "Stroke me." At his command, she curled her fingers around the heat of Joe's rigid cock. The handcuffs clinked against the table as the little thief's wrist settled into a slow rhythm.

Joe couldn't believe she actually went along with their farce. Usually the women lawyer'd up and wouldn't say another word. But not this one. This one wanted to avoid jail at all costs, even if it meant taking both guys at once.

He closed his eyes. The woman's soft hand slid up and down the length of his shaft. It'd been too long since the last time he got laid. He needed this. He only wished she wasn't cuffed to the table already.

"Is this alright?"

"Just keep strokin' it baby."

He reached across the table and brushed one finger over her plump lips. She gently bit the tip of his finger then sucked it into her mouth.

The suction made his cock longer, thicker. If she wanted something between those lips, he'd give it to her.

He backed out of her hand and positioned himself over her face. He cupped her chin and tilted her head back. He push the tip of his cock against her lips but she didn't immediately open for him.

On the other side of the table, Mac rubbed his hands down the inside of her thighs. She trembled but didn't protest. Maybe she liked being used by two guys at once.

Mac's fingers brushed across her belly then dipped down toward her pussy. He pressed a knuckle against the top of her slit. She moaned.

Joe took the opportunity to push into her slightly open lips. "Suck my dick, baby."

She slurped it into her mouth. Pleasure slammed into

him. The sucking about killed him. He fell forward and grabbed one of her perky breasts in each hand. He held on long enough to steady himself, and then he slapped one firm tit.

A gurgling sound exploded from her throat but she didn't even scrape him with her teeth. Damn the girl could suck cock. Her little pink tongue swirled over the top and lapped at the length before she gulped the entire shaft back into her mouth.

Joe flung his head back and pinched the pink nipples between his thumb and forefinger. He tugged and twisted and pressed harder.

She tore her mouth away. "Wait, oh God."

He rammed his cock back into her mouth and thrust deep. The little cocksucker didn't miss a beat and swallowed every inch of him. His balls slapped against her forehead as he drove into her mouth.

At the other end of the table, Mac's head dipped between her thighs. Joe watched his head bob and weave in time with her thrashing hips. Whatever he was doing with his tongue was driving her crazy.

Joe pulled all the way out then slid back in as far as he could go. He held his cock there until she sputtered then pulled out. She gasped for air then dragged him back in.

Tension built at the base of his spine. Her soft warm mouth worked the shaft then released it. She frantically lapped at his balls. A tingle of heat trickled from his spine into his balls and down the shaft to the tip of his cock.

As much fun as it was to fuck her face, he wanted to stuff his cock into her wet pussy. He stumbled back, grabbed the head of his cock and pinched hard to keep from coming.

Mac snickered. "Almost blew all over her face."

"Fuck you." Joe laughed.

Mac thumbed the length of her slit. "Sweet pussy."

On the table, the woman groaned. "Please, I need…"

Mac made a "V" with his fingers and captured her clit between them. "What was that?"

"I'm so close." She bucked against his hand.

"Oh not yet honey, you have a long way to go." Mac flicked the bud with his finger.

Her hips jerked off the table and she screamed.

"Sensitive."

"You think that's sensitive? Stick it in her mouth." Joe wanted Mac to get the hell out of the way. He needed to try out her hot pussy.

Mac traded places with him and stuffed his cock into her mouth. She slurped and sucked until drool dribbled out of the edges of her mouth.

Joe ran to his pants and grabbed a rubber. Always prepared. There should be a merit badge for having a condom ready at all times. He almost laughed out loud as he tore open the package and rolled it on.

He returned to the table, grabbed her hips and dragged them to the edge. He rubbed the tip of his cock against her slick entrance then slowly slid into ecstasy.

Kat's thighs spread under Joe's weight. When she heard the wrapper crinkle, she breathed a sigh of relief. She'd hooked up with the occasional guy in a bar but always brought her own condom. Apparently Joe did the same.

She couldn't see past Mac's balls but felt the tip of Joe's cock press into her sopping wet pussy. She arched to meet him and opened her mouth wider for Mac. She'd never been so filled in her life. Why hadn't she ever tried this before?

Two guys at once was a challenge. At first their rhythm was off and she couldn't decide what she liked better, the cock in her pussy or the dick in her mouth. She decided to match Joe's rhythm. Mac caught on quickly and within a minute, he would thrust into her mouth as Joe pulled out of her pussy. They were like some perverted version of a rowing team and she loved it.

Joe dragged her hips to the edge of the table. "Dammit Mac, this is a pain in the ass with the cuffs. Let's unlock her so we can really fuck her hard."

Mac drew back. "Sure. But I get to fuck her now."

Joe grabbed a set of keys from the floor. They jangled as the men unlocked her ankles and wrists. She rubbed the red marks. They'd fade by tomorrow, but in the meantime, she'd have to find a way to hide the marks from her sister.

Mac hoisted her off the table and flung her over one shoulder. He knelt and laid her on a pile of clothes. Her hip touched a cold patch of concrete. Before she could protest, Mac rolled her onto her belly then dragged her up by the hips.

His cock plunged into her aching pussy without warning. She cried out in surprise. A quick stab of lust made her moan and push back to meet him. She wanted every inch of him all the way inside. Deep. Hard. Rough.

He pounded her as Joe watched them from across the room. Her nipples scraped the icy floor. The friction heated the tips and sent warmth flooding straight to her clit.

She rolled her hips and pressed back to draw him deeper. He slapped her ass hard enough to sting the skin. Her eyes rolled back as he hit her other cheek. Back and forth, he pummeled her ass until it burned.

"Get the belt." Mac gestured toward the table.

Joe strode across the room, retrieved the belt then handed it to Mac. She twisted and watched as he doubled the belt over into a loop.

He didn't stop pumping her as he spanked her with the belt. The extra stimulation brought her to the brink of orgasm. She didn't know how much longer she could take the sting of leather on her ass.

Joe knelt down in front of her. "Give me the belt."

Mac handed it over.

"Get her face out of the way."

Mac grabbed a fistful of hair and yanked her head back. She arched back but he continued to pull until she sat back on her knees.

Joe rubbed the belt across her breasts. "You're very sensitive here, aren't you?"

"Yes." Her pussy throbbed around Mac's cock.

Joe flicked little hits across her chest and concentrated blows over her nipples. "You've been a very bad girl. Do you deserve to have your tits punished?"

She nodded.

"I didn't hear you." Joe dropped the belt and pinched her nipples so hard, a sliver of pain sliced through her pussy.

"Ouch. Yes. I mean, no." She couldn't think past the pain. Joe twisted and pulled so hard, a trickle of sweat worked its way down her back.

Mac released her hair. She fell forward and Joe relinquished his grip. Blood rushed into the sensitive peaks. They burned with scorching heat. Suddenly desperate for release, she thrashed against Mac. The animalistic need to fuck overwhelmed her. Nothing mattered but sensation. Pain, pleasure and the growing need to come overtook every thought.

Mac held her by the waist with one arm. Their skin slapped together as he pounded her pussy.

Rampant lust flashed in Joe's eyes. "Let's DP her."

"I get her ass."

She didn't know what they were talking about but before she could ask, Mac lay down and pulled her on top of him. He plunged into her soaked pussy.

Behind her, Mac rubbed his cock along the crease between her buttocks. The second she realized what he intended to do, she tried to crawl away.

"Where are you going?" Joe pinned her against his chest.

Mac parted her ass cheeks and spit against the puckered hole. "This is going to be tight."

"If you can't handle it—"

"I got it." Mac snapped.

The head of Mac's cock pressed against her asshole.

"You can't fuck me there." She swung her ass to the left to avoid his probing cock.

"We can fuck you any way we want. That was the deal."

Tears formed in the corners of her eyes as the piercing pain seared every nerve ending in her ass. The tip forced its way further into her tight little hole.

"Oh, God." She whimpered.

"Fuck this, it's too tight. I'm getting lube." Mac stood. He pulled on his pants and shirt then left the room.

Kat pleaded to Joe. "Please let me go."

"You know the deal. We get you until morning, then we cut you loose." He thrust into her quivering pussy as if to make his point.

The door swung open and Mac returned. Kat almost fainted when she saw who stood directly behind him.

∽

Ben threw the door shut and followed Mac into the interrogation room. He'd been under cover in a lot of places, but he'd never seen a suspect stripped naked and impaled on another security guard's cock.

"What the fuck is going on here?"

A look of relief washed over Kat's face. "Oh thank God. Get me out of here."

Joe grinned up at him. "Hey Ben, how's it hanging?"

"I thought we were busting this one. What the hell are you doing fucking a suspect?"

"We made a deal. She fucks us until sunrise then she's free to go. I'm guessing we have an hour to go?"

Ben washed a hand over his face. Everyone in the room could go to jail for one thing or another. Shit, he'd worked this thief undercover for a month and was on the verge of busting her. Now what?

Sweat pooled in the small of Kat's back. He'd wanted to fondle her luscious body for weeks but she'd never let him touch her. Now he had the chance. He'd be an idiot not to take it.

He stared at her. "You agreed to this?"

She flushed. "I can't go to jail. I was only stealing to pay for my sister's medical bills. I... I had to agree."

Joe bounced her on his dick. "Don't worry man, she liked every second of it."

"Not when you tried to fuck my ass."

Ben turned to Mac and raised an eyebrow. "Classy."

"What? She has a nice tight ass. Why not?"

Why not indeed. Ben cleared his throat. "Here's how this is going to go down. We all fuck every hole. Nothing leaves this room and no one tries pulling this bullshit again. Got it?"

The other two men responded in unison. "Yep."

Kat flinched. "No."

"This is a really good deal for you Kat. I recorded all of our conversations about the cheating. We have enough on you to get a felony conviction."

"It hurt when he tried."

Mac handed a bottle to Ben. "I was coming back with this when you spotted me."

"Nice." Ben flicked open the bottle. He set it on the table and began to strip. What a crazy night. He thought he was coming in to bust her ass, and now he was about to bust it. Literally.

His semi-erect cock sprung out of his pants. Just seeing her bare ass wiggle as Joe fucked her pussy made him hard.

Joe pointed to the pile of discarded clothes. "Condom in my pants."

Ben retrieved a foil package and quickly slid the rubber on. His knees cracked as he dropped to the floor. He grabbed the bottle and slathered the lube over his dick. With one finger, he scooped lube into her puckered hole. He set the bottle on the floor next to him in case he needed more. Anal was good as long as your cock didn't get raw from all the friction.

He positioned himself behind her and poked against her ass. "Relax Kat. It only hurts if you're too tense."

He continued to press forward until the head forced its way into her hole. He rubbed her ass cheek. "Good girl. Open up. Don't forget to breathe."

She responded with a whimper.

The tiny passage barely opened as he shoved a little more in. The muscles started to relax and to allow him to go deeper. He didn't let up. Inch by inch, he buried his cock into the woman he'd wanted more than any other woman in the world. He couldn't believe his luck. Good thing the other guys were such conniving bastards.

"Oh." She gasped as his cock slid past the tense ring of muscles that rimmed the inner edge of her ass.

Nice. A little further and he'd be balls deep.

"Ben, wait." She moaned.

He ignored her plea and crammed the last inch in. He waited as her body adjusted to his girth. The trembling, panting woman grabbed someone's discarded shirt and clung to it.

Joe pumped her pussy. She shuddered and moaned.

Ben pulled halfway out then stuffed her again. The vice-like grip was better than anything he'd felt in his entire life.

Kat gave up on escaping Ben. He violated her ass with thick deep strokes. Between his girth and Joe's relentless thrusts, she gave in to the haze of pleasure clouding her mind. The pain melted into something she'd never experienced before, a white space where she floated in a sea of ecstatic bliss.

Everything they did to her sent another shockwave through her pussy. Mac knelt in front of her and she opened her mouth for him. Every hole filled, she moved in perfect unison with them. Within minutes, the spacey sensation gave way to a rush of tension in her body.

Her muscles went rigid. She stopped breathing. The first clench of orgasm erupted throughout every cell in her body. Ripped apart, she came so hard, her heart slammed against her ribs.

Mac pulled out of her mouth.

A near inhuman scream echoed throughout the room as she thrashed violently on their cocks. The first splash of

Mac's cum landed on her cheek. It dribbled between her breasts.

Joe jerked up and his cock twitched in her pussy. The throbbing blended with her own until she couldn't separate one from the other. They came inside of her, all over her, still pounding, still jamming their cocks into her.

Ben pummeled her asshole with quick shallow strokes followed by one deep stroke. But the thrusts went deeper and faster until he grabbed her hips and rammed her so hard, her arms collapsed.

He continued to fuck her even as she lay flat on Joe's chest.

"Fuck, let me get up." Joe's cock slipped out of her pussy.

She pushed up enough to allow him to slide out from under her. Ben didn't stop fucking her ass. He pounded her so hard, her hip bones dug into the floor.

Finally, when she didn't think she could take another second, he growled and pumped a load into her ass. He shuttered and collapsed onto her. Their slick bodies stuck together as they both lay panting.

Ben's cock popped out of her ass as he rocked back. She crawled forward a foot then rolled onto her back.

Mac dug a watch out of his pants. "It's morning. Shift's over. See you guys tomorrow."

Joe and Mac dug through the pile of clothes, quickly dressed and then left the room.

Ben turned to her. "You okay?"

Kat's body buzzed with the aftermath of being taken by three guys at once. "I will be."

"Don't think about it too hard. You did what you had to do."

The reality of her situation crashed over her. "My sister... I'll never be able to help her now."

Ben opened his mouth as if to say something then closed it. He left the room.

Kat gathered up the tattered dress. She couldn't think. She just wanted to get out of the casino and go home but she couldn't leave half naked.

Ben returned with a wad of paper towels, jeans and a black t-shirt. "Here, you can wear these out. Clean up."

She used the damp towels to wipe the sticky cum off her face.

Ben looked anywhere but at her. He almost seemed embarrassed. "Look, I know your situation. About your sister. Nothing about tonight was by the book so I figure... Well, don't take all the chips to the cage at once. Send someone else in to cash them out. No one's going to say a word about what happened tonight. We could all lose our jobs."

"What are you saying?"

"You can keep the money. But never, ever come back here again."

She eyed him with suspicion. "Is this a trick?"

"No. You don't tell, we don't tell. Deal?"

She nodded slowly. She buckled the sandals then asked, "How do I get out?"

"Follow me." He led her into the hallway, along a series of corridors and out into a side parking lot.

She turned to thank him but he was already gone. The first rays of sunlight streaked the sky a pale pink and she knew she'd never step foot in that casino again.

PUNISHED BY THE VAMPIRE

Holly regretted the last glass of blood red Burgundy wine. Two hours into the Halloween party and already the grand ballroom was warm enough to qualify as the first level of hell.

She lifted ringlets of hair off the nape of her neck then fanned away the heat with a cream colored fan. When she'd chosen the Marie Antoinette costume, she assumed the autumn wind would curl across the ocean and race up the cliffs to Dragdon Manor to chill its occupants. She decided on the enormous 18th century dress thinking it would keep her warm.

She set the empty glass on the tray of a liveried waiter and cut through the crowd. The huge hoops of her gown brushed against the costumes of the other partygoers. A few of the men turned to glance at her as she passed. Their eyes fell from her face to the swell of her breasts. Several men approached her, but she ignored their requests to dance.

The first chords of a lone violin vibrated a haunting melody through the room. As the orchestra joined the soloist, the sound intensified the pounding of her heat induced headache. She just needed a few minutes outside, away from the crowd and in relative silence.

She drifted along an empty hallway at the rear of the mansion. She spotted a somewhat hidden doorway which led to a secluded veranda.

The door creaked as she opened it. She stepped out and the chilly air pushed the door closed. She drifted toward the edge of the balcony and rested her forearms on the cold stone.

A breeze whipped the first tendrils of fog across the ocean. The moon cast fingers of ghostly light across the fog as it seeped into the garden below. A shiver raced up her spine.

A man's voice cut through the silence. "Good evening. Are you enjoying the party?"

Surprised, she jumped and turned to him. She sucked in a breath then tilted her head up to take in every inch of his seductive beauty. Moonlight rimmed his hair in a silvery glow. His devilish features sent a ripple of desire though her body.

For a second, nothing moved, not even a breath of air. She couldn't hear the crash of the waves against the cliffs. The chill left the air. Even the ever present rustle of her skirts stopped.

He stepped toward her. A long black cape cracked behind him like a whip. His deep voice broke the spell. "I didn't mean to startle you."

Her hand fluttered to her neck. She twisted a long string of pearls between her fingers. "I didn't hear the door open."

A smile played across his thick sensual lips. "I can be quiet when necessary."

Somewhere in the back of her mind she knew something about the man was very strange. Completely secluded and alone, a whisper of warning tingled up her back.

"Were you trying to sneak up on me?"

"No."

Mesmerized by the flecks of gold in his eyes, she couldn't look away. The depth of passion contained in those eyes stunned her. She wondered what he was like in bed, and then quickly shook the thought away.

"I was just going inside." As she brushed past him, he caught her upper arm with one hand. Warmth flooded the lower part of her body.

"Stay for a moment."

She opened her mouth intending to say no. "Just for a minute."

"You have something that I want." His eyes locked with hers and he caressed the goose bumps on her arm.

She couldn't look away from the desire in his eyes. They captivated her and set her into a light trance.

She spoke in a whisper. "What do you want?"

"You, in every way imaginable."

A liquid heat pooled in space between her legs. She bit the edge of her bottom lip hard enough to draw a drop of blood.

He pulled her against the broad expanse of his chest. She could hardly breathe as he lowered his mouth toward hers.

His eyes, those strange flecks of gold seemed to glow as if ignited by an internal flame.

"Don't be afraid."

She heard him speak but could have sworn his lips didn't move. He brushed the softest kiss across her lips. She couldn't believe she was kissing a man she didn't know.

With his tongue, he parted her lips. He licked the cut then sucked the edge of her lip into his mouth.

Her knees buckled. He caught her in his arms. The electric kiss sapped all thoughts of resistance and left only pure unadulterated lust.

She returned his kiss with a passion she never thought possible. He scooped her into his arms and carried her to the balcony. He set her on the ledge and she clung to him to keep from falling over.

Her fingers tangled in his thick hair. His hands slid up the boning that created her hourglass waist. She cursed the thick corset. Suddenly the only thing she wanted in the world was to have his hands all over her naked body.

His tongue pressed against her demanding something she wasn't sure she could give. The intensity of kiss left her breathless and panting.

He lifted up the hem of her skirt. His hand found the back of her knees then slid up the sides of her thighs. She wanted his hands to go further, to part her thighs and reach for the delicate folds of her wet pussy.

Over his shoulder, the door creaked open.

He jerked back. His eyes flared with rage. "You shouldn't be here."

"What?" In a haze of need, she couldn't understand what he meant. Then a man stepped into the moonlight and she understood perfectly.

Adrian pushed the trembling woman behind him. Of course the other vampires would come at the first scent of blood.

"This one isn't for you." He glared at Marcos.

The older vampire glided across the veranda. He sniffed

the air. "Virgin blood. She's exactly what we need tonight. Our power wanes on the night of the full moon and it must be restored."

Adrian silently cursed himself for putting the irresistible woman in danger. He planned only to take a taste of her, just enough to keep the painful suck of the moon's energy from overtaking him.

"There are a hundred other women to choose from, many of them willing to offer up their necks to you."

Marcos' laughter cut through the night. "Yes, but none as sweet as this one."

Adrian shoved Marcos but was no match for the elder's power. Marcos backhanded him with full force. Adrian flew across the veranda and slammed into the wall. He stood just as Marcos caressed the cheek of the woman.

"What is your name child?" The wicked lust in Marco's voice made Adrian sick to his stomach.

"Holly." She murmured.

Marcos held out his pale hand. "Come with me. We have a very special party planned for you."

Holly clasped his hand. "Yes, a party."

Adrian recognized the glassy look in her eye. Marcos' magical enchantment was too powerful for any human to resist.

Marcos regarded him with a look of pity. "You may watch if you like."

Adrian clenched his fists. He pressed his lips together to keep from saying anything to enrage the other man. He needed to wait until it was safe to free her.

He trailed behind the pair as they made their way through the mansion. They traveled along the hallway and up the rear stairs to the third floor.

Adrian's gut clenched when he realized which room the

other man headed toward. Someone as delicate and gentle as this woman would never be able to stand the Dungeon of Pain. Maybe if he could convince Marcos.

Adrian grabbed Marco's shoulder. "Wait, allow me to punish her."

Marcos raised an eyebrow. "Quite a sudden change of heart."

"You're right. You've always know that I'm weak when it comes to hearing a woman scream. I try to deny this godforsaken hunger, but I need to drain her power. Virgin blood needs to be spilled to make us stronger." He grabbed the woman's arm and yanked her to him.

Marcos sneered. "I see you're finally coming around. Life would be so much easier for you if you would just accept what you are."

Adrian grasped Holly's hand and followed Marcos into the dungeon theatre room. He'd played in this room before, but always with a willing subject. This time, he hadn't given her a choice and the knowledge of this tore at his soul.

No. Not his soul. He'd have to be alive to have one. He shook his head then continued into the room.

The head of every vampire in the room turned to them. The sickening energy of their bloodlust rolled toward him in waves.

He walked down the aisle past rows of crushed red velvet covered chairs. The vampires seated along the aisle reached out to touch the entranced woman.

The house lights dimmed but the pale glow of their faces could still be seen. As Adrian walked up the steps, a different set of lights snapped on bathing the stage in a red tinted glow.

He surveyed the dungeon furniture. It had everything a vampire Dom could want. A punishment bench, a sex swing, a jail cell, a giant St. Andrews cross, a variety of spreaders, restraints, locking cuffs, and a wall of whips, paddles and other implements of discipline.

He decided on the spanking horse. Covered in black leather, it was one of the more comfortable pieces to play on. He needed to put on a good show, to make it believable enough that he could free her and escape at some point.

He pointed to the bench and in a clear, loud voice said, "Remove your dress."

A slight smile crossed her face. "Yes sir."

He stifled a groan. Anytime a woman called him sir, it stirred his blood and aroused him in a way nothing else could. He loved their complete obedience.

She struggled to lift the dress over her head so he moved to help. The creamy silk clung to her curves. He fought the giant dress and its many yards of fabric.

A woman in the audience cried. "Rip it off."

A murmur rose in the crowd. The palpable excitement in the room clicked up a notch.

Frustrated, he grabbed the front of the dress and tore it open. He pulled the tattered sleeves from her shoulders then stepped back.

Clad only in a corset and pantaloons, her innocent expression set the audience on fire. They clapped vigorously.

A man yelled. "And now the corset."

The entranced woman grabbed the ribbon between her thumb and forefinger and tugged. The pink silk corset loosened enough to reveal more of her ample breasts. They heaved as she let out a breath. She unlaced the corset until it was loose enough to pass over her curvaceous hips.

The lights cast a red tint over her milky white breasts. Her erect nipples begged to be licked and sucked, but he couldn't indulge yet. He needed to make sure Marcos believed the rouse.

"Take off your pantaloons." He commanded.

She complied and the undergarment pooled at her feet. He turned his back to the audience and swallowed. She stood naked except for a pair of pink satin panties.

He hooked a finger under the lacey trim and pulled them down enough to reveal her shaved pussy. Surprised, he stopped and stared. Maybe she wasn't a virgin. Maybe she wasn't as innocent as she seemed.

As he slid the panties further down, he caressed her thighs. When he dropped them at her feet, she kicked them into the audience.

A rush of vampires scurried to fight over them. They reminded him of piranha. Vicious, deadly creatures.

He pointed to the punishment bench. "Kneel."

The woman complied. They always did in this state, but after the first crack of a whip, they'd snap out of it and scream.

He removed a pair of wrist cuffs and ankle cuffs from the wall. He slid her hands and feet into the cuffs and locked them. They fit her perfectly.

The cuffs featured hooks which he used to latch her to the silver rings on the bench. Face down, she lay against the bench. Her perfect heart shaped ass pointed up toward the ceiling and her legs were spread so wide, he had an excellent view of her pussy.

He addressed the audience. "Punishment brings pain and excitement. Feed on her cries. Drink in the sight of her naked flesh."

The stage lights blocked his view of the audience. He wanted to pretend they weren't there, but couldn't. He needed to stay in complete control so he wouldn't hurt her too much.

He'd been a Dom for over one hundred years. With any luck, he could lead her into the darkest realm of her desires and into sub space. From years of experience, he knew that once a woman was in sub space, her pain transformed into exquisite pleasure. He needed to get her into that state as quickly as possible without arousing anyone's suspicion.

He chose a riding crop from the wall. The slaps would sting, but wouldn't bring the kind of pain a whip could.

The crop cut the air with a whoosh as he brought it down on her ass. She cried out. She turned her head toward the audience.

"What's happening? Where am I?"

The fear in her voice made his heart clench. More than anything, he wanted to release her, but to do so now would spell certain death.

He snapped the crop against her ass again. This time she yelled and struggled against the bench. She tugged at the bonds but couldn't move more than an inch in every direction.

He threw way the whip and slapped her ass with his bare hand. The contact of skin on skin reverberated throughout the theatre. He couldn't see beyond the first row, but the unmistakable sounds of zippers being opened told him exactly what was happening in the audience.

She writhed and trembled as he continued to spank her. But she didn't cry out. Her skin grew hot beneath his hand so he switched to her other cheek. He didn't pause until both sides were equally red and hot.

The beauty of her red ass sent a shot of desire from deep within his belly straight to his cock. A rush of blood filled his cock until the fully engorged hardness pressed against his pants.

He stopped slapping her and ran his fingernails over the sensitive skin. She moaned and stopped struggling. He cupped both sides of her ass and kneaded them together. Despite his plan, he wanted to bury his face between the plump cheeks and lick her until she came.

He slapped her hard to ward off the impulse. She screamed, but this time he realized her screams weren't of pain, but of pleasure.

Holly bit the black leather to stifle a scream. She didn't know where she was or who was spanking her heated ass, but she didn't care. A warmth unlike anything she'd ever experienced before spread from the burning flesh down her legs and up through her entire body.

She tried to grind her pussy against the bench, against anything to relieve the pressure building inside her, but she couldn't. The aching fold remained untouched and opened.

She was vaguely aware of being on a stage. She felt the audience's lascivious stares but couldn't see their faces. Maybe it was better that way.

A wave of shame crashed over her. To be so exposed, so aroused and so open to complete strangers shocked her to the core. What kind of woman wanted to be bound and spanked in front of a crowd of people?

A man's legs came into view. She knew he was the one who spanked and debased her. And he was the one who could give her the release she needed.

"Please." She whispered.

The man knelt down and she recognized him from the

veranda. He whispered in her ear. "I'm going to save you, but we have to make them think you're in excruciating pain."

She didn't know what he was talking about, she only knew one thing. "I need you."

"Don't worry, I'll figure out a way to free you."

Desperation entered her voice. "No, I need you to—"

He put a finger over her lips. "Everything's going to be alright. Trust me."

Her tongue darted out to lick his finger. She swirled her tongue around it and sucked it into her mouth.

The man's eyes went wide.

She stared into his eyes and mumbled. "I need you to fuck me."

Lust quickly replaced the look of shock on his face. He pushed a second finger between her lips. She greedily sucked both fingers into her mouth.

He pulled them out and unclasped his cape. He removed in with a flourish and tossed it to the other side of the stage.

A black shirt fell to the stage. Boots clattered where they landed. A zipper clicked down followed by the rustle of his pants as he shimmied out of them.

As he stood over her, she strained to look up but could only move her head high enough to get a glimpse of his enormous cock. The angry red head pointed up at the ceiling. More than anything in the world, she needed that cock between her lips. She longed to suck and lick the heavy balls that hung below the shaft.

She whispered. "Please let me suck you cock."

"Sir."

"Please let me suck your cock sir."

He moved just out of reach. She arched her neck and stuck her tongue out as far as possible but couldn't reach the head.

She groaned.

The man laughed and spoke to the audience. "Should I let her have it?"

The crowd cheered and a woman screamed. "Let her suck it."

Holly silently thanked the woman and stretched as far as she could. A drop of pre-cum glistened in the light.

The man stepped toward her just enough to allow her to lick the salty tip. She pressed the plane of her tongue against the head then flicked it a couple of times.

He grabbed her chin and slowly slid the length into her mouth. Her lips stretched to accommodate the girth. She tongued the ridge along the underside of his cock as he pushed deeper.

His hand moved from her chin to her hair. The first painful tug surprised her. She tried to look up but her position prevented her from seeing his face.

He pulled her hair to tilt her head back. At first she didn't understand why, but then his cock drove into her throat. She gagged and her eyes watered.

She tried to stay calm but his forceful thrusts made her panic. Just when she thought she couldn't take another breath, he pulled out. She panted. A thin trail of spit connected her mouth to his cock.

A moment passed before he rammed back into her throat. This time she prepared herself and took quick breaths as he thrust. He rewarded her with a groan.

A few men in the audience snickered.

His balls slapped against her chin. The rhythm slowed and he continued with long deep strokes. Air swirled behind her to cool her hot wet pussy. Sucking his cock temporarily distracted her from a desire so dark, so deviant that she could hardly admit it to herself.

She longed to be fucked in front of the audience. She never imagined she'd allow others to watch her. Not that she had much choice. But something about the energy coming from the audience made her want to display her pussy. It made her want to suck him deeper, to spread her legs wider.

But maybe it wasn't the audience. Maybe it was him, the mysterious stranger who spanked and used her like an object.

Adrian clenched his teeth and tried to think of anything but the heat of her mouth and the smoothness of her lips. He stepped back to keep from coming.

He couldn't believe the woman begged him to fuck her. How could he have been so wrong about her? She didn't give any indication that under her innocent façade, a wanton woman yearned to break free.

The telltale sound of rough sex came from the audience. Apparently, some of the vampires couldn't curtail their desires long enough to finish watching the show.

From behind, her swollen pussy lips beckoned. He dropped to his knees and inhaled the sweetness of her sex. He blew against the lips then licked the length of her slit from base to clit.

She wigged against his mouth and moaned. He lightly caressed the puffy folds with the very tip of his tongue before driving it into her.

She screamed and shuddered against his mouth. He pulled her hips back and buried his face in the slick heat. She tasted like a French pastry. Sweet enough to entice, but not so sweet as to be overwhelming.

He licked and sucked the folds until she shook so hard, the bench threatened to topple over.

"Sir, please. Make me come." She begged.

He loved the desperation in her voice, the raw need for release. But he wouldn't give it to her so easily. He wanted her on the brink of insanity before he'd allow her to come.

He sucked her clit between his lips and flicked it with his tongue. She gasped for breath and rocked back against his face. He swirled the length of her slit then with his fingers, he pinched the inside of her thigh.

She cried out. "Ouch. What the hell?"

Hell was right. He intended to torture every last drop of pleasure out of her.

He pulled back, stood and slapped her ass hard enough to leave a handprint. He delighted in her screams.

He strolled to the wall of instruments of pain and chose a paddle. Leather covered one side and faux fur covered the other.

He walked across the stage then presented the paddle to the audience. "A fine instrument indeed."

A woman ran up to the edge of the stage. "Beat me Adrian. Tie me to the cross and hit me until I faint."

He addressed her. "Flavia, darling, go find Marcos. I'm sure he'd be happy to punish you until you beg for mercy."

Marcos materialized and grabbed the woman by the hair. He sneered. "I'd be delighted to."

He dragged the woman into the darkness.

Relieved to see him leave, Adrian returned to the woman on the bench. He rubbed the fuzzy side of the paddle across her ass then down each thigh. He turned it on its side and slid it over her pussy lips.

She moaned. "Rub my pussy."

"Sir." He corrected.

He brought the leather side of the paddle down hard on her ass.

She screamed. "Harder sir."

He obliged and spanked her again and again until a slick trail of her juices ran down the sides of her thighs.

The glistening lips drove him to distraction. He threw the paddle down and positioned himself behind her. He drove into her hard and without any warning.

The walls of her tight pussy immediately clenched. She cried out as her pussy spasmed against his cock. The orgasm had her grinding against him. He pulled back slowly, then drove into her a second time. The bench scraped across the floor.

She whimpered. "Oh yes. Sir. God. Harder."

He met her last demand by burying his cock deeper into her than he'd ever been in any other woman. She thrashed on the bench. He leaned over and released the buckles that held her in place.

She slid to one side but he quickly grabbed her by the waist and pulled her against him. He rose up and changed his grip. He held underneath her thighs and raised and lowered her onto his cock.

He stood like this, fucking her tight, wet pussy until his thighs burned.

He pulled out and lowered her to the ground. She lay back and spread her legs so wide, she could grip her ankles with her hands.

He grabbed her hips and lifted her onto his thighs, then drove deep. The slurping sound of her pussy excited him.

He reached for her taut nipples and pinched. Her pussy clamped onto him. The tingling in his balls increased as she tightened around him. Her breasts bounced as he pounded her. The site of her was something he'd never get out of his mind, even if he lived a thousand years.

Sweat pooled in the concave sweep of her belly. He leaned down and licked the salty sweetness from her skin. She arched her back and groaned. After another minute, he wanted her in a different position.

"Get on your knees." He commanded.

She scrambled to her knees and faced him.

"Turn around."

She spun and put her head down. Her butt arched to the ceiling. "Please sir."

He entered her hot pussy and caressed the twin cheeks of her ass. He always loved this view of a woman, especially of the tiny puckered hole.

He licked the pad of his thumb and pressed it against the narrow hole. She yelped and tried to crawl away but he held her tight.

"So, you do have a virgin hole after all."

When she didn't respond, he slapped her ass hard.

"Yes sir. Please sir, not there." She stammered.

The plea did nothing to stop him. He applied more pressure until the tip of his finger entered the tight passage.

"Oh." She moaned and rotated her ass against him.

He looked around the dungeon and spotted a bottle of lube discreetly tucked under another table. He pulled out and hurried to get it.

When he returned, she frowned at the bottle. She probably didn't know what it was for and he chose not to enlighten her. She'd find out soon enough.

He set the bottle on the floor within reach and eased his cock back into her. He grabbed the lube and flicked open the cap. He squeezed a couple of drops onto his thumb, and then set the bottle down. The rim of her puckered hole resisted his finger.

She tried again to crawl away. "What are you doing?"

He slapped her ass. "Sir."

She turned her head to glare at him. "Sir, what the fuck are you doing?"

The fire in her eyes made his cock so hard, so thick with blood, that he could hardly pull it free from her tight pussy. "I'm going to fuck your ass."

Holly stared at his cock. Somehow it had grown in length and girth. There was no way in hell it would fit. She had to make him understand that.

"It's too big, Sir. It couldn't possibly—"

He pushed against her ass so hard, she stopped mid-sentence. One glance at his determined face and she knew she could never get away.

He spanked her ass. "Open up."

"I can't."

"Yes." He hissed through clenched teeth.

Her pussy ached from the pounding he'd given her, but she reached down and fingered it. The pleasure did little to protect from the pain, but she gritted her teeth and tried to get through it.

He shoved against her harder. Her knees buckled under his weight but he yanked her up.

"Be a good girl and open up." He nibbled on the edge of her earlobe. She melted against him.

Something about the invasion set her on fire. He reached around the front of her and swatted her hand away. He fingered her clit so hard it hurt, but in an amazing way.

Her eyes rolled back and fluttered. Possessed by lust, she'd never been so crazed in her life. She stopped fighting against the pain and instead spread as wide as possible.

He shoved the head of his cock past the ring of tight muscles. The resulting orgasm caught her by surprise. She screamed. He smashed her against the floor as he drove into her over and over. She didn't care. She grinded her pussy against his fingers and came so hard she stopped breathing.

She gasped for breath. The room swayed and her vision narrowed. Behind her, the stranger fucked her impossibly tight ass. Another orgasm ripped through her. She came until she couldn't think. Her whole world transformed into a crimson haze of pleasure.

Adrian pumped her with every ounce of strength in his body. Every sense was heightened. Every sound intensified. He could hear the chatter at the back of the audience. Comments about his virility, about how they never expected him to be so rough.

But above all of that noise, he heard the pulsing beat of blood as it rushed through her body. He strained to ignore it, but a savage beast rose up from within and demanded that he drink from her.

His fingers closed around her throat. She arched her head back and exposed her neck. A plump, pulsing vein beckoned. It mocked the life he would never live again. It reminded him that he wasn't human and would never be alive again.

His fangs extended. He licked the sharp peaks. Then he gave into his animalistic nature and pierced her exposed flesh.

A trickle of blood surged through his fangs. Her pure erotic energy flooded him with power so intense, so vibrant, he couldn't stop feeding.

Somewhere in the back of his mind, what little humanity he still had warned him to stop. But he couldn't. The pleasure was too great. All thought of right and wrong no longer mattered. The beating of her heart set him into a trance.

He sucked her neck as if it was his first taste of blood. The tightness of her ass on his cock and the sweetness of her blood pushed him over the edge.

He roared as he came. His cock pulsed deep inside, filling her with his seed. When the last contraction dissipated, he realized something was very wrong. Her cries of pleasure were inhuman. Horror washed over him when he realized what he'd done. He'd taken too much of her blood and in turn, she'd absorbed too much of his vile energy.

He screamed. "No. Not her."

He stumbled back and wiped a hand across his mouth. A trail of blood smear confirmed his greatest fear.

She touched the side of her neck then looked at him. Golden specks shimmered in her eyes as she whispered. "I'm thirsty for more."

PUNISHING THE BILLIONAIRE HEIRESS

From the deck of her yacht, Brittany glared at her bodyguard Antonio and stabbed a finger toward the Moroccan port. "What do you mean we're not allowed to dock? I wanted to go shopping in Africa. I'm sick of the same Paris fashions and I was hoping to get something different on this trip."

"The port is closed to all ships that have docked anywhere along the West African coast. They are taking the Ebola threat seriously. People are dying, and your little shopping trips mean nothing compared to the seriousness of this disease." In a typical display of insolence, Antonio's hands fisted at his sides. His emerald green eyes flashed.

"I don't like your tone," she snapped.

Antonio always had a way of speaking to her with a condescending tone and she was sick of it. She employed him, well technically her father employed him, but she could easily get rid of him. Even though she liked the way his white dress shirt enhanced his olive skin, she wasn't about to take his shit. So what if his khaki shorts clung to his rock-hard ass? She'd never respect a man who didn't respect her.

She put her hands on her hips. "I have plenty of money, so if you need to bribe the officials, do it."

Marco, her other Italian-stallion bodyguard, stepped forward. Unlike Antonio, Marco was clean-shaven. He never sported the perpetual 5 o'clock shadow Antonio favored. Marco's dark eyes fixated on her. "With all due respect ma'am, we can't buy our way into this port. Our best option is to wait a few days to see if the travel restriction is lifted. We don't really have another choice. We only have enough fuel to get to Spain, and they are also banning incoming ships."

She huffed. "I swear. I should replace both of you and find someone who can get me into that port."

Antonio's lips pressed into a thin, white line. Standing beside him on the deck, Marco's face remained passive.

With a flick of her hand, she said, "Dismissed."

As the bodyguards disappeared below deck, she stared at their tight asses. The noon sun beat down on her bikini-clad body. She swallowed and fanned her face with her hand. She'd fantasized about losing her virginity to one of the bodyguards, but couldn't decide which one she wanted more. Regardless, she'd never let a mere employee take her to bed. She was holding out for royalty. A Persian prince, or maybe a French aristocrat, someone worthy of her status.

Below deck, Antonio sat at the bar while Marco mixed a couple of martinis. The bartender had gone AWOL in India. Before he'd left, he'd screamed at Brittany calling her a stupid, vapid slut. As much as Antonio dreamed of yelling at the spoiled brat, he valued the job.

As heiress to her father's billion dollar sex toy company, she had an endless supply of money. The last two years consisted of a string of high-class parties and yacht trips around the world. Other than to deflect the heiress' occasional would-be lovers, he rarely needed to use his ex-Marine Corps skills.

"Want to lay odds on how long it takes before she becomes completely unglued?" Antonio smirked.

"Shh, if she hears you, you might end up like the bartender." Marco glanced at the door.

"What she needs is a big fat cock in her mouth."

"And I bet you'd be the one to give it to her?"

"Like you wouldn't want to?" Antonio asked.

"Who wouldn't want to?"

"The little cock-tease needs a good hard fuck. Maybe that's her problem." Antonio skewered an olive with a toothpick and popped it in his mouth.

"You better hope she never hears you say that."

"You've been with her longer than I have. What is it now, three years?"

Marco squinted and stared at the ceiling for a moment. "Yes, three, long, glorious years."

Antonio roared with laughter. "Glorious, hu?'

"Every second. Although, you have to admit this is a sweet job. We're getting paid a whole lot of money to babysit her."

"Not enough if you ask me."

Marco grinned. "Now you're just getting greedy."

"Just once, I'd like to take the spoiled brat, bend her over my knee, and give that tight little ass a good spanking." Antonio shifted as a rush of blood flooded his cock.

Marco's gaze darkened. "I'd like to fuck her tight little ass."

"Now we're talkin'." Antonio raised his glass and clinked it against Marco's.

Brittany's shrill voice screeched behind him. "You're both fired. How can you talk about me like that?"

Antonio nearly choked on the ice cube in his mouth. He spit it back into the glass. "How long have you been standing there?"

"Long enough to know that you're both fired." Brittany folded her arms underneath her ample chest. The barely there bikini only served to enhance her perfectly natural, perfectly round tits.

Marco's bravado faded as he ran a hand through his hair. "We were just kidding, please don't fire us."

"I can do whatever the fuck I want," she said defiantly.

Antonio leered at her. "Were all stuck on this boat, and now that were fired, we can do whatever the fuck we want."

Mario shot him a warning look. "You both need to calm down. I know tensions are high because we can't get off the ship right now. Everyone needs to cool off. Let's just go to our cabins, and wait this thing out."

In a haughty voice, she said, "Fine! You can both go to your rooms and stay there. As soon as we dock, you can both get the hell off my ship."

Mario stalked toward her. "You can't do that."

She smirked. "I just did."

Amused, Antonio was completely unprepared for what came next. Mario's hand shot out and grabbed her upper arm. His face took on a countenance Antonio had never seen before. Whatever dark need he had simmering just below the surface exploded.

In a low, menacing tone, Mario said, "I don't think you

know what kind of position you're really in right now. Now that we don't work for you, we can do whatever the fuck we want with you."

Antonio jumped to his feet. "Now we're talking."

She struggled to escape Mario's grasp, but his fingers dug into her skin. For the first time ever, fear infused her voice. "Mario, stop it right now. This isn't funny."

"Don't worry princess, we're about to have a whole lot of fun." Mario sneered.

Her eyes went wide. "What do you mean?"

Mario said, "Get her other arm. Let's take her to the master suite."

Still in a state of shock, it took Antonio a moment to process Mario's command. No shit, he was serious. Antonio couldn't believe the change in his partner.

"Are you sure? Five minutes ago you were calling me crazy, but now you're about to drag her ass down the hall to fuck her? I don't buy it," Antonio said.

A few steps ahead of him, Mario spun around. "You were right. I'm so sick of listening to her whine and complain about her endless privilege. She doesn't have a clue what the world's really like. But I am about to show her what happens to little rich girls who think money can buy everything."

Antonio trailed Mario down the hall. They crossed the threshold into the master suite, and then Mario tossed her on the overly girly ruffled bedspread. "Get naked."

Ever defiant, she tilted her chin up. "Get out of my room. I'll deal with your insubordination later."

Mario unbuckled his belt. "If that bathing suit's not off by the time I get there, I'm ripping it off."

She bristled and turned to Antonio. "You're not gonna just stand there while he does this, are you?"

Antonio shrugged. "You fired me. There's not a whole lot I can do at this point."

Mario's shorts dropped to the floor quickly followed by his boxers. After ripping off his shirt, he stalked toward the bed. "You're not naked yet."

Brittany blinked rapidly. Just beyond the fear lay something darker. The thought of being dominated by the rough, animalistic bodyguards made her drip with desire. But this wasn't her plan, they weren't sheiks or princes or even wealthy businessman. They were two lower class employees, and they intended to rob her of her virginity.

Mario climbed across the bed. The feral look in his eye seemed completely alien to the usually reserved bodyguard. She'd never seen him like this. He reminded her of one of the lions she'd seen while on Safari. The beast had attacked and mounted a female and fucked her from behind. The whole scene had made her so incredibly hot, that she couldn't help but wonder what it would feel like to be mounted by one of her bodyguards. As much as she wanted to deny it, she wanted both of them.

Mario climbed onto the bed and pushed her down. This was her last chance to protest, but she couldn't find the words. Her breath came in short gasps as he tugged the strings that held the bikini together.

Antonio stood beside the bed. His hands made quick work of the buttons on his shirt. After dropping his shorts to the floor, he walked around to the other side of the bed and climbed on.

"You're in a helluva lot of trouble, princess." Antonio grabbed her hips and lifted her off the bed.

Mario yanked the bikini bottom from underneath her ass and tossed it across the room. "Pull her up."

Still in a state of shock, Brittany stared at the men. They could easily pass for Italian models. Each man's abs rippled as they maneuvered her onto a pile of pillows. Eye level with their taut thighs, her breath caught in her throat. Both men sported enormous erections. Antonio's swept up with a slight arch toward the ceiling, while Mario's pointed forward.

Her mouth went dry. "Wait, can I have some water?"

Mario chuckled. "I have something else you can drink."

Without warning, he straddled her chest and pushed the tip of his cock between her lips. She made the mistake of opening her mouth to protest, which gave him full access. As he pushed forward, she couldn't see anything but the thick thatch of black hair above his shaft.

The salty taste of him overwhelmed her senses. Although she was a virgin, she had teased a few guys in the past. But none of them were as big as Mario. She forced herself to relax and sucked his cock deeper. Maybe if she let them come in her mouth, they'd leave her pussy alone.

Her stomach clenched at the sudden brush of hair against her inner thigh. She'd been so focused on Mario that she forgot Antonio was also in bed with them. The flick of his tongue against her clit sent a ripple of pleasure through her belly.

Mario crooned, "You like that, princess?"

She couldn't speak with his cock in her mouth, but the bastard knew that and was clearly taunting her.

He withdrew for a moment giving her the chance to say, "Fuck you Mario."

Antonio laughed against her clit. The vibration rippled down her legs in a series of tiny shivers.

"Open wide, you little slut." The commanding tone of Mario's voice made her secretly submissive side emerge. She opened her mouth and took in every inch of his huge cock. Her lips stretched wider, her jaw ached, but the part of her that wanted to please him wasn't satisfied until he was deep inside her throat.

Mario groaned. "Jesus, you're a good cock sucker."

Between her thighs, Antonio licked up and down the length of her slit. When he pierced the tight folds of flesh, she rationalized that as long as they didn't stick their cocks in her, she'd still be a virgin.

Mario's gentle thrusts became harder as he pistoned into her mouth. Trails of saliva dripped down her chin. As the sloppy blowjob continued, Mario grunted and swiveled from side to side hitting every inch of her mouth.

The shallow thrum of Antonio's lips against her increasingly wet pussy captured her full attention. His mouth was a thousand times better than any vibrator she owned. She moaned against Mario's cock. A surge of heat coiled and swirled deep inside.

Still thrusting, Mario hunched over and grabbed the back of her neck. "Suck it, that's right, eat that dick."

His filthy language coupled with the continuous purr of Antonio's lips sent her to the brink. Her entire body clenched, every muscle strained against the tension. As the first orgasm ripped through her body, Mario's cock twitched and shot a huge load of cum down her throat. She sputtered as she tried to scream. Overwhelming pleasure wracked her body. A convulsing shuddering mess, she had no choice but to swallow every ounce of his milky cum.

After the last ribbon hit the back of her throat, Mario slowly swung his hip across her body and collapsed onto the bed beside her.

Between heavy breaths, Mario gasped, "You're up."

Antonio sat back on his heels. "No sloppy seconds for me. I already know what I want."

Mario's chest rose and fell rapidly. "This was my idea, so I get to fuck her pussy first."

"You're going to have to fight me for it."

Brittany propped up on her elbows. "Nobody gets to fuck my pussy. It's off-limits."

Antonio's eyes narrowed. "I don't think you realize that there's nothing off-limits right now. Even that tight little ass is in play."

Brittany gasped. "No it's not. I mean, no one gets to fuck anything."

Antonio crawled across her body and pinned her arms over her head. "We've had to deal with your bullshit for years. A long, hard fuck is the least you can do to repay us."

She trembled. "But... I'm a virgin."

"Bullshit," Mario yelled.

"I'm not lying. Have you ever actually seen a guy spend the night? I might tease him a little bit, I might even suck a little cock here and there, but I'm saving myself."

Antonio's body completely covered hers. "Saving yourself for what?"

"A prince, or a sheik, or some other kind of royalty." As soon as she said it, she realized how ridiculous it sounded.

Mario roared with laughter. "You've got to be fucking kidding me."

She shook her head vigorously. "I'm serious. If Antonio really wants to, I guess I could let him fuck my mouth, but that's it."

Antonio shoved her legs apart with his knees. "Like I said, I don't do sloppy seconds."

He surged forward, the tip of his cock shoving between

the tight folds of her pussy. The barrier of her virginity blocked him, but he didn't stop. In one swift thrust, he tore the thin veil and buried himself in her pussy.

A mixture of shock and outrage excited every nerve ending in her body. She'd fantasized about being taken by force, but she never imagined how deliciously sinful it would actually feel.

The thick length of his cock dipped and withdrew. Between their bodies, the glistening evidence of her arousal coated his shaft. A tinge of pain radiated from her torn hymen. But with each stroke, pleasure pushed the pain aside. She arched to meet his wild thrusts. She released the death grip she had on the sheets and grabbed his ass. As he surged forward, she pulled him even deeper.

"I knew it," Mario snickered. "She just needed a good pounding. Look at her, begging for more. Give it to her hard, I want her nice and warmed up for me."

Antonio drilled her pussy. "She's so fucking tight, I haven't had pussy like this since Thailand."

"Enjoy it while you can, I'm about to tag in."

Antonio pulled out. "Get on your hands and knees."

She gasped. "You can't fuck me like a dog. I already gave up my virginity and I'm not about to give up my dignity too."

Antonio flipped her on her stomach, grabbed her hips and pulled back, forcing her to her knees. His hands slid up to her shoulders, and then he shoved them down. Her face pressed into the mattress effectively muffling her groans. She loved the rough grip of his hands. His fingers swirled and kneaded her pliant flesh before descending on her swollen nipples.

He pinched hard. She half screamed, half moaned. A lightning bolt of pain zigzagged down her hips. Her toes clenched as feverish desire enslaved her.

Mario reached over and slapped her ass. "Get the little slut."

"Oh God, harder!" She hardly recognized the raspy tone of her voice.

Antonio pummeled her pussy. Her knees sunk into the bed. His arm hooked across the front of her pubic bone to steady her. The pulling, pushing motion of Antonio's hips made her wetter than a tropical hurricane. The wild intensity pushed beyond her usual prim and proper attitude. The uptight façade cracked and she gave into him, relinquishing the last bit of control. She'd passed into the eye of the storm.

Every errant thought stilled. Every whisper of impropriety went silent. Every rule her ice-queen mother beat into her was replaced by the chaos of lawlessness. In that moment, the blue-blooded societal norms she'd been slave to for years didn't matter. All that mattered was the relentless grind of his cock in her pussy.

The pressure building inside became unbearable. She needed to come, to indulge her voracious sexual appetite. As if sensing her desire, he angled his cock down. The increased friction against her clit did it.

Her back arched as a convulsion ripped through her. She hardly recognized the high-pitched scream coming from her mouth. Each pulse of her muscles tightened her pussy until his cock could hardly move.

Antonio grunted. "Fucking so tight. I'm going to come. Fuck! Such a tight, virgin pussy."

From the hazy recess of her mind, a small voice protested. But instead of demanding that he stop, she spread her legs wider. The first hot splash of cum rolled through her. Molten heat radiated out from her core.

He collapsed. Crushed against the bed, she could only meow with satisfaction. She turned her head toward Mario.

His dark eyes raked across her body and she knew he had no intention of letting her out of bed.

Mario waited for the other man to get off of her. Unlike Antonio, he didn't give a shit about sloppy seconds. The more lube, the better, especially considering what he wanted to do next.

As Antonio rolled off, Mario replaced him. A trickle of milky cum dripped from her pussy. He scooped a glob onto his finger and mashed it against the smaller, puckered hole.

She whipped around. "What the hell are you doing?"

Mario didn't owe her an answer. He concentrated on the task at hand. With another scoop of cum, he pushed the tip of his finger into her ass. She squealed, her ass jerking from side to side in an attempt to escape his violation.

He slapped her ass hard enough to leave a bright red print. "Shut up. You know we're not stopping until we've had every hole."

The indignant look on her face was priceless. Too bad they weren't recording a sex tape. He paused as a devious idea formed.

Mario motioned to Antonio. "Go get the digital camera."

"Why?"

"For posterity. What the hell do you think? Let's record this shit."

Antonio's face lit up. "Blackmail?"

"Exactly. Not only can she not fire us, but now we can fuck her whenever we want to."

Brittany crawled around to face him. "No fucking way. I let you do this because... well, it doesn't matter why. But you are not recording it!"

Antonio glanced at her before walking out the door. "I'll be right back."

On her knees now, she wobbled toward Mario. "Please, I guess... I guess I could let you fuck my ass. But please, don't record it."

Mario narrowed his eyes. "Sorry, princess. If you hadn't been such a pain in the ass the last few years, I might reconsider. But, it's payback time."

She crossed her arms over her chest. "So I have no choice?"

"What's it feel like to have no choice for the first time in your life?"

Her face fell. "Will you at least use lube?"

He tilted his head as if considering her request. It would probably feel better with lube. Fucking a dry hole wouldn't do much other than rub his cock raw.

"Okay, get the lube," he commanded.

As she stepped off the bed, she teetered but quickly regained her balance. She opened the night stand. Inside sat a jumbled mess of sex toys including dildos, vibrators, nipple clamps and rope. His cock twitched at the sea of new possibilities.

Antonio strode into the room and whistled. "Damn, did you pack the entire empire?"

Mario held up an odd contraption consisting of a series of leather chords. "What do you suppose this does?"

"Give me that," she chirped as she snatched the toy from his hand.

"Looked like some kind of outfit," Antonio supplied as he set up the camera.

Mario shrugged and riffled through the drawer. Once he found the lube, he sat on the edge of the bed. "Come over here and lay over my lap."

She frowned. "Why?"

"Just do it."

The furrow in her brow grew, but she complied and lay across his lap. The rigid tip of his cock pressed against her warm belly. He wanted to ram it in her ass, but he needed to prep it first.

He uncapped the lube and spread a few drops on his thumb. The fattest finger was the best finger since it did double duty. Not only did it help spread her tight hole, it also spread the lube past the tight ring of muscles. And God, was she tight or what?

Across the room, Antonio fidgeted with the camera. Once he had it in place, he jokingly yelled, "Action!"

As Mario eased his thumb up her ass, she wriggled and hissed. "I can't believe you're recording this. Slow down. Oh, shit that hurts."

The streak of sadism he'd fought to keep under wraps for years reared up and he stuffed his finger in deeper. He swirled it around, spreading the lube evenly. His effort to resist temptation faded with each passing second. When he couldn't resist any longer, he gave her ass a hard smack with his free hand.

"Ouch!"

A red handprint emerged from her flushed skin.

She looked back over her shoulder and glared. "I didn't agree to a spanking."

"But you're getting one anyway." He sneered as he brought his hand down hard on the other cheek.

She hissed a breath. Antonio stood at the side of the bed, cock in hand, watching. Normally Mario wouldn't ever be in a room with another naked man, but threesomes didn't count.

"Get on your knees," Mario commanded.

Antonio said, "No, wait. I'll lie down, she can jump on my cock and we'll DP her."

"Sounds like a plan. You heard the man, princess."

Antonio lay on the bed and guided Brittany into a straddling position. As she eased onto his cock, she shivered and sighed. Good, at lease the little slut liked having a cock in her pussy. He'd find out how much she liked one in her ass in just a second.

He rubbed lube on his cock and positioned himself on his knees behind her. For a second, he watched as Antonio's cock slid out of her sopping pussy. The plump, engorged lips gobbled his cock up as he shoved it back in. She bounced on his cock like she'd been riding for years, a natural.

Mario strategically moved so as not to hit the other man's cock and pushed the head against her tight ass. She dropped down, stuffing Antonio all the way inside her. Mario took the opportunity to bear down on her. The head of his cock pushed against the tight hole. For a second, he wasn't sure it would get past the clenched muscles, but with a little extra force, he managed to pierce her virgin ass.

She fell forward, covering Antonio. "Oh, fuck!"

Mario grabbed her hips when she tried to crawl forward. He yanked back to impale her on his cock. The tightness fueled his already mindless lust. He ignored her whimpering and pulled almost all the way out before jamming it back in. He intended to punish her ass.

Brittany couldn't imagine how both men could be inside her at once. Everything between her legs was a crowded mess. She couldn't escape the pulsing waves of pleasure rippling through her ass. It wasn't the same as being fucked in the pussy, but as both cocks pistoned, she couldn't decide which sensation she liked more.

All sense of propriety vanished. As the lascivious act continued, the brutish way they worked her over excited the wantonness buried deep in her soul. She jerked and twitched as they hit erogenous zones far from the reach of her usual sex toys. She'd never even tried to stick anything up anywhere before. She'd been content with vibrators and only kept the other toys on hand in case she found a prince or sheik to give herself to. But that dream was over and she could care less.

She fixated on the rocking motion of the men and soon caught their rhythm. Her nipples, tight with desire, ached. But in her current position, she couldn't reach them. She had to make do with rubbing them against Antonio's chest. The friction helped, but she yearned for something just out of reach, something she couldn't even name.

Mario's cock battered her ass. But instead of being in pain, the tender flesh vibrated with an erotic energy so charged, she buzzed from within.

"Fuck me," she snarled.

They fucked her faster, harder, deeper, but she wanted more. She grabbed Antonio's hair and tugged. He responded by jack hammering her pussy. She seized up as an orgasm, stronger than any she'd ever experienced in her life, blasted through her.

Her eyes rolled back. Her neck arched and she screamed.

But, they didn't stop.

Possessed by rapturous contractions, she rode Antonio's cock. The violent jerk of her hips was beyond her control. A primal force consumed her.

Antonio said, "Jesus, she looks like she needs a fucking exorcism."

Mario laughed and worked his cock deeper. "I got some holy water for her."

Delirious from the spasmodic orgasm, she barely registered the twitch of Mario's cock in her ass. Warm, wet.

"Fuck... yes... don't stop. Oh fuck... more... more... yessss," she yelled as Mario filled her ass with cum.

When the twitching stopped, he pulled out. She sat back on Antonio's thighs and rode him until she couldn't take another breath. The orgasm didn't stop, even as she collapsed on his chest.

He jerked up and filled her pussy with cum. She shuddered but couldn't move. Completely limp, she could only roll to one side and collapse on the bed.

Antonio lay on her right side while Mario lay on her left. Flanked by her bodyguards, she finally drifted back to full consciousness and the implication of what she'd just done hit her. The blinking light of the camera caught her eye. She tried to sit up, but fell back against the bed.

"Turn it off," she murmured.

Mario crawled off the bed and hobbled to the camera. He hit a few buttons to end the recording.

"Delete it," she said.

A slow grin spread across Mario's face. "Not a chance, princess. Now that we have this recording, your ass belongs to us."

Every muscle in her body protested as she sat up. "I'm ordering you to delete it."

Antonio slid off the bed and stood beside it. "You fired us, remember?"

She looked from one man to the other, but neither looked like they'd relent. "What do you want?"

Mario said, "First, you reinstate us. Then you double our salary."

"But—"

Mario held up a hand to silence her. "We get to fuck you whenever we want to, however we want to."

She flashed back to the overwhelming orgasms they'd given her. How bad could it be if she let them make her come like that all the time? She never imagined sex could be so amazing and even though she was sore all over, she eyed their semi-limp cocks. Maybe this "arrangement" wasn't so bad after all.

She jutted her chin up. "Fine. Now, which one of you is going to bathe me?"

Mario and Antonio both said, "Me."

She smiled. Let them think they owned her. The joke would be on them. After all, they wouldn't be the first men she'd wrapped around her finger.

The shrill ring of the telephone by the bed jolted her. She picked up the phone. "Yes?"

"Ma'am, this is captain Jenkins. The quarantine will be lifted at noon tomorrow. Are you still planning to have us dock in Morocco?"

"Yes, and noon sounds good to me," she replied.

After hanging up the phone, she turned to the bodyguards. "That gives us plenty of time to see which one of you recovers fastest."

As the men eyed each other, a crackle of competition arced between them.

She smirked. She had them exactly where she wanted them.

DOUBLE STUFFED SPRING BREAK

Aiko stared at the tall black man across the dirt road. The harsh Jamaican sunlight defined every muscle on the street vender's ripped chest. Khaki shorts hung dangerously low on his hips. He skewered a piece of chicken and set it on a sizzling barbeque. The spicy scent of jerk seasoning drifted on the warm Caribbean breeze.

Aiko sipped a cup of Blue Mountain Coffee. It was better than she remembered. She hadn't tasted the exquisite beans in years, not since leaving Japan to attend college in America.

Mimi, her best friend at Yale, followed her gaze across the red plastic table cloth. "Nice view."

Aiko smiled behind the rim of the cup. "Indeed."

"Thank God your parents changed their vacation plans at the last minute. No offense, but bringing them with us to spring break would have been a total drag."

"I know what you mean. If my father ever caught me in a sarong and bikini top, he'd probably make me go back to Japan. He's so traditional."

Mimi gathered her flowing blond hair into a ponytail

and secured it. As she moved, the puffy peach sleeves of her airy, southern-belle-inspired dress flapped in the wind. She could have just as easily been sitting on the front porch of her family's plantation-style home in Atlanta. "What do you want to do today?"

"Other than him?" She discreetly pointed at the sexy stranger with her pinky finger.

Mimi smirked. "You wouldn't actually do him, would you?"

She shook her head. "Only in my dreams."

Mimi turned and waved at the fine Jamaican man. He grinned, revealing sparkling white teeth.

Aiko slapped her knee under the table. "Stop it. You're not supposed to encourage the men here. They can get pretty aggressive."

"I wouldn't mind getting a little rough with him."

Aiko bit the edge of her lip. She'd never been with a black man, but as his dark chocolate skin shimmered in the morning light, she couldn't help but wonder if the rumors about their size were true. Their cocks were supposedly so big, that some girl's couldn't even fuck them. The idea of spreading her legs for a twelve inch cock as big around as a Coke bottle made her pussy swell. Even if she couldn't get more than a few inches in, she'd love to try.

After surviving the first half of the spring term from hell, she was more than ready to let off some steam. The man across the street would be perfect. She wanted to lick him from his shaved head to his toes, but knew it wouldn't ever happen. Oh well, a girl could dream.

Aiko said, "I think we should go check out the coffee plantations. I hear the tours are cheap and really fun. I've always wanted to see how the beans are grown."

"Sounds like a plan."

As she finished the last drop of coffee, caffeine buzzed through her system. Alert and ready for an adventure, she stood and walked over to Kaela, the young woman who had served them. Kaela's braided black hair was held back by a large green and yellow head scarf. A white, gauzy dress rippled across her ample breasts and thick waist.

"You like the coffee?" Kaela asked.

"I loved it. I was wondering… my friend and I are looking for a guide to take us up to the coffee plantations. Do you know of anyone who could help us?"

"Dat man, De'ron." She pointed across the street at the sexy man. "That brother grows beans."

A rush of heat flooded Aiko's cheeks. "He looks busy. Do you know anyone else?"

Kaela waved her hand as if to dismiss the question. She yelled, "De'ron, this Asian girl be wantin' a trip to the farm."

De'ron flipped several pieces of chicken over before jogging to meet them. As he approached, his cinnamon colored eyes surveyed her from head to toe.

Aiko rubbed her suddenly damp hands across her sky-blue sundress. Nerves fluttered like cherry blossom petals in her belly. "If you're too busy—"

He took her hand and brushed his large lips across her skin. "Beautiful girl, I'll let my chickens dry out for you, no problem. We go now. Don't want sun roasting that smooth skin. Afternoon be too hot."

Mimi flashed him a salacious smile. In an exaggerated southern accent, she said, "We don't want to get too hot, now do we?"

He barely glanced at her before turning to Aiko. "We ride my truck. Come. Your friend, she come too."

Aiko hurried to keep up with his long strides. She admired the way his shorts outlined his firm ass and hips. It was so wrong to lust over a total stranger, but she couldn't help it. He was too hot to ignore.

De'ron helped Aiko into the front seat of his truck. She probably could have climbed up without assistance, but he couldn't resist the opportunity to put his hands on her petite body. Normally he liked his women with a little extra meat on their bones, but this young Asian girl inflamed his cock like no other woman had in months.

He loved spring break. It brought wild and sexy girls from all over the world right to his beach. Every year, he had his pick of the finest females. Their little string bikinis left nothing to the imagination, but he loved spreading their legs and looking at the only part of them they hadn't exposed to every man in Jamaica.

Aiko was different. He'd seen her on the beach the last two days but she always wore a modest one piece. The outline of her small breasts intrigued him. She'd ignored the other brothers who talked her up, but he wanted to crack her like a coconut. He wanted to suck on her fine white meat and drink her juices. He just had to figure out a way to get her naked.

Her annoying friend, Mimi, slid onto the seat. "I can't wait to see a coffee plant."

"The beans here be so good we ship all over the world."

He grinned. He couldn't be prouder of his family's farm. He and his brother Kaleb tended the plants during the early morning hours when it was slightly cooler. Then he'd head to the beach to run the jerk chicken stand. Fine women and a sizzling BBQ—what more could a man want?

As he turned onto a rocky mountain road, the truck

bounced and tossed from side to side. Aiko slid against him. His entire body burned where she touched him. He had to find a way to get her to spread her legs for him.

When they reached the center of the farm, he parked the truck under a large coffee tree. He helped Aiko out and waited until her friend walked to the side of the truck.

"Are you ready to see Jamaican gold?" he asked.

Mimi asked, "Is the coffee really expensive?"

"It depends on what you call expensive. Don't worry, we drink for free today."

Aiko smiled. Captivated by her mouth, he didn't realize he was staring until Mimi cleared her throat. He snapped his attention away from Aiko.

"Let's get on with the tour." He hiked under a series of banana trees. He wanted to keep the girls out of the sun as much as possible. Aiko's perfect skin would burn quickly. He hoped that the shade from the leaves would keep the scorching sunshine at bay.

A cluster of pineapple plants rose up along the side of the trail. Mimi pointed at them. "Oh wow, pineapples grow out of the ground? I always thought they grew on trees."

"They come up from the earth. Tastes sweeter than honey. You can try." He whipped a pocket knife out of his shorts and bent to grab a pineapple.

Aiko said, "Wait. We don't want you to have to pick one just for us."

He flashed a smile. "I would climb the highest tree to get fruit for you."

Aiko blushed. "Thank you."

After he plucked the pineapple, he sliced it and held it to her. When she tried to take it from him, he pulled back slightly. She grinned and ate the fruit from his fingers. In that moment, he knew he had her. It was only a matter of time before she begged him to drive his cock in deep.

He continued the tour, pointing at the various fruits. An unusually large coffee tree partially covered the path. He stopped and plucked a red berry from the tree. "This is the coffee cherry. We don't pick them until they're red and ripe."

He handed it to Aiko. The brush of her fingers against him made his cock thick and rigid with desire. Aiko's succulent lips pursed as she examined the fruit. An overwhelming need to shove his cock between her lips rocketed through him.

She said, "It's hard to believe that this becomes coffee."

"We dry the bean then roast it."

"The coffee I had this morning was amazing."

He leaned in. "How do you take your coffee? Black, or do you like a little extra cream?"

She blinked. "I... uh. Black. Really black."

She gazed at him with unmistakable desire. He just needed to figure out a way to get rid of her friend. Every once in a while, he'd fuck two girls at once, but not this time. He wanted to focus all of his attention on her.

Anxious to get Aiko alone, he led the girls back to the truck. They climbed in and he drove them back to town.

As Aiko slid out of the truck, the edge of her dress rode up her thighs. Her perfectly creamy skin peeked out, as did her pink panties. Damn, he'd love to tear those off with his teeth.

"How much do we owe you for the tour?" Aiko asked.

The edge of his mouth twitched. "I make you dinner tonight. You come at sunset."

Aiko tilted her head to one side. "I'm supposed to be repaying you, not the other way around."

"Beautiful lady, pay me back with your smile tonight."

She bit the edge of her lip as if to suppress a smile. The sexy move inflamed his cock. He knew he could talk her panties off. In a few hours, he'd slide between those smooth thighs.

∼

Clad only in a pair of pink cotton panties, Aiko held up one dress after another. "I don't know which one to choose."

Mimi sat on the edge of the second bed in the hotel room. A line of empty mini-bar bottles littered the sheets. "What effect are you going for?"

Aiko pressed a sultry red dress against her body. "Does this look too slutty?"

"Only if you're trying to be a good girl."

"I'm sick of being a good girl all the time. Just once, I want to do whatever I want."

"Or whoever you want?"

Aiko giggled. "Right."

"Well, be careful. You don't know anything about that guy and I want you to be safe. Where are you meeting him?"

"At the bar on the beach."

Mimi said, "I thought you were going to dinner."

Aiko shrugged and held up a dress in each hand. "Maybe we're walking. Anyway, do you like the blue one or the red one?"

"The red."

Aiko slipped into the gauzy red dress which clung to her chest but flowed out from the waist. She twirled in a circle. "I think this will do it."

Mimi tossed a tiny bottle of rum at her. "Drink up, for courage to actually go through with it."

Aiko grabbed it in mid-air. "I doubt I'll need it, but just in case."

She twisted the top off the bottle and took a long swig. She choked as the alcohol burned a trail of fire down her throat.

Mimi fell over laughing. "You're going to be a cheap date."

Aiko put her hands on her hips. "Now you're just being mean."

"You know I'm just messing with you. Have fun on your date."

Aiko slid her feet into a pair of sandals. After saying goodbye to her friend, she followed the concrete path leading from the hotel to the beach. The horizon cut the sun in half as it set. Red trails of fire rippled across the water. Entranced by the view, she didn't hear De'ron come up beside her.

"That be a tequila sunset," he said.

As she turned and smiled at him, he slid his hands into the pockets of his shorts. He was shirtless and looked good enough to eat.

"Tequila?" she asked.

"Yes, the more you drink, the redder it get."

She laughed. "Very true."

"Come with me. We go to my house. I cook for you."

He held out his large hand. She took it and followed him down the beach past palm trees and groups of tourists in bathing suits. The warm night air was slightly less humid, a welcome relief to the sweltering heat.

Sand slipped into her sandals and crunched through her toes. She'd dreamed about the beach throughout the icy winter. To finally walk along it with a sexy Jamaican man sent shivers of delight down her spine.

She glanced at De'ron. He wore the same relaxed expression as he had during the day. Life seemed simpler on the island. The hustle and bustle of city life grated on her nerves, but she was determined to finish college. Her Japanese parents would disown her if she did something as reckless as move to an island in the middle of the Caribbean without a job or an education. But sometimes she dreamed about escaping their expectations.

De'ron pointed toward a house in the distance. "That be my place."

As they drew closer, she studied the white-washed walls and sloped roof. The house couldn't be more than a few hundred square feet. As they stepped onto the wrap-around porch, she sighed. What would life be like if she could wake up to the sound of the ocean?

"Come inside. I'll get us drinks," he said.

She followed him into the modest home. Her sandals clicked against the clay-colored ceramic tile floor. The living room consisted of an older model television and a couch. An ornately carved oak coffee table seemed out of place in the room.

She stopped to run a finger across the carvings. "This is beautiful."

"I carved it."

"You must be good with your hands." She didn't miss the salacious look in his eyes.

He sauntered toward her. "I'm great with my hands."

She took a step forward. "Really?"

He wrapped his arms around her waist. Before she could talk herself out of it, she leaned in to kiss his full lips. Her hand pressed against the smooth skin on his chest. The solid wall of muscle flexed as he drew her against him. The evidence of his arousal pressed against her belly.

She surrendered to his scorching hot embrace. As he parted her lips with his tongue, she moaned. She hadn't been with a guy in over a year. She missed being wanted.

He explored her body with his hands. Every place he touched burned with need. His hands slid from her lower back to her ass. She didn't have much back there, but apparently he liked it anyway.

"You're so little," he whispered.

"You're so big."

He pulled back to smile at her. "Come, I'll show you."

She blushed. It hadn't taken much to get her into his bedroom. She wasn't sure why she'd gone from relaxed tourist to total slut mode today, but she didn't want to think about it. She'd fantasized about a thick, black cock, but never had the chance to see one until now.

Sheer white curtains rippled along the windows inside his bedroom. The crash and pull of the ocean sounded along the beach which was just steps from the window.

In the center of the room sat a large four-poster bed. Green sheets covered the mattress but there weren't any blankets. Although, she supposed he never needed one. The temperature was relatively stable throughout the year.

He guided her toward the bed. When they reached the edge, he stopped. He pulled her into his arms and planted a trail of kisses along her neck.

"You are the most beautiful woman," he murmured against her throat.

"Thank you," she whispered.

His hands slipped under the straps on her dress. As he slowly glided the straps down her arms, she trembled. Oh, God. It was really happening.

The dress slid down to reveal her small breasts. She wished they were bigger, but he didn't seem to mind. His hands found the soft flesh. He teased her nipples into taut peaks.

Her breath hitched as his lips moved to capture one breast. The swirling, tease of his tongue sent sparks of lust into her pussy. She rubbed her hand across his shaved head, wishing she had something to hold onto.

The luxurious scrape of his rough tongue continued down her belly. The lower he moved, the lower her dress dropped. When he reached her bellybutton, the dress pooled at her feet. She stepped out of it.

"Lay down." His low, gravelly voice sent a rush of blood into her already swollen pussy.

She lay back. Anticipation quivered along her belly. His hot breath swept up from the bottom of her pussy lips to her clit. He hadn't even touched her there yet and she was ready to explode.

His hands wrapped around her legs. His lips brushed the insides of her thighs. As he circled closer and closer with his tongue, she whimpered.

The first electric shock of his mouth on her pussy jolted her entire body. Heat flooded her core. She could hardly catch her breath as his tongue lashed against her. She couldn't find the strength to beg him to stop. The rush of sensation overwhelmed her. In a state of total erotic distress, she tried to push away his head, but he wouldn't relent.

His hands gripped her harder. His mouth closed over her clit. He sucked with just the right amount of force to make her pussy dripping wet. The scent of her arousal crowded out the ocean breeze. She gripped the sheets so hard that she pulled them off the edge of the bed.

"Oh, God," she cried.

His tongue vibrated against her. Suddenly her belly

clenched. Her legs twitched uncontrollably as a rush of orgasmic power pulsed throughout her entire body.

She came so hard, that the world faded into a gray haze for a few seconds. She screamed and convulsed against his mouth, but he didn't stop. He kept licking her until she became so sensitive it hurt.

"No more," she pleaded.

He sat back with a satisfied grin on his face. "Good?"

"Fucking amazing."

He stood next to the bed and slipped his shorts off. The biggest, thickest, most intimidating cock she'd ever seen sprung out. Fully erect, it swept toward the sky in a smooth arc. A roadmap of veins traversed the length. Twin shaved balls hung below the shaft.

She licked her lips. She had to taste him.

She dropped to the floor. On her knees, she looked up at the big, black cock. The cock of her fantasies come true. She knew she wouldn't be able to take all of it. For God's sakes it was as big around as a soda bottle. But she had to try.

After a tentative lick, she opened her lips as wide as possible. His briny scent curled into her nose. The heady aroma blended with hers to fill the room with the smell of sex.

He looked down at her through hooded eyes. "Good girl. Suck that cock."

She leaned forward to take the first few inches into her mouth. So far, so good. She pushed a bit more in then decided it was far enough. As she pulled back, she left a trail of drool. The extra lubrication made swallowing his cock easier as she pushed it back into her mouth.

She fell into an easy rhythm. Up and down, in and out. This was easier than she thought it would be... until he grabbed her head.

His hands laced into her hair. "More."

"I can't," she mumbled through a mouth full of cock.

He cradled the back of her neck in his huge palm. "A little more."

Before she could protest, he shoved his cock deeper into her mouth. She sputtered and gagged for a second before regaining control.

"Ahh." His thighs quaked against her shoulders.

He pulled almost all the way out before plunging deeper. Her nostrils flared as her eyes began to water. Trying to escape his grip was useless, so she did what she could to appease him.

He thrust into her mouth. Long deep strokes followed shorter strokes. She caught onto his rhythm and before long, she had the majority of his cock in her mouth. Well, her throat, really.

He fucked her face for a few minutes before his belly tensed. The second she realized he was about to come, she tried to pull back. He held on tight.

"Swallow," he commanded.

Her eyes went wide. He wasn't going to… Yes, he was. Hot ribbons of cum spurted against the back of her throat. Without thinking, she swallowed the enormous load.

After a final shudder he said, "Lick it off."

She lapped at the salty cum, cleaning his cock completely. She felt like such a dirty girl, but she loved it. She'd never been forced like that. The men she dated hadn't so much as forced a kiss, let alone deep throat.

He grinned at her. "Now I make you come."

He hoisted her up and tossed her onto the bed. As she lay back against the cool sheets, he crawled to cover her body. Although he'd just come, his cock still stood completely erect.

She eyed the massive dick. What if it didn't fit? She was a tiny Asian girl, not some super-slut with a loose pussy. Would he shove it in anyway?

He pushed her thighs apart with his knees then knelt back. He grabbed her hips and pulled her ass up onto his thighs. Well, this was a different position. Interesting.

He angled his cock down toward her pussy. He rubbed the tip up and down her slit, sliding in a little each time. She watched the head disappear. As it stretched her tight pussy walls, she moaned.

"Oh, God. Oh fuck."

He smirked. "You like the big, black dick, don't you?"

She nodded.

"Tell me what you like."

"Your cock. It's so fucking huge."

He forced it another inch deeper. "You're tight as hell."

She pushed against his belly. "That's all, I can't…"

A look of sheer determination crossed his face. She gasped. Oh shit!

He crawled forward until her ass fell back against the bed. She wrapped her legs around his waist and held on for dear life as he plunged his huge cock into her tiny pussy.

She screamed more from shock than from anything else. The feeling of being completely and utterly stuffed pitched her over the edge into a state of total ecstasy. She bucked against him as her pussy clenched and released his cock in rapid succession. Her mouth froze open in a silent scream as she came.

She stopped breathing as he fucked her with long, deep strokes. She was on the verge of coming again when someone walked into the room.

"What the fuck, Tyrone?" De'ron barked.

"I didn't know you had a lady up in here."

She turned to look at Tyrone. The black man stood in the doorway. His shorts tented with an obvious erection.

"I'm busy," De'ron said.

"Let a brother join in?" asked Tyrone.

She licked her lips. She'd already come this far, why not take both of them?

Before she could respond De'ron said, "She's mine."

She loved the possessive way he spoke, but she couldn't pass up this opportunity. "It's okay."

"What?" The men asked in unison.

"I've always wanted a hot black guy, now I can have two."

De'ron looked pissed that he'd have to share, but he relented and pulled his cock out of her sopping wet pussy.

Tyrone didn't need a warm-up. He managed to drop his shorts while walking across the room. After jumping onto the bed, he rolled her over and pulled her hips back. On her knees, she glanced at De'ron who was also on his knees, crawling to face her.

She opened her mouth to take De'ron. This time, it was so much easier to suck his cock. She hadn't known what she was capable of earlier, but now that she knew, she took almost all of him into her throat.

Behind her, Tyrone rubbed his dick against her pussy lips. As he plunged into her, she fell forward. De'ron pulled his cock out of her mouth which gave her a moment to adjust.

Back on her knees, she flashed a smile at De'ron. He took it as a sign that he could take possession of her mouth again.

With Tyrone in her pussy and De'ron in her mouth, she was double stuffed with two big, black cocks. She was such a dirty little whore and she loved it.

The men worked her good until her knees trembled and

her arms ached. After a while, her ravaged pussy shivered with another orgasm.

Tyrone whistled. "You got a vibrating pussy, girl."

She giggled around De'ron's cock.

A finger brushed her asshole. She jolted. "What the hell?"

Tyrone asked, "You like cock in your ass?"

She shook her head vigorously, no.

"You ever try it?"

"No," she managed to mumble.

"Then how do you know?" Tyrone dipped his finger into her pussy then spread the slick juices against her asshole.

She bounced her ass in an attempt to get away from his probing finger.

"Oh shit, bounce it, girl."

She froze as Tyrone laughed.

De'ron pulled his cock out of her mouth. "I know how to make it good. Come, climb up on my dick."

He lay on his back on the bed. Tyrone wrapped his arms around her waist and carried her over to his friend. He positioned her over De'ron's cock. She settled onto it, grateful that they'd apparently given up on her ass.

But just as she'd found a nice rhythm bouncing on his cock, Tyrone pushed her down so that her chest pressed against De'ron.

"What are you doing?" She turned to catch Tyrone spitting into his hand.

"Relax," he quipped.

She tried to crawl away, but she was impaled on De'ron's cock.

He held her hips. "Don't worry, he's good at this."

"But, I've never—"

Tyrone's cock pressed against her tight hole. Her eyes

went wide. Oh shit, they were going to double team her. She moaned as De'ron worked his cock against her clit.

Tyrone increased the pressure on her ass. When his cock pushed past the tight ring of muscles, she screamed.

"Ohhh, Gooooood."

Her eyes rolled back as an orgasm sent her into a spasming mess of pleasure. So stuffed, so filled, so dirty. She came again, this time digging her nails into De'ron's chest.

"Ouch," he yelped.

She couldn't help it. She couldn't stop coming as Tyrone worked his cock deeper into her ass. With one cock in her pussy and one in her ass, she was being pushed and pulled from every angle. She couldn't think, couldn't speak. She could only surrender to their enormous dicks, filling, stuffing.

"Ohhhh," she moaned.

Tyrone increased his pace. As he pounded her ass, the front of his thighs slapped the backs of hers. The obscene sound pulsed along with the blood in her ears.

Her arms failed and she fell onto De'ron's chest.

He grunted. "Let's change it up."

They pulled out simultaneously leaving her in a heap on the bed. They switched places so Tyrone lay on the bed and De'ron knelt behind her. They reclaimed her pussy and ass, working her over, forcing her to come again and again.

She couldn't do anything but take the savage pounding. But she loved it. She loved every second of it.

Dazed and half-conscious, she turned toward a sound in the doorway. A third black man stepped into the room. She gave him a lascivious grin. What difference did it make if she took one more?

He took it as an invitation to climb onto the bed. He tilted her head to one side and stuffed his cock between her lips. One in her pussy, one in her ass and one in her mouth. She couldn't wait to tell Mimi. Her friend would never believe what a dirty little slut she'd become.

The guys changed positions and took turns on her until she couldn't remember who was in which hole. But as another orgasm flooded her pussy, she looked down at the man below her.

De'ron's face twisted into a grimace as he jerked up, spraying his sticky cum into her pussy. The man behind her, God only knew who, blasted a white-hot load into her ass. The third man held her head in place as he blew a load into her mouth.

She crumpled onto the bed. The men took turns pulling their cocks out. She was covered in sweat and limp from coming so hard. The other two men left the room as De'ron curled up beside her. His heavy arm draped across her waist as he fell asleep. Although she needed to get back to the hotel, her eyelids were too heavy. She could just sleep for an hour, then go back.

When she woke hours later, the sky was still dark, but was growing lighter. She bolted upright. Oh, crap. Mimi was going to kill her for being out all night without telling her. They had an agreement that no matter what happened on the island, they'd both be back at the hotel room at sunrise to check in with each other.

She grabbed her dress and shoved it over her head. She had no idea where her underwear were and didn't have time to look for them.

De'ron's eyes opened. In a sleepy voice he said, "You coming back?"

She blushed. "Maybe."

"When do you leave?"

"Our flight is tomorrow night."

He grinned. "Then you come back tonight."

She winked. "I'll think about it."

She hurried out of the house onto the cool sand. As she ran up the beach, she debated how much she should tell Mimi. They usually shared every naughty detail of their dates, but what happened to her last night was a totally different situation.

As she unlocked the hotel room door, she turned to spot Mimi running down the hallway. A shit-eating grin spread across her face. "I thought you were going to kill me. But I guess we're both doing the walk of shame."

Aiko laughed as they walked into the room and fell onto their respective beds. "You are not going to believe what happened last night."

Mimi smirked. "You look like a hot-mess."

Aiko rolled onto her belly. "I'm kind of afraid to tell you."

Her friend said, "What happens in Jamaica stays in Jamaica."

"I thought that was Vegas."

"Whatever." Mimi waved away the response. "Spill."

Aiko began the story and she didn't stop until she'd described every last inch of the three men who'd triple stuffed her.

PUNISHING BRIDEZILLA

Blair hollered as she chucked the wedding cake topper across the hotel ballroom at Lenora, the event coordinator. "If I wanted an orange-colored bride and groom on top of my cake, I would have bought it from China myself. This is outrageous. Why can't you people do anything right?"

The waif-like, inept girl, who was way too young to be wearing a tailored Armani suit, responded through clenched teeth. "Mrs. Beaumont—"

"I'm not married yet, so you should address me as 'Miss Blair'. Although at this rate, I don't see how we're going to be ready by tonight. I should already be at the salon getting my hair finished and makeup done, but I'm stuck here doing your job for you," Blair snapped.

The rollers in her hair bounced for a second before settling down. She'd chosen a long, princess-style so that her Swarovski crystal tiara would sparkle under the ballroom lights. But at this rate, she'd probably need to have the stylist re-do her entire head.

Lenora said, "If the cake topper isn't to your liking, we

can change it. The hotel can provide a variety of options. If you just give me—"

"Well hurry up and get them. I'm don't have time for this nonsense," Blair huffed.

The event coordinator's lips pressed into a thin white line, but she kept her mouth shut, as she should. Who do these people think they are? Today, *her* wedding day, was supposed to be all about *her* and she'd destroy anyone who got in the way of her perfectly crafted soirée.

Out of the corner of her eye, Derek, the photographer, approached. As usual, his eyes dropped to the swell of her double-D cleavage. Apparently, he liked the red halter-top dress she was wearing because he could hardly tear his gaze away to look at her face.

The man practically drooled as he spoke. "Excuse me, Miss Blair. I wanted to run through the list of photos you want taken during the reception."

God, was everyone incompetent in this place? She put her hands on her hips. "Don't you already have the list?"

"I do, but I wanted to know if there were any last-minute changes. You've already had so many." He skewered her with a predatory look.

Something about him always made her nervous. Not only did he tower over her by at least a foot, but he was also built like a linebacker. He seemed ready to attack her, as if the rage seething just below the surface would explode at any moment. Even his jet-black hair spiked up in defiance of gravity. But she'd never let him know how intimidated she felt around him.

She grabbed the list out of his hands and skimmed it. Wrong, again! Ugh, she was so sick of having to constantly hold the staff's hand on every little detail.

She shoved the list against his massive chest. "This is the list from two days ago."

His eyebrows drew together, and his features twisted into a frightening countenance. "Is that right, princess? You've changed the photo list at least twenty-five times in the last two months."

"And I can change it again if I want. That's what I'm paying you for."

"You're not paying me; your daddy's paying me." He tore up the list and threw the pieces at her. "And from this point on, I'm taking whatever the hell pictures I want."

"You can't do that," she stammered.

"I can, and I will."

Lenora hurried into the room carrying a huge box. "I have more cake toppers to choose from."

Derek sneered. "Another thing the princess isn't happy with, right?"

Lenora suppressed a smirk, but hints of it pushed up the corners of her mouth. "She didn't like the cake topper she chose last week and wanted a new one."

Blair looked from one employee to the other. She couldn't understand why they were intentionally trying to turn her wedding into a disaster.

Derek took the box from Lenora. "She doesn't deserve to make any more changes. I know for a fact that the contract says that no changes can be made within 48 hours of the day of the ceremony. We've indulged her long enough. I'm done, and you should be too."

Blair grabbed the string of pearls at her neck and twisted them between her fingers. "I want to talk to the hotel manager. Now!"

Lenora turned to leave, but Derek stopped her. "Don't go

anywhere, Lenora. She doesn't need the manager, what she needs is to learn how to respect other people."

"I want the manager right now." Blair stomped her ballerina-style slipper against the tiled floor.

Derek grabbed her upper arm. "Shut up. I'm so sick of your bullshit. You're one of those pampered, demanding bitches that gets off on treating other people like shit."

"Maybe someone needs to teach her a lesson in humility." Lenora's typically mousy whisper was gone. Instead, she spoke in a rough, domineering voice.

Too shocked to speak, Blair's mouth hung open. She'd never been disrespected by hired help before and had no idea what to do. She was used to the staff catering to her every whim. Maybe she was having a pre-wedding nightmare. If only she could wake up.

Derek's grip tightened. "Lenora's right. You need to learn how to keep your mouth shut."

"Or maybe she just needs something in it." The low, menacing voice came from someone entering the room; someone she didn't recognize.

"Who the hell are you?" she demanded.

"Terry Waters, head waiter." He brushed an errant lock of curly carrot-colored hair from his hazel eyes. That hair color had to be from a bottle. Why would anyone intentionally do that to their head?

Derek slapped the other man on the back. "So you're sick of her shit too?"

"Yep, and I know exactly what she needs."

Blair took a step back, but Derek still held her arm. "What?"

Lenora pushed between the two men. "She needs to go to the 'debasement'."

Blair struggled but couldn't free herself from Derek's

grasp. "I think you mean basement, and I'm not going down into a smelly staff area. I'm leaving."

Terry pointed toward a partially hidden door at the rear of the ballroom. "We should take the staff elevator. If we go through the kitchen, too many of the guys will see us and it will turn into a cluster-fuck."

"What will turn into a cluster-fuck?" Blair asked.

She couldn't imagine what they were talking about. 'Debasement'… 'Cluster-fuck'… What kind of people were working here? This was supposed to be the premier boutique hotel in New York, but they were acting like Bronx hoodlums.

Lenora grabbed her other arm. "Let's go, cupcake."

"Where?"

Terry chuckled. "You'll find out soon enough."

Lenora clutched the bride's arm tighter. As Bridezillas went, Blair was above average on both the bitchiness level, and the hotness level. Lenora could hardly wait to get her hands on the uptight bitch's huge breasts. Oh, to be able to suckle those nipples.

She followed Derek into the staff hallway. With the quick glance in each direction, she breathed a sigh of relief. None of the staff were in the hallway. She hated sharing, especially the hot ones.

Blair whined, "Fine, I won't make any other changes. Just let me go so I can finish getting my hair and makeup done."

Lenora shoved her into the elevator. "It's too late. We're done with your bullshit. But don't worry, we know exactly how to fix spoiled little brats."

Derek pressed 'B' for basement. As the noisy freight elevator descended slowly, she glanced at the trembling bride. Good, she was already scared and would be easy to manipulate. Some of the Bridezillas would panic and collapse in a puddle of tears. Totally not sexy. But not this one, this one had some fight and she intended to find out exactly how much.

The doors opened into the immense underground storage area. Three years ago, she and the other staff took their first Bridezilla down here for a round of punishment. That first encounter was so successful, they'd made a pact. Never again would they put up with spoiled little bitches.

When she wasn't at the hotel, Lenora moonlighted as one of the few female Doms at Club Craze, a BDSM club hidden on the upper east-side. Her experience at the club came in handy in more ways than one. She knew exactly how to teach these Bridezillas how to become obedient wives.

Lenora steered Blair toward the furthest corner of the basement. Two years ago, they'd secretly crafted a dungeon behind a false wall. The entire room had been completely soundproofed, so even if other staff were in the basement, they'd have no idea what was happening just a few feet away.

They passed a huge storage area filled with tables and folding chairs. Hidden behind a towering stack of boxes, the door to the dungeon was secured with a padlock. Terry pulled the key from his back pocket. Apparently, he'd already planned to punish this bride. Sneaky bastard.

"You're like a fucking Boy Scout, always prepared."

As the lock clicked open, Terry smirked. "Come on, like you didn't know we were going to do her?"

"I predicted it after she changed the photo list the fifth time," Derek said.

Blair's whiny voice squeaked. "I don't know where you're taking me, but you can't do this. I'm going to tell my father and you're all going to get fired."

Lenora gave her an icy smile. "I highly doubt that."

"And even if she did complain, who'd believe her?" Terry snickered.

The door swung open to reveal the soundproof dungeon. The same gray foam used in recording studios lined the walls and ceiling. Plush crimson carpet covered the floor. They'd spared no expense, after all, this was a high-end hotel. Only the best for these coddled princesses.

Lenora pushed Blair into the room.

The bride's jaw dropped. "Oh my God, what is this place?"

"Tie her up," Lenora commanded.

"Where?" Terry asked.

"Let's use the leather handcuffs and the meat hook overhead," she replied.

While Terry and Derek restrained the whimpering bride, Lenora circled her like a tigress. She couldn't decide which part she wanted to sample first. Should she start with the girl's plump, milky-white breasts? Or maybe her delectable ass? Or maybe, she should start with the girl's silky thighs. The only thing she knew for sure was that she'd save her pussy for later.

Blair struggled against the bonds. Her head twisted as her gaze darted around the room. It looked like a medieval torture chamber. A giant cross stood in one corner next to a strangely shaped bench. An array of whips and riding crops, of all things, lined an entire wall. Bizarre contraptions were laid out on a long, steel table. But one set of devices captured her attention above all the others, nipple clamps.

She shuddered. The guy she'd dated before her soon-to-be husband was a total freak. He'd always wanted to experiment on her sexually, but she refused. One night when she was too drunk to resist, he'd clipped angry metal clamps on each nipple. Remembering that pain shattered her composure.

She begged, "Please, anything but the nipple clamps."

"Really?" Lenora tilted her head to one side and Blair realized she'd made a huge mistake.

"I guess I know what I'm using," Lenora said.

Terry tugged on the chain that held her arms overhead. "All set."

Blair glanced from him to the photographer to the wedding coordinator. All three displayed a confident, predatory grin. What had she gotten herself into?

Lenora stepped forward. She ran the tips of her fingers across Blair's belly. Blair wiggled and twisted to one side in an attempt to escape.

"Hold still."

Blair froze. The staunch command was impossible to ignore. It was the same tone her father took when he was mad at her.

Lenora's palm flattened against her belly. A cascade of trembling nerves rippled out from her core. No matter how much she wanted to break free of the cuffs, she couldn't. She could only submit. As the wedding coordinator ran the palm of her hand up and down her body, a strange warmth filled the room. Maybe the air conditioner wasn't working.

Derek stepped forward. "Let's get that dress off."

"You're always in such a hurry."

"We don't exactly have all afternoon," he said.

"She doesn't need to walk down the aisle for another three hours. We have plenty of time," Lenora countered.

"I just want to see those tits," he said.

"You'll see them soon enough."

Blair bristled, "The only person seeing my tits today is my husband."

"I highly doubt that." Lenora's hand cupped Blair's left breast. "You have great tits. Your husband's going to be a very lucky man."

Blair's jaw dropped. She'd never had another woman touch her in such a sexual manner. Lenora squeezed and caressed her breast until her traitorous nipple formed a taut peak. Her hand shifted to her other breast. The sleek caresses were so wrong, but her body betrayed her mental protests. As the unwanted contact continued, her pussy tingled.

"Good girl, I knew you'd like it," Lenora crooned.

Blair whispered, "I don't like it."

"Really?"

Lenora ripped the front of Blair's dress open. Her breasts heaved with each shaky breath. The utter humiliation of being exposed blanketed her and all she could do was hang her head in shame.

"You shouldn't be doing this," Blair insisted.

Derek advanced toward her. "We should. In fact, it's her duty to prepare you for your husband. He shouldn't have to deal with a demanding wife for the rest of his life. You need to learn some discipline."

As Lenora shoved the top down to her waist, Blair struggled. With her arms tied overhead, she couldn't cover her naked torso. Humiliation coated her body in a thin sheen of sweat. How could these people, these employees, think that they could get away with this?

Lenora pulled the dress to her hips. "You need to learn to stop being so selfish."

Derek grabbed her jaw and held her face. "Do you know what selfless wives like to do for their husbands?"

"No."

"They like to suck cock. Lots and lots of cock. So much cock, that their jaws get tired and their lips end up permanently puckered," Derek said.

Lenora laughed. "Okay, he might be exaggerating slightly."

"Not if she's doing it right."

"At least let me warm her up first," Lenora said.

"Get her dress off," Terry said.

Terry unbuckled the white cummerbund on his waiter's uniform. He carefully folded it and placed it on the steel table. He kicked off his shoes, but left his socks on. When he reached for his belt, Blair's eyes went wide. He wasn't going to get naked, was he?

The sound of his zipper answered that question. She could hardly believe it when his pants dropped to the floor. He'd gone commando. The tip of his huge cock hid beneath his white tuxedo shirt. It had to be eight or nine inches and it didn't even seem fully erect yet. She licked her lips and turned away. The only cock she should be salivating over today was her husband's. She stole another glance at Terry before quickly averting her eyes.

"I think she likes it," Lenora said.

Derek unbuckled his belt. Good God, both men were getting naked? Why? Maybe they just wanted to jerk off? Right?

Lenora pushed Blair's dress over her hips and down her

thighs. Her breath came in short gasps as the other woman tossed the outfit across the room.

"You'll get that back later," Lenora said.

"What... What are you going to do to me?" Blair asked.

Lenora slid the jacket of her suit off and hung it on a nearby hook. "Everything."

Although Lenora projected a timid, waiflike appearance, her lavender-colored, satin camisole revealed her underlying strength. Compact muscles rippled along her arms as she crossed the room. When she reached for a riding crop, Blair shuddered, but not from the threat of pain. She'd always secretly admired very fit women and although she wasn't a lesbian, deviant fantasies of being with a woman surfaced from time to time.

Wearing only her underwear, Blair couldn't escape the lust-filled gazes of the photographer and head waiter. They stood several feet away from her, but their looks caressed every exposed inch of her body.

Derek said, "I want to see everything. I want to see that pussy."

His vile language snapped her out of the hypnotic way in which Lenora captured her attention.

"How dare you!"

She was already trapped in the most humiliating situation of her life, but she'd be damned if she'd put up with his filthy mouth.

"How dare I? I think we need to find a way to keep that bitchy mouth closed."

Derek crossed the room and grabbed something that looked like a plastic tennis ball hanging between two straps. She had no idea what he intended to do with it, but it couldn't be good.

"Fine. I'll keep my mouth shut just keep whatever that thing is away from me."

"It's too late for that, open up."

As she opened her mouth to protest, he jammed the plastic ball between her lips and wrapped the leather straps behind her head. She tried to push the ball out of her mouth with her tongue, but he'd already secured it in place. There was nothing she could do.

Lenora tilted her head to one side. "Don't look so sad. I promise I'll take good care of you and by the time I'm done with you, you'll be begging for more."

Blair grumbled against the ball. Unable to form words, she settled for glaring at her captors.

"I'm going to start by warming up that tight little ass," Lenora said.

Blair was completely unprepared for the smack of the crop against her ass. Her scream came out a garbled whimper. A dribble of saliva dripped onto her chin.

"I'm going to spank you until you submit to me. The longer you resist, the longer I'll punish you."

Out of the corner of her eye, she watched Terry stroke his enormous cock. She'd been right when she'd guessed that it was only semi-erect. A dark desire curled in her belly. Her soon-to-be husband's cock was big, but not as big as the beast Terry held in his hand. For God's sakes, he could hardly get his fist around it.

Terry grinned. "I can tell you want to suck it. I see it in your eyes."

She shook her head vigorously.

"It's okay. You can pretend you don't want it. Eventually you will be on your knees begging," he said.

She glared daggers at him for a moment before the hard whack of the crop caught her attention. Lightning bolts of pain shot through her ass straight to her pussy. She couldn't believe it, but being spanked had awakened a twisted, mysterious desire. As much as she wanted to resist, her body warmed and tingled where the crop struck her ass.

The corners of Lenora's eyes crinkled as she smiled. "Heating up already?"

Lenora tossed the crop across the room. For a second, Blair thought the punishment was over, boy was she wrong. Lenora renewed her vigorous assault with the palm of her hand. The walls muffled the smacking sound, but they couldn't contain the hellfire burning in her belly.

She twisted and writhed, her moans silenced by the ball gag. When she realized the uselessness of her feeble protests, she stopped thrashing. Raw heat blazed across her scorched ass. The endless slaps folded into each other until they merged with the pulse of her swollen pussy. As much as she wanted to deny it, the spanking turned her on.

A full minute passed, maybe two, before Lenora stopped. She scratched her nails across Blair's inflamed ass. The sensation was unlike anything she'd ever experienced. Part pleasure, part pain, all desire. She didn't know what was happening to her, she just knew that something deep inside was breaking.

Lenora dragged her nails under her ass and along the sides of her thighs. "I bet you didn't even know that you'd like this."

Lost in a sea of conflicting emotions, Blair didn't attempt any form of communication. She simply stood, waiting for whatever came next. Her mind raged against the sudden turmoil. What kind of woman enjoyed being beaten?

Lenora caressed the inside of her thighs. "Try not to think too hard, you'll only drive yourself crazy with questions."

The woman's deft fingers swirled and circled ever closer to Blair's panties. At least she still had those, that and her bra were her last barriers of protection. She figured she'd be okay as long as she could keep some clothing on, so when Lenora's fingers dipped below the white lace, Blair panicked.

She mumbled against the ball gag. "Oh my God, what are you doing?"

Terry slowly stroked his cock while he watched her. "I think we should let her talk."

"It is amusing, the things they come up with when they're completely freaking out." Derek wrapped the palm of his hand over the head of his cock and gave it a few light tugs. As long as he kept his hands to himself, she didn't care what he did.

To her relief, Lenora removed her hands from her panties and unhooked the gag. "Don't try to scream, it's pointless. No one can hear you down here."

"Can you at least uncuff me?" Blair asked.

"No. Any other questions?"

"Why are you doing this?"

Lenora walked behind her. Her hands deftly unhooked Blair's bra. "I'm doing this because there are two things in life I love more than anything else. Pussy, and punishing princesses."

"I'm not a princess."

As Lenora slid the bra up to Blair's bound hands, she said, "Hold onto these, we wouldn't want them to get lost."

Blair gripped the bra in one hand. "Please, let me keep my panties on."

"If you keep your panties on, how am I supposed to touch that shaved little pussy?" Lenora returned to face her.

"You can't... You can't touch my pussy," she sputtered.

"Be good, or we'll gag you again," Derek said.

The thought of drooling all over that disgusting piece of plastic kept her momentarily silent. She was tied up, naked, and at the mercy of a dominant lesbian. This was the furthest possible scenario from her ideal wedding day, but a twisted part of her wanted to know what would happen next.

Lenora leaned in and captured her lips in a soft, utterly erotic kiss. She'd never been kissed like this before and all thoughts of resistance vanished. When Lenora slipped her tongue into Blair's mouth, she responded by stepping closer to the other woman. As the kiss deepened, Lenora slid her hands into Blair's panties. Caught up in the kiss, she didn't protest when Lenora slowly worked them down over her hips. After they fell to her ankles, Blair kicked off her shoes and panties.

As Lenora pulled back, her hand rested on the string of pearls at Blair's neck. "I think we'll leave these on. It's somewhat poetic, don't you think?"

Blair nodded and stared at the other woman through hooded eyes. Sapphic desire coursed through her veins. Even though it was unnatural to kiss another woman, she couldn't help but want to taste the sweetness of her lips again.

"Kiss me," she whispered.

Lenora's mouth descended on her lips, hungry and demanding. Blair's breath caught in her throat as the other woman reached for her breasts. Lenora lightly pinched each nipple between her thumb and forefinger. When she tugged, the sharp pain of her overly sensitive nipples made her gasp.

"Shh... Sensitive, aren't you?" Lenora asked.

"Yes."

"Is that why you freaked out about the nipple clamps?"

"Yes, it's too much, too tight."

"You just have to leave them on until you get used to it." Lenora smiled and released her. She glided across the room toward the dreaded implements of torture.

When she picked up the nipple clamps, tiny bells affixed to their ends jangled. An involuntary shudder rippled through Blair's body. She already knew she couldn't escape. The best she could do was endure the evil little monsters. She had a feeling that the more she protested, the longer she'd have to wear them. The other woman's sadistic streak could be far worse than she knew.

Lenora tweaked one nipple, then the other. "The trick is to make sure they're nice and hard. It will keep the clips from falling off."

As Lenora fastened the first clamp, Blair cursed her rock-hard nipples. The slight jiggling motion of her breasts made the bell clang. The high-pitched ring continued with every tremble.

She hissed a breath as pain rocketed from her nipples to her pussy. Whatever invisible connection between them became overly apparent as the second clamp snapped closed. To her horror, a trickle of her juices dripped from her pussy down her thigh. She prayed no one else noticed.

With the clips in place, Lenora traced the thin patch of hair pointing toward her pussy. She splayed her palm against the hair and flicked the pad of her thumb along the slit. Blair shivered with pleasure. For a moment, she forgot the unholy nipple torture.

Lenora's thumb pressed deeper into her pussy. She'd breached the delicate folds of her labia and worked the wet juices until she was coated in her own desire.

She'd never been touched by another woman. Something strange and terrible was happening. The more Lenora stroked her clit, the wetter she became. She couldn't deny her arousal any longer. Somehow, her captors had forced her to debase herself. Everyone in the room knew exactly how much she liked what was happening. She hung her head in shame so they couldn't see her eyes.

When the slick dampness swirled against her clit, she moaned. Lenora stroked her faster and harder. Blair's knees trembled, but she stepped wider to give the other woman better access.

One finger, then another slid into her pussy. Lenora fucked her with her hand. Blair's muscles contracted as if trying to pull her deeper. Her hips arch in a greedy attempt to press the extraordinarily seductive fingers against her clit. She'd given up on propriety. If they wouldn't let her go, she'd take the filthy pleasure they intended to inflict on her.

Feverish with lust, she writhed against Lenora's hand. Somehow, the diabolical nipple clamps added to the growing storm in her body. She bit the edge of her lip and whimpered. Even if she wanted to stop the impending orgasm, she couldn't. They'd unleashed a force long buried deep inside her and there was nothing she could do to stop it.

Her head whipped back as her muscles convulsed. Undulating waves of release wracked her body. She screamed as the orgasm crashed over her. A shuddering mess, she hung from the handcuffs until Derek reached overhead to release her. She'd nearly forgotten the two men in the room who'd witnessed her shameful display of passion.

She raised her head and locked gazes with Lenora. The self-satisfied look on the other woman's face was humiliating. She'd come for a complete stranger on her wedding day.

Lenora licked her fingers. "I knew it. You are an obedient little slut, aren't you?"

⁓

Derek loved this part. The part where the Bridezilla broke and realized she'd fallen under their spell. He admired the way Lenora could control a woman with a single finger. The girl had skills he wished he could partake in. Unfortunately, Lenora only liked pussy, so he'd always had to keep his cock in his pants unless they were breaking a Bridezilla.

He dragged the bride across the room to a punishment bench. Before he continued, he unclipped the nipple clamps. He didn't want her wrecking her tits. He bent her over the waist-high, black leather-covered, wooden bench.

"What? I thought it was over," Bridezilla whimpered.

"Not even close. There are two cocks in this room that you haven't serviced yet."

"But, I can't have sex with another man on my wedding day."

As he attached leather straps across the backs of her knees, he said, "I'm sure your fiancée won't mind. After all, he's going to have a very obedient bride when we're done with you."

Her legs were bound to the bench, but she kicked and flailed her feet. As if they could free her. He laughed at her futile attempts to escape.

After walking around to the front of the bench, he grabbed one waving hand and wrapped a leather strap around it.

The bride's head whipped up. "Not my hands."

Losing control distressed every Bridezilla. At this point, they typically resigned themselves to the process. But not this bride. She repeatedly slapped at him with her other hand until he captured and secured it.

Terry grabbed a paddle off the wall and stalked toward her. The paddle whooshed through the air before connecting with the girl's plump ass.

"Ouch," she yelped.

Lenora said, "You'd better cooperate. If you make them mad, you won't be able to sit at your reception."

Out of the corner of his eye, he watched Lenora strip. She removed her bra to reveal twin mounts of small, yet firm breasts. They matched the rest of her thin, waif-like body. She packed a ton of power in her small frame and he respected her sadistic tendencies. Too bad she wouldn't let him shove his cock into her tight little pussy.

"What do you guys want? Do you want to humiliate me?"

He returned his attention to the complaining bride. "We want you to learn obedience. The world doesn't revolve around you. If you weren't such a bitch, we wouldn't have to train you. But you are, and we will."

To thwart further discussion, he grabbed her chin which was eye level with his cock. "Do you suck your fiancée's cock?"

She drew back. "No."

"Have you ever sucked cock before?"

"A few times. But, why?"

"Seriously? You have to ask?"

"I'm not going to suck yours." She spit on his cock.

He lightly slapped her cheek with his shaft. "Thanks for the lube. Make it nice and slobbery. I want to see drool dripping from your chin."

"Wha—"

As soon as she opened her mouth, he shoved his cock in.

The wet, hot softness enveloped him. His eyelids fluttered at the sudden rush of pleasure. Most of the Bridezillas were excellent cock suckers; after all, they were used to using their mouth a lot.

He grabbed the back of her head and worked his cock in deeper. To his surprise, she didn't resist. She stared up at him with the submissive gaze he knew he could coax out of her. He just hadn't realized how easy it would be. Could she be faking her protests and secretly be getting off on all the attention?

As he pulled out to let her take a breath, she swirled her tongue around the head. Yep, she liked it.

He relaxed as she sucked and licked the length of him. Not bad considering she claimed not to suck off her fiancé.

The rollers in her hair bobbed with the movement of her head. She'd have to have her hair redone for sure. He glanced at the clock on the wall. They had a few more hours before they'd have to let her go, plenty of time to fuck her.

Terry waved the paddle in the air as if to ask if he could use it. Derek nodded slightly and pulled his cock out just as the other guy smacked her.

"Oh, fuck," she yelled.

But the cry didn't sound like a cry of pain, it sounded like a cry of pleasure.

"Again," he said.

Terry brought the paddle down hard. Bridezilla moaned and clawed at the legs on the bench.

Lenora moved in behind the bride. After each whack of the paddle, she waited until the girl stopped groaning before she rubbed her thumb against the girl's clit.

Soon they found the perfect rhythm and the bride's eyes glazed over. He knew that look. Sub-space, that warm, fuzzy place where submissives went after they relinquished control and let their Dom take over. The subs were very open to suggestion while they were in that space.

"Open your mouth. You're going to suck my cock while they spank you, and you're not going to bite."

She nodded and stretched forward, as if eager to let him bury his cock in her throat. He wasn't one to deny a horny woman, so he spread his feet into a firm stance and slid his cock between her lips.

The sloppy, wet blowjob worked his cock into a state of total arousal. He'd never been so hard in his life and more than anything in the world, he wanted to come in her mouth. Instead of trying to hold back, he welcomed the tingling sensation in his balls.

He locked gazes with her and said, "Swallow every drop."

Her nostrils flared. Her eyes went wide. His thrusts muffled her garbled response. He didn't give a shit about what she'd said. He only cared about one thing - filling her mouth with a huge load of cum.

As the first contraction rippled down his cock, he clenched his thigh muscles to keep himself steady. A blast of cum jetted into her throat and then another and another. She dutifully sucked as much as she could, but he'd been saving his cum for two days. He'd known she'd end up down here and had planned for it.

Each blast of cum, stronger than the last, shot into her throat until she'd swallowed as much as she could. She tried to pull away and a ribbon of cum drizzled onto her cheek. Her tongue lapped at the sticky cum as if she was desperate to taste every drop.

As the orgasm subsided, he stumbled back into a chair. "Fuck, that was good."

Lenora rubbed the girl's pussy. "You should feel how wet

she is right now. I wish I had my strap-on with me. Do you think I have enough time to run home and get it?"

Terry responded, "No. There's not enough time. But I bet you won't forget it next time."

"Asshole," she said.

Terry winked. "Is that an offer?"

Lenora rolled her eyes. "Not in this lifetime."

"So I have a chance," he quipped.

Derek said, "If you two don't shut the fuck up and get that pussy, I will."

Terry shook his head. "Not a chance. I've been standing here with my cock in my hand while you two fuck her. It's my turn."

Blair's breasts pressed against the bench. She inhaled the scent of new leather and knew she'd always remember this day as the day she realized she liked being ordered around. Relinquishing control wasn't as bad as she feared. It didn't make her weak. In fact, she was the one who'd made Derek come. So what if she was tied up, she still had the power to make him moan. But, another form of fear still hung over her head.

At first, when Derek told her to suck his cock, guilt crept up to shame her. Then she realized that her husband would never find out. The staff would lose their jobs if they ever told anyone and Blair sure as hell wasn't going to reveal her dirty little secret. She could get away with this just like she'd gotten away with so many other things in her life.

A brush of something against her pussy grabbed her attention. "What's going on back there?"

She heard the door to the room open as Terry replied, "Just lubing up my cock so I can fuck you."

"What? NO! I'll let you do anything but that. The only man who can fuck me on my wedding day is my husband."

"I'm glad you think so." The deep voice she'd recognize anywhere belonged to her fiancé, Craig.

She wilted on the bench. Oh God, he'd caught her. Wet, naked and with a cock inches from her pussy, he was going to be furious.

"It's not what it looks like," she said.

He stood in front of the bench in full view of her depravity. "Your mother came looking for me when she couldn't find you. I asked Avery, the bartender, where to look for you and she told me about the staff's secret dungeon."

Too shocked to speak, she stared at him.

"I have to admit. At first, I was furious. How dare they do this without my permission? But then I realized that, in a way, this is their wedding present to me. You've always been uptight in the bedroom. I'm glad they're breaking you before I marry you."

She gasped. "You don't care that another man is about to fuck me on our wedding day?"

"No. In fact, I can't wait to watch."

"Don't you want me all to yourself? Most men would never allow something like this."

"I'll have you to myself for the rest of my life, so I'm perfectly fine with sharing you once. It's always been a fantasy of mine. Besides, you don't exactly look very distressed," he said dryly.

Lenora said, "Just say the word and we'll stop. This is more about getting her ready for you than it is about us getting to fuck her."

"I'll watch for now," Craig said.

Blair dropped her gaze to the floor as her fiancé slid into a nearby chair. She couldn't believe he was condoning the staff's behavior. Maybe he'd hidden his perverted tendencies for the last two years and had been waiting until they were married to unleash them.

Avery drifted into view. She looked less like a bartender and more like a librarian. Wire rimmed glasses framed her face. A long, chestnut ponytail hung halfway down her back. The only indication of her less than prim and proper façade was the huge green dragon tattoo on her right thigh.

The dragon undulated and flowed as if filled with life as she walked. Blair couldn't look away from the expertly inked tattoo. She barely noticed as the girl unbuttoned her white dress shirt and black pencil skirt.

As soon as she was naked, Avery clapped her hands together. "It's like a fucking buffet. I can't decide where to start."

Lenora embraced Avery. "I recommend her pussy."

"Mine." In a single word, Terry staked his claim. And to keep the other women away from his prize, he slipped the tip of his cock between her pussy lips.

Blair fought the urge to moan. She refused to let her fiancé witness her disgraceful behavior. They could fuck her all they wanted. As long as he was in the room, she wouldn't make a sound.

Terry thrust his cock into her. Oh God, it was unprotected.

"Wait," she yelled.

Terry ignored her and in one swift thrust, buried his cock deep inside her. She bit her lip to keep from screaming. The sudden, forceful invasion blasted pleasure along the walls of her slick pussy. Still, she refused to make a sound.

Lenora and Avery were locked in a passionate kiss. Both

women groped the other's ass and breasts. They seemed very well acquainted with one another. When they finally broke the breathless kiss, they giggled like two school girls.

Avery said, "Can I put the anal beads in?"

Lenora traced the areola on the other girl's left breast. "I did last time, so it's your turn."

Avery squealed. "Small, medium or large?"

"Large, of course."

Derek still sat in the corner recovering from the blow job. "As if you had to ask…"

Blair shuddered. Thank God the girls were occupied with each other. If one of their tongues landed on her pussy, she'd scream for sure.

Avery opened a drawer in a large dresser and pulled out a string of beads of increasing size. As she walked back to Lenora, the dragon on her thigh coiled as if preparing to strike. Blair shook her head. The craziness of the situation was clearly making her hallucinate.

Avery swung the beads over her head. "Want to help me?"

"Absolutely," Lenora replied.

They disappeared from sight. At least she didn't have to watch them doing strange things with those beads.

Terry stroked his cock in and out of her pussy. She bit down on the bench to keep from begging him to fuck her harder. Too bad she didn't have that ball gag anymore. She never would have believed she'd want it again, but she did now. Dare she ask for it?

As she struggled with that question, she felt something drip onto her ass. Ew, probably Terrry's sweat. She was about to turn and tell him to wipe it up when she felt something hard press against her tightest hole.

"What the fuck?"

Avery said, "Don't clench, we already dripped some lube onto your ass. If you relax, they will go in easier."

Blair lurched forward and the bench scraped a few inches across the floor. "No way. I've never had anything in my ass before."

Her fiancé said, "I can guarantee that. The second I try to get near it, she freaks out."

She glared at him. "It's not natural to put things in there. It's for getting things out, not in."

He smirked and unbuckled the belt on his pants. "We'll see about that."

"We have your blessing, right Mr. Beaumont?" Avery asked.

Craig peeled his shirt off and standing in just his boxers, he replied. "Be gentle."

"Of course."

Blair jerked against the restraints. "No way. Not my—"

Her words dissolved into a shriek as Avery shoved the first anal bead into her ass. It awakened every nerve ending and she frantically grasped the legs of the bench. The evil beads popped into her ass one by one until she couldn't take anymore.

"No more," she whimpered.

A drop of sweat formed over her top lip. She fought the urge to moan and ground her pussy against Terry's cock. The beads clinked against the walls of her ass awakening sensations she'd never experienced before. It felt so amazing; she bounced her ass to make them move even more.

"Yeah bitch, ride that cock," Terry bellowed.

Avery shoved one more bead into Blair's ass. "All done. See, it wasn't that bad."

Blair panted and silently congratulated herself for not

moaning. Her fiancé returned to his chair and stroked his cock slowly. He stared at her with lust-filled eyes.

She'd just gotten used to the feeling of being completely stuffed with the beads when they vibrated to life in her ass.

"Ahhhh..." She screamed as an orgasm ripped through her body. The completely unexpected buzzing sensation ricocheted through her. She jerked and churned her ass, desperately trying to escape the sensation.

It was no use.

She collapsed against the bench, screaming, coming on another man's cock while her fiancé jacked off. She'd almost recovered when a scratchy tongue stroked her clit, unleashing a new wave of spasms.

She didn't even know who it belonged to. She just knew she wanted more.

Derek came out of nowhere to unlock the cuffs that held her hands and wrists. She tried to crawl away. It was too much, too intense. She had to escape before her heart exploded in her chest.

Strong arms grabbed her around her waist and lifted her in the air. Terry's cock slipped out as he spun her toward him. She held on for dear life as he scooped her up by her ass and impaled her on his cock. Still standing, he thrust up into her. Her legs wrapped around his waist. Her hands grabbed his strong shoulders.

"Fuck me," she yelled.

All sense of shame scattered along with half of her consciousness. They could do anything they wanted to her as long as they could make her come this hard.

Derek said, "Get the anal beads out. I want in."

Avery rushed to pull the beads out. One by one, they stretched her hole and made a wet, popping sound as they burst free. Every time another ball was freed, the continuous orgasm intensified for a second. She'd never come this long, or this hard in her life.

Derek stood behind her and stabbed at her ass with his cock. "Get her on the floor."

Terry pulled out. She staggered over him as he lay on the floor. "Jump on my cock, baby."

She straddled him and eased his cock into her quivering pussy. "More."

Derek knelt behind her. "You want more, you greedy little slut?"

"Yes, oh God, yes."

Derek forced the head of his cock into her ass. A searing pain lasted a few seconds but was quickly replaced by the overwhelming feeling of being completely, utterly stuffed.

She rode Terry's cock. Rollers uncoiled in her hair but she didn't care. Fuck the wedding, fuck looking and being perfect. She wasn't anyone's princess anymore, she was their fuck-slave and she loved it.

"Give it to her hard." She could hardly hear her fiancé's voice over her endless moans.

Derek pummeled her ass with his cock.

Avery stood over Terry's head and said, "Eat my pussy."

Blair had never eaten pussy in her life, but she licked and sucked the succulent folds as if her life depended on it. Avery grabbed the back of Blair's head and ground her pussy against her tongue.

Lenora knelt down beside her and snaked her hand between Blair and Terry's bodies. When the other woman found her clit, Blair tossed her head back and screamed. Rollers flew in every direction. Long curls unfurled across her breasts. Lenora pushed Blair's hair out of her way and latched onto one nipple with her mouth.

Blair jerked her hips and the whole room grew hazy and

grey. Lightheaded and about to pass out, she whispered. "Come in me."

The first spurts of cum filled her pussy and ass at the same time. Her peripheral vision was gone. Blood pounded in her ears. She came over and over until her pussy ached. Avery's sweet cream filled her mouth. It was the last thing she remembered before passing out.

Seconds later, she regained consciousness. Derek's cock popped out of her ass. Avery's pussy was gone and Terry was rolling her off him.

Lenora held her fiance's hand as she walked him over to his bride. "We've broken her for you. She's an obedient bride and will do anything you want right now."

Craig smiled. "I can't thank you guys enough. I never imagined seeing my future wife fucked by two guys and two girls at once. This is better than anything we could have put on our gift registry."

Avery chuckled. "Sure beats china."

From her place on the floor, Blair watched as Derek and Terry shook her fiancé's hand.

Terry said, "Hell of a girl you have there. I hope you spend a lifetime together."

Lenora checked the clock. "You have about twenty minutes before we need to take her up to hair and makeup. We'll be back to take her then."

Craig said, "That's plenty of time."

The four staff members filed out of the room. Blair looked up at her husband, completely unsure of what to say.

"You look beautiful right now," Craig said.

"I just let four people fuck me and you're telling me I look beautiful?"

He sat on the floor next to her. "Seeing you give up control is beautiful. I want you to be happy and insisting that everything be perfect all the time doesn't bring happiness. It brings misery."

She clasped his hand in hers. Her bottom lip trembled as she asked the question to which she feared the answer most. "Do you still love me?"

He tucked an errant strand of hair behind her ear. "I love you even more now."

She sighed with relief.

He said, "I do have to ask you one thing."

"What?"

"Is it true, are you going to be my obedient wife?"

She grinned. "Maybe in the bedroom."

"Or a dungeon?" he arched a brow.

She shot him a shy smile. "Are you considering one?"

"Now that I've seen what we can do in it, hell yes…We have a few minutes until they come back. I'm going to lay you down and fuck you until you get rug burns on your ass."

"Right now? But—"

"Consider it an obedience test."

He crawled across her body and slid into her still trembling pussy. As he pushed his cock in deep, the slick cum of the other man made a sucking sound, evidence of her debauchery.

She tensed up for a second, but her fiancé kissed her trepidation away. He rocked her with long strokes. And true to his word, her ass scraped across the carpet until it burned. But she didn't care. She had the man of her dreams in her arms and she couldn't wait to marry him, and to obey him, for the rest of her life.

TAKEN HARD BY FIVE BILLIONAIRES

I'm on hour four of the longest, most boring open house on record. If I wasn't trying to step up my game as a real estate agent, I would have pulled the plug on this over-priced monstrosity of a house hours ago. But, if I can sell this Stepford-wives-ready mansion, I can finally go on my dream vacation to France.

The doorbell rings. Who doesn't know that they can just walk into open houses? I'm not a butler. I sigh as I walk to the door. When I open it, my jaw drops. Five of the hottest internet millionaires I've ever seen stroll into the house. I know exactly who they are because they were on the cover of Forbes last week.

Holy shit, they're hotter in person than they were with all the air brushing. Their backs are to me so I take the opportunity to straighten my tight red pencil skirt. I also discretely unbutton the top button on my crisp white blouse. Good thing I'm dressed to kill. Although, I'm not really sure what I'm expecting. It's not like they're all going to line up and fuck me on the pool table upstairs, but a girl can dream.

I hand each of the hotties a brochure. "It's twenty thousand square feet and includes a movie theater and fully appointed game room."

"And a pool?" asks Andrew Barley.

His jeans are a size too small but in all the right places. I'm guessing he's at least 8" and thick if the bulge in his pants is any indication. He gives me a look that says, my eyes are up here.

I smile broadly. "It's right outside. I'll show you the backyard."

As I turn toward the sunken living room, Jared Lawson follows a little too closely. I wonder if I'm swinging my hips for nothing, after all, how the hell can he see my ass if he's breathing down my neck?

Jared steps outside and whistles. "Tennis courts too?"

"Designed by Frank Dunken, the best in L.A."

While the guys walk around the huge swimming pool, I take in the view. And I don't mean the expansive vista overlooking downtown L.A. I mean the glorious view of five tight asses. Mmm, it's been way too long since I got laid. I should probably hit a bar, but when do I have the time? Between taking care of my sick mother and my sniveling ex-husband, I hardly have time to eat. Which is probably good since I've managed to keep my waistline in check.

At thirty-two years old, I'm hovering somewhere between being a hot co-ed and a naughty MILF. Not close enough to either end to qualify. But I stay in shape with morning runs and drink the god-awful green smoothies that are all the rage right now. Yuck!

Perry Neilson turns and gives me that up and down look that means he likes what he sees. "I like the view."

"It's hot."

"And tight."

Kyle Pinkley says, "Let's go see if we can bounce a quarter off the beds."

For a second I think he's propositioned me but then I come to my senses. Unless I'm dead and in Heaven, I'm not going to get fucked by five hot guys during an open house. I mean, who does that? I'm a professional, dammit.

I allow the guys to walk past and marvel at their hot twenty-something asses. I seriously need to get laid.

As we enter the house, I rattle off the details of the mansion. "The kitchen was completely upgraded by the current owner and includes a gas range and double oven."

Andrew Barley, who made his fortune selling a video game app, smiles. "I'm sure our chef will like it."

"You're all planning on moving in together?" I ask.

"We do everything together," Dylan Yaley says.

He reminds me of a fictional Dylan from this zip code. He even has the same leather jacket and James Dean hair. He'd be a woman's wet dream in any era, especially with that cocky swagger.

As we climb the stairs to the second floor, the folds of my slick pussy rub together. I'm already wet and ready, but I'm so far from closing the deal it's not even funny.

Perry stops to inspect a few bedrooms. "How many total?"

"Seven plus the master."

"One for each of us and two left over."

"You're going to have to fight me for the master," Dylan says.

I use my best 1950's housewife voice, "Now boys..."

Kyle finds it hysterically funny. "Nice one."

"I thought you might like that," I say.

We reach the movie room. I flick on the overhead lights and show them the dimmer switch. "You get the same surround sound and movie experience without the hassle of driving downtown."

"I can't wait to crank up a porno in here," Jared says.

I try to suppress a smile, but Dylan sees it. In fact, he's looking at me with dangerously sexy intent. I couldn't possibly be imagining it, could I?

The men file out leaving me with Dylan. As we're about to walk out, he turns and blocks the door by holding the door frame with his hands. "I have a question for you."

A flutter of anticipation bounces through my chest. "Okay."

"Have you ever had sex in public?"

My jaw drops. I can't catch my breath long enough to get a word out.

He continues, "Because you're fucking hot, and if I took you to the movies, I wouldn't be able to resist pulling your panties down. I'd slide you onto my lap and make you ride my cock until I shoot a load of cum in your pussy."

"I..."

He cocks his head to one side. "You're even cuter when you're flustered. I like the prim and proper suit and bun-thing on your head. It gives you that naughty librarian look. But I wonder what you look like when you're not at work. Are you secretly a little sex kitten?"

He releases his grip on the door and stalks forward. The sway of his hips is almost as mesmerizing as the lust in his eyes. Okay, I wanted him before, but now I'm dripping with slick juices. A trickle runs down the inside of my thigh.

"Do you want me to fuck you?" he asks.

"I..."

Without warning, he spins me around and folds me over the back of one of the plush leather chairs. One hand yanks up my skirt while another pulls my panties down. Thank God I have lace on and not my white cotton granny-panties.

"Spread."

He's not asking, he's ordering. It's so fucking hot that I don't hesitate. My skirt is bunched around my waist. My panties are wrapped around my sensible pumps. I didn't even wear my come-fuck-me-heels today and I'm about to get a dick stuffed into me.

He leans over and presses me forward. He whispers, "I hope you like it rough."

"Yes," I croak.

"I knew it. I could see it in your eyes."

I hear his zipper come down. With every notch, I get a little hotter, a little wetter, a little more desperate to be stuffed full of millionaire cock. Shit, I don't even care that he's rich. I steal a glance over my shoulder just as he's pulling out all ten inches of his massive dick.

He grins and strokes it a few times. A drop of pre-come glistens on the tip. I lick my lips. I'd suck the hell out of his cock if he let me. But he has other plans.

He pushes me back over the chair and pulls my legs apart. I'm so far forward that I'm barely touching the ground anymore. The chair's wide and rounded at the top so it doesn't dig into my belly too hard. But Dylan, shit, he wasn't kidding when he said he hopes I like it rough.

In a single, savage thrust, he drills deep into my quivering cunt. I let out a scream which brings the other four running. They burst into the room but I can tell they aren't shocked.

"Fuck," Jared says.

"Yeah, he won the pool," Andrew grumbles as they each whip out a crisp $100 bill.

Dylan's balls deep in me. "Put it on the chair. I'm a little busy if you can't tell."

He pumps into me a few times before really giving it to me hard. My feet fly off the ground. The only thing that keeps me from toppling over the chair is Dylan's death-grip on my hips. His nails dig into me giving me that pleasure-pain sensation. I don't even think he knows he's doing it.

Kyle quietly unbuckles his belt and sets it on the chair. He drops his khaki shorts and steps out of them. He folds them neatly and sets them on the chair just under my face. I look up to see another massive cock. It's the same size at Dylan's, maybe bigger. But I'm not really in the position where I can whip out a tape measure or anything.

"Suck it."

I open my mouth eagerly. His cock's briny scent fills my nose with the smell of young, hot flesh. Jesus, I'm hard up.

I'm so out of practice that his cock barely fits between my lips. I'll need to remember to stretch my mouth before I do another open house. Not that I expect this to ever happen again, but who the hell knows.

His cock fills my throat so fully that I have trouble breathing. It doesn't help that my diaphragm is being crushed by the chair. But, I do what I can and he seems to like it. He pulls my chignon loose and a cascade of long blond hair spills over my shoulders and down across my shirt.

Andrew says, "Get your cock out of the way for two seconds. I want her naked."

Kyle pulls his sloppy wet cock out of my mouth. A trail of drool extends from it to my lips. It's over a foot long before it breaks off.

Andrew kneels on the couch and makes quick work of the buttons on my shirt. I expected him to rip it open. But, I guess that would be hard to explain if I got pulled over by the cops on my way home. I might drive like a drunk by the time they're done plowing me.

The second Andrew takes off my shirt, Kyle's back in my face with his cock. I bounce forward as Dylan works his dick deep into my slick hole. It's so hot, so dirty, so forbidden that I'm only seconds away from coming. The added friction of the leather from the couch against my clit is enough to make me explode.

"Fuck, I'm coming," I babble around Kyle's cock.

He just laughs. As my eyes roll back and I convulse harder than an epileptic, Kyle goes for the deep throat. I'm so gone I don't care. Forget breathing. Who needs it when you're double stuffed with cock?

Behind me, Dylan yells. Hot jets of cum shoot into my still quivering cunt. I try to dislodge Kyle's cock from my throat but he's got a grip on my hair that shows me he means business.

"Hey, let her up for a second," Perry complains.

He must have some semblance of authority over the group because Kyle begrudgingly pulls his cock out. I slide over the front of the chair in a crazy summersault and land on my ass on the floor. There's plenty of room between the aisles so I don't hit anything with my flailing legs.

Kyle slides into a seat and all I can think is, holy shit, I hope we don't stain the chair. How would I explain that to the homeowners?

"Come jump on my cock," he says.

My pussy feels surprisingly empty after being stuffed with so much cock, so I'm happy to straddle him. I lower myself onto his thick, wet cock and lean back to show off my tits. I'm fucking proud of them. They're just as firm today as they were when I was eighteen.

Jared, Perry and Andrew all have their cocks out now. I'm about the ride them like a train and I can't fucking wait. Stuff it in boys, momma needs some more cock.

Jared walks up behind me. "Lean forward."

I don't know what he's up to until I hear him spit. Oh, wait a minute. The tip of his cock brushes up against my puckered asshole.

I gasp. "Don't you guys have lube?"

Perry says, "Fuckin' animals. Of course I remembered to bring the lube this time."

This time? So they've done this before. Not that I'm surprised. I mean, they weren't exactly shocked to come in and find Dylan bending me over the chair.

An exchange of lube is made and Jared's cock is back to attempting to invade my ass. I sigh, anal's not my favorite, but I can get into it if I'm really feeling dirty. I'm surrounded by hard cocks getting fucked in my client's home theater. Yeah, it's dirty enough.

The tip of his cock pops past the tight ring of muscles and in slow, painstakingly hot progression, he fills me.

"Oh, shit," I gasp.

It's so big and hard and…

"Argghhhh…"

He pulls back then slams into me. He reaches around to hook his pointer fingers in my mouth. I moan and lean into him. I love being treated like a dirty little slut. He's riding me like a beast.

The slapping staccato of his hips against my ass is sucked up by the soundproof walls. I'm starring in my own porno now, Angela Hinks Takes on the Millionaires. I can't see myself, but I can imagine what it looks like and it's scorching hot.

Kyle reaches up to squeeze my tits together. I'm pretty

busty, but pushed together, it's obscene. His mouth descends on one nipple. He tugs and bites gently at first, then he sucks until I'm writhing with overwhelming pleasure.

"Ohhhh," I moan.

Jared releases his grip on my mouth and slaps my ass. "Yeah, take it, you naughty bitch."

Kyle lashes his tongue across my swollen nipples. They're raw with need. He doesn't disappoint. Rather, he sucks them again, back and forth until I'm bouncing like a maniac on his cock.

I need to come.

"Oh, God."

The link between my breasts and my cunt is driving me wild. I'm so close, just seconds away from an explosive release. But then Kyle beats me to it.

He hollers as hot cum spurts into my pussy. A dazed look passes over his face. His mouth drops open as the final jet splashes into me.

Jared lifts me off of Kyle. "Mine."

I love the way he's possessing me and controlling me like a doll. Objectify me. Use me. Hell, they can do whatever they want as long as they can make me come this hard.

Jared's wrecking my ass. A buzzing sensation flows from my ass to my pussy. Oh, wait. Is it... Oh shit!

The first anal orgasm of my life sends me into a convulsive mess. I lose my balance but Jared's ripped. He's strong enough to hold me up against him while I come.

Ragged jolts of erotic release blast through me. I'm screaming and trying to lunge for the couch. My feet are so high off the floor that I'm flailing. Then I go completely limp.

Jared plunges into me. My eyes bulge as he reaches uncharted territory. Even my pervy ex-boyfriend couldn't hit that spot. My ass immediately throbs and squeezes his cock as if trying to milk it.

Jared groans and rotates his hips against me. The swirling motion ratchets up the intensity of my long, continuous orgasm. Undulating waves put me into a state of complete ecstasy. I didn't even know I could come this hard for this long. Jesus, I'm probably ruined for all eternity now that I know how good it can get.

Two swift jerks later and cum bursts out of Jared's cock to line the walls of my ass. His fingernails dig into my hips to pull me tightly against him. A second later, he stumbles toward a chair and lands on his ass. The acrobatic move keeps me impaled.

When Andrew and Perry flash me lecherous looks, I know I'm not done yet. Andrew advances first. Impatience surrounds him in an aura of wicked intent. Jet black hair, dark eyes, a devilish smile and twelve inches of hot, rigid flesh come at me.

I stand there like a fool, staring. How can I not? He looks like he walked straight out of hell and I'm ready to get my demon on.

"On your knees," he commands.

While I drop to the floor, my mouth falls open. The briny, ultra-masculine scent assaults my senses. I want him to use me. Oh, God, I need it.

"Wider," he snaps.

I wish I could unhinge my jaw like a snake. But I do what I can as he shoves his cock between my lips. My nostrils flare. My eyes flash with fear. Oh, no. I totally underestimated the girth. It's still growing in my mouth, pressing dangerously close to my teeth. I open wider and press my teeth into the soft sides of my mouth. Please let it be enough.

"That's a girl, suck it harder."

Mmm, a rough blowjob. I'm into it even before he starts giving me orders.

"Deeper, baby. Yeah, right there. Fuck."

He groans and jabs the back of my throat with his monstrous cock. Normally, I don't have a gag reflex, but for some reason I start gasping around his dick. He loves it. Instead of pulling out, he grinds in deeper. I can't believe how much I've taken. I eye the remaining two inches and decide I'm up for the challenge.

After sucking in as much air as I can, I grab his ass and pull him toward me. His knees hit my chest but I cling to him in a desperate attempt to take it all. And I do. I fucking win. I should get a prize, like, the full asking price for this house.

How I can think of real estate transactions in this moment is a testament to my focus. I didn't make it to the big leagues without breaking a few rules. But I can honestly say I've never fucked anyone during an open house. Maybe I should take this as a lesson.

Andrew groans and strokes his cock against my tongue in a slow, deliberate motion that sets my pussy ablaze. Although my mouth is crammed full, my pussy is empty and alone. I need more.

I tear my face away for a second to gasp, "Fuck me."

Andrew thinks I'm talking to him, so he forces his cock back in. He grabs the sides of my face and rolls his hips in a perfectly rhythmic fucking motion. If only he was doing that to my cunt.

Not to be outdone, Perry lays on the floor next to me. "Straddle me."

A lock of sandy-blond hair falls across his eyes. He's so tan, I suspect he spends a lot of time at the beach, probably surfing. And why not? His parking lot app sold to Intercorps for fifty-million dollars.

His abs ripple as he leans over to caress the inside of my thigh. The deft brush of his fingers across my slick pussy lips is more than I can handle. I let Andrew's cock slip out of my mouth. I need Perry's gloriously curved cock, now.

As I straddle Perry, I shiver with lust. Never in a million years would I have imagined I'd be taken by five hot studs during the most boring open house on record. Today couldn't possibly get any better.

But as I ease Perry's cock into my needy pussy, it does. Oh, God. He's hitting me in all the right places. I writhe on his enormous cock. It's so good I'm getting deliriously light-headed. This is better than even my wildest fantasy. And I'm not done yet.

I reach for Andrew's cock and stroke it in my fist. He doesn't seem to mind that I'm jacking him off instead of sucking. His eyes are closed, his jaw slack. He's the picture of blissful surrender.

Perry, on the other hand, is driving into me with such force that I have trouble holding onto Andrew. The hard pounding vibrates throughout my entire body. My eyes roll back as my pussy clenches in rapid succession. A scream tears from my lips. My tits bounce as tremors of pleasure wrack my body.

Andrew says, "I want to fuck your ass."

"Do it."

He kneels behind me. With one hand on my back and another on his cock, he pushes me forward and claims my ass at the same time. My thighs quiver but there's no place for me to go. I'm trapped between two cocks and I know I'm going to be here until they come inside me.

In an instant, I realize how completely wrong this all is. I hadn't even insisted on condoms. Perry had lube so he probably had condoms too. But the thought is fleeting. Whatever. It's too late now.

Dylan comes into view. "Have you ever had two cocks in your ass?"

His question knocks the air from my lungs. Oh hell no. Two? One is enough to stretch me almost to the point of pain. Two would ruin me.

He leers. The playful smile is gone. Now I see the feral darkness inside. But my own restless need rises up and suddenly I'm convinced that his proposition is a great idea. Why the hell not? It's not like I'm going to have an opportunity like this again.

"Use lots of lube," I say.

"Oh, I will."

He grins as he drips several drops onto his cock. I'm not entirely convinced there's any extra room in my ass, but the second his cock pops past my defenses, I know I'm wrong. Horribly, painfully, blissfully wrong. It hurts so good.

I scream as Dylan works his cock deeper. It's too big, too much, too hard, too... oh shit. Another orgasm sends me into a twitching display of depravity. Below me, Perry isn't moving much, but he's still firmly entrenched in my cunt.

I glance up to find Jared and Kyle stroking their cocks. Kyle steps forward. He grabs the bottom of my chin. "Open up, baby."

His cock is thick and hot against my tongue. I do my best to lick the underside of his shaft as he's stuffing it in, but all of the thrusting makes it impossible.

Jared grabs my hand and squeezes it around his cock. I have one in my mouth, one in my hand, two in my ass and one in my cunt. I'm astonished that I can keep up. But then I realize, I'm not really doing anything. I'm their plaything. I'm their toy and they're having a hell of a time using me.

I've lost complete control of the situation, not that I had any to begin with, but instead of being frightened, I'm elated. Five guys wanted me enough to fuck in front of each other. Five guys thought I was sexy enough to risk being caught by other house hunters. Anyone could walk in on us at any moment, but no one cared. They wanted me that badly.

A rush of power arcs along my back. I meet Jared's eyes as if to say, yeah, you want me. I fucking know it.

Behind me, Andrew groans. He's been fucking my ass the longest and I know he's close. I can hear it in the way his breath catches then whooshes out.

"Oh, fuck," he screams.

A flood of cum flows into my ass and almost immediately, Andrew sides out. He staggers to a chair and slumps into it.

Dylan takes full advantage of his newfound freedom to pound my ass.

Kyle pulls his cock out of my mouth. "Lift her up so I can fuck her too."

Wait, what?

Dylan hooks his arms around my waist and stands. He's so strong that I'm as light as a feather in his arms. My legs splay open for a second. I've never been in this position in my life. Dylan's knees are bent slightly and my thighs rest against his. His cock is still balls-deep in my ass. He should be in the sex Olympics. Is there a sex Olympics? I should find out later. Right now, I'm too stunned to do anything but wait as Kyle advances.

As Kyle pushes into my cut, Dylan grunts and grabs the undersides of my thighs. He lifts me up. I wrap my arms around Kyle's broad shoulders and my legs around his narrow waist. The men bounce me on their cocks. It's so completely unexpected that I come instantly.

Thick spools of heat radiate out from my pussy. Or maybe it's Dylan's cum from earlier. I'm not sure. I don't really care as long as they keep fucking me like this. I realize Perry's standing off to one side with a murderous look on his face. He's pissed that Kyle took his spot in my pussy. Someone's going to pay for that. I can see it in his narrowed eyes.

Kyle's face screws up. "Ohhhh… UGhhhh."

He jerks in a final thrust before coming deep inside my cunt. I'm a slippery mess but Perry doesn't care, he shoves Kyle aside and surges into my pussy. He slams into me so hard that Dylan swears. "Fucking slow down or I'm going to drop her."

"You've already fucked her twice so pull your dick out and fuck off."

Dylan retaliates by pulling me off of Perry. I kick and flail as he kneels on the floor. I'm face down, ass up and being fucked so hard I'm probably going to get rug burns on my tits. I'm also loving every second of having them fight over me. I've never felt so desirable in my life.

After pounding my ass for a few more minutes, Dylan comes. I can't believe he came twice in an hour. What a hot piece of—

"Ohhh," I yelp as Perry shoves Dylan aside. I'm about to get hate-fucked. Oh, shit.

Perry grabs my long hair in his fist and yanks back. "You like this, bitch?"

"Yes," I gasp.

He thrusts into my pussy and rides me like a bull rider. I buck and twist and moan in a crescendo of orgiastic ecstasy. I can't stop coming. My head starts to pound in time with his vicious jabs. I don't want him to stop, ever. This is the most intense fucking I've ever experienced in my life.

Within two minutes, he floods me with sticky cum. Perry rolls away to be replaced by Jared. He opts for my pussy and slides into the throbbing recess. I moan and roll my hips back to meet him. He's slow, deliberate, infuriatingly controlled. It's enough to make me scream in frustration.

"Harder," I demand.

He increases his tempo. Soon he's hitting it with enough force to make me have to press back to keep from collapsing. My arms shake from the effort. My whole body is slick with sweat. I'm dripping inside and out.

Jared jerks into me with a war-cry, as if he's conquered an army. And maybe he has.

He falls away and Andrew takes his place. Another cock, another man, another round of delicious orgasms wrack my body. Strength drains from my arms. In slow motion, I slide to the floor.

Andrew grabs my hips and pulls them up. My cheek is pressed against the floor. I don't care if I walk out of here looking like a disaster victim.

"I love it," I moan.

"Yeah."

"I love it." I chant over and over as I descend into ecstatic madness.

The only thing that brings me back is the river of cum flowing into my cunt. Andrew slides out with an obscene pop.

I collapse fully against the ground. I can't move a muscle. The men are breathing hard and fast. I'm worn out, but so are they. This gives me some measure of pride.

I lay there for several minutes. I'm not even going to attempt to get up until I'm sure I can make it.

The silence is finally broken by Dylan. "Maybe you should show us the master bath."

I laugh and laugh until my ribs ache. I'm borderline hysterical as the enormity of what just happened sinks in.

Kyle leans down to help me up. "Are you okay?"

"We didn't hurt you, did we?" Dylan asks.

"No. I'm just… it's… shit."

Perry smiles. "Yeah."

We all laugh.

Andrew says, "So, about that bath…"

I gather up my clothes. The guys follow suit before trailing me to the master bath.

In an attempt to regain my composure, I start rattling off the amenities. "The master has a large shower with a built in stone bench and eight shower heads. An adjacent Jacuzzi tub gives you the option of taking a long, hot bath if you have the time."

Dylan's behind me as we walk into the bathroom. I'm careful not to look at my reflection in the mirror. I'm sure I look like I was just gangbanged by a group of hot studs. I'm sure it's not a pretty sight.

Andrew turns on the water. As steam fills the room, Kyle asks about the list price.

"It's thirty-five million dollars."

"Does that include you?"

"What?"

"We've been looking for a permanent… companion for the group," Andrew says.

"Someone who can keep up with us," Perry adds.

"I… well."

Dylan says, "The position includes a salary and of course, vacations with us."

"We're hitting the Bahamas next week," Jared says.

I arch a brow. "I already made enough as an agent."

Kyle laughs. "Between the five of us, we have over a billion dollars. If you agree to our offer, we'll buy the house, you keep the commission, and you get laid any time you want it."

I step into the shower as I contemplate the offer. Fortunately the owner left liquid soap. As I lather myself up, the rest of the men join me. What they're proposing sounds almost too good to be true.

"What's the catch?" I ask.

Jared says, "You'll have to be willing to fuck, a lot."

I smirk. "You have no idea."

Dylan says, "I think I do. I could see it in your eyes. You're fucking hot. You'd be perfect for our group."

As I rinse my hair, soap swirls at my feet. It mingles with sticky come before being swallowed by the drain.

I have a huge decision to make and I'm not sure what to do. On the surface, it sounds appealing. Spend the rest of my life surrounded with more money and more cock than I could ever need. Or, be trapped. I have no idea which way this will go. But I want to find out. I can always call it off later.

"I'll do it."

Perry grins and holds out his hand. "Then we have a deal?"

"Only if you pay asking price." I say with an impish grin.

"Done."

We shake on it.

As we're stepping out of the shower I say, "Be careful not to get water on my new floor."

The guys laugh and high five each other.

After we're all dressed, I walk them to the foyer. "It's been a pleasure doing business with you."

Dylan says, "The pleasure was all ours."

I shake my head. "Trust me, I've never come so hard in my life."

"You didn't faint," Andrew points out.

"Why would I?"

The men look at each other knowingly. Perry finally says, "We'll get to that later. First, we need to sign the papers and get moved in. Then we'll make you faint in ecstasy."

I smile. "You'd better keep that promise."

WILD AND WASTED SPRING BREAK

On the first morning of Spring Break, Ruby ran along the Cancun beach. Her hair curled into blond ringlets which whipped through the salty sea air. Warm sand squished between her toes. She couldn't believe she'd finally made it to Mexico, home of the biggest frat party of the year.

Becoming a member of the hottest sorority on campus had solidified her place among the elite co-eds at Arizona State University, but she wanted more. She'd heard scandalous things about the Spring Break Bash, but couldn't believe the student body would get that crazy.

A palm tree stretched across her path. Its fronds hung less than a foot over the glistening azure water. As she jogged around the obstacle, she spotted another early morning riser. Robert Overton.

God, she could roll his name around in her mouth like a chocolate bonbon. That's not the only part of him she'd eagerly take into her mouth if given the chance.

The six foot tall senior's chest rippled with power as his long legs propelled him across the beach. He jogged just inside the waterline, his feet kicking up wet sand in his wake.

Ruby quickened her pace and pushed her shoulders back. She'd intentionally chosen a near transparent white bikini. She worked her ass off for a good body and tried to show it off whenever possible.

As Robert approached, his gaze sizzled across her chest and down her curves. He grinned and slowed to a walk.

She stopped and laced her fingers together. She stretched her arms overhead, thrusting out her chest in the process. "You're up early."

His grey-blue eyes sparkled with mischief. "I haven't been to sleep yet. I figured I should get a workout in before I go to bed."

"You've been up all night?"

As she dropped her arms, she glanced at the slight bulge in his black swim shorts. What she wouldn't give for a peek.

"I like to stay up all night." The deliciously sexy tone of his voice hinted at a double entendre.

She licked her lips. "Are you going to the party tonight?"

"Which one?"

"There's more than one?"

As he smiled, twin dimples created divots in each cheek. "There's the main Spring Break Bash hosted by my frat, but there are other, more private parties."

"Really?"

He bit the edge of his lip and narrowed his eyes for a second. "But they're not the kind of party we'd invite a freshman to."

Her stomach dropped. "Don't you ever make exceptions?"

"Sometimes, but the girl has to be up for anything.

These parties can get a little… rough. There usually aren't many girls there. Only the really special ones get invited."

"What does a girl need to do to get invited?" She asked coyly.

He stepped close enough for her to smell a hint of alcohol on his breath. "She'd have to do something really kinky in public."

She glanced up and down the beach. The sun had barely crested the horizon and there wasn't another soul in sight. "Would a BJ on the beach be kinky enough?"

He arched a brow. "That would qualify."

Although no one else was on the beach, she didn't want to be completely reckless. She spotted a cluster of flowering tropical bushes.

She grabbed his hand and pulled him toward the secluded area. "Come here."

"Whoa." He dug his heals into the sand.

"What?"

"You want to blow me on the beach?"

"I want an invite to the party tonight."

He chuckled. "I don't know, I'm about to fall asleep on my feet."

She stepped behind a short palm tree. She peeked around the corner and flashed her most flirtatious smile. "You don't have to stay on your feet."

He grabbed her and pushed her up against the base of the tree. He pulled her arms over her head. Pinned between the tree and him, she shivered with desire. She'd been with rough guys before and loved the way they dominated her. She'd gladly submit to anything Robert wanted.

He stared down at her, his eyes more blue than gray now. "Is this what you had in mind?"

"No, you were on your knees in my fantasy." She joked.

He released her hands and pressed his rock-hard body against hers. A thin sheen of sweat shimmered on his upper lip. She stood on tiptoes and laced her fingers behind his neck.

"Kiss me," she whispered.

He descended on her like a hurricane. His mouth crushed hers, his tongue parted her lips. A tempest swirled in her belly as he eased up. The expert, yet tumultuous kisses stole her breath. Her senses went on full alert. Every inch of her skin begged for more contact.

When he broke away for air, she also took a greedy gasp. "Shit you can kiss."

He smiled. "I can do a whole hell of a lot more than that, but I think you had something in mind for me, right?"

She dropped to her knees into the cool, shaded sand. "Take off your pants."

He backed up against the tree and jutted his hips. "You take them off."

She hooked her fingers in his shorts and dragged them down slowly. She wanted to savor the first look at the part of him she'd been coveting for weeks.

The fabric caught on the top of his shaft. She gingerly pulled the clothing down, inch by inch, to reveal a hot, thick, throbbing, ten inch cock.

She swallowed and prayed she'd be able to take it all.

He stepped out of his shorts. "You want to suck it, don't you?"

She rolled her eyes. Way to go Captain Obvious. "I wouldn't be on my knees if I didn't."

He laughed and thrust his hips. "Well?"

She bit the edge of her lip. She wanted to burn the image of the enormous, mushroom tipped head into her mind. Although she wasn't a total whore, she loved cock and had seen a dozen or so. But nothing like this. Nothing so big, so perfect.

Swollen veins lined his magnificent shaft, a set of shaved balls hung below. She couldn't decide where to start, so she began at the base.

She licked the briny sweat from the underside of his shaft before descending to swirl her tongue across his smooth balls. His sharp intake of breath made her chest swell with pride. She knew she was a good cocksucker, so she couldn't wait to show him everything she could do.

She lapped at the seam along the bottom of his shaft before dragging her flattened tongue across the length of it.

She approached the tip with what bordered on reverence. She loved that shape. The way it pulled on her pussy lips as a guy withdrew made sex so intense. But she wasn't ready to fuck him. Not yet at least. She intended to drive him insane and make him beg her to attend the private party.

She circled the base of the head and nibbled a path to the tip. She savored the salty taste of him for a moment before opening her mouth as wide as she could. As she gobbled up the length of his cock, he groaned and tangled his fingers in her hair.

She dragged her lips across his skin as she slowly withdrew. His hands tightened on her head and he shoved her face back onto his cock. She swallowed almost every inch of him, only a little bit remained.

As she started to pull back, he shoved her face against him. Her nostrils flared. Her eyes watered, but she didn't struggle. She loved the sensation of a forced blowjob. She slowed her breathing, determined to stay on him as long as he wanted.

"Jesus, you can suck cock," he growled.

She smiled as much as she could and gazed up at him. Their eyes locked. He moistened his lips with the tip of his tongue, never taking his eyes off her. In that moment, she knew they'd descended into an erotic calm more powerful that the eye of a storm.

A surge of heat dampened her pussy. She longed to touch her swollen lips, but this wasn't about her. This was for him. Only for him.

He finally released her head and allowed her to pull back. She gasped for air. He smiled in that cocky, frat-boy, kind of way that made her pussy beg to be filled. She wanted to spread her legs and let him pound her into the sand. But giving everything up wouldn't earn her an invitation.

After giving her a moment to collect herself, he gripped her chin. "I want you to suck my cock and swallow every drop."

She nodded and relaxed as he plunged his cock into her mouth. He ground against her, searching for the back of her throat. She smirked, knowing he was trying to make her gag. She didn't have a gag reflex. Her ego soared as she took all of him without a single sputter.

"Suck it," he groaned.

She grabbed the backs of his thighs and pulled his knees against her shoulders. Slobber dripped from the edges of her mouth. Every thrust created a pornographic slurping sound. She hoped no one passed them on the beach. Even though they were hidden, it wouldn't take more than a curious tourist to blow their cover.

His rhythm increased. His knees trembled. A rush of power hardened her nipples. She rubbed her breasts against his thighs while savoring the rush of pleasure flooding her pussy.

He abruptly pulled out. "I want to fuck you."

She bit the edge of her lip as if considering his request. "I don't fuck on the first date."

"This isn't a date."

She smiled. "Maybe tonight. Maybe I'll let you fuck me at the party."

He scooped his hand around the back of her neck. "If you don't miss a drop of cum, you're invited."

She pinched her lips closed around his cock and sucked as if her life depended on it. His breathy cries of pleasure encouraged her to suck harder.

"Ahh. Oh fuck." He groaned in time with his hips.

She tickled the underside of his balls with a fingernail. That did it. His hand gripped her neck, holding her in place. The first spurt of cum splashed against the back of her throat. She swallowed it quickly, ready for more.

Each jet of cum shot down her throat and she hadn't missed a drop. But as he pulled out, the final stream landed on her lips.

He stumbled back and leaned against the tree. "Fuck yeah."

She waited until she had his full attention. When she did, she slurped the milky cum from her lips and swallowed the last drop.

Between heavy breaths he said, "Yes. Tonight. Ten p.m. Room 516."

She grinned. She'd just scored an invite to the ultra-private Spring Break party. Her heart fluttered with excitement. She could hardly wait to run back and tell her best friend Tess.

"I'll see you tonight," she said.

He ogled her breasts. "Come in a bikini. But be ready to take it off."

She tilted her head to one side. "How many people will be there?"

He smirked, pulled his shorts on and turned to leave. "You'll see."

How cryptic.

She shrugged as she watched his tight ass walk back to the hotel. Whatever. She couldn't wait to get back to her room.

She bounded up the beach and took the stairs two at a time. She jogged down the hallway and used a magnetic key to access her room.

She shut the door and skipped across the room. She jumped onto her best friend's bed, landing on all fours. "Guess what?"

"Death." Tess grumbled.

"I know, you're going to kill me for waking you up, but something big happened." She giggled. "Something huge."

Tess brushed a veil of auburn hair from her face. She cracked one emerald green eye open. "What?"

"I ran into Robert on the beach and he invited me to the private Spring Break party."

Tess rolled from her side onto her back and pushed herself up against the headboard. She didn't bother to cover her nudity.

Ruby crawled under the covers and snuggled against her friend. They'd been sleeping together since December. Ruby wasn't a lesbian, but she couldn't resist Tess' tongue. The woman had skills.

Tess stroked Ruby's hair. "You owe me coffee. What's going on?"

"Robert invited me to the frat party tonight."

"So? Everyone's going to that."

"Not the main party, the private party."

Tess' hand froze mid-stroke. "You can't go to that."

"What? Why not?"

"I've heard things about it. It's not something you want to mess with."

Ruby frowned. "What have you heard?"

Tess traced the curve of Ruby's cheek and reached behind her neck to untie her bikini. "It's a filthy party. The guy to girl ratio is ten to one."

Ruby sucked in a breath as Tess pulled the bikini down. Her exposed breasts flushed in anticipation.

"That doesn't sound like a bad ratio." Ruby let Tess roll her onto her back.

The other girl traced the outer edge of Ruby's areola. "I heard that things get really rough."

Ruby moaned as Tess dipped to suck one nipple into her hot mouth. She laced her fingers in Tess's hair and pulled her face up to kiss her. What began as a gentle kiss intensified into a storm of Sapphic desire. Although Ruby wanted to hear more about the party, Tess' distracting lips shattered her train of thought.

She moaned and parted her lips. The other girl's kitten tongue darted into her mouth and melded with hers. They blended together so well that she didn't know where Tess ended and she began.

Tess tugged the string on Ruby's bikini bottom and freed her from the damp swatch of cloth. Warm, Caribbean air streamed into the room. Gossamer white curtains billowed then fell back into place.

Even with the windows open, no one could see them. They'd secured a coveted corner room and their balcony pointed directly at the ocean. Because they were three stories up, no one from the beach could see their entwined bodies.

Tess broke the scorching kiss and burned a trail of kisses across Ruby's throat. The girl consumed her with the intensity of her focused passion. Ruby tossed her head back and whimpered as Tess' head dipped into the valley between her breasts.

Tess' lips and teeth grazed the concave plane of her belly. She writhed against the girl, wanting her lips between her thighs. But Tess never rushed their encounters.

Her languid kisses inflamed the inside of one thigh, then the other. Ruby moaned. "Please, don't make me wait."

"You're always so impatient."

"Because I want you."

Tess' throaty laughter floated through the room. "You just want me for my tongue."

Ruby propped up on her elbows. She met the other girl's steady gaze. A spark of lust ignited an inferno of longing. "Please, baby. Please lick my pussy."

The corner of Tess' luscious mouth turned up. "Tell me you want me more than some stupid frat boy."

Ruby would have agreed to anything. "Right now, I want you more than I've ever wanted any man."

Tess' breath fluttered against her clit. "You're so sexy. I love the way I can coax your clit out with my tongue."

"Show me."

Ruby jolted as Tess' tongue swept across her pussy lips. She sighed as the girl swirled her tongue around her clit. And when she finally stroked the tip, she cried out.

"Shh, you don't want to scare the girls next door."

Ruby clutched the sheets in balled up fists. "More, oh God, I need your tongue."

Tess settled her face between her thighs and licked the folds of her sopping pussy. Her long, luxurious kisses made Ruby's thighs fall open even more. She wanted to spread as much as possible. She wanted to give Tess' masterful mouth all the space it needed to bring her to the mindless ecstasy she craved.

Ruby released her grip on the sheets and pushed Tess' long hair to one side. She gathered Tess' locks into her hand and rested it against her knee. She played with the silky strands while her lover's eyes gazed up at her.

Ruby's eyelids fluttered closed. Over the sound of the rustling curtains, ocean waves broke against the shore. She'd never imagined such an amazing paradise. She was just a small town girl from Oklahoma. Everything had changed when she'd been accepted at ASU, a huge party college. She couldn't imagine any other life.

Tess' lips captured her delicate clit and sucked gently. She knew exactly how much pressure Ruby liked. They'd only had sex a handful of times, but she knew Tess wanted more. She just couldn't have a monogamous relationship yet. Not with a girl, not with a guy. She'd finally had a chance to really explore life and didn't want to be tied down.

Hum, tied down?

Ruby glanced around the room. Her gaze settled on the ties holding the curtains back.

"Do you want to tie me up?" she asked.

Tess' head snapped up. "You'll let me?"

She shrugged. "You've been begging me to do it."

"Lay down, flat on your belly."

While Ruby followed her command, Tess raced to grab the ties. She returned and bound Ruby's hands to the posts on either side of the bed.

"Why face down?" Ruby asked.

Tess' dark laughter sent shivers down her spine. "Because, I'm going to punish you for making me want you all the time."

"I don't make you do anything."

"Oh, but you do. The way you prance around in your panties. The way you roll your hips when you walk. I know what you're up to."

Ruby giggled into a pillow. "You caught me."

"And now, it's time for your punishment."

Tess' hand came down hard on Ruby's ass. She yelped. The sting of the slap warmed her flesh.

Another smack landed against her other cheek. Her breath hitched. Tess hit harder than she'd expected.

"You've been such a tease. But not anymore. When I'm done with you, you'll never want to leave me again."

Ruby tensed. Tess had to be joking. If not, she was acting really weird.

Another open-handed whack burned the already tender skin. As Tess spanked her, Ruby wondered at the strange sensation building in her pussy. She never imagined that being punished would make her so wet.

She ground her pussy against the bed, aching for release. "No more, please make me come."

Tess rubbed spirals across each cheek. "I love it when you beg."

"Please, eat my pussy."

"On your knees," Tess commanded.

Ruby complied as well as she could. With her hands still tied, she had her face pressed against the sheets while her ass pointed skyward.

Behind her, Tess rustled through the closet. Ruby tried to turn her head to see what she was up to, but she couldn't.

As Tess climbed onto the bed, Ruby trembled. She couldn't wait for the other girl to put her mouth on her pussy. What she got instead was completely unexpected.

A hard dildo pressed against her slick folds. She gasped

but wriggled back to meet it. If Tess wanted to use a vibrator on her, great. Whatever. As long as she got to come.

"I've wanted to fuck you like this since I met you," Tess murmured.

"What?"

Her confusion only lasted a second before she realized what was happening. Tess had a strap-on. The front of her thighs pressed against the back of Ruby's.

"Wait. Don't we need some lube?" she asked.

"But you're already so wet, baby."

Tess thrust forward, driving the dildo into her pussy. Ruby screamed as her pussy clenched around the invading cock. Undeterred, Tess drove into her again and again.

Still in shock, Ruby bit the pillow to keep from crying out. Electric sparks of pleasure shorted the nerve endings in her clit. She couldn't think, couldn't move. She couldn't do anything but let the other girl plunder her quivering pussy.

Her breasts ached as they bounced against the sheets. Tess grabbed her hair and pulled hard enough to make Ruby's eyes moisten. When Tess smacked her ass, she yelped. And when Tess hooked her hand around her thigh to fondle her clit, Ruby's back went rigid.

A tidal wave of release crashed over her. The pulsing, dripping, throbbing energy radiating out from her pussy drowned out everything else. She hollered and jerked back, eager for more cock.

Tess fell forward and grabbed Ruby's breasts. As she pinched her nipples, Ruby convulsed. She didn't recognize the high-pitched screams as her own.

The entirety of her focus rested on her vibrating pussy. She'd never come so hard in her life.

As she collapsed against the bed, Tess thrust harder. The

girl worked her pussy until Ruby's back arched and another orgasm tore through her.

"I can't—" she gasped.

"So close," Tess moaned.

Ruby bucked to try to get Tess to stop but the other girl kept going and going. Finally, Tess screamed and collapsed against Ruby in a shuddering mess.

Tess reached up and released Ruby's hands. When Ruby tried to crawl away, Tess hooked an arm around her waist. She slowly eased the dildo out of Ruby's tender pussy.

Ruby flipped over. Her eyes widened as Tess withdrew the double-sided dildo from her pussy. "Holy shit, I didn't know you had one of those."

Tess tossed it toward the end of the bed. "I was hoping I'd get to use it on this trip."

Ruby let Tess pull her into her arms. "You were a little rough."

"I'm sorry. I got kind of carried away. Your pussy's so beautiful and your ass was still red from the spanking. You'll forgive me, right?"

Ruby asked, "What was all that talk about not leaving you?"

Tess turned away slightly. "I guess I get a little possessive."

"You know we're just messing around, right?"

Tess slid out of the bed and padded toward the shower. "I get it. Do what you want."

"Hey, don't act like that."

"Like what?"

Ruby walked into the bathroom. "We're just having fun. Wasn't that the deal? You know I'm not one for commitments."

"Don't I know it." Tess snapped. She stepped into the shower and closed the door behind her.

Ruby frowned. What the hell was wrong with her? They'd been messing around for months with no strings, but over the past few weeks, Tess was becoming more and more possessive.

She decided to let the argument drop. "I'm going to take a nap. We can talk later if you want."

"Sure, whatever."

Ruby turned to leave as Tess called, "Just don't say I didn't warn you about that party."

Robert glanced at the clock by the bed. Almost ten p.m. and the party was bumping. Thick smoke wafted in from the balcony where his frat brothers were smoking fat joints. Beer bottles littered the floor.

His cock twitched. Ruby would arrive at any moment. She was only one of three girls invited to the party. One chickened out and the other was across the room on one of three beds.

Mandy, or Candy, or whatever her name was, slurped up her fifth cock in a row. The wasted sorority slut loved to eat cock. Good for her. He wasn't interested. He'd already had the cock-sucking of his life that morning and he wanted more.

He glanced around the huge room. The whole frat, all forty guys, were in one state of undress or another. Normally, only fags would hang out naked, but this was different. When pussy was involved, all bets were off.

He almost didn't hear the knock over the pulse of discoteca music. His buddy Bret scored a pack of CD's from a street dealer in downtown Cancun. Since they only had an older CD player in their room, they had to make do with it.

He swung open the door to find Ruby dressed in another white, transparent bikini. The girl sure liked to show off her tan. "What's up? Come on in."

She grinned. "Thanks."

He closed the door behind her and ushered her past the oral orgy. Her mouth dropped open but she didn't comment. Good. He'd always pegged her as a prude, but maybe not. He'd know soon enough.

He yelled over the din of music. "Can I get you a cerveza, or some Patrón?"

"Beer's good."

He handed her a cold one. "Drink up."

They clinked their bottles together. He took a huge swig while watching her over the top of the bottle. Her hazel eyes roamed around the room.

"What do you think?" he asked.

"My friend said it might get a little crazy here."

"And?"

"And she was right." She laughed.

When she didn't turn and leave, he asked. "Have you ever been to a party like this?"

"Never."

He put his arm around her shoulders. "Don't worry. I'll take good care of you."

She giggled and pressed against him. "I bet you will."

He guided her to the makeshift sitting area they'd constructed out of a pile of pillows. He sat cross-legged with his back to the wall.

She settled in across from him and pointed toward the occupied bed. "How'd she get invited?"

He glanced at the sorority girl. "Last weekend, she pulled a train at the house."

"A what?"

"She fucked ten guys in a row while we all watched."

He flashed back to that scene. God, what a little whore. She'd been spread wide by two brothers while one fucked her pussy and another fucked her mouth. They'd lined up and taken turns on her until she tapped out.

He turned his attention back to Ruby. "Would you ever do anything like that? I'm not gonna lie, you surprised me with that BJ on the beach today."

She grinned sheepishly. "Doesn't every girl have secret fantasies?"

"Most do, but not all of them will act on them."

"Hum," she murmured.

"You didn't answer my question."

"Would I ever fuck ten guys at once?"

"Yep."

She bit the edge of her lip and grinned. "Maybe. I think I'd have to be really drunk though."

He stood and took the empty bottle from her hand. "Well then, let me get you another one."

Two hours and countless beers later, Ruby didn't flinch when Robert suggested she strip and put on a little show for the boys.

She stood on wobbly legs and teetered toward the closest bed. She kicked off her sandals and climbed onto the mattress. She used the bedpost as a stripper pole.

Someone had changed the music to gangster rap and she gyrated to the beat. Sometime in the last hour, the other girl had disappeared leaving Ruby alone with about twenty guys.

She wasn't worried at all. Robert said he'd take care of her.

From across the room, he yelled. "Take off your top."

She licked her lips as she tried to untie the strings. Her damn fingers felt like lead pipes and she couldn't get them to work the way she wanted.

Robert jumped up. "I got this."

She stumbled and fell into his arms. She slurred, "You're undressing me."

"That's right."

"I'm doing a show."

"Yep."

The other brothers began a low chant. "Take it off. Take it off."

As he untied the back of the bikini and lifted it over her arms, the other guys whistled and hollered.

She giggled. "They like it."

"It's because your tits are so perfect."

"My ass is perfect too." She winked.

"Let's see her ass," someone yelled from the audience.

"Ass. Ass. Ass," became the resounding chant.

Robert untied her bikini bottoms and suddenly she was naked in front of a room full of frat boys.

"Woooohooo," she screamed.

Robert whispered in her ear. "Why don't you show them what a good little cocksucker you are?"

She opened her mouth. "Awweeee."

He tugged his shorts down, revealing the cock she coveted. In the back of her mind, she knew she was completely trashed, but she didn't care. She'd come to the party knowing things could get nuts, but she was up for anything.

Fuck Tess. Possessive bitch. She didn't belong to anyone. Not a woman. Not a man. No one.

She teetered toward Robert. "Gimme your cock."

He stepped out of his shorts and pulled his white tank top over his head. "Here you go, baby."

She dropped to her knees to worship the perfect cock. It hadn't even been twenty-four hours since she'd had it in her mouth and she wanted it again. After the weird fuck-fest with Tess, she couldn't wait for a predictable guy. No bullshit here. Fucking only. She liked that.

The tip of his cock disappeared from her hazy view. She slurped it into her mouth and rolled the tip of her tongue around it.

"Suck it," someone yelled.

What the fuck? She was sucking it. These bastards needed to calm the fuck down.

She dragged her mouth off his cock and lapped at the head. He pushed it between her lips and down her throat. Even wasted, she still didn't have a gag reflex.

"Jesus, she's good," someone commented.

The crowd closed in. They inched forward until they formed a ring around the bed. She gobbled his cock while random thoughts flitted through her head.

Was she being a total whore? Who cares. She'd be queen of sorority row after this performance. If the other frigid bitches didn't like it, fuck 'em.

God, she was drunk.

She realized his cock wasn't in her mouth anymore and looked around. He'd climbed onto the bed and was beckoning to her.

She crawled toward him. "Where'd you go?"

"I'm right here, baby. Want to ride my cock?"

She waved toward the group. "But everyone's gonna see my ass."

"They already did."

"Oh, right." On her knees, she straddled his huge cock. "I already got fucked by my girlfriend today so be nice 'cause I'm sore."

He arched a brow. "Your girlfriend?"

"She likes me but I don't like her like that but I like her tongue on my clit and she fucks me good sometimes and..." her voice trailed off as his cock pierced the slick heat between her legs.

She sat down slowly. Her eyes rolled back as his thick cock filled her aching pussy. It wouldn't take much to make her come.

"Come on. Fuck me," he coaxed.

She rode him slowly at first, but as the group chanted "faster, faster," she complied.

She went wild on his cock, riding him like a cowboy. He grabbed her hips and ground her against his cock. The increased friction snuck up on her and suddenly her pussy clenched with a violent orgasm. She screamed and convulsed. She dropped down hard, impaling her ravaged pussy.

As she jerked, he rolled her onto her back. He stuffed his cock back in and went to town on her. His thrusts pushed her hips deep into the bed. Her legs flailed as he forced his cock in deeper.

She gasped for breath. It was all too much. Too deep. She needed a second. A break. She pushed on his chest. "Can't breathe."

He climbed off her and flipped her over onto her knees. Head down, ass up, she gasped for air. He grabbed her hips and plunged his cock back inside her. He worked her until her pussy dripped with desire. She'd never been fucked so thoroughly in her life.

He rotated his hips and pummeled her with quick thrusts, then slowed and stroked her steadily. She couldn't take the intensity of it and tried to crawl away a few times.

The second time he pulled her back, he turned to the group. "Someone get up here and keep her face occupied."

A tall, thin black guy knelt in front of her face. She looked up at a cock so big, she burst out laughing. "No way. That's impossible."

The guy grabbed her jaw and shoved his cock into her mouth. "Make it happen."

She gurgled on the huge cock but managed to suck it.

Behind her, Robert pounded harder and faster. His breath whooshed across her back. She could tell he was close, so she squeezed her pussy lips hard and clenched his cock.

He hissed. "Oh fuck."

She would have laughed because she'd made him come, but she couldn't. Not with a huge black cock in her mouth.

Confident that she'd only have to get the guy in her mouth off, she wasn't prepared for the sudden intrusion of another cock in her pussy. She tore her mouth away from the guy and looked behind her.

A ripped guy with short black hair dug his nails into her hips. His cock wasn't quite as big as Robert's, but he wasn't small either. It scraped against the walls of her vibrating pussy. Even though it wasn't as intense as before, she hadn't stopped coming since Robert stopped fucking her.

Every stroke from the new guy stoked the firestorm in her pussy. She loved the endless push and pull from the guys. The one in her mouth pulled out and slapped her face with his cock a few times.

She waved her tongue around while trying to capture the head. When the fucking tease wouldn't give her the cock, she glared at him.

He laughed and began fucking her mouth again. It didn't take long for his cock to swell and spew milky cum down her lips. She'd been pushed from behind so hard that she'd half-spit out the cum. Damn guys were throwing off her rhythm.

Another guy replaced the black guy, this time an average sized ginger. She stared at the thin patch of red hair over his cock, mesmerized. She'd never fucked a ginger before and hoped he'd fuck her pussy.

After two more guys busted a nut, her arms trembled.

Someone said, "Give her a break."

Everyone else laughed.

She slumped against the bed.

A new guy lay down. "Climb up on me. I'll do all the work."

Grateful for the reprieve, she spread her legs over him and lay her head on his chest.

"Get the lube," Robert said.

She raised her head a fraction of an inch. What did they need lube for? Was Tess here? Did she have that evil little dildo again?

Behind her, something poked against her ass. "What the fuck?"

Robert said, "Relax, baby. I said I'd take care of you, right?"

"What are you doing?"

"I'm going to fuck your ass and you're going to love it."

"I am?" Confusion slanted her eyebrows. How could she

like getting fucked in the ass? Hadn't one of the sorority sisters warned her against it?

She tried to remember the ancient conversation but couldn't think, not when another cock appeared before her eyes like fucking magic. She was in fucking magic cock land and loved every second of it.

Her snicker turned into a yelp as Robert pushed the head of his cock against her ass. She screeched, "Wait. That doesn't go there."

He grabbed her hips and pushed forward relentlessly.

"Ouccchhhh," she whined.

"Just relax."

She tried to, but she couldn't. There was too much going on at once and that, plus all the alcohol, made her completely confused.

Her bewilderment vanished as a sharp pain sliced through her ass.

"I'm in," Robert gasped.

Her eyes went wide. Another cock plunged between her lips and she sucked without thinking. On autopilot, she took another guy in her mouth and one in her pussy. But as the guy shoved his cock into her pussy, she suddenly felt too full.

"Oh shit," she yelled.

"Bust that pussy." A few guys snickered.

She had three guys in her, one in each hole and they thrust like a well-timed rowing team. She flailed her hands until a cock appeared in each one. Now she was servicing five cocks at once. The coordination effort was totally lost and she jerked and sucked while the other guys fucked her.

Then lightening seemed to slash through her body. The overwhelming fullness broke into undulating waves as she came so hard, she nearly fainted.

Robert thrust deeper and harder. He dug his fingers into her hips and went rigid as he shot an enormous load of cum into her ass.

"Who wants sloppy seconds?" he asked as he stumbled away.

Another frat boy replaced him and another and another until an endless stream of men and cum filled her.

When the last guy finished, she didn't even know her own name. She rolled onto her back in a daze and passed out.

She woke up hours later on the floor outside her hotel room. She had no idea how she'd gotten there and couldn't remember half of what had happened the night before.

The door opened to reveal a horrified Tess. "Oh my God, what happened to you?"

She scooped Ruby's ravaged body up and carried her into the room. She set her on the bed. "I'll run a bath."

Ruby couldn't lift her head. Exhaustion made every limb heavy. Even her eyelids hurt. But she remembered enough to know she'd never regret it. She'd never imagined a party like that and although she wasn't sure she wanted to do something like it again, she was glad she did it.

Tess carried her into the bath and settled in behind her. "Want to tell me what happened?"

"No."

"Come on."

"You'll just judge me."

Tess gently washed her with a soft wash cloth. "No, I won't. I realized something after you left last night."

"What?"

"I love you because you're such a free spirit. If I tamed you, you wouldn't be the same. So I promise I won't ask you for more than you're willing to give."

Ruby rested her head back against Tess' shoulder. "You're the first person who's ever accepted me for who I am."

"I love you, even if that means I have to sit back while you fuck an entire frat house."

Ruby smiled. "I love you too."

Tess tipped Ruby's head back and kissed her softly. As she ended the kiss, Tess whispered, "Hell of a Spring Break."

Ruby closed her eyes. "I'll never forget it."

MAID FOR PUNISHMENT

Krista struggled to free her slender neck from Dirk's rough grasp. Her boyfriend completely crossed the line with this stupid porno reenactment.

"You're so fucking hot when you panic." Dirk drove his cock deeper into her pussy.

She rolled her eyes, so lame. If he wasn't the hottest, most connected guy at the university she'd dump him. But being with him elevated her from lowly freshman to campus royalty so she'd endure some of his crap.

Dirk ground his pelvis against her. "Take it deep like a good little slut."

She tried to tell him how stupid he looked but his fingers clenched tighter. A tingle of fear rippled along her spine. He'd never taken the game this far before. Usually he'd put a hand around her throat and although he used a firm grip, he never squeezed. This was getting way too weird.

His fingers coiled tighter. "God, you're wet. You like this don't you?"

She shook her head but it barely moved. He laughed and pounded her pussy harder. Done with his bullshit, she grabbed his wrist and yanked.

He released her neck and clutched her shoulders. His nails dug into the tender flesh. "I'm gonna dump a load in you, get ready baby."

She sucked in a breath. "Get the fuck off of me."

"Stop being such a bitch."

Dirk grabbed a pair of lacy white panties off the bed and wadded them in his fist. "If you don't shut the hell up—"

A deep male voice cut him off. "What the hell do you think you're doing in my bed?"

Krista froze at the sound of her employer's voice. Grant wasn't supposed to be home from the boxing match in Atlanta for two more days. She'd only agreed to have sex with Dirk in Grant's bed because she was sure he wouldn't come home and catch them. And, she hadn't even stopped partying long enough to clean the mansion. Strike two. Her job as a maid for the most famous boxer in the world was basically gone. She'd be back to cleaning disgusting hotel rooms before the end of the week.

Dirk's already pale skin flashed lightening-white. Two broad hands grabbed the younger man's shoulders and tore him off her. He landed in a heap on the floor.

Grant towered over her idiot boyfriend. Rage rippled along his ridiculously sexy arm muscles. "Who the hell are you?"

Dirk held his hands up in surrender. "Sir—"

Grant addressed her. "Was he hurting you?"

She hesitated. Hurting? Not really, well kinda. She probably could have handled Dirk, but he was acting so weird, who knows. Everything was happening so fast she wasn't sure how to respond. If she said he was hurting her, then

Grant would probably kill him. But she couldn't exactly admit to liking rough sex either. She nodded but didn't say a word.

Her employer advanced toward Dirk. "You're lucky I don't kill you. You have two seconds to get out of my house."

"I was just—"

"Leaving before I fucking kill you?"

Her boyfriend scrambled to his feet and grabbed his jeans. After he jammed both legs in and zipped up the fly, he opened his mouth to speak.

Oh god, shut up. The stupid jerk needed to hurry up before Grant's rage exploded.

One look from the ripped boxer and he closed it without a sound. Tension crackled between the men. It reminded her of a Mexican standoff, only she knew exactly who'd win. Dirk didn't stand a chance against a man with an entire room dedicated to his boxing trophies.

The half dressed moron stumbled over his shoes as he backed toward the door. He scooped them up along with a black t-shirt then turned and ran.

When Grant didn't follow, she breathed a sigh of relief. At least she wouldn't have to drive Dirk to the hospital.

The front door slammed. The walls rattled for a second, and then he turned to her.

"Jesus Krista, are you okay?" His gaze traveled from her face to the swell of her ample chest.

She clutched the black satin sheet and dragged it to her chin. She'd have to play this up to keep from getting into a ton of trouble. She was getting fired for sure, but in his house and completely at his mercy there were far worse things he could do to her.

"Thank god you came in when you did. I thought he was trying to kill me." She ended with a dramatic sniff.

"I'll handle this." He stalked toward the door.

"No!" Still holding the sheet, she jumped off the bed and raced toward him. "Don't leave me. Not right now."

She buried her face in his chest and prayed he'd stay. If he left right now, Dirk would end up hamburger, or worse. Her boyfriend, well, soon to be ex-boyfriend, could be a jerk sometimes, but he didn't deserve to be maimed.

Grant's arms encircled her trembling shoulders then pulled her close. "Shh. Don't cry."

Between sobs she whispered. "I was so scared."

"It's okay baby, I got you."

She suppressed a smile. So far, so good. He seemed pretty damn convinced she needed to be comforted and not reprimanded.

She brushed her cheek across his strong, masculine chest and sighed. So sexy and so off limits. Mixing business with pleasure could only end in total disaster. She'd learned that at her last job.

"You've got goose bumps." He briskly rubbed her arms.

The friction from the calloused pads on his fingers sent shivers of delight straight through the slick folds of her pussy. She didn't even get to come before Grant busted in on her and Dirk. That little spectacle stole the orgasm she desperately needed. Tension hummed in the pit of her stomach. She'd give anything to have Grant shove two rough fingers against her clit. That's all she'd need to come all over his hand.

"You need a nice warm bath."

He crossed the room and opened the door to the master bath. She followed him into her favorite room in the house. Whenever he left for a match, she'd sneak into his bathroom and take a long hot soak in the Victorian style tub. Pure luxury.

Grant twisted the brushed copper knobs and a cascade of steaming water splashed against the bottom of the tub. She could hardly wait to wash away the thin sheen of sweat collected on her skin.

He turned and perched on the edge of the tub. His gaze rested on her lips. "I should fire you for fucking that guy in my bed."

"I'm sorry about—"

"No." He put a finger to his lips. "Don't say another word."

"But I need this job to pay my tuition. Please, don't fire me. I swear I won't do anything like this again."

"I'll consider it."

He dipped a finger into the bath then turned the cold water faucet on for a few seconds. He turned both faucets off then grabbed a bottle. The cap popped open and he poured a stream of liquid into the water. As he swirled his hand through the water, a sea of frothy bubbles formed.

"It's ready."

She didn't want to appear too wanton, so she waited for him to leave but he didn't move. "Are you staying?"

"I think I'll stay and watch. After all, it is my bathtub." A hint of a smile played at the edge of his sensual lips.

"I'd rather you didn't."

"I've already seen you naked and you don't seem to have any shame."

"If I'd known you were coming home, you wouldn't have caught me and wouldn't have seen me naked."

He crossed the room and grabbed the top of the sheet. "I only saw you in all your naked glory for a few seconds. But it only took a second to see that you have a great body."

He tugged the sheet out of her hands. She took a step

back but he quickly wrapped an arm around her and drew her closer.

"First you'll take a bath. Then you'll repay me."

"How?" She whispered.

His amber eyes sparkled. "I have some ideas."

He slowly guided the satin sheet down the length of her body. The heat from his palms seared a trail over her breasts, along the hollow of her belly and done her thighs. He was almost on his knees when he finally released the sheet.

She hurried toward the tub and stepped into the hot water. Despite the near scalding temperature, she quickly submerged herself until only her head remained dry.

His amused smirk carried into his tone. "I'm going to prepare a few things. Take as long as you need."

After he closed the door, the breath she'd been holding whooshed out. She had no idea what he was planning but she'd have to go along with whatever it was. Next semester's tuition was due in a week and without the money from her job, she'd have to quit college.

Grant whistled as he wrapped a pair of handcuffs around a bedpost. How many nights had he lain in bed fantasizing about tying the little tart up and making her come until she begged for mercy?

It was sheer luck that the other boxer cancelled the fight. Grant caught the next flight out of Atlanta and happened to come home at the perfect moment. Any sooner and he wouldn't have found her in such a compromising position. Any later and, well that frat boy couldn't have lasted very long with prime pussy splayed out underneath him.

Now he had the opportunity to do anything he wanted to her. But he wasn't about to do anything to someone unwilling, so he had a few tricks up his sleeves.

He returned to the chest at the end of the bed and riffled through it. He shoved a riding crop to the side and lifted a black leather paddle out of the way. It had to be in here somewhere. He pulled out a brand new feather duster and snickered. Ironic considering she's the maid, maybe for later.

A small blue egg shaped vibrator lay hidden underneath a ball gag. He fished it out then set it on the nightstand. A perfect implement of torture. It never failed to elicit the most delicious screams from his partners. He couldn't wait to hear her cries of pleasure.

She seemed to be taking her sweet time in the bath. He wanted to join her but resisted. He couldn't appear too eager or she'd think she was completely off the hook for tainting the bed with a decidedly pedestrian sexual encounter.

Encounters? God he hoped it was only once. And who fucked in missionary position anymore. With all the porn available on the internet, she should be a little more creative.

He gathered the soiled sheets off the chair where he'd tossed them and stuffed them into a hamper in the closet. She could wash those later.

The sound of water being sucked down the drain drifted from behind the bathroom door. He debated undressing just to see her reaction, but he wanted her to remove each article of clothing, slowly.

The bathroom door swung open. A white towel covered Krista's curvaceous body. The creamy swell of her breasts rose and fell with every breath. Tendrils of damp auburn hair clung to her heart shaped face. Her hazel eyes regarded him with trepidation.

Her voice wavered when she spoke. "Did you decide?"

"On what?"

"On how I can repay you."

"Yes. You can spend the rest of the night in my bed."

She cocked an eyebrow. "By myself?"

He chuckled. "Well that wouldn't be any fun."

"So I'll be in bed with you?"

"Exactly."

"How's that a fair deal?"

"It seems completely fair. You violated my space by bringing that boy into my bed and now I will reclaim it. Besides, I don't think you're in a position to make any demands right now."

She crossed her arms under her breasts which only pushed them further toward the top of the towel. "Fine. One night."

He sauntered across the room to where she stood then ran the back of his hand down one shoulder. "You'll probably enjoy it."

She brushed his hand away. "I'm only agreeing because I need this job."

"You'll keep your job, but not until you've been punished. Now, drop that towel and lay down on the bed."

When she hesitated, he grabbed the corner and yanked. The towel dropped to the floor. He grabbed her wrists and held them over her head then backed her into the nearest wall.

"What the hell?" Her eyes blazed.

"When I tell you to do something, you'll do it."

"Well it's off now."

Her defiant attitude sent a ripple of need straight to his cock. Her spirited response made him want to tame her.

Grant cursed the layer of clothing separating them. He should have undressed too, but the prospect of having her do it for him was too enticing.

He leaned forward and whispered in her ear. "I'm going to release your hands and you're going to use them to undress me."

"Yes sir." She snapped.

He liked the sound of that. Sir. Powerful. He loved power and control more than anything in the world. Those two qualities made him a hell of a fighter. In the ring, power will only get you so far, control is the key. Without it, you waste all your energy throwing punches.

He wasn't about to waste all his energy sparring with Krista. He needed to finesse her until she willingly surrendered.

He released her wrists and took a small step back from the wall. He intentionally crowded her to maintain control.

Her fingers fumbled with the buttons on the shirt. Her nails grazed his naked flesh. He sucked in a breath as a tingle of desire coursed across his chest.

The air conditioning kicked on sending cool air throughout the room. His nipples formed taut peaks.

"Someone's cold." She teased as she released the last button.

"Why don't you put that hot mouth of yours on them? Warm them up."

With her palms, she pushed the shirt over his shoulders. It slid down his back and landed on the floor. She dipped her head and sucked one hard nipple between her lips.

He swayed then grabbed her shoulders to steady himself. The velvety inside of her mouth closed around him.

He tipped his head back and reveled in the delicate ministrations of her tongue.

She licked a wet trail across his chest and sucked the other nipple. This time, she pulled it between her teeth and gently tugged. Blood rushed to fill his cock. The little minx brushed a shoulder against the bulge in his pants. She knew exactly what she was doing to him.

"Take my—"

Before he could even finish, her hands worked to unhook his belt. She bit down on his nipple hard enough to cause a shock of pain.

He tangled his fingers in her still damp hair and yanked her head back. "You're a dirty girl, aren't you?"

"Maybe?" She responded with an impish grin.

"Show me how dirty."

Her eyes sparkled. "Yes sir."

She pulled the belt completely out of his jeans and tossed it onto the bed. Only a thin pair of boxer shorts prevented him from being totally naked. She dropped to her knees then hooked her thumbs into the waistband and pushed down. The underwear caught on his rigid cock.

She smiled up at him.

The sight of her on her knees made him impossibly hard. He wanted to stuff his cock into her mouth and make her suck until he came deep in her throat. But there would be time for that. Right now, he wanted to touch her.

He kicked the boxers away. "Get up against the wall."

She stood and took a step back.

"Turn around and put your hands on the wall."

She complied.

He's gaze traveled up from the sleek curve of her calves to the taut firm thighs he couldn't wait to part. The curve of her ass made his mouth go dry. He knew she had a great body under that maid uniform she liked to wear. But he had no idea she was this perfect.

"You have a great body."

"Thank you sir."

"Spread your legs a little wider."

She did and arched her back to expose her pussy. He moved forward and planted a kiss on the nape of her neck. The silky perfection of her flawless skin teased his lips as he nibbled a trail of desire down the length of her spine.

Her sighs of pleasure made him want to taste her. The flick of his tongue against the small of her back elicited a moan so primal, he wanted to push her to the ground and shove his cock all the way up into her hot pussy. But he restrained himself. Instead, he chose to savor every inch of her trembling body.

His head dipped lower. He kissed each cheek of the most perfect ass he'd ever seen. A perfect heart shaped ass just begging to be spanked. There would be time for that later.

He wanted to see all of her and gripped her hips to turn her to him. She leaned against the wall, a look of lust smeared across her features. Any hint of defiance had vanished.

Her belly quivered as he brushed feather light kisses across the taut skin. Then his lips trailed to the thin patch of hair covering her pussy. She smelled ripe with sex.

Krista gazed at him through her lashes. His warm breath swirled against her swollen lips. Another inch and his tongue would touch the most intimate place on her body. She shivered with need.

He glanced up as if to confirm the effectiveness of his

teasing. She tried to hide behind a mask of indifference but it was no use. One look at her face and he'd know exactly what she wanted.

He spoke and the warmth of his breath tickled her. "I knew you'd enjoy it."

She bristled and responded with a complete lie. "I'm only doing this because I need to keep my job."

"You'd make a terrible liar."

Before she could respond, he lashed the slick folds of her pussy with his tongue. She tried not to cry out but it was useless. Every lick drew moans of pleasure from deep in the pit of her stomach.

She laced her fingers into his thick black hair and pulled him closer. He smoothed his hands across her hips then reached behind to grab her ass.

The tip of his tongue stabbed into her. Her head snapped back and hit the wall but the pain barely registered. The sensations quivering deep within were unlike anything she'd ever experienced.

Grant was right. Dirk was a man-child and Grant was a real man. Her limited experience with men hadn't prepared her for the expert tongue pressed against the core of her being.

His lips nipped at her pussy lips. She arched into him. She wanted more. She wanted everything he could give. She wanted to drown in the ecstasy of his kisses.

He pulled back and blew a long breath against her scorched lips. The air cooled her slightly but did nothing to stifle the yearning in her body.

"Grant." She whispered.

"Yes?"

"Take me to bed."

He stood and placed one arm behind her knees and one

behind her back. As he scooped her up, she wrapped her arms around his thick neck. He carried her to the bed where he unceremoniously dropped her.

She frowned. "Not exactly gentlemanly."

"Who said I was a gentleman? I haven't even begun to punish you so save your assessment of my character until sunrise."

"I could get up and leave right now and never come back."

"You could. But you won't."

He was right. Even if she could scoop her pride off the floor, her body would never let her. He'd awakened an erotic appetite that demanded to be sated.

He pointed to the bed. "Face down."

She crawled onto the giant bed. A floral scent wafted off the sheets. At least he'd changed them.

He wrapped something around her ankle. She propped up on one arm and twisted to look. "Handcuffs? You can't be serious."

He smirked. "Oh, I am."

A mixture of dread and desire kept her still. She'd secretly wanted to be tied up but never trusted Dirk enough to let him. So far Grant hadn't done anything to hurt her, and for some reason, she trusted him far more than she'd ever trusted Dirk.

She pushed the thought away as Grant clicked the last handcuff into place. At the least these were lined with a thin strip of leather. Not exactly comfortable, but the thrill of being restrained overshadowed any discomfort.

"You've been a very bad girl Krista. Fucking some guy in my bed while I was away."

Totally unprepared for the slap of his hand against her ass, she yelled. "Ouch."

The second crack of his hand against the other cheek sent red hot shockwaves straight through her pussy. She strained against the cuffs.

"I like the look of my handprint on your ass. I almost want to take a picture and hang it on my wall."

Through gritted teeth she replied. "Fuck you. You better not take any pictures."

His palm connected with the first cheek. She screamed into the sheets as the pain radiated out in waves. She ground her hips into the bed. It was the only way she could escape the blows.

His weight lifted off the bed. She tried to see what he was up to but couldn't. He was directly behind her. The sound of her ragged breath filled the room.

He returned to the front of the bed where she could see him. In his hand lay something she couldn't quite identify. It looked like a ping-pong paddle but one side was covered in black leather and the other side with faux fur.

"What is that?"

He brushed the leather side across the tip of her nose. She inhaled the intoxicating scent of leather. It brought back the memory of her first kiss. The trainer who taught her to jump dressage style horses led her into a barn filled with hay, horses and leather saddles. He'd taken her into an empty stall, pressed her again a bale of straw and kissed her so lightly, she nearly melted into the floor.

The crack of the leather against her ass brought her back to the present. As he continued to smack her, something dark within blossomed. A deviant desire opened a new state of consciousness and suddenly she floated on a sea of sensation. She felt everything and nothing at the same time. As if her soul and her body shared two completely different experiences simultaneously.

The whoosh of the paddle and the whack of it against her humming skin sent her into a state of bliss so perfect, she didn't want to ever return from it.

A minute passed before she realized he'd stopped. He stared down at her with a look of triumph.

"I can spot a submissive woman a mile away. It's in your eyes."

She didn't want to argue, she only wanted the thick heat between her thighs to dissipate. "Grant, shut up and fuck me."

He smiled and opened the nightstand drawer. "Not yet. I want you desperate, begging, pleading with me to shove my cock into you. You're not there yet, but you will be."

Her eyes went wide at the toy in his hand. She'd coveted the ridiculously expensive Japanese vibrating egg for over a year but wouldn't ever be able to afford it.

He held the blue egg in the palm of his hand. "Spread your legs wider."

She immediately complied. The egg would free her from this erotic torture.

He climbed onto the bed. With his knees, he spread her legs even wider. She pointed her ass toward the ceiling to give him better access to her aching pussy.

A faint buzz filled the room. He touched the vibrating egg to the back of her knee. She jerked to one side. The sensitive flesh shivered under the egg. Tendrils of desire curled in her belly.

The egg traced a path up her thigh but stopped just inches from her engorged lips. She bucked and thrust her hips back trying to reach the egg but it was too far away. He had her completely aroused and totally at his mercy.

"Grant, please."

"Begging, but not desperate yet."

She wiggled toward him. "What? I am. Make me come. Please Grant."

"Please sir."

"Please sir. Please fucking make me come."

The vibrating egg caressed the crease of her ass and finally dipped lower. When it touched the delicate folds of flesh between her thighs, she groaned.

She ground her pussy against the egg. It undulated around the edge of the lips then he pressed it into her. She thrashed against the bed.

The tiny egg pulsated within her. She couldn't breathe, couldn't think. On the tip of ecstasy, she drove back shoving it deeper. The orgasm began to build from the center of her body. Just seconds away from mind shattering bliss, he pulled the egg out of her.

"No. Please. Fuck, I'll die if you don't make me come." Her pitiful cries for mercy were devoid of ego. She didn't care if she sounded like a desperate, pathetic fool. Her mind fixated on one singular thing, release.

"Pleading, but not desperate yet."

"Nooo." She whined.

He swept the egg across her pussy lips. She almost fainted when he pulled it away. Why? Why was he doing this?

His voice took on a deeper tone. "I love watching you like this. Spread wide, shaking."

The egg thumped against her. Her eyes rolled back as if she'd been hit by a knockout punch. Her hands became fists as she jerked on the bed. Her heart pounded in her chest.

Her juices trickled onto the bed. The wet spot growing wider with every minute that passed. She didn't know how much more of this she could take. An animalistic hunger overcame her. She was nothing but a twisted bundle of nerves begging desperately for relief.

"Grant." She panted. "I need to—"

The egg pressed against her clit and she screamed. Violent shockwaves pulsed though her pussy. Her back arched so hard she came off the bed. Tremors wracked her body. She came over and over as he pushed the egg in and out of her pussy.

She didn't ever want to stop. The room went hazy as her field of vision narrowed. Close to passing out, she wanted to speak, to tell him to take the egg away, but she couldn't. The muscles in her stomach clenched hard and the egg slipped out of her.

Mercifully, he turned the egg off and set it on the nightstand.

A trickle of drool slid down the side of her mouth. He licked it up before thrusting his tongue between her lips.

Still caught in the throes of the most amazing orgasm of her life, she let him suck her tongue into his mouth.

Grant reveled in the power he had over her. The indescribable look on her face made his chest swell with pride. He loved the screams she made when she came, a siren's song.

But he wasn't through with her yet. Not by any means. His cock stood completely erect, almost brushing his abs. She may be temporarily sated, but now it was his turn.

He climbed back onto the bed and knelt behind her. He grabbed the top of her thighs and pulled her back until she was on her knees. Her pussy still pulsed and he took a second to watch it. Then he rubbed the tip of his cock against her soaked lips.

Krista moaned and spread her legs wider. He considered unlocking the handcuffs, but seeing her completely helpless and at his mercy was better than any aphrodisiac.

Without warning her, he shoved forward into her quivering pussy. Balls deep, he reached around and flicked the pad of his thumb over her clit. She bucked and tried to crawl away but his cock sealed them together.

He thrust into her then swirled his thumb, then repeated the process until once again her body shook violently. The muscles in her pussy clamped down on his cock. The tight grip forced a rush of blood into his balls. He didn't want to come too soon, so he pulled back and dipped a few shallow strokes into her.

She stopped trembling. A thin sheen of sweat covered her back. He leaned over her and gently grazed the back of her neck with his teeth. He licked a path down her spine. She tasted like sin. So sweat and wet with desire.

He reached for her breasts and cupped each one in a palm. He massaged them as she moaned the sound of ecstasy.

The hard tips of her nipples were pliant between his thumb and forefinger. The pressure in his balls had decreased slightly so he forced his cock back into her. When he pinched her nipples, she cried out and the tight walls of her pussy clenched around him.

She rocked against him and soon they were fucking in a slow, leisurely rhythm. He loved the way her ass bounced against his stomach. The slapping sound grew louder as he thrust harder.

She moaned and rolled her head to one side. Their eyes locked. He tried to read the look on her face but couldn't see past the lust written all over it.

He swiveled his hips against her and increased the pace.

The pressure in his balls built each time he penetrated her. The way she writhed beneath him increased the friction until he couldn't hold back another second.

He thrust as deep as he'd ever been inside a woman and rubbed the tip of her clit. The first shot of cum exploded into her just as she exploded beneath him. The suck of her pussy on his dick was unreal. He felt the orgasm from the tip of his toes to the top of his head. Every nerve ending fired at once until a glorious haze blurred his vision.

After the last twitch of his cock, he pulled out of her and sat back on his heels. He watched the creamy cum ooze out of her. Perfection.

He stood on shaky legs and found the key to the handcuffs. He released each one then climbed back onto the bed.

Krista crawled into his arms and he leaned back against the headboard. She nuzzled his chest while he stroked her back.

"I think I'll let you keep your job." He joked.

She turned and punched him lightly on the arm. "You better."

"On one condition."

"What?" Her eyes sparkled.

"We're adding one duty to your list."

"Tree trimming?"

He laughed and drew her closer. "Not quite."

"Cleaning out the gutters?"

"Tempting, but no."

She glanced at his semi-hard cock. "Polishing your trophies."

"You already do that."

"Well then maybe you want me to polish something else?"

The first thing that popped into his mind was too cliché.

He wouldn't say it out loud. Instead he said. "What I want is really simple. I want you in my bed, ready and waiting to take every inch of me when I get back from a boxing match."

She grinned. "I can do that."

"Yes you can."

DOUBLE TEAMING AUDREY

I love anal. I crave it. Even now, sitting in a coffee shop full of unsuspecting college students, I can't stop thinking about getting pounded in the ass. Maybe it's an addiction, but ever since my boyfriend popped my anal cherry a few years ago, I can't get enough.

As I twirl the end of my long blonde pigtail around my finger, I search their faces. Who might make a good partner? A group of nerdy science geeks are huddled in the corner. If I walked over there right now, one of them would blast a load of sticky cum in his jeans. Guaranteed. Sometimes shy guys are the biggest freaks in bed.

Before I can make my choice, my phone rings. I glanced at the number and smile. I have a dirty little secret that none of my friends know about. They think I pay for school with a late-night waitressing job but really, I'm a coed escort. And my favorite client is calling for a session.

"Hey baby, I missed you in December," I say in a pouty tone. "I had three weeks off from school and I spent the entire winter break pounding my pussy with my vibrator. You are a very bad boy for not calling me."

"I deserve a spanking for making you wait." His gravelly voice slides through me like honey. "How soon can I see you?"

"I have class in an hour, but I guess I could skip it for you," I say in a flirty tone.

I'm lying. Classes don't start until tomorrow, but he doesn't need to know that. It's so much more fun when they think I'm doing something naughty. As if I'd ruin my education for a quick fuck. Not a chance. I've got two years left before I get my Bachelor of Science in nursing. As much as I love fucking strangers for money, this isn't a career choice. I may be young and hot as hell right now, but I have far loftier goals. One day I'm going to meet an insanely hot surgeon and become a doctor's wife. But until then, I intend to fuck whoever I want, whenever I want, however I want.

"Can you meet me at the same hotel?" He asks in a tone thickened by lust.

I wouldn't be surprised if he already has his hand on his cock. I've never met anyone with so much stamina. For a guy in his 40s, he sure can fuck. My ass clenches with need. Maybe he'll pound me up against the wall, or over the edge of the balcony. Either way, I can already taste his cum in my mouth.

After telling him I'll meet him in an hour, I chug what's left of my coffee and head toward the door. Several heads turn to watch me walk past. Too bad boys, you had your chance. I can't understand why they're so intimidated by me. It's as if they've never seen a girl in a tight black miniskirt and a red halter top. Like I'm some sexy version of a mythical creature. Untouchable and yet they're dying to fuck my tight little hole.

In California, beautiful women aren't rare. But I've been told I have a special aura about me. It's as if they can see every filthy thought in my head. If only they knew how much I love being bent over tables, how much I love sucking cock in broad daylight, or how much I love being taken by two guys at once.

My stilettos click across the sidewalk as I wind a path through campus. I always meet David at one of the ritziest hotels in town. Although this is a huge college town, it's also full of large corporations. David is the CEO of a huge pharmaceutical company. He's filthy rich, but I'd never date a client. This is strictly business. I know better than to fall for these guys.

Forty-five minutes later, I've shaved, plucked, and primped until I'm as smooth as ice. My pussy quivers in anticipation. When I reach the hotel, I stroll past the liveried doorman and walk across the lobby as if I belong here. And I do. I can't quite afford such lush accommodations right now, but one day I will. As soon as I land my doctor husband.

During a quick trip in the elevator, I check my lipstick in the reflective glass. Perfect cherry red lips, as always. Sometimes I think about changing the color, but men seem to love seeing a red ring of kisses around their cocks. What can I say? I do good work.

I don't even have to knock on the hotel room door. It swings open and David reaches out and grabs me by the back of my neck with one huge hand. Standing 6' tall, he easily towers over my petite 5'3". He drags me into the room and manhandles me around a corner. As he pushes me up against the wall with one hand, his other reaches up under my skirt.

"Good girl. No panties," he growls.

Oh man. I'm in for it. He's in one of his moods. Something must have gone wrong at work because I hardly take a breath before I hear the tell-tale slide of his belt. Now don't get me wrong, I like it rough, but a little warning would have been nice.

"Have you been a good little slut?" he asks.

"Yes, Daddy."

I shiver. Did I mention I have daddy issues? Don't ask. It has nothing to do with my own father. He's a great man who'd be horrified if he knew what I really did for work.

Behind me, David's pants drop to the floor. His shirt follows. He's stark naked and I'm dying to take a quick peek. I try to turn my head, but he grabs the back of my neck and shoves my face into the wall.

"Be a good girl and spread wide for Daddy."

I step out far enough to make my balance precarious. Any further and I'll fall over. Men don't understand the delicate laws of physics required to walk in stilettoes.

"Wider!" he barks.

When I don't immediately comply, he yanks my tight skirt up around my waist. His hand thwacks against my ass once. Twice. Three times before I cry out. Stinging needles of pain fan out across each ass cheek. He takes his time warming up my bottom until I'm squirming and dripping wet.

"Don't tease me," I whisper coyly.

He grabs a fistful of my hair and tugs my head back until my neck's arched and aching.

"I'm not going to be gentle," he says, as if that's not already obvious.

"I can take it," I murmur.

Inside, I'm dancing for joy. I've been in need of a good pummeling for weeks. Winter break was my longest dry spell in ages. I had a smattering of clients after Christmas, but not enough to keep me satisfied. I could fuck five times a day and still be ready for more. I'm insatiable. Some might call me a nympho, but I'm just a normal, healthy twenty-one year old coed slut.

David's fingers trail down from my ass to part my pussy lips. I'm already soaking, so he slides one finger into my needy cunt. A second finger follows, then a third. I arch against his hand and moan. I can't hold back as he stuffs even more fingers into me.

"Did you bring my toys?" he asks.

"Yes."

I point to the bag I dropped when he'd pulled me into the hotel room. He releases me and I turn to lean one hip against the wall. I roll my neck to get the kinks out. I should have done some yoga before coming over. I'm tense and too riled up to relax. And when he pulls a big black dildo out of the bag, I know what he's going to do to me.

"Oh no." My eyes flare wide as if horrified. That couldn't be any further from the truth. I can't wait to be double stuffed by David and my big black cock. He's a white guy, so I love the contrast of colors plunging in and out of me.

"Oh yes." He thrusts the toy out toward me.

I take it with a sheepish smile.

"Bedroom?" I ask.

"Boardroom."

"Boardroom?" I glance around the room and for the first time notice we're in a huge suite. A living room complete with a full bar and sitting area takes up most of the space. Closed doors flank the walls.

He crosses the room and opens one of the doors. I step in to find a huge boardroom table. There's a closet with mirrors on one side of the room and a huge wall of windows on the other. I look across the street directly into another hotel room. A man sits in a chair while idly looking out the window. When he spots me, he winks.

Now I know what David wants. He planned this little show. I don't know who the other man is, but my nipples harden at the thought of being watched.

"Get on the table," David demands.

I hoist myself up and scoot back a few inches. He motions for me to move closer to the edge. I do.

"Untie your top," he says.

I tug on the halter and the ties fall down to my breasts. I'm not wearing a bra. He reaches for my shirt and yanks it down around my waist.

"God, your fucking tits," he mutters. "Perfect DD's."

As he cups my breasts, I set the dildo down. I place my hands on the table as if I'm about to do a pushup. I turn my head and wink at the man who's watching us. A wry smile spreads across his lips. He slowly lowers the zipper on his slacks. He unbuttons the top of his white dress shirt and leans back. His pants are still on. Fucking tease. He's basically issuing me a challenge.

Well don't worry, buddy. I'll give you a reason to finish stripping.

I grab the big black dildo and slowly lick the tip. Behind me, David's leans over and kisses one throbbing butt cheek. It still smarts from where he spanked me. His lips graze the heated flesh before nibbling along the length of my little slit.

When his mouth finds my pussy, I moan. His lips grasp and tug my swollen lips. The man eats pussy like a demon. He works a tantalizing spell on my body, licking, sucking, and nipping until I'm half-mad with lust.

I groan and circle my ass. Across the way, the business man in the chair pulls out his cock. It's pink, thick, and he can hardly close his hand around it. I cream. David laps at me, devouring my musky arousal as if intoxicated. He's holding out much longer than usual. Maybe it's because we have an audience. Or maybe he's just reveling in this sweet torture.

He stands and wraps an arm around my waist. As he hauls me off the table, I yelp. He drops me to the floor. I land like a cat. This isn't the first time I've been dragged off a boardroom table. The black dildo bounces and rolls out of sight.

I look up, my face a mask of shocked innocence. He loves my expression. Fire dances in his eyes as he strokes my cheek.

"How can you be so perfect?" he asks.

"You make me like this," I demure.

It's not entirely a lie. He ignites my intrinsic passion. Most of my clients are sweet and the vast majority are rather shy. But not David. He's a CEO and knows exactly what he wants, so I'm not surprised when he brushes a finger across the seam of my lips before forcing my mouth open with his thumb.

His cock juts up in a graceful sweep toward my lips. I lick the tip. His hand cradles the back of my head. His fingers slide through my hair and then he thrusts his dick into my mouth. My nostrils flare and I struggle to breathe around him. All ten inches are crammed into me. He's halfway down my throat and the impulse to gag rises up. But I'm a fucking professional.

He likes to play this game with me. It's his way of making sure I know that he's in control. As if I could forget it. He wants me to push him away. He wants me to surrender to his authority. But I don't. He loves my defiance. Even now, with his cock jammed down my throat, I challenge him.

Powerful men seldom meet their match in bed and that's part of the allure of being with a high-class escort. We can hold our own when it comes to cock.

I'm proud as fuck when he finally relents and slides back to give me room to take a breath. I smile around his dick. He sees my triumph and forces his cock back in. He uses my pigtails as handlebars as he fucks my face. The filthy slapping sound of his balls against my chin adds another level of debauchery. I love the soundtrack of his shallow breaths coupled with the slurp of my lips against his cock.

"Fuck you give good head," he hisses.

I slide back onto my heels and smile politely. "Thank you, Daddy."

Our gazes lock in a steamy exchange of lust. My pussy's dripping and throbs in anticipation. I don't have to wait long. He drops to all fours and crawls behind me. I turn my head toward the mirror and assume my favorite position: doggy style. He grabs my hips and hauls them up. When I try to lift my head, he pushes it down toward the floor. It's a subtle form of domination, but he gets his point across. He's in charge and I'm just his fuck toy.

The tip of his cock brushes against my ass cheek. It leaves a trail of precum which quickly dries in the cool air. He's marking me, making me his, if only for an hour. No matter how much I love being plowed by his huge cock, he'll never own me. No one will.

I must have radiated my defiance in some way because he thrusts deep without warning. He forces his cock between my delicate pussy lips, ravaging me with a quick succession of plunging beats.

"Take it you fucking whore," he growls.

It's not an insult, it's validation. I am the best damn whore in Boston and I'm going to give him the most mind-blowing sex of his life. My ultimate mission in the bedroom is to destroy men. I want them to dream of me, long for me, lust after me, and beg me to meet them for a quick rendezvous between business meetings. I adore the attention they bestow on me and lap it up like a ravenous cat.

David works his cock in with ever increasing fervor. I pant and gasp but it's not an act at all. He's pushing me toward a singular point of total ecstasy. Electric sparks of passion race down my nerves to coalesce in my cunt. The energy builds and coils into a tight ball of agony. I'm dying to come all over his huge cock. But even as he changes the angle to hit my clit harder, I can't reach the precipice.

I toss my head back in frustration. Across the way, the mysterious man is furiously beating his cock. His face screws into a tight mask of pre-orgasmic focus. The firm line of his lips and furrowed brow tell me he's reached the same point. We're both writhing desperately, searching for the final push. And then it happens.

He looks up and our eyes meet. His lips part and his head falls back as the first thick spurt of cum jets from the angry red tip of his cock. Jets of cum splash on his belly and chest. The erotic sight shoves me over the edge. I scream as spasms of release wrack my pussy. My cunt clamps down on his dick, sucking at the condom like a greedy bitch.

Behind me, David grunts and continues to pound me into the rough carpet. My abraded nipples scrape across the fibers as he forces me to the floor. I listen for the tell-tale sound of his orgasm but nothing comes.

Confused, I turn my head toward the mirror. He pulls out and bites his bottom lip. My pussy shivers from the sudden loss of him. But when I see what he's up to, my cunt pulses with delight.

Audrey has no idea how much I need to fuck her tight little asshole. By the time I'm done, she'll be begging me to stop. The man in the window watching us is an executive from a fortune 500 company. I've heard about his voyeuristic predilections for years. Normally I wouldn't let another man watch me fuck my favorite toy, but if Jack enjoys the show, he'll greenlight a trade deal between our companies that will make me millions.

I'm not about to leave anything to chance, so I pull a small bottle of lube out of my pant pocket. Fucking Audrey's hot little pussy should have been enough for Jack, but it never hurts to err on the side of caution. Anal should seal the deal. It's not the first time I've claimed her ass, but I won't be gentle this time. I want to hear her scream.

Maybe I have sadistic tendencies, but I love pushing the envelope with her. She never complains. I can stuff my cock in any and every hole. She just thanks me and asks for more. If I could wrap her up and take her home with me I would. But my life is too busy and a wife requires a certain level of maintenance. I don't have time for it.

After lubing my cock, I coat my finger with the viscous fluid and swirl it around her puckered hole. She wriggles her ass. My cock jumps in response.

I drive the tip of my finger into her ass. The muscles contract and try to force me out but I'm relentless. Inch by excruciating inch, I forge a path deeper. She moans and pushes up on her hands. When she arches her back and tilts her ass up, I slide a second finger inside. Two should be enough to get her started. I don't want her too loose. Where's the fun in that?

Satisfied with the level of tension in her hole, I set the

lube aside and position the head of my cock over my intended target.

"Be gentle," she pleads.

I don't know if it's part of her coy act, or if she's truly not ready. Either way, I don't care. I'm shaking with unchecked lechery. Her ass is mine. All mine. And I intend to pummel every inch of it.

Without warning, I thrust my hips forward. She gasps as half of my cock disappears into her tight little hole. I don't give her time to adjust. Instead, I pull back a few inches before pushing deep. This time, all but an inch is wedged firmly inside.

Unacceptable.

I drive into her again and again until her ass rests firmly against my hips. She screams and claws at the ground as if trying to escape. Her ass clenches hard in an attempt to dispel me. It's useless. I'm in as far as anyone's ever been. Triumph courses through my veins.

Jack stands and walks toward the window. His cock swings between his legs. I'm surprised he's as well-endowed as I am. And then I get an idea. What if we took turns filling Audrey? We could even double stuff her. The possibilities are endless.

I wave at Jack and indicate that he should come over. He quickly gathers up his clothes and disappears from sight.

"My friend is going to join us," I tell her.

"Oh, God, Yes," she moans.

I pound her ass for several minutes, making the most of the time we have alone. By now, I could have come ten times, but I'm holding back. My stamina is unparalleled. I doubt she's ever met a man who could go for hours like I can. But she loves it. I can see it in her glassy-eyed stare when she stumbles out of my room after our sessions.

A knock sounds on the door.

"Don't move," I murmur as I pull out.

I open the door for Jack and quickly return to the boardroom. Audrey's right where I left her. Spread wide and waiting.

"I'm impressed that you're willing to share your friend," Jack says.

"It's not a common practice for me," I say. "But I don't mind the occasional romp."

"What's your name?" Jack asks.

"Audrey."

"Pretty name for a pretty girl," he says.

"And what should I call you?" she asks demurely.

"Jack."

"Are you going to fuck me too?"

"Would you like that?" Jack asks as he sheds his clothes.

"Yes. But my rate doubles."

"You'll make a great businesswoman someday," I say.

"Thank you, Daddy."

"Daddy?" Jack asks.

"It's our thing," I say. "Sometimes she needs a strong hand to guide her. "Don't you, sweetie."

"He likes spanking me when I'm a bad girl."

"Have you been a bad girl?" Jack asks.

"Always," she replies.

I laugh before turning to Jack. "How do you want her?"

"We have so many options."

"I know."

"I want to take both of you at once," Audrey says. "One in my pussy and one in my ass. I've dreamed about doing it that way but I've never had the chance."

"Sounds good to me," Jack says. "I can't wait to feel your tight little pussy."

Jack lays down on the floor and Audrey slides a condom onto his cock. She positions herself over him, and then guides his cock into her slick cunt.

"Fuck, you're so tight," Jack gasps.

"I like to stay in shape," she says. "Inside and out."

She rocks her hips back and forth as she rides his dick. Every inch of her creamy white skin is covered in a thin sheen of sweat. I want to lick it off her and worship her perfect, curvy body. God, she's incredible.

Blood rushes into my cock making it impossibly hard. It never gets like this with anyone else, only her. Maybe I should make her my wife, or at least my girlfriend.

"Are you coming?" Audrey casts a salacious glance over her shoulder.

"Hell yeah."

I drop to my knees behind her, careful not to rest on Jack's thighs. Her plump ass bounces up and down as she grinds on his cock. I press down in the middle of her back to get her to angle her ass up at me. She instantly complies.

Stuffing my cock back in proves to be much harder now than it was the first time. But I'm a man on a mission, so I keep at it until I'm balls deep. It takes a minute to find the perfect rhythm and soon we're a sweaty, thrusting, writhing mess of orgasmic lust.

I've got two cocks buried to the hilt and I couldn't be any happier. I cry out a garbled mess of nonsense as they continue to fuck me harder, deeper, and faster. This isn't the first time I've been double stuffed like this, but these two are working me like they've been doing it together for years. And maybe they have. I still don't know a damn thing about

Jack, but I'm intrigued because let me tell you something—the man can fuck!

All sense of time and space disappears as quaking shockwaves rise up to claim my pussy. My ass clenches around his cock which throttles up the intensity. It's like being double teamed by two of the fastest vibrators on the planet. I'm being split in two but I don't care.

I grab a handful of Jack's hair and bend down to crush my lips against his. Normally I don't kiss on the mouth, but this is the only way I can stop screaming in ecstasy. The walls must be sound proof because we're making such a racket that I would have expected security to bust the door down twenty minutes ago.

They jam their cocks in over and over until I can't breathe. Absolute bliss rushes up to consume me. Jack's cock swells against my tight walls and all I can do is let them use me. I'm their plaything and I love it. Nothing gets me hotter than having a powerful man take me like this. And now I have two.

I'm gasping for air when David roars. His cock twitches in my ass, releasing streams of hot cum. He jerks violently against me, nearly knocking us all to the floor. One last twitch rattles my hole before he falls back. I turn to make sure he hasn't passed out. He sits on the floor, a smile of absolute satisfaction smeared across his face. I can tell he's done for the day.

Jack, on the other hand, is just getting started. He rolls me onto my back and I instinctively wrap my legs around his waist.

"Your fucking tits are amazing," he growls.

Before I can respond, he leans down to capture one plump nipple in his teeth. I arch and moan as tendrils of white-hot heat arc between my breasts and my pussy. My nipples are the most sensitive part of my body. He swirls his tongue around the taut peaks before cupping my tits. As he leans to brush sloppy kisses across them, I squeeze the muscles in my pussy.

"Fuck," he gasps. "Jesus, your pussy's so good."

I know. That's why I get the big bucks.

"Goddammit I want to fuck you forever," he groans.

Good luck with that. I know how to make a man come when I'm ready, but I'm not done with him yet. The man is a beast. He jackhammers his hips, driving me into the floor with every thrust. I'm going to be covered in rug burns after this but I don't care. Screwing him is a fucking dream. I'll never admit it, but he's one of the best I've ever had.

"I want to fuck you on the table," he says.

"Okay."

He wraps his muscular arms around me and hauls me up as he stands. I can't believe it. I'm still impaled on his dick when he walks me over to the table.

The polished table is cool against my feverish back. I can't imagine what it looks like right now. It's probably a mess of carpet burns. But they'll heal. And I'll have a funny story for the other girls at the agency. We love sharing stories about our "dates".

Jack grabs my ankles and pulls them over his shoulders. I'm splayed out like an erotic buffet. Hunger blazes in his eyes. His hands roam across my breasts and belly. I shiver and grab one of his wrists. I bring his fingers to my lips and suck the tip of each one in turn. Maybe I have an oral fixation, but I love sucking a man's fingers as he fucks me.

David takes a seat at the table and watches us fuck. I've never seen him with such a silly grin on his face. It's charming. He's a very handsome man and if I was looking for a sugar daddy, I'd probably pick him. But I like being independent.

As Jack drills me, I let my thighs drop open. My legs quake and my pussy tightens around his cock. I know what's coming but even I'm shocked when my whole body tightens up into a ball of tension. It only lasts a second before an orgasm races down my spine. My pussy trembles and vibrates around his cock.

"Look at that pussy," Jack whispers in awe.

His fascination only lasts as long as my pussy's shaking. The moment it stops, he pulls my hips down over the edge of the table. I start to sit up, but he pushes me back down.

"I'm going to fuck your ass too," he says. The tone of his voice leaves zero room to question his demand. I love it. I bet he's just as bossy with his subordinates.

"Yes, Sir."

His cock probes my throbbing asshole. The last ripples of orgasm keeps my muscles tight and he's having trouble entering me.

"Relax, baby," he coos.

I try to calm down but my heart's beating in double time. And just when I think he's going to give up, he plunges forward. The enormous length of him turns me inside out. I'm screaming his name and coming all over again.

Deep, percussive strokes render me completely helpless. I'm a slave to his cock. He can do whatever he wants and I won't say no. Not after this. I've never been so out of my mind with pleasure. It radiates throughout every cell in my body. A sensation of floating lifts me up and then I crash down with each thrust. It's like being on a sensual rollercoaster.

I lose track of time completely. I never knew how much I needed to be fucked like this. It's a revelation. Minutes pass and everything becomes a hazy, endless rolling wave of ecstasy.

Jack sucks in a huge breath. It whooshes out as a loud grunt as he comes in my ass. He buries himself to the hilt and stays there. His face is crimson and rivulets of sweat roll down his chest.

When he eventually pulls out, I sit up. My legs are shaking and I can hardly walk to the bathroom. After a long hot shower, I find my clothes in the entryway. Both men are seated on white sofas facing each other. Once everyone's dressed, I take a seat next to David.

"How are you doing?" I ask.

"Amazing." He gives me a soft kiss on the cheek. "I have something for you."

He passes me a plain white envelope. I thumb it open. A fat stack of hundred dollar bills peeks out. I can't wait to get home and count my tip. It's got to be a few thousand extra.

"Thank you, Daddy." I glance at Jack. "It was nice to meet you."

"Here's my card. Call me some time," he says.

That's not how this works, but I don't want to correct him and embarrass him in front of David. He'll tell Jack how to contact me after I leave. He needs to call the agency first to get screened. I won't take anyone who hasn't been through that process.

After slipping into my strappy heels, I stand.

"I'll walk you to the door," David says.

"Thank you."

As I stroll out of the room, I cast a quick glance over my shoulder and smile. I had one hell of a time and I hope they'll call me again. I can't wait to get double stuffed by their corporate cocks. And maybe if I'm lucky, they'll even bring an extra friend.

BRITTANY'S MENAGE

I'm painting my nails electric green when I get call from the agency. A new client has ordered a two girl special and they're teaming me up with Jade. We've both been working for the agency for a couple of years while I finish college. I'm working on my post-doc in Greek History with an emphasis in Sapphic love stories. Now don't go getting all excited. I'm not a lesbian per say, but I do love a good pussy licking and Jade's the best I've ever had.

My appointment isn't for two hours so I take a steamy bubble bath. I shave my long legs until they glisten in the water. They're so enticing that I can't help trailing my fingers across their silky surface. My fingers linger at the top of my thighs. Although I only have an hour before I need to leave, I might have time for a quickie. I haven't masturbated yet today and I'm already hotter than molten lava.

As I glide my fingers down toward my bald pussy, I shiver in anticipation. I could come ten times a day and still not be satisfied. Maybe I'm a nympho, but I don't hear my clients complaining.

The pad of my thumb teases the length of my slit. I'm already wet, and not just because I'm sitting in a bathtub full of soap bubbles. The temptation to draw out my private session is overwhelming but I'll get in trouble if I'm late to my appointment. So I press two fingers against the top of my pussy. My clit jumps in response. Greedy little thing.

My tiny nub swells with yearning. The more I stroke the sensitive bundle of nerves, the wetter I get. Slick with need, I quicken my tempo until I'm frantically rubbing my clit. My full double-D breasts jiggle sending a torrent of bubbles over the edge of the tub. Oops. I always make such a mess when I'm in this state. But I can't help but pound my hot little cunt into submission.

I'm seconds away from coming when my phone vibrates on the shelf over the bath. I grab it before it falls into the water. It's Jade, so I quickly answer.

"Hey sweetie, I can't wait to see you," I say seductively.

"Brittany! Are you masturbating?"

"Maybe."

"I can't understand how you can do it so much and not have carpel tunnel," she says.

"It's a gift."

"Are you at least thinking about me?"

"Of course," I say, even though I didn't have any particular fantasy in mind. It never hurts to stroke her ego. "I was imagining how good it's going to feel to have your tongue on my pussy. It's been a few weeks since our last double date."

"And I've been thinking about you every day since," Jade says.

Of course she has. I gave her a toe-curling, soul annihilating orgasm that had her screaming for an hour. My tongue almost fell off, but it was worth it. I love making her come over and over until her pussy aches. I consider it a hobby.

"We'll be together soon," I say.

"Is your hand on your pussy right now?"

"Yes," I whisper.

"Tell me."

We've played this game before. It's a pre-date warm-up. She loves listening to me describe every single caress. I was so close to coming before she called that I need to step things back a bit or I'll come too soon. See, it doesn't just happen to guys. Women want to hold back too. We're greedy that way.

"I'm putting you on speaker phone." I'm going to need both hands for this.

"I'm listening."

"The water is cool on my nipples. They're hard as pebbles and just begging for me to tweak them."

"Do it," she murmurs.

"Oh God," I groan as I pinch each nipple simultaneously. "It's so good."

"I can't wait to suck your tits."

"Mmm," I moan. "Now I'm cupping my breasts and squeezing them together. I have to taste them."

"It's so hot when you suck on your tits. They're so perfect."

She sighs and I wonder if her fingers are in her panties. Probably.

"I'm gliding my hands down my chest and across my belly. It quivers as little tendrils of desire stretch down to my pussy."

"You're always so good at describing this. You should be a phone sex operator," she says.

"But then I couldn't be pounded by a big fat cock while I'm eating your pussy."

"Good point."

We both laugh.

"My fingers are slipping lower. I can't resist curling my fingers into my cunt."

"How many fingers?" she asks.

"Two. No. Wait. Three. Oh yeah."

"Get it nice and loose. I hear the new guy's got a BBC."

"A big, black cock?"

I stuff my fingers into my pussy. There's nothing hotter than a brother with a monster dick. Sometimes I can't believe I'm getting paid to be plowed by those guys. If my plan to become a professor falls through, I'll just keep serving my cunt up to BBC.

"Close your eyes," Jade says. "I want you to imagine the thickest, longest, most plump cock you've ever seen. Now see it sliding into your tight little hole."

"Oh, it's too big," I whisper, playing along.

"Just let him shove it in."

"I can't."

"Grind your pussy all over his cock. Do it," she commands.

"Yes, Ma'am."

"Good girl."

"It's sliding in," I gasp dramatically. In reality, I've got three fingers stuffed up my pussy and I'm rubbing my clit with my thumb. "Oh, I think he's going to...oh fuck!"

"What?"

"It's so fucking big. It's so deep."

"Do it," she groans. "Pound that fucking cunt. I want to hear you come harder than you've ever come in your life."

With the way things are going, I might actually give myself a tension headache from the strain. I suppress a giggle and refocus my effort. My fingers plunge in over and over. My thumb jams against my clit as my ass lifts up. Water splashes all over the bathroom as I arch and writhe. I'm so caught up in the passion that I can hardly hear Jade over the ruckus.

"Come for me," she commands. "Come all over your fucking hand. Do it."

"Oh, fuck!"

"Do it you naughty fucking girl."

"Ugh!"

I shatter as an orgasm rips through my body. My pussy clamps down on my fingers, pulsing faster than I ever thought possible. My mind is completely overwhelmed with ecstasy as wave after wave of absolute bliss crash into me.

When the trembling finally subsides, there's only a few inches of water in the tub. The floor is saturated. Oops.

"I might be a few minutes late," I say. "It's a bit of a mess in here."

"I can imagine."

"I'll see you soon."

I hang up and attempt to get out of the tub. Nope. My legs shake for another minute before I can finally move. God I needed that. And to think, I'll get to come again in an hour. I love my life.

Brittany's such a fucking tease on the phone. I couldn't listen to her describe her masturbation session without stuffing my fingers up my skirt. I'm already dressed for the session with our client. But now my perfectly ironed wrap dress is a wrinkled mess. It's bunched up around my waist and draped over the arm of the sofa I'm sitting on. My living room window faces the street but I don't care. Give the nosey neighbors something to talk about. Their quaint suburban lifestyle bores me. I should move downtown like Brittany but I hate all the traffic.

I glance at the clock. I don't have enough time to finish unless I rush and I'd rather get to our appointment horny and ready to fuck. We don't always get BBC when we go on dates so I want to make the most of this one. It might be a few weeks before we get another one.

After smoothing my skirt as much as possible, I rearrange my scarlet lace panties. My pussy begs me to reconsider. But I ignore her pleading.

"You'll be satisfied soon enough."

Yes, I talk to my pussy. Why not? Sometimes I need to put my demanding little cunt in her place. If I let her take over I'd spend every hour on my back with a cock stuffed inside me. It might sound glorious to someone who's not getting laid enough, but trust me, the girl needs a night off from time to time. I don't want her getting stretched out wider than a watermelon. I take pride in maintaining my tight little hole.

I grab my keys off the table by the front door and head outside. A thin layer of snow covers the grass. Spring can't come soon enough. It's almost here. I can feel it in my blood. I swear I want to fuck ten times more in the spring than in the winter. The cold, dark months are for cozying up by the fire with a cup of hot cocoa. They aren't for getting naked and freezing your ass off. Well... I guess you could fuck in front of the fire, but I prefer to hole up in my house and read books.

Halfway to my Ford Expedition, Mrs. Jenkins from next door hollers at me from her porch. She's in her late fifties but through the magic of Botox doesn't look a day over forty.

"Where are you off to today?" she asks.

"I'm running errands." And getting my pussy pounded.

"Will you be stopping by the market?"

"I'm not sure," I say truthfully. It all depends on whether or not I have any energy left after our date.

"If you happen to be near a market, could you be a dear and pick up a bottle of merlot? I'll pay you back."

Did I mention she's a drunk housewife? It's not uncommon here. Most of the other residents on our street are moderately wealthy. I inherited this house from a sweet older man who wanted nothing more than to find a nice girl to suck his shriveled cock. Sounds gross, but I did get a house out of it so…

"I'll see what I can do," I yell across the hedge between our homes.

"Thank you, dear."

"Anytime."

I don't mind running errands for her from time to time if it keeps her off the streets. She's had at least one DUI that I'm aware of but I wouldn't be surprised if there were more. I'm pretty sure her license was revoked last year but I don't follow the neighborhood gossip. The only time I even engage with the other women is when I'm out running and can't avoid them.

Cross town traffic is a bitch. I make it to the address provided by the agency two minutes before we're set to arrive. Punctuality is a huge deal in this business. We live and die by the clock. Even though we're careful about not making it a huge deal, we never go over our allotted time. Even if the guy's dick is magical. Sigh.

I pull into the designated space in front of the building and the doorman runs over.

"Are you Jade or Brittany?" he asks.

"Jade."

"Mr. Jackson is expecting you."

I hand my keys to the man.

"When you enter the lobby, you'll find the penthouse elevators on the right. Will you be needing anything else?" he asks.

"No. Thank you."

Most of our clients are upscale businessmen, but this building is unbelievable. White and grey marble floors stretch across the entire lobby. On the right side, a sitting area full of overstuffed chairs and a crackling fireplace gives off a welcoming vibe. But that's not the best part. The walls are filled with built-in bookshelves. There are volumes upon volumes of books from floor to ceiling.

I'm standing there gawking like a kid in a candy store when Brittany arrives.

"My God this place is amazing," she says.

"So many books."

"One day I'm going to have a library like that," she says.

"I should install one in my house."

"Yeah. If you have the room for it, why wait?"

"We should get going," I say. "We can check it out again when we leave."

"Ha! As if we're going to want to do anything other than stumble over to our cars."

I laugh and loop an arm through hers. The subtle scent of her floral perfume curls up to entice me. I can hardly wait to strip the prim and proper business suit off of her curvaceous body. How she can hide those stunning breasts is beyond me. If I had a rack like hers, I'd show them off as much as possible. I'm a solid C, which actually works well with my petite frame. But maybe one day I'll get the girls enhanced.

We take the elevator up to the penthouse. As we step out into the hall, a door swings open and the most gorgeous black man I've ever seen steps out.

"Ladies."

"Oh my God, you're Brock Jackson!" Brittany shrieks.

"In the flesh," he says.

I turn my blank expression toward Brittany.

"He's the quarterback for the greatest football team on earth," she gushes.

"Or at least the east coast." He grins. "Come on in and make yourselves comfortable."

We follow him into a room straight out of a palace. An enormous oriental rug covers the floor. Gilded walls lit by golden sconces set a seductive scene. Small stylized sofas in a variety of shapes are positioned throughout the room.

I run my fingers over one covered in a Damascus silk brocade with images of naked people entwined in a variety of sexual positions. The designer clearly had the Kama Sutra in mind when she created the pattern.

"Can I get you a drink?" he asks.

"White wine," I respond. Normally I don't drink much when I'm on the clock, but wandering around such luxury without wine somehow seems uncivilized.

"A Jack and Coke for me," Brittany says.

"Coming right up. Feel free to get acquainted, girls."

Apparently the agency hasn't told him that Brittany and I are already well acquainted. I wink at her and walk over.

"I'm Jade." I offer her my hand.

"It's nice to meet you," she says. "I'm a little nervous. I've never done this before."

I almost choke on a laugh. She's such a great actress.

"Don't worry. I'll take good care of you," I say.

Brock looks up from behind a bar tucked in the corner of the room. "Did I hear you say this is your first time?"

"With a girl," Brittany demurs.

I stroll over to her and brush back a few strands of her soft honey-blonde hair. When I lean in to kiss her, she lets out a little gasp. I delve into the kiss, licking the edge of her bottom lip before sliding it into her mouth. She moans against me as I wrap my arms around her. She tastes like cotton candy. I can't get enough of her pliant lips.

We're well into our make out session when Brock returns with two glasses.

"Don't let me interrupt." He sets the glasses on a glass table in the center of the room.

I draw Brittany toward a pink silk chaise. She sits on the end of it. I straddle her and wrap my legs around her waist. Her curves melt into mine as I reclaim her sultry lips.

Brock settles into a chair a couple of feet away. He swirls a glass of amber cognac and takes a sip. Since he seems happy enough to watch, I resume my exploration of her petal-soft lips. It only lasts a second before she slides her tongue into my mouth. The kiss becomes a firestorm of lust and soon we're rubbing our breasts together and wriggling our bodies to create friction.

"Undress," Brock says.

I reach for the tie at my waist and tug. My wrap dress falls away from my body in one swift motion. God I love how fast I can go from dressed to naked.

Brittany pushes me onto my feet. She stands and turns her back to me.

"Would you unzip me?" she asks.

"Of course."

I make a show of pulling down the zipper. Each soft click of metal on metal increases the anticipation in the room. I peel the dress over her shoulders and slide it down past her hips. It puddles on the floor. She turns to show off a stunning black lace bra and panty set with a matching garter. I should have worn a garter too. Oh well, the red satin set I'm wearing will be a nice contrast to hers.

Brittany prances over to Brock and sits on his lap. I sashay over and strike a pose.

"Do you dance?" he asks.

"Do you have music?" I reply.

He reaches into the pocket of his slacks and pulls out a remote. In seconds, the pulsing slow beat of a song worthy of a strip club fills the room. I can work with this. No pole necessary. I've taken a bunch of stripper-style dance classes and can't wait to show off my moves.

As Jade begins a seductive strip tease, I slide off of his lap and lean down to unbuckle his slacks. He leans back in the chair and lets me tug them off. Boxers! I knew he'd be a boxers not briefs guy. I can't wait to dive it and find out how big his cock is, but his T-shirt's long and in my way. It only takes a second to rectify that problem. I pull his shirt over his head and drop it on the ground next to his pants.

He's all muscle. Ripped arms covered in tribal tattoos. Taut thighs that you could crack a walnut on. Every inch of his body is a testament to testosterone. I want to lick every inch of his rock hard body already. But not before I check out his package.

I hook my fingers into his boxers and tug them over his slim hips. The biggest cock I've ever seen in my life pops out to rest on his thigh. Already semi-erect, a drop of pre-cum drips from the tip of the bulbous head. I can't resist diving right in.

As I wrap my hand around his shaft, he groans. His cock swells, growing in length and girth until I can hardly hold it all. When I move closer, the scent of clove and cinnamon sparks from his skin. And he tastes even better. I don't know what kind of edible oil this is, but it tastes like a cinnamon roll. Smart man. I could nibble on his dick all day.

My tongue snakes around the tip before slathering his shaft with saliva. I love giving really wet, really nasty blowjobs. Did I mention I have no gag reflex? It's a fucking gift.

I wrap my lips around him and slowly slide him into my mouth. His hips arch slightly but I shove them back down. He needs to know that I'm in complete control of the situation. I won't let him face fuck me until I'm good and ready.

The more I take into my mouth, the louder he moans. When I've gone down as far as I can, I push myself to take a little more. Trust me, when you think you've done as much as you can, you're only at ninety percent.

Ten percent later, my nostrils flare and getting any oxygen becomes a challenge. I love challenges. I stay like that, tonguing the underside of his shaft for a full minute before letting up. As I glide my lips up toward the tip, he shutters. I've reduced him to desperate man who can't wait for me to swallow his cock again.

I suck, lick, and eventually let him face-fuck me. It's hot and my pussy's wet by the time he eases me away.

"I want to fuck you," he says in a breathy tone.

I straddle him and guide his cock into my tight little hole. He's so big that I can only slide down an inch at a time.

My body struggles to take it all but I've got gravity on my side.

"You need some help?" Jade asks.

She walks up behind me and reaches around to cup my breasts. I'm not exactly sure how this is supposed to help me but who gives a shit? The minute she starts pinching and tweaking my nipples I'm a goner. I rock my hips and slip up and down his cock. Jade nuzzles the back of my neck before dragging her teeth across my shoulder. I groan as all of the sensations pool in my cunt. Sex is so much more fun with three people.

"Kiss," he says.

I turn and find Jade's mouth just inches from mine. We meet in the middle in a scorching hot kiss that melts the muscles in my belly. I tremble and work my hips in a circle, always making sure to keep my focus on him as well as her. I wouldn't want anyone to feel left out.

Her tongue parts my lips and we're going at each other with unchecked passion. If I had to guess, I'd say she hasn't been with another girl in a long time. She seems almost desperate for it.

I reach for her prefect breasts and tug on her nipples. She moans into my mouth and laces her fingers in my hair. We kiss until our lips are swollen and bright pink.

When she trails her mouth down my throat and across my breasts, I clench around his dick. He's lifting his hips now, holding me in place with strong hands and a firm grip on my waist. I don't have to do much because he's bouncing me on his cock. The sheer muscular strength is enough to make me cream all over his dick. A wet, sucking sound fills the air as my pussy rides up and down the length of his shaft.

"I want to see you eat out your friend," Brock says.

Jade lays back on the chaise and spreads her thighs. Her tiny pink pussy winks at me from between her legs. I get on my knees in front of her and brush my nose across her slit. She reaches down and pulls my hair away from my face.

She smells like strawberries and tastes like sugar. I don't know how she manages to taste so fucking good, but I could eat her for hours. I tongue open the folds of her lips and find her tight little nub. When I close my lips around her clit, she arches and presses against my face. I grab her hips and hold her still.

Brock takes a pillow and shoves it under my knees. My ass is pointing up and my pussy is waiting. When he pushes his cock into me, I gasp against Jade's cunt. Even though he was balls deep inside me earlier, my pussy isn't ready for the pounding he gives me. My tits slap against the edge of the chaise and I can hardly keep my mouth on Jade's pussy.

After a few minutes he relents and slides in and out in such perfect rhythm that my orgasm builds steadily. I've never had this happen before, but he brings me to the edge over and over without pushing me beyond it. He's a fucking master at edging and I'm going mad with lust.

Suddenly, he plunges deep and pistons against my clit. I scream and come so hard that my knees buckle. He hauls me up with his hands and shoves in deep as I convulse on his cock. A shrill keening blasts from my lips but I can't contain it. It's not pretty, but I haven't come this hard in months and I can't stop screaming.

When he pulls out, I fall onto my side and curl up into a twitching ball of ecstasy. I'm only half-conscious as I watch him drag Jade's ass toward the edge of the chaise. He takes her with long, slow strokes. I realize he's preparing her for the same level of pounding I just enjoyed. I'm almost jealous as I watch his firm butt clench and drive with each thrust. Even though I couldn't possibly take his cock again for at least a few minutes, I want it.

"Come here and sit on my face," Jade says.

I try to stand but my legs collapse.

"I need a second."

"Did I wear you out?" Brock asks smugly.

"Yeah."

"Good."

I smile and bite the edge of my lip. I adore this man. His mission to please us makes him even sexier.

Sweat drips down his dark skin making it glisten in the low light. Every muscle in his arm flexes as he grabs her hips and pulls her back into him. Even the chords in his neck stretch with the effort. I can't stop staring at this beautiful man.

"Oh fuck," Jade yelps.

I spring to action and crawl toward the chaise. I use the tallest part of it to drag myself up off the ground. As I straddle her face, my legs shake uncontrollably. There's a good chance I'm going to end up sitting on her face and smothering her, but my pussy's ready for more action.

I brace my hands against the top of the chase and lower my pussy toward her waiting mouth. The moment her tongue makes contact I jolt and pull away.

"Still sensitive?" she asks.

"God yes."

"I'll be gentle."

I graze her lips with my cunt. Sharp tingles of left over orgasm spark down through my thighs. I lean against the chaise a bit more to keep from falling. Jade grabs my hips and tugs me lower. When her lips meet my pussy, I moan.

Behind us, Brock whispers, "You two are so fucking hot."

"Thank you," we respond in unison before dissolving into a fit of giggles.

The vibrations of her mouth on my pussy sends tendrils of hot need into my core. I grind my cunt against her. When her tongue pokes up to tease my clit, I whimper. I've never been so turned on in my entire life. This isn't the first time she's eaten me like this, but something about the whole scene is getting to me. Maybe it's the way Brock completely wrecked my pussy or the enthusiasm with which Jade is eating my cunt. I don't know. I just know that I never want this to stop.

The chaise starts to slip across the rug as Brock begins his rhythmic, deep pounding. I know Jade won't be able to hold back long. The girl can come on a dime. So I move my clit to her tongue. She swirls and curls around my hot button until the room goes hazy.

A scream builds up somewhere deep in my chest and explodes from my mouth. My entire body clenches in a fit of contractions as an incredible orgasm seizes me in its grip. I fall forward against the chaise, knocking it back another inch.

Jade cries out once, twice, and then goes silent. I look down to find her eyes wide and her mouth twisted into a shocked display of bliss. Soft gurgling noises come up from her throat as she rolls her head from side to side. She's clearly caught up in the same orgasmic ecstasy.

I carefully swing my leg over the chaise and drop to my knees beside her. Every pent up sound seems to spill from her lips at once. She's screaming, sighing, and moaning until her eyes roll back and she falls limp. Did she seriously just faint?

Brock pulls his cock out and blasts a load of hot cum all over her breasts. I can't believe how much spunk he can hold. A trail of cum slides down her nipple, curves around her breasts and drips down her side. I'm mesmerized.

He steps back a few paces and falls into a chair. Jade sucks in a breath and her eyes flutter open. She gazes around the room with a disoriented look.

"Hey, sweetie," I say. "Welcome back."

"Did I faint?"

"Yep."

"Oh my God that's so embarrassing," she mutters.

"I think it's hot," Brock says. Of course.

"I can't even move," Jade says.

"Give it a minute. I'll go find a towel," I say.

"Second door on the left," he says.

I manage to haul my ass off the floor and find the bathroom. After a quick sponge bath at the sink, I grab a couple of towels and cover the corners with warm water. You can't get cum off with cold. It just doesn't happen.

I return to find Jade sitting up. I hand her a towel before heading over to clean Brock's cock. The blissful smile on his face is priceless. I love making my clients happy. I have an intrinsic need to please so I take pride in a job well done.

After we're clean and dressed, Brock hands me an envelope stuffed with cash.

"When can I see you both again?" he asks.

"Just call the agency. We had so much fun," I say.

"It was amazing," Jade says.

"Thank you ladies. Can I get you anything else? A drink for later?" he asks.

"Actually, yes," Brittany says. "You wouldn't happen to have a bottle of red wine laying around would you?"

"I have a whole wall of red. Take your pick."

I shoot her a questioning look and she winks. I know she'll tell me later.

With the wine in tow, we head down to the lobby filled with books. As much as I'm tempted to spend an hour browsing, I'd rather head home.

"Want to come over for a bit?" Brittany asks.

On second thought, I wouldn't mind spending time in her huge bubble bath. I'm sure we'll end up getting water all over the floor again. We usually do.

CLAIMING CANDY

It's two p.m. and I'm flying down a California freeway with my sunroof open. My golden blonde hair streams behind me as I sing along to a nasty Two Live Crew song. The base bumping from the speakers rattles my white Jeep Wrangler, but that's nothing compared to what it's doing to my pussy.

I'm on my way to a client's office. I've seen him more times than I can count but I've never really paid much attention to what he actually does. The minute he whips out his cock, I don't care about anything but getting it into my tight little cunt.

This guy loves to pound me on his desk with the door closed. His coworkers are in the next room but he doesn't seem to care. Dirty boy. I love men who are completely unapologetic about their desires. It makes me so hot.

Out of the corner of my eye, I notice a truck in the lane to my right. It's pacing me, so I glance over. It's a nondescript work truck, but the guy has the kind of tan you can only get from spending your life working outside. I'm intrigued.

He grins and gestures at me. I don't know what the hell

he's trying to tell me so I simply smile and return my attention to the road. He starts flailing his hands so I look over. With both hands off the wheel, he mimics an hourglass shape. Oh, he's talking about my hot body.

Now it might sound conceited, but I know I'm hot. I don't get five hundred an hour for nothing. And trust me when I say that this body doesn't come easy. I spend at least two hours in the gym every day sculpting my ass to perfection. The muscles in my chest are so tight I can hardly see over my tits to drive. They're a totally natural D-cup. No matter how ripped I get, my boobs never get smaller. It's a gift.

Mr. Highway's tongue is hanging out of his mouth already, but why not give him a little show? I'm wearing a black halter-top dress with little red cherries all over it. It would look perfectly innocent on anyone but me.

I reach behind my neck and untie the halter. When the fabric slips down to settle over my breasts, I flash him a shocked smile, as if I can't believe it just fell down. A grin splits his face and lust sparkles in his eyes.

"Should I take it off?" I mouth.

"Fuck yeah," he yells.

I roll the window down and arch my back. The slight movement sends one strap tumbling over my breast. I quickly grab it and pull it back up. My fingers linger on the swell of my breast. I peel the fabric down to just above my nipple.

"Take it off," he shrieks.

We're still barreling down the road at sixty-five miles an hour, so I check to make sure no one's around us. I don't want to cause an accident.

After determining that the coast is clear, I push the cherry dress down to reveal one plump breast. The guy swerves slightly and his eyes bulge out of his head. He probably didn't expect me to actually show him my tits.

"Pull over," he hollers.

A slivery laugh spills from my lips. Not a chance. I don't know this guy so there's no way I'm pulling over on the side of the freeway for him. Besides, what does he expect me to do? Fuck him in the bed of his truck?

He's still pacing me so I look over. I'm sure he's going one hand on his cock but I can't see that far into the truck. I'm about two exits from my off-ramp so I decide to really fuck with him. With a quick yank, I pull my dress down to my waist. My creamy white breasts pop out and bounce as the jeep blazes down the highway. I'm not gonna lie, this guy's making me wet. I've never been much of an exhibitionist, but this is fun. I'm flashing a total stranger in broad daylight. Anyone could drive past me and see my tits but I don't care.

I glance up at the exit sign. One more to go. Oh well, it was fun while it lasted. I pull up the straps and tie them behind my neck. The guy honks at me.

"Pull over," he yells.

I laugh and shake my head. Sorry buddy, not today.

He takes the next off-ramp. Hum…

I glance at the clock. I'm about twenty minutes early to my client's office and it's only two minutes away. That gives me about eighteen minutes to kill. I could go get some Starbucks, or…

The guy pulls into a parking lot just off the freeway. We're in an industrial complex full of storage units and huge warehouses. I pull into the lot behind him. I can't exactly give him a business card for my agency. Besides, it would be a miracle if he could afford me. But I've got time to kill so why not have some fun teasing him.

I park and slide out of my jeep. My dress slides up to

reveal my red lace thong. It's already soaking wet. Flirting with this guy has made me super horny. Thank God I have a client in a few minutes.

"What's up?" I say.

When he gets out of his truck, all of his machismo is gone. His honey-brown eyes dart toward the floor as he pushes shaggy brown hair from his face. Clad in a pair of tight jeans, I can see the outline of his cock. He's hard as hell. My fingers twitch. I want to unzip his pants, whip his cock out and slurp it into my mouth.

"Hey," he says.

"You wanted me to pull over."

"I didn't think you'd actually do it," he stammers.

I almost laugh out loud. Men are so funny sometimes. They wave their dick at you from a distance but the minute you mean business, they turn into scared little boys.

"So... I'm on the clock." I arch a brow and search his expression to see if he gets my meaning. His eyes go wide. Yep. He gets it. "But if you want to call me later, I can give you my number."

He's silent for a moment. I'm convinced he's about to jump in his truck and flee. But he doesn't.

"My company has a storage unit around the corner," he says.

"Give me your wallet."

"What?"

"Your wallet. I told you I'm on the clock."

Maybe he didn't believe me when I said it the first time. But he believes me now. He hands me the wallet. I flick it open with my candy-apple red nails. As I fish through the bills, I count. It's not nearly enough, but I can't stop thinking about how funny it would be to blow this guy in a storage unit. It would make one hell of a story someday.

"I'll need all of it," I say.

"Okay."

"I've only got about ten minutes."

"I'll be fast. Wait. I didn't mean it like that," he stumbles over his words.

"I know what you meant."

I don't tell him that my record is getting someone to come in under sixty seconds. I can be such a bitch sometimes but I love fucking with clients and making them insta-come. I'll stay and let them pop off again if they're not a dick about it.

After I take all of the money out of his wallet, I hand it back.

"Lead the way."

I follow him around the corner and down a long alley. A public storage facility comes into view. His unit is two doors down from the office. Well shit. Maybe this wasn't such a good idea. But I've got his money in my purse now so it's time to follow through. I'm not a trick-roller. That's just fucked up.

He parks his truck across the front of the storage unit and I park behind him. After he opens the unit, I follow him inside. Pool equipment and the scent of chlorine permeate the air. Ah, he must work for a pool repair company.

As I stroll around the twenty by twenty unit, he pulls the roll up door halfway down. In a way, I'm kind of glad he didn't close it completely. I know this is crazy and totally stupid, but I'm so turned on that I can't help but see it through.

"Come here," I say.

He walks over.

"Um, I have a blanket."

"I won't need it."

I drop to my knees and reach for his pants. Don't think I haven't forgotten about the ticking clock. I've got a time limit. I'm never late for an appointment. Never.

As I slowly lower his zipper, he sucks in a sharp breath. I can already tell he's going to be an easy one. He's probably going to come in my mouth the second I wrap my lips around his dick.

I hook my fingers in his jeans and pull them down around his ankles. When I go back for his boxers, my eyes widen. His dick is huge. It's poking out of the slit in his boxers. Technically, I don't even need to take them off, but I like having unobstructed access to cock. I reach into his boxers and fish out his cock with one hand while I shove the offending garment down with the other. That's better. Now he's all mine.

As I lean in toward his cock, a car drives past the open door. Technically the other driver probably can't see me, but the thrill of the possibility of being caught makes my cunt wet as hell. If I had more time, I'd let this guy fuck me all over this storage shed, but I don't.

The car outside passes without incident, so I return my attention to his cock. The briny scent of sweat curls up to turn me on even more. There's nothing hotter than a man who's good with his hands who comes home from work demanding a quick fuck. At least that's one of my favorite fantasies. I'll settle for Mr. Freeway's cock instead.

I snake my tongue out to lick the tip. Salty. Mmm. Just the way I like it.

When I wrap my lips around his cock, his knees wobble. I smile as much as I can with a dick in my mouth. It doesn't take long for me to get into the perfect rhythm. I'm giving the kind of wet, sloppy blowjob guys love. Who knows, he might even end up becoming a regular. Maybe. I'm still not sure he can afford me.

I swirl my tongue across the tip before sucking him deep into my throat. He grabs my head and hold me down until I'm about to gag. The he growls and pulls back enough to face fuck me. My teeth are rattling in my head but I'm not scraping his flesh. I've got my lips wrapped over my teeth and I'm taking long slow breaths through my nose. Good luck trying to face-fuck me until I pass out. Not gonna happen.

When he grunts and plunges deep again, I decide I've had enough. I cup his balls and glide my wet thumb around each one in little concentric circles. His knees knock against my tits as he hisses a breath. The more his balls tighten up, the closer he gets to blowing his load all over. Now's the time to decide where I want it. If I didn't have another client right after this, I'd let him come all over me. But I don't have time to get cleaned up, so I suck him deep and give his balls a little squeeze.

He moans and jerks his hips forward as hot spools of cum blast out of his dick. I slurp up almost every drop, but let some dribble onto my chin. It's a strategic move to give him the experience of coming all over my face without the messy clean up.

As he steps back to lean against the wall, I stand and brush my skirt down. I adjust my tits in my halter-top. When everything's where it needs to be, I glance at him. A shit-eating grin is smeared across his face. I use my tongue to lick up the dribble of cum on my chin. He shakes his head.

"God you're fucking hot."

"Thanks. Want my number?"

"Of course. Here." He hands me his phone and I program it in.

"Candy?" he asks as he looks at the name I put in.

"Yep."

"That's not your real name, is it?"

No, genius.

"Nope," I say with a smirk.

"What is it? I have to know," he says.

I don't really have time for this but it's fun to watch them grovel and beg for my real name. As if I'd ever give it out. I roll my eyes.

"Can't say. Sorry," I tease.

"Come on. I might never see you again."

Probably, but let's not kill the mood with the truth.

"Next time I see you, I'll tell you," I say.

"I'll call you soon."

Sure he will.

"Sounds good," I say. "See you around."

On the way out of the storage unit, I stop to check my reflection in the mirror on the side of his truck. I definitely don't look like I just sucked dick. Nobody would believe it, especially not with my innocent little smile.

I hope back in my car and stuff his pile of money in my glove box. The clock reads five minutes until my appointment time. Good thing I'm only three minutes away.

As I drive away from the storage units, I glance in my rearview mirror. God that was fun. The best thing about my life is that it's completely unpredictable. One minute I'm driving down the freeway and the next I'm in a storage unit with a dick in my mouth. How could life get any better?

Oh wait, it can! Because I'm about to get a cock stuffed into my sopping pussy.

I pull into the parking lot next to my client's business.

The key to getting past the receptionist is to act like I'm a repeat customer. If only she knew. Or maybe she does. If she does, she'd damn good at hiding it.

Inside the building, I stroll up the front desk.

"Ms. Pavolva to see Mr. Handley," I say.

"Of course. Can I get you coffee or water?" she asks.

"No, thank you."

"Very well. He's been expecting you."

I'm sure he has.

I follow her down the hall to the corner office. Mr. Handley stands as we enter.

"Good afternoon." He extends a hand as if I'm actually a business associate. I grasp it and try to stop grinning.

"Will you be needing anything else?" the receptionist asks as she moves toward the door.

"No. Please close the door and hold my calls," he says.

"Of course, sir."

After she shuts the door, I turn to him.

"I should start calling you that," I say.

"What?" He stalks around the edge of his desk.

"Sir. It's hot."

"You're hot."

"Why thank you," I say.

He slides his hands across my hips and tugs me against him.

"Nice dress," he whispers in my ear.

His hot breath curls down my neck in a seductive caress. He knows better than to try kissing me on the lips unless he wants a spanking. Apparently he doesn't want one today because he's already walking me back toward his desk. He lifts me onto the edge of the desk and sweeps the rest of his paperwork onto the floor. It's pretty damn funny that he does this every time even though he knows I'm coming over.

As I lean back on my forearms and jut my tits out, he runs his hands up my thighs.

"Pink?"

"Nope." This is a game we play. He's trying to guess what color panties I have on.

"White?"

"You know I don't wear white. Lightning would rain down from the sky and kill us all," I joke.

"Okay…black."

I shake my head and laugh. I'm beginning to suspect he's just fucking with me. I have this OCD obsession with matching my panties to my outfit and I'd never go with something as boring as black.

"Well then, I guess I'll just have to take them off and find out," he says.

I press my legs together and lift my ass up. He moves between my thighs and reaches under my dress. When his fingers hook over the edge of my panties, a shiver of lust shimmies down my thighs. Sucking that other guy's cock made me so hot I can't wait to fuck. I wish he'd hurry the fuck up and rip my panties off with his teeth.

As he slides my lacey red panties down my thighs, I lick the edge of my lip and narrow my eyes at him. I give him my best come-fuck-me smile. He doesn't need to be seduced. His cock is already stabbing the front of his jeans. I guess there are benefits to being the boss. He can wear whatever the hell he wants. It's usually jeans and a T-shirt like today.

He tosses my panties onto a chair and bends down to shove his head under my skirt. I giggle and spread my legs. I hook my heels on the sides of the desk but they fly up the second his lips find my pussy. Holy shit. He'd not wasting any time. He dives right in with his rough tongue.

"You're already so wet," he mumbles against my pussy.

"I've been thinking about you all day."

It's not a lie. I have been thinking about his cock and how much I can't wait to get fucked on his desk. I'm just extra wet because of Mr. Freeway—my own personal fluffer.

"You taste so good," he says.

I want to tell him to shut the fuck up and eat me, but I'm a polite girl.

"Thank you, Sir."

"I like that. Keep calling me 'Sir'. It's hot."

"Yes, Sir."

He rewards me with a thorough tongue lashing. I don't know if he's been practicing his moves on that new pussy-licking app or what, but he's way better than normal. Or maybe I'm just much hornier?

As his tongue whirls and circles my clit, I squirm on the desk. I clamp my lip shut to keep from crying out. Even though his receptionist probably knows he's fucking me, there's no point in making it obvious.

He licks and sucks and fucks me with his tongue until I'm shaking and about to fall off the desk. My thighs quiver against the side of his head. He stands up and reaches behind my neck to unhook my halter top. He pulls the top down to expose my breasts. With a quick growl, he descends to suck one plump nipple into his mouth.

The friction of his jeans against my pussy is driving me insane. I want his cock so bad that I'm ready to beg him to fuck me. But his lips are doing crazy things to my tits. He reaches up to pinch one nipple before swiping over to torture the other.

While tugging, plucking, and nibbling on my little nubs, he somehow manages to unzip his jeans and yank them down. His boxers quickly land in the same heap. He steps out of it, never releasing my tits from his mouth, and kicks his clothes out of the way. I yank his shirt over his head while he reaches behind my back to unzip my dress.

He grabs my dress and pulls it over my head. Instead of dropping it to the floor, he tosses it across a chair. I know this is going to sound really weird, but he's such a gentleman about my clothes. I totally appreciate the care he takes in not fucking up my dresses. Some guys don't care and I end up sheepishly handing my cum-stained dresses to the disapproving Asian lady at the drycleaners. She probably thinks I'm a total whore. Occupational hazard.

"Get on your knees and suck my cock," he demands.

"Yes, Sir."

I drop to my knees and spit on his cock. The saliva slides down to dribble across his balls. My pussy clenches and creams. I'm dying to have him take my little cunt, but not yet. I'm ready to earn it on my knees.

My eyes flutter closed as I glide my tongue up the seam underneath his shaft. When I reach the tip, I slurp up his entire dick in one swift move. He grunts and his knees press into my shoulders. I suck harder and he nearly stumbles over. He's my personal marionette and I love controlling him with his cock.

The more I lick, suck, and swallow his cock, the more he whimpers and moans. I'm so into it that I decide to go for the deep throat earlier than normal. I also want to hurry him the fuck up so he'll pound my cunt faster.

I open my eyes and give him a worshiping smile. He groans and laces his fingers into my hair. When he presses me forward, I take all of his cock. I take it deep, and even when it bounces against the back of my throat, I don't stop. I want it all, every last inch.

My nose presses against his skin. I inhale the scent of

desire and sultry heat. A few drops of salty pre-cum drip from the tip to tickle my tonsils.

Our gazes are locked in an expression of mutual lust. I'm not faking it at all. Freeway Guy turned me out and now I'm ready to do anything. He could bend me over and pound me in the ass and I wouldn't complain. No lube? No problem! Just fuck me every which way to Sunday.

I'm shaking with need by the time he pulls his cock out of my mouth. He drops to the floor behind me and pushes me onto all fours. My arms tremble in anticipation. Oh God he's going to do it. He's going to shove his dick in hard enough to make me scream.

Without a second to spare, I shove my face into the carpet and try to muffle my scream when he plunges into my cunt. No pretense. No warning. Just hot and fast. I needed this so bad. It's almost as if he could sense it.

He grabs one ass cheek and digs his nails into my flesh. He can't spank me. My firm ass makes too much noise, so he takes his aggression out in more subtle ways.

While his cock pummels my pussy, I gasp and try to hold myself upright. He grabs my arms and pulls them behind me, forcing me up so that he can fuck me even harder. The slap of my ass against his stomach is obscene and so erotic that I'm already on the verge of coming.

My cunt tightens around his cock, sucking, tugging, and taking him with greedy abandon. Sometimes I don't think I'll ever get enough dick. But when someone like Mr. Handley fucks me this thoroughly, I'm almost satiated. Almost.

He releases my hands suddenly and I fall face first into the carpet. I reach one hand up and start sucking my fingers. I'm a screamer, so I need to do something to keep myself from hollering like a banshee.

I must have inspired him because the next thing I know, he's rubbing my asshole with the tip of one finger. I squirm and try to angle my ass out of reach but I can't escape. He's going to fuck my ass and my pussy at the same time.

His finger moves away. A slurping sound punctuates the staccato slapping of my ass. And then his finger returns. This time he presses until my muscles can't fight back. I glance back just as the tip of his thumb violates my ass.

"Oh, shit," I say through clenched teeth.

"Look at that fucking little hole," he growls. "You like it don't you?"

"Ohh..."

"Yeah you know. I know you do. Dirty girl."

His thumb penetrates me deeper, awakening thousands of little traitorous nerve endings in my ass. The jerky motion sends bolts of electricity from my ass to my pussy. My eyes go wide as a second finger prods my ass.

"Wait," I whisper desperately.

"You can take it."

"Oh, shit."

"Yeah. Take it. Open up your ass for me."

I writhe as something clicks over in my head. All thoughts evaporate as my body becomes a sea of conflicting sensations. My ass aches as he forces a second finger inside, but at the same time it throbs with pleasure. My cunt's a sopping wet mess of desperation. I need to come so bad that my heart's about to explode right out of my chest.

The tempo of his fingers increases. My ass fights back but it's no use. He's going to fuck my tight little hole until I come. I have no choice but to accept my fate. I'm going to come so hard that I'm actually scared.

Tension builds as he pushes his dick deeper. The walls of my pussy close around him as he plunges into me again and again. A low keening spills from my lips. He uses his free hand to reach around and clamp it over my mouth.

"Quiet!"

I mumble curses against his hand. How in the hell can he expect me to be quiet when he's fucking me like this? How is he able to stuff one hand in my ass and hold my mouth shut with the other without falling over? The man's got thighs of steel.

The relentless invasion of his fingers tickles parts of me no man's ever fingered. I know that's hard to believe given my profession, but my ass is usually off limits. Maybe I should rethink that rule. Maybe it's not really even a rule since I didn't stop him when I figured out what he was up to. Maybe I like it.

His hand slides of my mouth and down my throat. He wraps it around my neck and squeezes. After a split second of panic, my cunt buzzes with unexpected lust. Apparently I like being choked. He's never done this to me before, but he's doing it now and I don't even want to resist. It's so hot, so dangerous, but I don't care. He can do anything he wants to me as long as he keeps fucking my pussy.

When he finally releases my throat, I gasp a deep breath. I want to beg him to do it again but it seems to dirty. I can't bring myself to ask for it. Fortunately, he doesn't need me to. His hand closes around my throat again and this time he squeezes until the edges of my vision start to blur. I can't even find the words to explain what this is doing to my pussy. It's literally throbbing so hard that I can't believe I haven't come already. Something about the way he's choking me is prolonging it. He's stretching everything out—how long we're fucking, my ass, my cunt.

I've never been so tense in my life. My spine is rigid and locked in place. My thighs shake and my chest heaves, but other than that, I can't move. Part of me wants to crawl away to escape the overwhelming sensation but I can't.

And I don't have to because when he starts to release my throat, a tidal wave crashes over me. An orgasm unlike anything I've ever experienced absolutely destroys me. I scream until he slaps his hand over my mouth. Even then, I can't stop my muffled screams.

I jerk and twist as convulsions steal my soul. I'm coming so hard that I'm convinced my spirit has somehow left my body. It's as if the shock of this level of orgasm is too much for me to handle. I float on a cloud of total ecstasy until he grunts behind me.

Hot jets of cum fill my cunt. I completely forgot to get a condom. He's turning me into a filthy creampie and I love it. My pussy sucks at his twitching dick, gobbling up every last drop of cum. His fingers are still in my ass which also pulses with orgasmic vibrations.

Neither of us move for a full minute. I think all of our muscles are frozen in place. He finally pulls his dick out. His fingers slide out of my ass to leave a gaping, shivering hole.

I flop onto my back and drape a hand over my eyes. I'm raw and shocked by how thoroughly he's worked me over.

"Not bad, hu?" He slumps into his chair.

"I don't even...I can't even..."

"Take your time."

I lay there for a few minutes until my heart stops pounding in time with my throbbing ass. When I try to sit up, my stomach clenches and my pussy vibrates with an aftershock.

"God, I'm still coming," I moan.

A grin spreads across his face as he hands be a box of tissues. Cum dribbles out of my pussy as I roll onto all fours and attempt to get up. It takes another half a minute before I can get my feet under me.

"Come here and clean me off," he says.

Normally he just puts his pants on and carries on with his day, but how can I refuse him after what he just did to me?

I walk over on wobbly legs and drop back to my knees. I lick up a mixture of his cum and my pussy juices. I'm thorough and make sure to take care of his balls too. When I finish, I'm able to stand and dress myself. He gets dressed too and moves toward the office door.

"Same time next week?" he asks.

"Yes," I respond enthusiastically.

"Good girl." He hands me an envelope filled with crisp $100 bills which I stuff in my purse.

As I waddle—yes waddle—past the reception desk, I have no doubt that she heard us that time. She arches a brow and smirks as if to say—I know you just got fucked harder than you've ever been fucked in your life.

And I arch a brow as if to say—that's right bitch, and I got paid more than you make in a week.

As I walk out into the California sunshine my phone rings. I check the number. A slow smile spreads across my face. It's another client, and I'm ready to get to work.

DELIA'S DUNGEON

I like to be spanked. And I'm not talking about a light pat on the ass. I mean really pummeled. Whacked until my ass cheeks burn and tears fill my eyes. Dominated until I'm begging him to stop, but not quite ready to holler my safeword. The harder he slaps my firm bottom, the hotter I get. I'm wet just thinking about it.

Today, a very special client is requesting a public punishment session. I've never allowed a man to spank me in public before, but today's his birthday, so I'm willing to step out of my comfort zone.

I tap the address into my phone and wait for a rideshare car to arrive. A nondescript four-door arrives within minutes. The man driving leans out the window.

"Delia?"

"That's me."

His eyes go wide as his gaze sweeps from my face down my body. I'm trussed up in a tight steel-gray corset, thigh-high boots, and an almost nonexistent mini-skirt. Normally I don't go to my escorting dates dressed like a total hooker, but this was part of his request. Maybe it's my client's way of preparing me for my impending humiliation. Lucky for me, I get off on dressing up. The sluttier the better.

I slide into the backseat and the driver pulls away. His eyes flash in the rearview mirror several times as he navigates the roads into a seedy part of town. We pass rows of warehouses, some with neon signs flickering in the darkness. It's eight p.m. on a Friday night. I don't know if those are dance clubs or bars, but the people lingering in the shadows give me pause.

How much do I trust Ken? He's been my client for years, but do I really know him? He's never given me a reason to worry, and I've never had to use my safeword with him. Usually I don't let anyone tie me up, but I've known him for years. What could possibly go wrong?

"Are you sure you have the right address?" the driver asks as he pulls into a dark alley.

"Yes."

I have an obsession with checking and rechecking addresses so I don't end up at the wrong house. But as I step out, I can see why he's questioning the location. A single flickering bulb hangs over a staircase that descends below street level. It doesn't look like a sex club. Maybe I transposed a number?

My phone rings. It's Ken. Thank God.

"Hey sweetie, I'm here. I think," I say.

"I'll come out and get you."

"Okay."

"Do you mind waiting?" I ask the driver, not quite ready to let go of my only safety net.

"No problem. I hope you know this guy pretty well."

"I do."

The driver flashes me a look that says he doesn't quite

believe me. I don't bother arguing with him. Although I appreciate his concern, there's nothing to be worried about.

I hope.

When the top of Ken's head appears in the dimly lit stairwell, I breathe a sigh of relief. He's hotter than the desert sun and more deadly. Black hair, black eyes. A midnight blue shirt and leather pants. Everything about him screams darkness and danger. I'm already wet, and he hasn't even touched me.

"Hey there, gorgeous."

"Hi Sweetie."

I stand on tiptoes in my strappy silver sandals and give him a long, wet kiss. He shoves his tongue into my mouth and grabs a fistful of my hair. My knees go weak. I sag against his rock hard chest. He always knows how to take control. How to dominate me.

"Have a good night," the driver calls.

As the car pulls away, Ken breaks the kiss long enough to bite the edge of my neck. Normally I don't let people mark me, but Ken's different. I'm not sure why, but when he dominates me, I let him do anything he wants. His confidence is intoxicating. Even now, in this filthy alley, I'd let him shove me to the ground and stuff his cock so far down my throat that I choke on it.

But he has other plans.

He steps back and surveys my outfit.

"Very nice, Delia. I knew you'd look great in that corset."

"Thank you for sending it."

"You make everything I give you look a thousand times better than it did on the rack. Are you wearing the garters?" he asks.

"Yes."

"Turn."

I obey his command.

"Bend."

I brace my hands on my thighs and spread my legs. As I bend at the waist, his breath whooshes across my ass.

"Open."

I move my hands to my ass cheeks and spread them. Even though I can't see his face, I know he's pleased. I sense it. With him, I know what he's thinking and can anticipate what he wants before he asks. I don't understand this connection we have, but I don't question it.

His fingers graze the crease of my ass. As he palms one cheek, I shiver. He's going to spank me. Right here. Right now. And I'm trembling in anticipation.

Although I know what he's about to do, I'm not prepared for the sudden slap of his hand on my ass. I yelp and jerk forward. He grabs the laces on the back of my corset and tugs me upright. His lips graze my ear.

"Have you been a good girl this week?"

"Yes, sir." My voice quivers.

"I don't believe you."

He never does. Convenient, isn't it?

"I should slam you up against the wall and force my cock in your ass, shouldn't I?" he asks in a dark tone.

This is the other side of him. The Dom. Whatever sweetness he possesses is gone the minute his tone changes. The sadist has taken over.

"Answer me," he demands as he spins me around to face him.

"Yes, sir."

"Master."

"Yes, Master."

For whatever reason, I picture Barbara Eden from the show "I Dream of Jeannie". I stifle a laugh.

"What's so funny?"

"Nothing," I murmur.

"I'll punish you for that later."

I bite back a moan as he slides one hand behind my neck. He drags me forward, but instead of pressing his lips against mine, he brushes them with a feather-soft kiss. He does this to throw me off because a second later, he tosses me over his shoulder and carries me down the stairs.

The black door opens and we walk into my darkest fantasy.

Delia's become my obsession. I've had subs before, but nothing like her. She's sweet, innocent, and filthier than a two-dollar whore in Thailand. Don't ask me how I know. I won't be telling that story anytime soon.

As I walk through the club, other doms turn and nod in my direction. I don't typically bring new playthings to my favorite haunt. Delia's special. I've kept her hidden, away from the seedy Vegas sex club scene. But tonight, I'm going to display her. I'm going to make everyone in this place wish they could have a woman worship them the way she worships me.

Sure, I might have a bit of an ego, but I deserve it. In a club full of deviance, I make these people look like nuns. But not my Delia, this girl's the devil in disguise.

My dick is already rock hard when I drop her to the floor in the middle of the club. I reserved the main stage. It has everything I'll need to bring her to tears.

She rolls onto her knees and bows her head like a good slave. I turn away from her, mostly to get control of my raging need to pound her delicate cunt, but also to survey the implements at my disposal.

The usual whips and riding crops are lined up, but tonight I've requested several switches. They're nasty little fuckers, but I love the sound they make when I swing them through the air. I haven't used one on Delia yet, but I will. Tonight.

As I turn back toward my sub, several couples filter into the room. There's a red velvet rope around the edge of the play area. Per the house rules, no one can cross the threshold unless the dom running the scene grants permission. I've already gone through a list of Delia's hard limits. No fire play. No electricity. I can live with that. What I can't live with is defiance.

"Back straight," I bark. "Ass out, fingers splayed."

She adjusts until she reaches the perfect submissive pose. Several people in the growing audience whisper about her beauty. She's stunning. Perfect alabaster skin. Sassy short ebony hair. Bee-stung red lips. A classic beauty. She could have walked out of a 1920's silent film. I should photograph her one day. With her permission, of course.

"Stand."

She rolls up from her feet to stand before me.

"Pick your poison," I say.

She swallows and walks toward the wall. Although we've never played with switches before, she must know how they work because she quickly walks past them in favor of a leather, wide-tipped riding crop. We've played with this before, so she knows what to expect. As much as I want to flay her with a cane, she needs to be warmed up.

"Lay on the sawhorse."

She obeys. As she drapes her still-clothed body across the sawhorse, I grab four zip ties. I bind her wrists and ankles, leaving just enough room to let her thrash. The sawhorse is bolted to the floor so there's no fear of it toppling over.

A pair of surgical scissors gleam from their place on the wall of tools. I grab them and walk over to my sub. I give her ass a hard whack. She yelps in surprise. Clearly she wasn't expecting that.

I set the scissors aside for later, just in case she wants to be released from her bonds early. I doubt she will though. Thus far, Delia has never backed down from anything I've tried. That's one of the things I love about her; she isn't afraid of very much.

I pick up the crop and use it to slide her skirt up to reveal her ass. I wait several seconds to avoid the predictability of striking her right away. When I'm sure she won't expect it, I bring it down on her ass. She yelps and jerks her ankles against the bonds. Each time the crop makes contact with her flesh, she makes a different noise, but it gets quieter and quieter as she acclimates to the leather.

When she starts to get used to it, I bring the crop down harder and faster, until her backside is bright red. More and more people gather to watch. It won't take long before every person in the club is gathered around to watch. My cock grows harder in my pants. Just the thought of all those people watching us has me on edge.

I bring the crop down again, this time even harder. I'm rewarded with another squeal.

"You like that?" I ask. When she doesn't answer, I bring it down again. "I asked you a question."

"Yes," she manages to squeak out.

I bring the crop down again. "Yes, what?"

"Yes, I like it, Master."

I can't see her face, but I suspect her cheeks are almost

as red as her backside. It takes some coaxing, but I know just how much of a slut she can be, and I'm looking forward to bringing all of it out of her tonight.

Eventually, I grow bored of the crop. It's time to spice things up. I return the crop to where it belongs and grab one of the switches. When I glance at Delia, her eyes are wide. I wait for her safeword to come out, but it never does. Instead, she just watches me and sucks her bottom lip between her teeth.

Those luscious red lips will be wrapped around my cock soon enough. Everyone will see that she likes more than just the toys. She lives to service men, in every way she possibly can.

But I'm saving those lips for later. I'm not quite done with our warm up just yet.

Walking back around to her backside, I smack the switch against my hand a couple times, getting a feel for it. It can definitely cause some pain if you don't use it right, but luckily for her, this isn't my first time.

When I bring it down against her already tender ass, she shrieks. She squirms against the zip ties, but not too hard, and the safeword stays tucked away.

My cock strains hard and harder each time the switch hits her ass. She continues to squirm and moan and squeak. The audience seems to be thoroughly enjoying themselves. Many people are already rubbing their crotches, clearly turned on by the display we're putting on for them.

"You like that?" I ask Delia, loud enough for everyone to hear.

She nods, but doesn't respond.

I bring the switch down again. "I can't hear you."

"Yes," she says, loud enough for our audience to hear.

I grin. It makes my cock throb. This is starting to become

too much for me to handle. I have to get my cock inside her soon. Otherwise, I'm going to empty my nuts into my leather pants, which is not where I want this night to go.

I walk around to the other side of her. There are tears at the corners of her eyes, but they don't fall. Instead, she looks up at me. Lust burns in her eyes. Her gaze travels lower to lock onto the bulge at the front of my pants. She licks her lips.

Oh yeah, she's a super slut—and I love it.

I rub my crotch as she watches. She doesn't even blink. What she wants is blatantly obvious. I reach over her and bring the switch down on her ass one more time. She squeaks, but keeps her gaze locked on my hard cock. I can do anything I want to her, and she won't look away.

She wants my cock.

I can't really blame her either. My cock wants her just as badly.

Undoing the front of my pants, I smirk at the watching crowd. Most of them have seen my dick before, but when a couple of them get their first look at it, they audibly gasp. I never get tired of that reaction. It was the same reaction I'd gotten the first time Delia laid eyes upon it.

She licks her lips again, still not looking away from it. When I bring my hips forward, her tongue darts out to flick against the head. I suck in a breath and grit my teeth. There's a reason I keep going back to her. None of the other girls I've been with ever compare to her.

She sucks my cock like she was born to do it. She doesn't even need her hands to work her magic. Every few seconds, I smack her ass with the switch. I love the feeling of her moans and squeals against my cock.

Not only is she one of the best cocksuckers I've ever encountered, but she's also one of the few that can take my entire length in her mouth without gagging. No matter how hard I face fuck her, she takes it like a true champion.

The audience is loving it almost as much as I am. Men have their cocks out now, stroking as they watch us. Women are fingering themselves, eyes wide as they watch Delia suck me off while I swat her backside. Each and every one of those women looks envious as they watch her, which makes me even hornier.

My cock throbs in her mouth as I move my hips back and forth. I can feel her throat loosening up with each thrust until I'm face fucking her, all the while smacking her ass with the switch. As the audience begins to pleasure themselves in earnest, I fuck her face harder and harder.

Pressure builds up inside me. I won't last much longer, but that's all part of the plan. If I empty my nuts down her throat, I'll be able to spend as much time as I want with my cock shoved up her ass.

Delia knows the drill by now. She moans around my cock, her own orgasm building as I play with her. She's the only woman I know who can come while giving head. Just knowing how close she is turns me on.

"Suck harder," I growl.

I bring the switch down against her ass. She bucks and glares at me with mock-anger.

A hush falls over the audience. Delia's moans mask the sounds of skin sliding against skin coming from the audience. The faces in the crowd contort with pure lust. It won't be long before the floor is covered in cum.

Delia's going to love it, and so will I. If there's one thing she loves almost as much as pleasuring a man, it's seeing how much other people get turned on by her actions.

I smirk at the horny onlookers and fuck her mouth harder and faster until the tension inside becomes unbearable. It won't be long now. It won't be long until she gets to swallow her first load for the night.

If I have my way, it is going to be the first of many cum shots. By the time she walks out of here, she'll have rivers of cum dripping from every hole.

She's already covered in a thin sheen of sweat and we've hardly even started. I'm not quite sure she's going to be able to walk out of here tonight—at least, not without some help. That's fine with me. Maybe I'll even bring her back to my place afterwards for some extra fun.

I can't get enough of her. I could have her three times a day and still want more.

"Here's it comes," I grunt, loud enough for the audience to hear. They're all watching without blinking now, like they're afraid of missing a single second of action.

I can't really blame them. Delia's one hot slut. If I was one of them, I'd be clawing at the rope for a chance to touch her. This is the only club I'd ever consider taking her too. Everyone here knows how to keep themselves under control. They all know the rules, and wouldn't dream of violating them. The only thing between them and the hottest fuck on the planet is a thin, velvet rope, but they'll stay on the other side of it.

I thrust my hips forward, shoving my entire length down her throat. Her nose is buried in my crotch. My groans echo throughout the club. She relaxes her throat just in time for the first rope of cum. As it shoots down her throat, she gags. I come even harder, continuing to empty my nuts in her mouth. It's the first orgasm I'd had in two days. I've been saving a huge load for her and I want to feed her as much cum as possible.

Despite her slight gags, she's an expert slut. She doesn't

let a single drop of cum dribble out of her mouth. She swallows every last ounce.

When I pull out of her mouth, she looks up at me with an expression that nearly brings me to my knees. Flames of lust burn behind her beautiful blue eyes. She wants more. She wants me to ram my cock back down her throat and feed her another load of hot cum.

Could a guy ask for a better woman than that?

I glance at the crowd. Many of the men now hold their limp dicks in their hands, cum dripping from the heads. They enjoyed the show almost as much as I did. Now it is time for round two.

After setting the switch down, I walk around to check out her ass. It's bright red from all the abuse it's taken. Pussy juice dribbles down her thighs. My cock twitches. I lick my lips and fight the urge to drop to my knees and lick up every last drop.

I take a breath to regain control. I slowly squat until I'm eye level with her delicious sex. It's puffy, dripping wet, and begging for attention. The scent of her arousal makes my cock stiffen. I'm already good to go again.

When I reach out and run a finger along her slit, she lets out a gasp. She bucks against me, desperate for more. I have no doubt she wants me to fuck her brains out, but I'm saving that for later. Right now, I'm going to give her a little taste of pleasure, just enough to calm her down.

As I rub her slit, she fights against her bonds. She pushes her ass backward, trying to get more. Always such a greedy little cunt. I can't help but grin as I watch my slut struggle to come. Despite her need, she never makes demands. She trusts me to give her what she needs when it's time.

My fingers find her clit and I start to gently caress it. This drives her wild. Her moans bounce across the play area. When I pinch her clit, her voice echoes around the entire club. She's so turned on, I could probably make her come in two seconds. But that would be too easy.

Instead, I release her clit and spread her legs wide open. Leaning forward, I blow a breath of air against her exposed flesh, making her entire body quake. Her knees wobble, and I know she won't be able to stand much longer.

Time slows to a crawl as I inch my face closer and closer to her pussy. The scent of her juices fills my nostrils and brings my cock to full attention. I want to stand up and ram my cock into her, but I'm a patient man. I prefer to wait until she's begging for it.

I stick my tongue out and run it along her puffy slit, tasting her for the first time tonight. She's sweet and succulent and even better than I remember. Her juices continue to flow freely. I lap them up, devouring the delicious nectar.

She thrashes harder and harder against her bonds, trying to push herself up against my face. I grab her hips to hold her still as I tease her cunt with my tongue. Her body trembles. I don't know how much more she can take. And yet, other than her moans of pleasure, she hasn't said anything. She hasn't started to beg yet, but she will. Soon.

She's fighting back her orgasm as much as she possibly can. I'm impressed she's lasted this long, considering how horny she gets when we're alone. Maybe she's holding out for the audience. Maybe she wants to put on a memorable performance.

A sardonic smile spreads across my face.

I back away, leaving her desperate and needy, writhing on the sawhorse.

"Come for me," I whisper.

She moans and tries to grind against the sawhorse. I

wait until she sobs in frustration. This is it, exactly how I want her.

When I resume sucking her pussy, her body jerks from the unexpected contact. I have to fight to keep her still. Her moans are deafening. Members of the audience whisper to each other, their gazes riveted on Delia.

Seconds later, an ear-splitting scream bursts from her lips. She practically smothers me with her cunt as she comes. Her juices flood my mouth. She jerks and shudders so hard, I'm worried she'll rip the sawhorse from the floor.

She comes for what seems like an eternity. I do my best to swallow everything, but she could've drowned a person with the flood coming from her sex. I've never seen her like this before. I'm glad I'd decided to bring her here. Not only do I get to show off for everyone in the building, but I know she'll never forget this night as long as she lives.

I gasp for air, my knees buckling and threatening to give way. Opening my eyes takes too much extra strength; I collapse into a quivering heap.

Ken is always one of the best at making me come, but this was on a whole new level. This was more than just knowing which buttons to push. He's just taken me to heights I've never imagined. And that was only the first part of tonight? Jesus, what else does he have planned?

When he releases my hips, I have to steel myself to stay in position. It's tough, but I don't want to disappoint him. He stands in front of me. I can barely open my eyes, but when I see his hard cock hanging out of his leather pants, I can't look away.

He grins at me for a moment, his lips glistening with my

juices. Once he sees I'm watching him, his tongue darts out and licks his lips clean.

I moan as a tremor rips through my body. My breath comes out in ragged gasps. I silently congratulate myself for not fainting. This is surreal. Far beyond my expectations for the night. And we're just getting started.

When he picks up the scissors, I instinctively try to squeeze my legs shut. I can't move. I'm completely helpless and at his mercy. As he releases my bonds, I slide over the edge of the sawhorse and drop to my knees. I gaze up at him while whimpering. It's not an act. He's already reduced me to a puddle of wanton need.

He stands in front of me, staring at my face as if assessing me. I don't know where to look, his face or his hard cock. He solves the problem for me by hoisting me up and mashing our lips together. As I moan against his mouth, he grinds his hard cock into my belly.

God, I want him to fuck me. I want to feel his juices dripping from my already soaked cunt. I want all these people watching to see him treat me like the whore I am.

But he has other ideas. He sits in a metal chair, spins me around, and pulls me into his lap. He grinds his hard cock against my ass. All I can do is moan and squirm and stare at the crowd of people watching us.

They all look at me like wild animals. I know if that little velvet rope wasn't hanging there, they'd be on me like a pack of hounds. And to be honest, a small part of me wants to service every single person watching us, but a bigger part of me only wants Ken.

He reaches up and grabs my breasts, tweaking the nipples and making me squeak. Fire rushes into my pussy. I can't believe I'm still this turned on after the orgasm I'd just had.

With his right hand still tweaking my breast, he reaches down with his left to pinch my clit. I squirm even more. At this rate, I'm going to come again.

He coats his fingers in my juices, then reaches between us to stroke his cock. Over and over his repeats this process until his slick cock is sliding easily against my ass. I take a deep breath, knowing what's coming next and trying my best to prepare for it.

No amount of mental preparation is enough. When he lifts me like I'm a rag doll and points his thick cock at my asshole, I shudder. The lube from my juices helps, but I still yell out as he impales me on his dick.

He's so long and thick, it seems like an hour passes before he's balls-deep in my ass. Despite the pain, my pussy quivers. My juices flowing down my thighs. I wanted him to fuck my pussy, but nothing compares to having his cock in my ass.

I am grateful when he pauses. It gives me a chance to catch my breath and adjust to having him so deep inside me. But he only gives me a few seconds of reprieve before he starts bucking his hips.

He's fucks me mercilessly, as if my ass was my pussy. I'm barely able to take. Tears form in the corners of my eyes. Pain and pleasure mingle until I can't separate one from the other.

His hands slide all over my body, sending jolts straight to my cunt. I grit my teeth to try to keep myself under control, but I can only do so much as my master fucks me with rough strokes.

When he leans forward to bite my earlobe, I squeak. His breath is hot against my skin and I instinctively lean against him.

"You. Like. This?" He accentuates each word with a thrust.

All I can do is nod, but that's not enough for him. He reaches between my legs and pinches my clit. I shriek. He doesn't need to ask the question again for me to know what he wants.

"Y...yes...."

I writhe in my master's lap. My body's on fire.

"Tell these people what you are," he whispers.

The room is frozen, silent, as if everyone's holding their breath. All eyes are on me now. The fire intensifies, and I don't know how I haven't already melted into a puddle on the floor.

"A dirty, filthy whore," I murmur.

"What?"

He rams his cock into my bruised and violated asshole.

"A dirty whore," I sniff, trying to hold back a fresh wave of tears.

"Louder."

He drives his cock deep, tearing apart whatever vestige of self-respect I have left.

"I'm a dirty whore."

"Why?"

I hesitate. I don't know what he wants from me.

"Because...because..."

He reaches around and pinches my clit. I wail and a waterfall of tears spills down my cheeks. I can't hold back any longer.

As suddenly as he grabbed me, he releases me. Blood rushes back into my clit. I'm swollen, dripping, and desperate.

"You're a fucking slut, aren't you?"

His fingers thrum against my throbbing clit. Pleasure rushes through me.

"Yes," I gasp.

"You come all over stranger's cocks, don't you?"

"Yes."

"Because you like being used."

"Yes."

He pounds my ass, faster than any fucking machine I've ever encountered. The slurping grip of my ass is loud enough to carry into the next room, bringing in a new wave of people. It's standing room only, and all of these people—these strangers—are witness to my utter humiliation. I can't hide anymore. They know who I am. They know *what* I am.

And just when I think I can't be any more debased than I am right then, my pussy explodes. A shrill keening bursts from my lips. My cunt pulses with a mind-shattering orgasm. I can't stop screaming and crying. I'm squirting everywhere. Liquid heat spills down my thighs to form a puddle below me.

I look up through a haze of tears and see their faces. The strangers. Some look on in awe. Some smirk as if agreeing that I'm a filthy slut. But others, others gaze at me with envy. They want to be me. They want to be on display, spread completely open for all to see. They want to be objectified and humiliated and controlled.

And those people...those are the ones who truly know me.

TRAINING TEMPTATION
CHAPTER 1

The 1959 Dom Pérignon Rosé soured in Caroline's mouth. "I've only missed one payment. I don't see how the bank can start foreclosure proceedings."

Anton reclined on the plush sofa and laced his hands behind his head. "Banks can begin the foreclosure process the second you miss a payment."

She gazed into the flames slithering in the fireplace. "I'm going to catch up on my payment as soon as the race is over."

His lips curled into a smirk. "I'm offering to buy you out."

"You can't put a price on this estate." Her mother would shudder in her grave. Caroline imagined ancestral specters looming amongst the towering bookshelves in her library glaring with disapproval.

He oozed off the sofa, leaving a deep indentation in the cushions. He towered over her and the wine on his breath nearly gagged her. "Everyone has a price."

She wouldn't let him intimidate her. "I'll never sell."

His sudden grip on her arm startled her. Leaning close,

he whispered, "Everyone has a price. The bank will be all too happy to hand the estate over to me. But maybe we can come to a certain agreement."

The lecherous glint in his eye told Caroline the type of agreement he had in mind. She yanked her arm from his sweaty grasp then retreated to the far side of her enormous oak desk. When he didn't follow, a trickle of relief slid down the back of her neck. "So you're the one pressuring the bank?"

"Pressuring?" He laughed. "They just want to get paid. Money is money."

"You won't get this estate."

"I always get what I want. It's really only a matter of time."

"Not this time!"

He pulled an envelope from his tuxedo pocket and dropped it onto the desk. "Let me know if you're interested in my *friendly* offer."

Before she had a chance to say anything, he sauntered out of the room. She crumbled the envelope into a ball then hurled it into the fireplace. The contents didn't matter. She could never sell the legacy her mother left when she died.

The gilded walls of the study seemed to close in on her. No one could know about the threat. If even a hint of financial strain twisted in the rumor mill, people would stop bringing their ponygirls to her world-class training facility. She'd lose the last thing her mother gave her before she died, Sheridan Estate.

A log cracked and sparks exploded amongst the flames. Her ponygirl Tiffany Rose was her only hope. If she didn't win the final race, she would lose everything.

Footsteps shushed on the carpet behind her. Caroline

jumped as a deep male voice whispered into her ear. "Canapé?"

She spun to face Edward Hastings. The son of the man who'd just threatened her stood before her, grinning.

"What are you doing up here?" The last thing she needed was taunting by her arch-rival. Through the pony circuit they'd know each other for years, but his silly jabs still annoyed her.

"I came to escort you to the ball." He leaned his hip against the sofa and hooked his thumb into the waistband of his slacks.

Ignoring the way the fabric hung from his hips, she grabbed the precariously balanced tray from his free hand and set it on the desk. The last thing she needed was to be distracted by his delectable body. An occasional fantasy was manageable, but she'd never act on her desire.

"I don't need an escort." Caroline's gaze strayed to the contours of his broad shoulders. A thousand hooves galloped across her heart. The week's festivities hadn't officially stated and he'd already ruined her plan to ignore him. And even worse, she'd suddenly forgotten how to breathe.

The corners of his bottomless amber eyes crinkled, a slow smile formed on his sensuous mouth. "You remembered."

"Remembered what?"

His gaze caressed her body traveling from her eyes, to her lips, to the deep V of her neckline. "Burgundy is my favorite color on you."

She willed her face to remain passive. "Oh? I had no idea."

"Denying it makes things more fun, doesn't it?" He grinned.

Clenching her fist, she fought the urge to slap him. He

needed to learn that women were more than just playmates for spoiled rich brats. An assumption he'd clearly learned from his father.

"I have to see to my other guests." She turned to walk away but his strong warm hand clasped her elbow.

"You know," he leaned closer to her, "I've been looking forward to beating you in the race for, what is it now, the third year in a row? You could say I've been chomping at the bit."

She rolled her eyes and yanked her arm out of his grasp. "When you see Tiffany Rose race, you'll realize you have no chance."

"Really?"

"She's the fastest pony I've ever trained."

"Care to make a little wager on the side?" His eyes seemed to hypnotize her. Maybe that's how he lured so many women into bed.

"You know the rules, we can't bet on the races." She stole a quick glance at his chiseled forearms then averted her eyes.

"It doesn't have to be money." The sparkle in his eye implied he wanted something money couldn't buy.

Caroline swallowed. "What exactly did you have in mind?" The second the words became airborne, she regretted them. Too late to pull them back. The race was too important to let anyone, especially him, cause such a disruption. It wouldn't help the situation. The bottom line: If her ponies didn't win, all remaining connection to her family would be lost.

"Well, I think…" His gaze drifted to the door where her maid stood.

"You may enter," Caroline said.

She sauntered into the room. "Excuse me Lady Caroline, the first guests are arriving."

"Please show them to the ballroom."

"As you wish."

The maid's curvy hips gave an exaggerated sway as she left the room. Choosing the younger woman for the dressage competition would ensure a victory. The $100,000 First place prize would help, but she really needed to win the final race if she was going to pay off her debt and continue to preside over Sheridan Estate.

Nothing could be done about it now. Guests were arriving.

"I have to attend to a few matters before I go downstairs." She waved her hand toward the door but he grasped it mid-air.

Brushing his lips across her knuckles, he whispered, "I look forward to a dance."

A shiver of pleasure slid like sweat between her breasts. The look in his eyes left her speechless. She quickly turned away from him to hide her face.

The soft click of the door closing signaled his departure. She smoothed her palms against the satin on the bodice of her gown. She needed to collect herself and stop acting like a schoolgirl in heat.

Caroline took a deep breath and closed her eyes. She visualized a brook meandering through a valley then released a pent-up breath. Picturing herself in a serene place always helped to calm her. The tension headache threatening to ruin her night eased into a dull ache. She willed the muscles around her mouth to transform from a scowl into a smile. A mask of happiness fell into place. She'd spent years hiding her true emotions and today wasn't any different.

As she strolled the length of the east wing, the edge of

her gown lapped at her ankles. She half expected to find Edward waiting as she rounded the final curve of the hallway. No one stood near the winding staircase.

She dismissed the flutter in her chest as nerves, not disappointment. From the top of the stairs, she looked down at the crowd gathered in the foyer. She waited until her newly arrived guests tilted their faces to look up.

Edward watched from the crowd below as she raised her slender arms. Her stance reminded him of the fountain of Athena in Austria.

Caroline carried herself like a goddess as she addressed the crowd. "Ladies and gentlemen." Her voice cast a silken spell over the guest who fell silent. "Welcome to Sheridan Estate."

The crowd responded with enthusiastic applause. She surveyed the room and smiled while slowly descending the staircase. He took a sip of his martini and watched as a group of women adorned in glittering dresses flocked to her. Maneuvering through the crowd, he got within earshot of her conversation. With his back to her, he turned slightly to catch her reflection in the French doors.

One of the men stepped forward to greet her. "Lady Caroline."

"Senator Garvin, it's so nice to have you here," she said.

The senator grasped her hand and brushed his lips across it. "The pleasure is all yours, of course."

"Of course." Her silvery laughter echoed through the room as he released her hand.

Edward skewered an olive and jammed it into his mouth. She flirted with everyone but him. This year, no matter what it took, he would charm her into his bed.

"Edward Hastings." The smooth southern drawl tickled

his ears as he turned to face a sultry blonde in a tight black dress. She looked vaguely familiar but he couldn't place her.

She tapped her long red nails against her whiskey glass. "You never called."

Where did he last see her? Think. "Darling, I've been so busy. I just got in from Switzerland two nights ago."

Sliding closer, she rested her hand on his shoulder. Her breast pressed against his arm and a subtle musky perfume enveloped him.

She whispered, "You might be able to convince me to meet you on the beach again. But bring a towel this time. You don't want to scrape your back against the rocks again."

He instantly remembered the moaning vixen. The scars from that night were still fading and it had been over a year. He smiled. "Slamming me against them left quite the impression."

"I'm sure it did."

Over her shoulder he caught a glimpse of Caroline. Would she be a moaner or silent? His eyes caught hers and they gazed at each other over their conversational partners.

"What time should I meet you?" The vixen leaned into him, her hand trailing across his chest.

Caroline frowned and turned her attention back to the senator. Terrible timing, as usual. He tore his eyes from the tight curve of her hip and discretely adjusted his tux to hide his arousal.

"Excuse me. I see the senator has arrived." He flashed his most dazzling smile then brushed the woman aside.

She sputtered behind him, "Later then?"

"Mmm," he mumbled as he walked toward his intended prize.

As he crossed the room, he stopped to grab two champagne flutes from a liveried waiter.

Shifting closer to the senator, Caroline gazed over his shoulder at the reflective glass in the French doors behind him. She spotted the reflection of the man staring at her and the smile faded from her face.

She had to get away, fast. "Excuse me senator, allow me introduce you to Prince Franco. He just arrived."

"Trying to get rid of me so soon?" he joked.

She leaned in and whispered, "Franco just acquired Bareli Enterprises. The announcement will come Monday, but you might want to discuss the details of his intended merger with Denning Corp."

The senator arched an eyebrow. "Merger? It seems that the prince and I do have something to discuss."

Attempting to disguise her distress, Caroline played the proper hostess and steered him toward the prince. After introducing them, she turned to escape.

Blend in. She could blend into the party if she hid amongst the other guests in the ballroom. With over two hundred guests at the party, she could avoid him.

Caroline threw open the heavy mahogany doors to the ballroom and her eyes darted around the room. No sign of him. Excellent.

The rhythmic beat of drums and the soulful singing of the sultry woman draped across the piano filled the ballroom with electric energy. Laughter carried through every corner of the enormous room.

A sigh escaped her lips. She knew he would be here, so why was she nervous about seeing him? Caroline had spent the last five years ignoring him. Not an easy accomplishment. Their particular fetish du jour, sexy athletic women dressed like horses, ensured they'd see each other at almost every event. This week marked the 13th Annual International

Ponygirl competition. Everyone who was anyone would be here.

The sound of shattering glass smashed through the ballroom snapping her into the present. Conversations sputtered then roared back to life as the piano singer continued her song. The carnal hunger of the crowed swirled around her. Everyone's eyes seemed misted with anticipation for the race.

Overwhelmed by the energy in the room, she threaded her way through the crowed to the safety of the kitchen where broken wine glasses littered the floor. The chef barked orders as the kitchen staff scurried to clear the mess.

She leaned over to help pick up a shard from the floor. The glass bit into her hand. Dammit. Pain slashed across her fingers and blood dripped from the wound.

The chef grabbed a clean dishrag and wrapped it around her hand. "Are you okay?" he asked.

"I'll live."

"Let me call a doctor."

"I'll be fine," she lied. She hadn't been fine since Anton's threat and she wouldn't be fine again until she was sure she wouldn't lose Sheridan Estate. Tears formed in her eyes but she blinked them away.

The staff stared at her. She followed their attention downward to where droplets of red stained her dress. She needed to change.

She turned to leave and Edward appeared out of nowhere. "There you are."

Great. He'd cause an even bigger scene if she didn't get rid of him quickly. She brushed past him. "Excuse me."

The chef stepped between them. "Sir, you can't be in here."

"It's okay, I'm a doctor."

Aware the staff was listening, she lowered her voice. "You never finished med school."

"It doesn't take med school to slap on a bandage."

She thrust her wrapped hand toward him. "Blood is dripping everywhere. Please get out of my way."

"Wait, let me help you."

She shoved past him and stomped down the hallway.

"I was pre-med at Stanford," he said.

She paused. Maybe he could be of some use after all. Avoiding Edward for the rest of the week would be pointless. Why was she trying so hard to avoid him anyway? It wasn't like he was a serial killer. Men like him were always around the stable with their latest flavor of the week, so why did she get so rattled when he was around?

She stood up straighter and pushed her shoulders back. She wouldn't let him get to her. "All right doctor, I have a first aid kit in my bathroom but you better behave."

"I finally get to play doctor with you." He grinned.

Caroline put her injury-free hand on her hip. "This is exactly why I don't think you should come up."

He held his hands up as if he was surrendering. "I promise to be on my best behavior."

"The only reason I'm letting you come up is because you're the only doctor here, and I hate hospitals."

He gestured toward her hand. "From the way it's bleeding, it may not be minor, but I need to look at it to be sure."

"Fine." She could tolerate him for a few minutes.

He remained silent as they climbed the staircase to the third floor. Her room occupied the end of the east wing of the mansion.

"Sit here." He pointed at her crushed blue velvet settee. Her hand throbbed as he unwrapped the kitchen towel.

"The bleeding has slowed considerably but we need to wash it out to avoid infection."

He grabbed a bottle of hydrogen peroxide, cotton balls and a gauze wrap. His eyebrows furrowed and his lips pressed together. Interesting, he actually seemed concerned about someone other than himself.

"This is going to sting." He held her hand over the sink and poured the liquid onto the cut.

Shocked by the burning sensation, she yanked her hand back. "Damn, that hurts."

His expression softened. "I know, but I want to make sure it's completely disinfected."

She allowed him to grasp her hand again. His fingers encircled her wrist and warmth spread up her arm.

Their eyes met in the mirror and for a moment, neither of them moved. The corners of his eyes were softer. His full sensual lips relaxed into an inviting smile. She couldn't look away.

"Thank you." Maybe there was more to him than just an arrogant playboy.

He dropped his gaze to her hand then brought it up to his lips. As he brushed his smooth lips across her knuckles, he seemed to be searching for something in her eyes. The pain in her hand was forgotten as her heart threatened to explode in her chest.

The tense edge of her mouth relaxed when he looked down to wrap gauze around the wound. "You need to apply ointment twice a day. If you see any redness or swelling, or if the pain gets worse, you need to see a doctor right away, okay?"

In a daze, she nodded.

A twinkle lit up his eyes. "You realize you owe me now, right?"

His question snapped her back to reality. "I'd say name your price, but I don't think I want to know." Of course, he wasn't doing this out of the goodness of his heart.

He sat next to her and turned to face her. "I'll settle for a kiss."

She sat perfectly still as he leaned toward her. Her pulse leapt when his fingers grazed her sensitive earlobe as he settled a lock of hair behind it.

He whispered, "You can say no."

Mesmerized, she wouldn't stop him. His tongue flicked out darting across his bottom lip. She wanted more than anything in that moment to taste him, to suck and nip at his lips, to tangle her fingers in his thick, luxurious hair.

Intoxicated by the subtle scent of his cologne, she inhaled deeper, pulling his essence into her lungs. Her eyes locked on his face as he shifted closer to her. Closing her eyes in anticipation, she could hear the sound of her breath mingling with his. His wine laced breath caressed her face.

"Excuse me, Lady Caroline?"

She smacked her head against his hand as she jerked back. Scowling at her maid, she said, "Amanda, you need to knock when you enter my chambers."

"I did knock."

"Did you wait for a proper reply?"

The maid stared at the floor. "No, Lady Caroline."

"I should send you to the groom the ponies in the stable this week. What do you want?"

The maid glanced from her to Edward and back to her. "The guests who are staying on the property wish to retire for the night."

Caroline stood and towered over the maid. "You have the list of who is staying in each room."

The maid nodded toward Edward, a wry smile crossed her face. "Does he know where he's staying tonight?"

"He's staying in the blue room in the west wing, not that it's any of your concern." She raised an eyebrow and glared at the maid.

"Should I show him to his room?"

"That won't be necessary. I was just about to escort him out."

What was this girl up to? She wasn't jealous of the maid, was she? The maid excused herself then sauntered out the door.

Caroline turned to him. "It's been a long night. I trust you remember how to get to your room?"

She struggled to read his expression and it bothered her.

He stood. "I guess it has been a long night. Until tomorrow?"

As soon as he stepped into the hallway, she closed the door. She sagged against the wall as tremors rippled along her spine. The stress of being behind on mortgage payments coupled with the stress of organizing the competition killed the ability to think clearly. She'd fallen right into a trap like all of his other playthings.

TRAINING TEMPTATION
CHAPTER 2

Edward slipped on his sunglasses to block the morning sunlight. Scanning the various training rings, he watched dozens of beautiful ponygirls and their trainers go through their pre-competition workouts. The first time he'd seen a woman dressed like a pony, he'd been enthralled. Years later, he still marveled at all of the women dressed like ponies. The elaborate ponygirl costumes included everything from bit, to bridal, to reins, to a tail and it all cost a fortune. Good thing there were no actual animals on the grounds to ruin the outfits.

Where was she? He turned as a lithe ponygirl stepped out from the shadows of the stable. The sun's rays highlighted the long smooth muscles of the woman. She tossed her head causing her braided chestnut hair to brush the back of her taut thighs. A content smile spread across her face as the groomsman led her toward the warm-up ring. This was one hot race pony, but it wasn't *her*.

Two hours of prowling the grounds and he still couldn't find her. Maybe the injury kept her inside. Worry creased his brow.

As he headed toward the mansion, he sensed several ponygirl's eyes on him. He smirked. If he hadn't been so distracted by Caroline last night, he would have followed his usual tradition of finding the hottest ponygirl and screwing her all night in one of the stalls.

Twisting to look at the ponies, he smacked into Caroline as she hurried down the dusty trail.

"Watch where you're going. Knock over one of the ponies and you'll be paying a pretty penny to the woman's owner." She tugged her riding shirt down and brushed at her pants.

"I've been looking for you all morning, where have you been?"

"I'm been attending to various business needs." She maneuvered past him.

Following her down the trail, his eyes moved from her black leather boots to the tan riding britches. A quarter could bounce off that firm round ass. Her tight, white riding shirt molded to her athletic curves. The wavy bounce of her hair made him want to sift his fingers through its softness.

At the bottom of the trail, he caught up with her. "So, are you training your secret weapon today?"

"Yes, she's waiting for me in the warm-up ring."

"I can't wait to see my competition."

"Patience was never one of your virtues."

"It's always good to size up your competition, don't you think?"

She stopped at the edge of one of the rings and pointed toward a chestnut ponygirl. "There she is."

The pony scratched at the ground with her boots. She was the same ponygirl he'd spotted coming out of the stable earlier, the one with the long legs of an Olympic runner.

He whistled. "Nice pony."

"Fast pony." A dimple appeared on her cheek as she smiled at him. How had he missed that in all the years that he'd known her?

Caroline swung her leg over the metal bar to enter the ring. He reached out to steady her.

"Thank you," she said.

"How's your hand?"

"Better than last night." She extended her hand so he could examine it. His fingers brushed across her skin, awakening every nerve ending.

"It's healing well. But continue to apply ointment until it's completely healed. It should prevent any scaring."

Her green eyes met his. "Thank you."

"May I watch?"

"I always considered you a joiner, not a voyeur. You're more than welcome to watch anytime. Unfortunately for you, no one stands a chance against her."

"We'll see about that," he whispered under his breath.

He stood near the fence while she put the pony through the basic paces. It wasn't long before he started to worry. Caroline hadn't exaggerated. The pony would be fast out the gate. This could be a problem. Half the battle of a race is getting momentum out of the starting gate and she seemed like she would fire out as soon as the gun went off.

But, it was a middle-distance race, so she would have to maintain that stamina for a mile and a half. He'd seen a lot of fast starters over the years, but not all of them could maintain the pace. Relaxing slightly, he turned his attention to Caroline.

She gave a slight nod and the pony slowed to a trot. "Tiffany Rose is a filly. She's only been racing for three years."

"Why haven't I heard of her before?"

"Her owner kept her at his estate and had his personal trainer break her in."

"Where has she raced before?"

"Meadow Wilds, Paradise Downs, and Oakwood Bay."

He nodded. They were all small second-tier venues. Sometimes the huge crowd at the International Ponygirl Competition scared the ponies. He hoped that would work to his advantage.

Caroline asked, "Why aren't you training your pony? Has she arrived yet?"

"She's coming in from Redwood Estate tonight. I planned on having a little more fun than I did the first night here."

Her expression darkened. "I hope cutting myself didn't ruin your fun."

He chuckled. "Your maid ruined the fun."

"I think she arrived just in time."

"Only if she planned on joining in." Weird, a threesome would have been his go-to fantasy in the past, but he hadn't considered it last night.

Her cheeks turned pink and her eyes narrowed. "Your reputation precedes you. You really are a jerk."

He roared with laughter. "My reputation?"

"Women talk."

"Apparently I have quite the reputation." Women fell at his feet most of the time. He eyed her. Why did she resist him when other women threw themselves at him? It wasn't the first time a woman called him a jerk but coming from her it stung. "Who's been spreading tales about me?"

"The list is long, but your conquests are hardly distinguished." She tiled her head to one side, obviously enjoying his frustration.

Of course she wouldn't tell him. The first rule of gossip is to never divulge your sources. It didn't matter. Once he took her to bed, she'd forget all about the gossip. He'd finally have her out of his system and could go back to his very willing stable of women.

She brushed her hand across her forehead. "It's getting really hot out here." She turned her back to him and made a clicking sound with her tongue. "Tiffany Rose, come."

The pony cantered to the edge of the ring to join her trainer. Caroline stroked the pony's hair. "Good girl."

"In a few days, we'll see how good she is," he said.

"I'm sure we will." She grasped the pony's reins and led her toward the barn.

Leaning his hip against the ring, his eyes feasted on her until she disappeared into the barn.

Heading away from the stable, he meandered down the winding path to the beach. The ocean always helped him wash the cobwebs out of his head. Caroline wove threads of need into his brain. The image of her plump pink lips pursed and waiting to be kissed ignited his desire. Of all the women at Sheridan Estate, Caroline was the only one that scorched his brain and made him burn to kiss her.

Caroline paced the driveway. Her stomach churned, threatening to send her dry heaving into the bushes. Coming to an abrupt stop, she bent forward as her chest lurched, her hands braced against her knees. What was taking Henry so long to bring the car around?

Footsteps crunched in the gravel. She peeked through her wet lashes spotting Edward across the driveway. Great, he was the last person she wanted to deal with right now.

He paused mid-step and after a second of hesitation, he sprinted to her. "What's wrong?"

Her voice trembled. "Tiffany Rose was in an accident."

His eyes widened. "What happened?"

Tension constricted her chest. "It landed on her." She paused to draw in another shaky breath. "They were delivering carrots and hay and one of the hay bales fell from the second floor and hit her."

"Is she okay?"

"No, I don't know. An ambulance came. They wouldn't let me ride with her."

"Where did they take her?"

"St. Rosenbloom Hospital." She hated the way her voice broke. Not wanting to appear weak, she straightened her shoulders and stood erect.

He tilted his head and he opened his mouth as if he wanted to say something. Instead, he pressed his lips together. "I'll get my car, I'm driving you there. Now."

"I can drive myself. Henry's bringing mine around."

A sleek black sports car followed the curve of the circular driveway and stopped in front of them. Her butler exited the driver's side then handed the keys to her. "Anything else Lady Caroline?"

"No Henry. That will be all."

Edward snatched the keys out of her hand. "You're in no condition to drive."

"Give the keys back." She gave him her best death-glare.

"I'm driving. Get in the car."

Sarcasm crept into her tone. "When did you get a driver's license? Doesn't your driver take you everywhere?"

"Not everywhere. A driver wouldn't be able to enter some of the establishments I frequent." He winked at her as he opened the passenger door.

In no mood to deal with his smug entitlement, she ignored his comment and she slid onto the smooth leather seat. The door clicked shut and an image flashed through her mind. She was standing in front of the mansion holding her suitcases while the mansion doors slammed closed. Without Tiffany Rose, she wouldn't win the race. She would lose Sheridan Estate and with it, the only tie she had left to her mother. Her heritage would be lost.

Grief's gnarled hand squeezed her heart. She sucked in a breath. It took ten years to earn the society's respect; to prove she wasn't her mother; to prove she wouldn't end up committing suicide because her wealthy playboy boyfriend dumped her in the gutter like a hunk of rotting sewage. To prove she was a force to be reckoned with, and most importantely, to prove that the prophetic whispers she heard as she passed by her "old friends" would never come true.

Edward slipped her hand into his. "It's going to be okay."

"No, it will never be okay."

"People have accidents all the time. She may just need a couple of days rest."

She only had six days before the race and if Tiffany Rose couldn't race, Caroline was doomed. Her secret burned her stomach like a ghost pepper. At least he wasn't being a jerk right now. He seemed to be genuinely worried about Tiffany Rose.

His jaw was clenched and determination radiated from him. Right now he was being a good friend. Maybe friendship was their destiny.

They arrived at the hospital and rushed to find Tiffany Rose. A silver haired doctor told them she was in surgery with a broken leg.

Caroline crumpled into a chair in the waiting room.

Edward's warm, firm grip on her hand calmed her but the medicinal stench overwhelmed her and nausea set in.

"I have to get out of here." She ran for the entrance doors, which slid open to let her pass. Gulping the sweet fresh air, she realized she was shaking and slid onto a bench. It was as if the entire world closed in on her.

"Hey, it's okay." Edward's knee brushed against hers as he sat by her side.

"I'm going to lose everything," she blurted.

"She'll be all right in a few months." He rubbed her back and she began to relax.

His touch soothed her. She looked up and he wiped a tear from her cheek. "I'm broke."

"Excuse me?"

"I'm broke. Bankrupt. Destitute. Without money. Penniless." She could hear the hysteria creeping into her voice.

His head tilted to the side as if she spoke a foreign language. "What do you mean broke?"

"I missed a payment on the mortgage and your father is pressuring the bank to foreclose on me. He wants Sheridan Estate and he'll stop at nothing to get it."

He took both of her hands and gave them a gentle squeeze. "I can talk to my father."

"Would he listen to you?"

He looked away. "I don't know."

"I can't base my entire future on 'I don't know'."

"What other options do you have?"

"It's taken every penny of my boarding fees to pay the mortgage the last two months. All I have is my reputation and the reputation of my stable."

"I can't imagine you being broke. How is that even possible?" he asked.

"The fire last year wiped out my savings."

"No insurance?"

"The insurance adjustor decided it was negligence and denied the claim. He said faulty electrical started the fire and since the addition to the barn wasn't built to code. Apparently builders do this all the time, so he refused to approve the claim. I explained that I had no idea it hadn't been built to code, but he said it was my responsibility as the estate owner to ensure additions to any existing property were approved by the city planning department and built to code."

He leaned back and laced his fingers behind his head. "There has to be a way of catching up on payments. You still make money when clients bring ponygirls for training, right? Stable fees and such?"

"Yes, but it's not enough. I need at least $250,000 to keep the place running long enough to get out of this mess."

"That's easy, just tell everyone what happened and I'm sure you can raise $250,000."

A car honked in the distance and a pack of nurses walked by complaining about work. "Do you remember what happened to Frank Anderson when the community found out he was broke?" Caroline asked.

He twisted the hem of his pants with his fingers. "They turned their back on him."

"If that happens, I have nothing."

He stood and paced in front of her. "I could loan you the money."

She considered it for a moment before rejecting the idea. "Senator Garvin is on the board at your bank. Gossip would spread the second I signed the loan."

He looked at her and gnawed on his lower lip with his teeth. "There is one way. Win the race."

Peals of laughter rolled off her tongue. The statement

was so ridiculous, she wasn't sure she could stop laughing until he frowned at her. Between clenched teeth she asked, "How the hell am I supposed to win the race when the only chance I had is in there?"

"Do you have another pony that could do the race?"

"No one else is fast enough."

"You're fast enough."

She crossed her arms over her chest. "You're kidding right? I'm a little past my prime for racing. Dressage maybe, but not racing."

"I'm serious. The last time you ran was during the 9th Annual Ponygirl, right?"

"It's been four years."

"Do you still run every day?"

"I do if I want to stay sane."

Imitating a conspirator, he lowered his voice. "Let me train you."

"No." She paused. "No way. Absolutely not."

He frowned. "What are you afraid of?"

"Nothing." *Everything.*

"You know I'm the best race trainer in this competition."

She bristled. "I'm the best. If I was going to run, I'd train myself."

"You can't push yourself the way a race pony needs to be pushed. You need a trainer."

She considered what he said. He was right; no one in their right mind would force themselves to train as hard as a race pony trains without someone to push them. But if she agreed, her entire future would depend on him.

Everything about him screamed trust fund playboy. He never worked for a single minute in his entire life. What if he got sick of her after two days and ran off to find a shiny new toy? A Buffy, or Bunny, or Honey, or whatever ridiculous name his arm candy called themselves.

Or worse yet, what if she came to depend on him for more than just training? Her mother believed in her lover until the day he humiliated her. She had refused to talk about what happened that day. Instead, she had woven her secret into a rope, strung it around her neck and took it to her grave.

She sighed. Maybe he wouldn't humiliate her. But, did she believe in herself enough to complete the training regime when he inevitably dumped her?

She raised a single skeptical eyebrow. "What's in it for you?"

"No one else is really competition for my pony and I really wanted to beat you for the fourth year in a row. But..." A Cheshire cat-like smile spread across his face. "...training you with only six days to go will be a challenge, and I love challenges. Besides, my father shouldn't get everything he wants."

He seemed sincere, but she still hesitated. "If I were to accept your offer, there would have to be a few ground rules."

"Like what?"

"This is a business arrangement. I can pay you for your time once I win the money."

He laid his hand on her shoulder. "I wouldn't think of taking a penny from you."

"I can't let anything get in the way of training. No other entanglements."

"No entanglements. I promise."

As he trailed his hand down her arm, her skin tingled with awareness. Being nearly naked with him for six days, *that* would be the real challenge. She stole a glance at his tailored jeans. They hugged him in all the right places and she couldn't help but wonder what they hid. She was a grown woman, she could control herself and she would never be as weak as her mother. No man could ever make her love him enough to destroy her.

"Fine. Tomorrow morning. Six a.m."

"Five."

"Five-thirty."

He tapped the tip of her nose. "Done. Don't be late or you get the whip."

If she didn't have so much riding on this race she'd be tempted to arrive intentionally late. She had no doubt he'd be skilled in punishment. Four years since a riding crop smacked her ass. Being late might be fun.

TRAINING TEMPTATION
CHAPTER 3

The screeching alarm clock jolted Caroline awake. She opened one eye and fumbled around until she managed to slap the snooze button. The first rays of sunlight streaked across her room illuminating the clock. How could it be five-thirty already? She never liked crawling out of her warm bed before ten. Rolling away from the windows, she yanked the blankets over her head.

Her sleepy haze yielded to a soft tapping on the bedroom door. She hurled the pillow across the room where it landed with a thump. Pushing back the lilac embroidered duvet cover, she grumbled under her breath. She swung her legs over the side of the bed and slid into her slippers.

"Come in," she called.

Amanda entered with a large white box wrapped in silk and tied with a lavish red bow. "Seems you have a secret admirer."

"Who's it from?" Caroline asked.

"If I could take one guess, I'd say Edward Hastings."

"Ridiculous."

"That's not how I'd describe the way he looked at you last night."

"He was helping me with the cut. Nothing else."

"It's pretty heavy." The maid's eyes shimmered with expectation.

A creamy linen card peaked out from under the ribbon. Caroline shot her a sidelong glance then slid the card from the gleaming silk box. She paused. Opening it in front of the maid was a bad idea. If it was from Edward, who knew what was inside?

"You may go now," she said.

"Seriously? I'm dying to know what's in the box."

Caroline set it on the bed. "I'm not opening it right now. I have to go running."

The maid glowered at her, stomped across the room and swung the door closed. Caroline chuckled. *That'll teach her for interrupting me.* Payback can be so much fun. Besides, the girl needed to learn to respect her privacy.

She slid her nail along the edge of the envelope. It opened with a slight tear. She slipped the enclosed card out. *For my new pet, Edward.*

She bristled, tossing the card onto her bed. He made it sound like she belonged to him, but she was nobody's pet.

She frowned at the gift. Opening it would put her into even more debt with him. But, she also knew that if she left it sitting on the bed, she wouldn't be able to focus on training. And, she'd probably have to explain to him why she didn't open it. Or, she could give it back.

Deciding to return his gift, she entered her closet and walked to the back corner where she kept her workout clothes. Not wanting anyone to know what she was up to, she placed a black running outfit along with her running shoes into a backpack. She stuffed the gift into a large garment bag.

Armed with her items, she dressed in black jeans and a black blouse. If nothing else, she'd find out if she could still run the way she did four years ago. Did she still have the same speed? The same stamina? She'd told Edward to meet her at the beach house, away from the crowd. If this ended up a total failure, at least all of her clients wouldn't be laughing.

She tiptoed down the back staircase. The loud creak of a worn step echoed along the wall. She peeked around the corner. All clear. She had no choice but to sneak out. The alternative was to embarrass herself in front of the more conditioned ponies. Too bad this wasn't a game. As a child, she'd loved playing hide and seek. Her father, the only man she'd ever loved, played the game with her. She smiled remembering the hours spent playing with her father before he died in the car accident. So many years had passed. The searing pain in her heart had finally settled into a dull ache. *Rest in peace, Daddy.*

She sprinted out the back door and into the woods. At the edge of the tree line, she stopped and looked back at Sheridan Estate. She yawned and stretched her arms high overhead. For once, she'd escaped the barrage of questions her staff fired at her within the first hour of waking. Smiling, she skipped along the path toward the beach house.

But the grin on her face dissolved with every step she took. The grim reality of the situation wrapped her in a cloak of fear. She couldn't afford to think this was anything but a fight for her very livelihood. If she lost Sheridan Estate, where would she go? Both parents were dead. The only relationships she had were the superficial social friendships with the women and men on the pony circuit. Those connections would vanish. Overseeing the estate allowed her to surround herself with people. Without them, she would be entirely alone.

Caroline rolled her shoulders inward and dropped her head. The gift seemed to weigh her arms down like the fifty-pound bale of hay she'd heaved off Tiffany Rose. The immaculate polished boots on her feet turned grey with dust as she dragged them along the trail. A cold wind groaned through the trees.

At the end of the trail, the secluded cottage where she intended to meet Edward appeared to have sunk into the tree line on one side and stretched to drown in the sea on the other. A white picket fence encircled the cottage. Flecks of storm gray paint had peeled off the base of the home but she didn't have the time or money to have it repainted. Caroline sighed. Worrying wasn't helping anything and she would have plenty of time to obsess about her situation later. *Time to make the best of this.*

Whistling drifted from the kitchen window and rode the wind. She peeked into the kitchen and spotted Edward. He held a large carrot in one hand and a peeler in the other. A pile of carrots sat in a crystal bowl next to him. *Mr. Playboy cooks?* What other secrets hid beneath his skirt-chasing façade?

As he worked on another carrot, the well-defined muscles on his forearms rippled under a crisp white trainer's shirt. Tan britches hugged his thighs. Her lips curled into a smile. He was all male and definitely fun to look at. With a body like that, no wonder women were hurling themselves at him. She couldn't really blame them. Maybe turning him into a plaything would help her get through the next week. Being pinned under him could be a great stress reliever.

She entered the cottage and walked past the spacious living room into the kitchen.

He waved a carrot in her direction. "I'm glad you arrived on time. We have a lot to cover and not a lot of time to do it in."

"The faster we get this over with, the faster I can get back to my guests. What's with the carrots?"

"Just getting these ready for you."

"I don't like carrots. My skin turns orange."

"You'd have to eat about fifty pounds to turn orange." He chuckled.

She tossed her backpack and garment bag onto the kitchen table where they landed with a thud. Just because she intended to morph into a pony didn't mean she planned on eating like one. She unzipped the garment bag and retrieved the gift.

The peeler clanked against the stainless steel sink. He turned his back to her and lifted the faucet lever with his elbow. He scrubbed his hands like a surgeon.

"You didn't open it," he said.

"Consider this a business relationship." *For now.*

He reached into a drawer and pulled out a towel. The corners of his eyes crinkled as he smiled. "I take it you don't want to mix business with pleasure?"

Maybe, especially if he continued to undress her with his eyes. "This is a serious business relationship. You're training me."

"I never named my price."

She leaned against a carved oak chair and crossed her arms. Of course he wanted something. She didn't expect him to agree to work with her just to fuel his ego.

"You said you'd do it for the glory, now you want to name a price?"

"I was thinking something along the lines of complete obedience." The last word curled off his tongue taunting her.

She snatched up her backpack. "This is ridiculous. I don't have time for games considering what's at stake. I'm about to lose everything, so if this is nothing but a joke to you please let me go. I can't risk my entire life for your amusement."

"Wait." He grabbed an arm strap and tugged her against him. "I'm just teasing."

"I don't have time for your games."

Releasing the backpack, he said, "I'm sorry. That was a really stupid approach. I was just trying to find a playful way of explaining my training method. I do take this seriously which is why I need you to do everything I say without question."

Her fingers tapped against her upper arm. "I need to win. I'll be obedient as long as you don't make absurd demands."

"Agreed." He picked up the package. "Please, open the gift."

"You can't buy me like one of your other women."

"I'm currently, happily single. And trust me, I don't have to *buy* women." He leaned against the wall, hooked his fingers in his belt loops and jutted his hips forward.

The edge of the red ribbon lay like a fuse between her index finger and thumb. She hesitated. Would accepting his gift be like opening Pandora's Box?

She tugged. The ribbon unfurled then slithered to the floor. Her fingernail caught the edge of the silk. As she peeled the wrapper from the box, his eyes fixated on her.

Inside the box lay the most beautiful handcrafted Italian leather bridle and bit she had seen in years. She picked up the chocolate colored bridle and caressed the smooth edges. Several straps attached to the silver rings on each side of the bit. She pressed her finger into the bit and sighed. Hard enough for her to feel any changes in direction, but enough give to keep her mouth comfortable. A chin-strap hung from the silver rings. The extra support would be welcome. The last time she wore a bridle was four years ago. Would she even remember how to be a pony?

Mesmerized by the beauty of the harnesses, she forgot he was in the room until his fingers caressed her hand. She sucked in a breath as her heart reared in her chest.

He slid the bridle from her hand. A new intensity entered his voice. "Do you like it?"

"It's beautiful." She reached into the box and pulled out a tangle of matching leather strips connected by a series of small silver rings. Holding it up one way, then another, she couldn't quite figure out what form it would eventually take.

"It's the rest of your pony outfit," he said.

Leather strips dangled from her fingers. "As long as you can figure out how to put it together…"

She set the contraption on the table then lifted a layer of tissue paper. Soft leather pony boots lay in the bottom of the box. Each curve blended into the next, a mark of exquisite Italian craftsmanship. Anyone with a foot fetish would lick a thousand mistress' boots clean to own a pair of these. They matched the rest of the ensemble perfectly. Her fingers trembled as she lifted the boots to inspect the soles. Custom metal horseshoes had been driven into the boots.

Reverence infused her tone. "How did you know my size?"

"I guessed."

"Can I put them on now?"

"Not yet." He took the boots and motioned for her to follow.

In the living room, he placed the boots on the glass table in front of the sofa. Her eyes shot from the boots to his face and back. Damn gift, maybe she could be bought. An unsettling flutter coursed through her chest.

"I want to see you." His matter-of-fact statement hung in the air for several seconds.

She pointed to the leather outfit. "Well, if that's what I'm wearing, you will."

The outfit would leave her very exposed, but she had mentally prepared herself to be brave, to be naked in front of him. After all, she would be all right as long as she remembered her mantra: *He's just another trainer.*

"Now. Strip." His voice dropped. So deep. So demanding. She shuddered while reaching for her blouse. He'd never used that voice with her before.

"Boots first."

Bending at the waist, she balanced herself and slid each dusty boot from her feet. She folded the socks then tucked them into the boots. Unhooking the top button of her blouse, she glanced his way.

"Eyes down," he commanded.

She studied the floor and unhooked another button. *Stay detached, professional, he's just another trainer.* As he continued the inspection, her apprehension grew. It was as if she exposed more to him than her body. Was the stress of this week getting to her already? It seemed like a reasonable explanation.

Another button unhooked revealing her intentionally conservative black bra. The irony of her choice broke some of the tension in her spine and she relaxed.

"Stand up."

She thrust her shoulders back and stretched her neck higher.

"Good." He stood and took a step towards her then stopped as if considering something.

After releasing the last button, she let the blouse flutter to the floor. She swallowed. He scrutinized her with such intensity.

His hands were on her so fast the motion seemed a blur. She gasped as he placed one palm below her breast and the other on her back. Pushing her chest up and her back forward, he guided her into an even better posture.

"Never settle for anything less than perfection." He stood close to her, unmoving.

At first, the subtlety of the change was unnoticeable because it was so minute. The muscles in her back went rigid as she unhooked her cotton bra. Red lace would have been better. A costume could have insulated her. She could have retreated into herself and simply played a part.

The bra slid down her arms catching on her fingertips before falling to the floor. As she pivoted towards him, her breath escaped in shallow puffs.

"Eyes forward."

The rough hitch in his voice snapped her forward. She was used to giving the commands. Compliance felt unusual, unnatural...and yet a ripple of excitement traveled up her spine. The strong voice of a master trainer could lull her into deep pony space.

"Pants." He snapped his fingers.

Her zipper seemed to crackle with audible energy. She sensed his impatience and hitched her fingers into her jeans. When she dropped them, the zipper scraped the polished wood floor.

"Now the panties."

Oh God, she pressed her knees together, *they're wet.* Her hands trembled as she slid her panties over her hips. They fell to floor. She hooked one of her polished toes into the crotch and kicked them under the sofa. Maybe he didn't see the damp patch.

"Well done. Although, rather damp?"

A slow heat spread through every inch of her exposed skin. His expression established a thread of connection between them. Knowing that she couldn't hide from him intensified her arousal.

"Don't move." His warm palm touched her shoulder and she jumped.

"Easy. Jumpy aren't you?"

Remembering her posture, Caroline straightened. His hand roamed from her shoulder down her back and settled at the base of her spine. She shuddered and wished he would let her put on her pony gear. As a pony, she could detach and focus on him as a trainer, not as a man. *He's a trainer, not a man. Don't let him get into your head.*

"Your posture will be an issue. But I we can fix that." His hand lightly caressed her butt and then he slapped her right cheek.

She yelped. "What the—"

"Silence! Nice muscle tone, but you could use some lunge work."

Her eyes narrowed. He could use a slap himself.

The light caress of his palm against her ass soothed the sting. It awakened a restlessness she hadn't succumbed to since Thomas. Had it been three years? Catching him with her last maid had been humiliating. She had dismissed the maid but before that, she watched the tramp pack every last one of his socks into boxes and dump them onto the back driveway.

Edward pinched her thigh. "You will stay present while we work. Eyes down."

His hands traveled her legs evaluating, pressing and pinching until she wasn't sure she could stand it anymore. He woke her up, made her feel. She hated it and wanted it at the same time.

He produced a brown leather crop from his bag, and flicked it across the tip of her right nipple. A wave of pain intertwined with pleasure arced between her breast and her pussy. She shot him an indignant look.

"That was for disobeying. I expect complete silence while you are my pony."

She wanted to tell him she would never be *his* pony, never belong to a man. Instead she bent one leg and traced an X on the floor with her toe. What if she couldn't resist him? If she lost control? Maybe it would be better to just give up Sheridan Estate than put up with this humiliation.

She looked past him through the floor to ceiling glass window. Outside, the ocean churned. If she gave up, where would Henry, or Amanda or any of her staff go? As annoying as they could be sometimes, they were her family. Determination bubbled up from Caroline's core. She couldn't let them down.

"I'll give you my evaluation and then you can speak." He paused. "You're in pretty good shape, but will need a lot of work and focus if you want to win. You're detached from your body, but we'll work on that today..."

"I'm not detached." If anything, his thorough evaluation had fed her awareness.

"We have six days. Normally I'd say it would be impossible, but your determination will make up for not having nearly enough time."

She let out a frustrated breath. *Remember why you're*

doing this, don't get emotional.

He handed her the pony boots. "Time to get dressed."

"I can't run in those. They're too perfect."

"So you plan on running completely naked and shoeless?"

"No."

"Well?"

She yanked on the first boot, then the second. Fine, she could run off the frustration. The horseshoes clicked against the wood floor. The familiar sound began her transformation.

"Arms straight out." He held up the leather contraption and slipped it over her arms. His fingers grazed her right breast and her pussy clenched. A series of buckles clicked shut along her hips and back. For the first time in years, a veil seemed to descend over her. The smooth leather grazed her skin and she shuttered. Caught between being a woman and a pony, she shifted her weight from side to side. Impatient.

He wiggled the buckles until they settled into place. "Very nice," he said.

A profound new awareness trickled through every cell in her body. The only thing that mattered was her trainer's voice.

She stood taller. Pride encouraged her to maintain correct posture.

A brush appeared and he stepped behind her. Every nerve ending fired as he pulled the bristles through her hair. Every stroke untangled a mess of human emotions. Fear, desire, anger, greed, jealousy, envy, all transformed. As he gathered her hair into a ponytail, his fingers brushed the back of her neck. She shivered.

In front of her again, he picked up the halter and the

bit. "Open."

Her jaw went slack. His eyes consumed her. She lapped at his fingers as he slid the odorless, tasteless silicon bit between her teeth. He drew back then tugged the silver ring on the right side of her face making the bit more comfortable.

Inhaling the leather, she pressed her tongue against the bit. The slight give caused a ripple of pleasure down her throat. He settled the chin-strap into place. At the base of her head, he tightened two locking buckles.

His voice undulated through the buzzing in her ears. "I always work with a safe word, but with a bit we're going to use a motion. If at any time you want me to stop, tap your right foot three times. I will stop immediately. Do you understand?"

She shook her head up and down.

"Show me."

She stretched her leg toward him then tapped the floor three times.

"Good girl," he crooned.

He produced a set of reins that weren't in the box. "I'm going to start with a shorter set so I'm close to you." He hooked the reins onto the silver circles at each side of her mouth. "We're going to work on form today, not speed. If your form is wrong, your speed will suffer."

Impatient, she scratched at the floor with her boot.

Edward's cock pressed painfully against his pants and he discretely shifted into a more comfortable position. She'd make an amazing pleasure pony. Very responsive and he'd barely touched her. Unfortunately, his current task didn't include throwing his new pony over the back of the sofa and spreading her legs to see how far they would go.

Great rewards could be enjoyed from a patient pursuit. The intensity of ponygirl training would play right into his seduction plan. Eventually every woman who tried resisting him surrendered.

Edward gripped the reins. With a flicked of his wrists, he guided her to the door. The scent of her arousal drifted on the air. If he didn't get her out of the house soon, he might come up with too many interesting ways to use the furniture.

Focus Hastings. By the end of this week, you will be nibbling on your treat.

"Lift your knees."

A good warm-up would prevent injury so he directed her toward the beach. At the edge of the sand, he pulled her to a stop. He removed their boots and set them on the grass. Early morning sunlight cast her in an orange glow. He'd seen and been with some of the most beautiful women in the world, but something about her was different.

"Walk."

She responded to him by turning and stepping lightly across the sand. The graceful stretch of her leg, the curve of her hip and the peaceful energy radiating from her made him smile. Her beauty encompassed more than her physical attributes. Seeing the way she cared for Tiffany Rose intrigued him. Her staff was more than just employees; they almost seemed like family. Growing up, he'd followed his father's example. The male staff was available to serve him. The female staff, well, they seemed to fall into his bed more often than not. They were fun dalliances, but nothing more.

The morning breeze warmed his face as the sun rose in the sky. With every step, he buried his toes in the cool sand. His mind started to drift as the tide pressed and pulled at the beach. After thirty minutes, he directed her back to the edge of the grass where they slid their boots back on.

From the beach, he guided her onto a secluded forest trail, he tapped the reigns against her and she broke into a trot. Time to see what she could do.

Her legs stretched creating proper positioning but her rigid back hampered her movement. "Loosen up. More bounce," he called.

She lifted her knees higher and sprang from foot to foot. Her ass bounced from side to side. Better. He longed to cup those luscious cheeks in his hands. In time, in time.

Edward called out a series of commands and observed her movements, tempo and reaction times. Working together would help with the reaction time, but something still seemed off about her movements.

As morning slid into afternoon, the air hung hot and thick in the forest. Over the next hours, the heat intensified so he decided to return to the cottage to finish the lesson. He pulled her reigns. She slowed to a halt. Tugging on the left rein, he guided her into a turn and then snapped both reigns. In a full gallop, her boots pounded the ground flicking dirt clods towards him. They would both be a mess by the time they got back. But he didn't mind. The beach house shower was built for two.

Sunlight trickled through the trees, illuminating her. Her back reminded him of the nude Degas hanging in his study. Rivulets of sweat dripping down her back became the strokes of an impressionist painter. They formed an elusive scene. If he could capture her image, he would hang it in his bedroom.

Faster than expected, he found himself breathing heavy. Whether it was from the run, or from the tantalizing view, he didn't know. They returned to the cottage where he pulled her to a stop. She tossed her hair and snorted then pawed the ground.

"That's enough for today, girl." Edward patted Caroline's head then looked into her eyes. Clear and sparkling, they took his breath away. Caressing her cheek with the back of his hand, he realized she wasn't just racing to save her stable. She actually liked being a pony.

Once inside the cottage, he let the reigns drop to the floor. He grabbed the bowl of carrots from the kitchen and returned to her. Still in deep pony space, she wiggled her mouth when he removed the bit.

"Treat?"

She whinnied. The carrot rested in his palm. He fed her they way he'd feed a regular pony. Her teeth grazed his palm sending ripples of pleasure into his cock.

After a few more carrots, she pushed away his hand with her nose. He set the bowl on the table and began unhooking the buckles on her bridle. As he removed it from her, he caressed her head.

"Good girl," he murmured.

Reluctant to release her from her pony state, he paused. A regal calm infused her face. She never looked that peaceful and he wanted it to last.

In the kitchen, he grabbed a clean dishtowel and ran warm water over it. As he loosened the buckles that held her leather pony outfit together, he wiped sweat from her glistening skin. With each buckle, her eyes became clearer. As she emerged from her relaxed state, tension contracted her shoulders. The trance-like glaze in her eyes evaporated and a deep sense of loss settled into him. She'd be so much happier if she could just relax for a few hours every day. He loosened the final buckle and the last vestige of her pony persona disintegrated.

He sighed. Time to get back to business. "Not bad, but not good either."

She frowned. "This is just the first day."

"When we don't have many days, every second counts." Something still bothered him about the way she moved, but he couldn't quite pinpoint the issue.

"Where did I fail?" Her hands flew to her hips.

Edward realized what had eluded him out on the trail. Her arms moved while the rest of her body remained rigid. "You're disconnected from your body. It's a stranger to you."

"I live in my body. I'm hardly a stranger to it." Her chin lifted in defiance.

"You need to get back in touch, reconnect with your animalistic instinct. When was the last time you touched yourself?"

"Excuse me?"

"I want you to touch yourself." She needed to get back in touch with her body. If she didn't know the purpose and function of every muscle in her body, she wouldn't improve. Also, she'd look scorching hot.

"That's ridiculous."

"Now." He heard the hitch in his voice and hoped she missed it.

The look in her eye screamed indignation. "I can't."

He lunged at her, grabbed her wrists and pressed her against the wall. Every inch of her delectable naked body writhed against him in protest.

With molten rage in her eyes she yelled, "Get your hands off me!"

"You promised obedience."

"This is not part of training."

He tightened his grip on her wrists. "Everything between us is part of your training."

TRAINING TEMPTATION
CHAPTER 4

Restrained against the wall, Caroline glared at Edward. His calm gaze unnerved her. No way would she cave to the burning need ignited by his proximity. She wiggled from side to side trying to escape but he held her captive with more than just his body. The scent of his sweat curled into her lungs, invading and inviting. She expelled a breath trying to push his essence away. She couldn't lose control, refused to lose control. But his firm grip excited the part of her that longed to give in.

The friction between their bodies intensified the lingering effects of being a pony. Her dormant animalistic side demanded release. How long had it been since she'd relinquished her leadership role? Could she even follow another person's lead?

A sardonic smile spread across his features. "Tell me."

"What?"

"You want me to fuck you."

"I. Do. Not." *Liar!*

He released one wrist. She slapped her hand into his chest and pushed against the solid wall of muscle. Part of her wanted to let him to crush her in his strong arms. To let him take over. To let him take her. His determination, the way he knew exactly what he wanted excited her. To simply give into a base need was a freedom she never allowed.

As she struggled, his muscles flexed and contracted in a display of pure masculine energy. She swallowed the sudden rush of lust. No matter how much she wanted to deny it, she craved him.

His palm pressed against the wetness between her thighs reminding her of her nakedness. Amusement sparked in his eyes. "Soaked."

Heat built in her chest and radiated into her cheeks. She wished her clothes were on her body, not folded across the room. How could she deny desire, when the evidence lay in his palm?

She glared up at him while wanting to slap the self-satisfied expression from his face. The truth ensnared her tongue. She'd never reveal her longing. If he took her without permission, without her compliance, she could deny the ache. Deny the ravenous hunger. She wouldn't have to bear the consequences of whatever happened between them.

Her eyes searched for a point beyond him. "I don't want anything from you."

"I think you do. Say it."

Edward released her hands, leaned into her and brushed his cheek against hers. Rough stubble grazed her skin scratching at the final tendrils of resistance. She dissolved against him.

He'll screw you, use you, and dump you. The loud protest she'd planned came out a whisper. "No."

"Say it, Caroline."

The soft caress of his lips on her throat unleashed a tidal wave of thirst. She wanted to drink him in.

A moan escaped her lips. Icy resistance melted into a damp puddle of need. Darker desires flooded drowning out any logic. Any protests. Blood pulsed through her neck following the trail of his lips. *Get him out of your system and the feelings will go away*. Her final rationalization faded as she pressed her hips against him.

She raised her lips to the edge of his earlobe. "I want..." Her voice trailed off as he pressed his erection against her. Was his intention to drive her mad with desire?

"What?" His eyes searched hers as his breath went ragged. "What do you want?"

Caroline shook her head refusing to speak. *Kiss me, kiss me now.*

The way he lowered his lips, incrementally toward hers was maddening. She wanted to scream. If he held back a single second longer, she'd dissolve into flames.

"You," she murmured as she rose and brushed her lips against his. A jolt of electricity sizzled down the nape of her neck.

A strangled groan escaped him as he tangled his fingers in her hair. She shivered with delight. Oh, to feel so desired after so long. The tip of his tongue slid across her bottom lip. She sighed. Why had she resisted feeling this good?

Refusing to give up all sense of control, she took charge by breaking the kiss. She pushed him toward the bedroom. He responded with an arched eyebrow. Amusement radiated from him.

A devilish smile played across her face. "Laugh all you want, we'll see how good your stamina is."

"Hours baby... I can go for hours."

She planned to wear him out, so he'd better have excellent stamina. As they crossed the threshold, she slipped her fingers between his shirt and pants. She wanted him equally naked and exposed. But, she had to go slow.

The corner of her mouth pulled up as she freed the shirt from his pants. She meant to undress him slowly, to savor revealing every inch of his body. But there were too many buttons in her way and the starched lapels of his shirt were too tempting. She grabbed them and tore his shirt open. The popping buttons clicked against the wood floor like rain on a tin roof.

His chest rose and fell in rapid waves. Her breath kept pace with his as she traced the smooth lines of his muscular chest. Its hardness contrasted with the soft line of hair traveling from his navel to beyond the edge of his pants. Fascinating. So hard and so soft at the same time.

As she explored, she realized the nervous flutter in her belly had vanished. Completely in her element, her hands traveled over his chest. For the first time since she'd met him, she felt in control.

She trailed her braid across his chest in slow circles causing his nipples to flush a deep red. They clenched into hard pebbles. Stronger than any aphrodisiac, the effect radiated over her own nipples. They clenched rising from the tips of her breasts. A profound ache from deep within her demanded fulfillment.

The trail of hair descending from his bellybutton enticed her. How far down did it go? She hooked the button on his pants under her thumb and flicked it open. Between her fingers, the zipper clicked like a car on the rising side of a roller coaster. As she lowered the zipper, anticipation had her biting the edge of her lower lip.

He sucked in his breath. Tension rippled across his belly. She loved having power over him. Putty in her hands, she could mold him into the perfect partner. A marbled Greek god reanimated solely for her pleasure.

Her hands caressed his tight ass then trailed down his muscular thighs. She crouched, slid his pants off then tossed them across the room. They landed with a thud on a rustic carved oak chair.

She stepped back as he kicked his boots off. Her gaze traveled down to his thick cock and she licked her bottom lip. Would it taste salty like the sea? Could she consume him the way his eyes consumed her?

"Lay on the bed," she commanded.

"Yes ma'am." He stretched across the four-poster bed, lay on his back and laced his fingers behind his head. Tilting his head to the side, his eyes traveled the length of her body. Raw energy rolled off him. He seemed ready to strike.

She regarded him for a moment trying to decide what she wanted to do to him. The antique oak chest at the foot of the bed opened to reveal her favorite toys.

Caroline reached into the box and pushed aside a riding crop, paddle and nipple clamps. Now wasn't the time for parlor tricks and exhibitionist games. A more subtle form of erotic torture was necessary. This might be her only chance to get him back for all the years he'd spent teasing her. The perfect implement presented itself. She pulled a white silk scarf from the available options. Payback time.

"Arms up." The edge of the scarf trailed across his body as she leaned over him. She forced his hands together and wrapped the scarf around his wrists. A highwayman's hitch knot would let him struggle all he wanted but he wouldn't get loose. A favorite amongst safety knots, one tug and the loose end would immediately release him.

He smiled. "So you really are a naughty girl, aren't you?"

"You have no idea."

"I suspected. You can't run a pony ranch without a little raunchiness in you."

"True."

She crawled across him and straddled his waist. He tried to buck her off but she wrapped her legs around him and held on.

"Bad boy." He deserved a little punishment. She reached behind her and slapped his cock. His back arched and he groaned.

She leaned toward him intentionally pressing her breasts against him. She whispered, "I can break even the roughest stallion."

"I have no doubt you can."

She brushed her fingertips across his full lips. A shiver of pleasure traveled up her spine as he sucked each fingertip between his teeth. He nibbled at the sensitive pads before releasing them.

"Untie me," he growled. A breeze rippled along the crimson curtains sending a streak of sunlight across his face. Intensity flashed in his eyes.

She climbed off of him, strolled to her toy chest and grabbed a feather.

"You wouldn't."

She brushed the feather across his thigh. "I would. And I am."

He thrashed against the bed. "You're going to get it when I get free."

Amused, she teased and tickled every sensitive place on his body. He writhed. His teeth clenched.

"Stop," he gasped.

To have such a big strong man reduced to begging for

freedom gave her a heady sense of power. Her throaty laughter filled the room. "If I don't?"

He yanked his wrists away from the bed. "You'll need a new bed."

A smile played across her lips. She tossed the feather onto the nightstand. She tugged the end of the knot freeing him. "Now, be nice."

She gasped when Edward grabbed her by the waist, flipped her underneath him and pinned her arms over her head.

"So bad, but so sexy," he murmured as he lowered his lips to hers. The bed seemed to drop out from under her. Everything she'd held back was unleashed as he crushed his mouth against hers. Her hands flew to his back and she pulled him against her. The solid weight of him became her lifeline as the kiss deepened.

A feral groan escaped her. The slight parting of her lips became a gateway for his demanding tongue. Its wet warmth mingled with hers. In way over her head, she drowned in his embrace. The harder he kissed her, the more she wanted. Desperate to end the endless cycle of anticipation, she wiggled beneath him finally settling him between her thighs.

He pushed up on his forearms. "Impatient, aren't you?"

"Maybe I like it hard and fast." She undulated her hips against his, welcoming his advance.

He sat back on his feet and watched her. Breathing hard, his eyes were riveted on her thighs. She left them drifted open. Just because he wasn't tied up anymore didn't mean she couldn't still tease him.

She trembled as he traced his thumb down the inside of her thigh. He lowered his lips to the inside of her knee where he blazed a trail of fire with his teeth, with his lips, with his tongue. If he made her wait another second, she'd combust.

As he traveled closer to her molten center, she groaned. "Oh yes."

Her fingers curled into his hair as she drew him closer. The first electric shock of his tongue on her lips sent a blaze of desire through her belly. She arched her hips taking everything he gave. And he gave.

His hands gripped her hips and puller her closer. Relentless, he licked and sucked and nipped until she held her breath. About to die from pleasure, she tried to catch her breath. A shallow series of gasps and moans offered little reprieve as tension built between her thighs.

His relentless tongue curled around her clit. His name tumbled from her lips. "Edward. Please."

She arched her back trying to escape. It was too overwhelming. He was too good. She could hardly breathe. She clutched his wrists. Had to stop him. About to faint, she couldn't hold on much longer. He changed tempo and the world cracked open. Her nails dug into his wrist. She screamed as waves of pleasure tore through her. Wracked with tremors, she writhed against his mouth finally collapsing.

She froze. A final shudder left her as she pressed her eyelids closed. What had just happened? She'd completely lost control. Panic welled in her chest. One minute she'd had total power over him and the next she'd been reduced to a helpless, wanton woman. And even worse, she wanted more. This wasn't the plan.

She looked up and his eyes locked with hers. For a moment time stood still, then Edward eased her thighs apart and her fears fell away. The way he gazed at her awakened a long denied yearning. She wanted to be desired, to incite the fire in his eyes. Didn't she have a right to lose control from time to time?

"You're so beautiful when you come," he said. Her embarrassment transformed into satisfaction. She had every right to receive pleasure from him.

He tore into a condom packet then rolled it on. *Where did that come from?*

She pushed aside her fears. He never took his eyes off of her as he eased his hard cock into her. The gentleness stole her breath. She molded herself to him enjoying the connection.

Passion took over as a slick sheen of sweat coated his arms. She matched him thrust for thrust and breath for breath. They were connected in a way she hadn't experienced in years. Heat rolled off her body. Sweat trickled between her breasts.

She melted into perfect synchronicity with him. His rigid stomach coiled above her. Raking her nails across his back, she watched his lips grow taut. He sucked in a breath.

His fingers pressed into her hips as he drew her closer. Arching his back, he groaned thrusting deeper. His earthy scent enveloped her, pushing her closer to the edge.

The taut lines of her belly clenched as the pleasure racing through her body built into a crescendo. Minute tremors fluttered along his arms. His snapped his head back, stretching toward the ceiling. "Caroline!"

Everything she'd been holding back erupted as she soared across the threshold. She wanted to sob with relief as he collapsed against her. The intensity of the sex, the all consuming passion, still frightened the control freak in her. But, the rest of her was a puddle of satisfaction. His weight anchored her to the bed. The sensation of floating away dissipated as the seconds passed.

As his breathing returned to normal he caressed her cheek with the back of his hand. "You're amazing," he whispered.

The gentleness in his eyes surprised her. She didn't expect him to have a sensitive side. Maybe the rumors about him were wrong. Caroline snuggled closer.

"I'm going to jump in the shower." He pushed her away, slid from the bed and padded across the room.

She frowned. Expecting cuddle-time from a notorious playboy? A ridiculous expectation, and yet a wave of disappointment washed over her.

The sound of water coming from the bathroom grated on her nerves. Of course he jumped out of bed and into the shower the minute it was over. He probably wanted to wash every trace of her off of his body. Edward took what he wanted then left, just like the man who'd destroyed her mother. Just like all men.

Even though she knew better than to expect more from him, she hated the way her heart clenched in her chest.

TRAINING TEMPTATION
CHAPTER 5

Edward turned his face into the stream of water pelting him from the showerhead. He washed the taste of Caroline's salty skin from his lips. The pulsing droplets stung but he embraced the discomfort. Anything to ward off the sensation of falling.

With a bar of sweet scented soap, he scrubbed his skin. He'd seduced her, had gotten what he wanted, but walking away from her now was impossible. He wanted to explore her, find out what made her happy, what made her sad, and what made her burn with desire. The sudden need terrified him.

He shut off the water and wrapped a towel around himself. Droplets of water fell from his hair onto the tiled floor. Somehow, she'd inched her way into his mind, taken over his soul.

But, he warned himself to go slow. To be careful. Caring too much about a woman was dangerous. He learned that painful lesson from his mother. One day she just disappeared and neither he, nor his father, ever heard from her again. Women could vanish without a trace. They could leave heartbreak in their wake. Loving them involved an enormous risk he wasn't sure he was willing to take.

He paused as indecision radiated from his mirror image but the more he deliberated, the more he asked himself, what was life without risk? Fear didn't rule him in any other part of his life, so why should it rule his relationships? She was worth risking the hurt.

He swung the door to the bathroom open and looked for Caroline. The previously rumpled duvet had been pulled tight enough to make a military sergeant proud. All physical evidence of their pleasurable romp had been erased.

"Damn," he muttered. He ran his hand over the tightly made bed. The musky scent of their passion hung in the air.

As he dragged his pants on, he caught the right foot in the fabric and had to hop to stay balanced.

In the living room, the roar of crashing waves greeted him. Caroline stood with her back to him gazing up at a painting of a woman.

"You made up the bed pretty quickly," he said.

Silence stretched between them. He shifted from one foot to the other as he waited for her to speak.

He followed her transfixed gaze and looked up at the painting. The woman's haunted eyes matched Caroline's. A relative? Pain pinched the woman's features. Her lips pressed into a thin line.

"Who is she?"

"My mother."

"She looks familiar."

Her voice came out a whisper. "She's been dead for years. You would have been a child when she was alive."

She turned away from the painting. The strained look on

her face melted into rage. She stabbed her finger toward the front door. "You got what you wanted, now get out."

He combed his fingers through his hair. What was her problem? She'd gone from content to pensive to enraged in ten minutes.

"You seem—"

She cut him off. "What happened between us was a lapse in judgment. It won't happen again."

"But..."

Her blazing brown eyes cautioned him against arguing with her.

"Fine," he muttered. "I'll see you tomorrow."

"That won't be necessary."

He stopped at the door. "You still need to be trained. Business, remember?"

"Our business is over." She folded her arms across her chest and turned toward the painting.

He crossed the room to stand next to her. In a soft voice he asked, "If I don't train you, who will?"

She cleared her throat. "I'm fully capable of taking care of myself. I always have, and I always will. Agreeing to work with you was a mistake—*my* mistake."

His brow creased. "What is going on? One minute we're rolling around having a great time and the next you're like this."

"Men like you only want one thing and now you've had it."

He grabbed her shoulders and turned her toward him. Looking into her eyes he said, "Give me some credit, not all men are assholes."

"Maybe." She shot him an irritated look. "You jumped up pretty fast. What was I supposed to think?"

"I needed a shower. After all the running, I was a sweaty

mess." He ran his fingers through his hair. Lying to her felt wrong, but he wasn't about to admit that sleeping with her messed with his head.

"I don't think we should train together anymore."

"You need me to train you or you're going to lose the estate."

She pulled away from him and wrapped her arms across her stomach. "This was my mother's estate. It's all I have left of her and I mean to keep it."

"You will."

"If I lose Sheridan Estate I will have nothing and no one. This is my life. Training and showing ponygirls is all I've ever done. This is such a different world from the 'normal' world. I don't know how to do anything else."

He gently took her into his arms. "It won't come to that. I know you think I'm an ass, but I really do want to help you win this race."

"For the glory?"

"More than glory. I want to help you win to save your estate. You project a tough persona. Pretend you're a hard ass. But I saw the way you were when Tiffany Rose got hurt. You're a not some ice queen living in a magical castle. You genuinely care about her."

She sniffed back her tears before burying her head against his chest. "I'd like to go check on her."

"I'll take you."

"Hey honey, the doctors say your leg set well and you should be up on crutches in no time." Caroline stroked Tiffany Rose's forehead as her eyes fluttered open.

"It still hurts like hell. Good thing I'm not a real horse,

you'd have to shoot me. Speaking of shooting someone, did I hear Edward's voice?" She rolled her head to the side of her pillow facing the door.

Caroline sat on the edge of the bed careful to position herself to avoid hitting her injured friend's legs. "I don't even know where to start with that one."

"So, there's somewhere to start?"

She smiled, relieved to see the twinkling in her eyes. "He's my trainer now."

"You're kidding?"

"No, I'm afraid I'm not."

"How on earth did that happen?"

As she relayed the visit from Anton and his threats to take the estate, her friend grimaced.

"You trust his son to help you?" She brushed her fingers across her forehead.

"He says he wants to do it for the glory. It doesn't hurt that winning would also be a slap in the face to his father. I don't think they have the best relationship."

"His father is scum. I wouldn't want to be in a dark hallway with that man."

She nodded in agreement remembering the claustrophobic feeling she'd had in the library. "Edwards says he also just wants to help me for the sake of helping me."

"More like help himself to a serving of you," she laughed.

Caroline shifted causing ripples to form on the blanket. Before she could stop herself she blurted, "He's already had a serving."

Her friend shot up in bed then groaned, rubbing her thigh. "Damn leg. Details."

"Our first training session was today. And, well, after..." Her voice trailed off.

"After, you did the nasty with super playboy."

Heat flooded her face. "It was hot."

"It bet."

"I mean outside. It was hot and I was all sticky and he was hot and sticky…"

"Then you got *really* hot and sticky."

The grin on her friend's face spread to her own. She picked at imaginary fuzz on the blanket. "I plead temporary insanity."

"Uh-huh."

"Anyway…" Caroline waved her hand. "It was a mistake. Fun for one time, but that's all."

"Well, I'm glad you're finally having some fun. Besides, you'd be a complete mess if all you did was obsess about losing the house."

"I guess you're right."

"As your oldest and wisest friend, I highly recommend riding that ride while it's hot. Don't start analyzing the relationship. Just have some fun until Saturday's race. Think of it as a week of debauchery and then you can go back to being the woman with the iron crop."

"I'm not that bad, am I?"

Her friend arched an eyebrow. "Some days, you could turn coal into diamonds."

In the pre-dawn light, Edward checked his watch. Being late would set a bad example so he hurried toward the beach house. He didn't want to do anything to mess up the new camaraderie between them. During the drive from the hospital to the estate the night before, he'd been relieved to see the more relaxed expression on Caroline's face. She'd even laughed at some of his jokes.

Footsteps pounded on the earth behind him. As she passed him, Caroline yelled, "Better keep up."

He picked up the pace and raced toward her. "Not a chance, sweetheart."

"Maybe you need some coffee." She leapt over a clump of gnarled roots.

Pumping his arms, he gained momentum. "I'm on your heels."

Her laughter rang through the forest. He'd just turned the last bend before the path to the beach house when his foot caught on something and he slammed into the ground. "Shit."

"Man down," she joked as she came around the corner.

"Stupid tree, I would have caught you."

She reached down and pulled him up. "You were losing, admit it."

"Never." He grinned while hobbling into the beach house.

"Sit on the sofa, I'll get some ice."

While he waited, he stared at the painting. A memory sparked and he suddenly knew her identity. A cold claw of fear sliced at his gut.

As she returned from the kitchen, her smile faded. "What's wrong, it's not broken is it?"

"What? No. It'll be fine after a few rounds of ice." He took the ice pack and pressed it against his knee.

She bit the edge of her lip.

"I remembered where I saw her," he said.

Caroline turned her full attention on him.

"When I was thirteen, my father threw a huge masquerade

New Year's Eve party. There had to be five hundred guests. The society's elite, the best of the best, all dressed in ball gowns and tuxedos. All with elaborate feathered and sequined masks."

Impatience saturated her voice. "What does this have to do with my mother?"

He shot her a silencing look. "I remember the clock striking midnight and hearing a commotion in the foyer. Security wouldn't let a woman into the party. She was stunning in a red ball gown and silver and white feathered mask."

She swayed turning visibly pale. He patted the sofa next to him and she sat.

"Are you okay?"

She nodded. "Go on."

"I was upstairs hiding on the landing. My curfew had passed. I overheard her talking to security. At first she maintained her composure and explained that there had to be a mistake with the guest list. If she could just speak to my father, he'd straighten things out. When the guards refused to let her talk to him, she screamed my father's name over and over. Anton. Anton. Anton."

Caroline shifted away from him. The oddest expression marked her face.

"My father came to the door, grabbed her by the elbow and dragged her up the staircase. I'd ducked into one of the rooms and hid in the closet to avoid getting caught. I overheard everything."

He stopped. The cramping in his stomach overwhelmed him. He'd never revealed to anyone what happened next. Part of him wanted to stop, but the secret had burned in his chest for years. Maybe she was the wrong person to tell, but someone had to know. Somehow, his father had to pay for what he'd done.

"Caroline," he grasped her hand, "I don't know if I should tell you more."

"Tell me," her voice came out a whisper.

"My father dragged your mother into the room and tossed her onto the bed. Through a crack in the closet door, I watched him smack her across the face."

His memories emerged from his mind like raw cotton and as he told her about that night, the memories wove into a thick chord to choke the story out of him. Images he'd never wanted to remember flashed through his mind. He didn't realize he'd stopped speaking until Caroline's piercing eyes brought him back to the present.

"I need to know," she said.

His voice cracked as he continued. "He hit her over and over yelling about how she was a whore and he would never leave his rich wife for her. He said she was nothing to him."

Bile rose into his throat. "And then he tore off her clothes and..."

"And what?"

"My father raped her." A tear traced its way along his cheek.

"And you did nothing." The chilling accusation in her voice froze him in place.

"I was thirteen. What could I do?"

"Call for help. Stop him." Her voice rose. "You could have stopped him and you did nothing."

He jumped to his feet. "He would have killed me."

Her eyes narrowed, and her features pinched inward as she rose from the sofa. "What year was it?"

He choked on his response. "2002."

The fury in Caroline's eyes grew as she spat, "Six months later, my mother killed herself."

TRAINING TEMPTATION
CHAPTER 6

Caroline raced into the bathroom and slammed the door. As she fell to the floor, her knees cracked against the tile. She leaned over the toilet retching.

Finally everything made sense. Her mother's depression, the way she refused to leave the house, the nightmares that had her screaming at 2 a.m. If only she had known, she could have done something to help.

Sobbing, she slid to floor then pressed her face against the cool tile. Images of the last months of her mother's life seemed to imbed themselves in the reflections in the tile.

"Let me in." Edward rattled the door.

"Go away!" She hardly recognized her voice. It sounded so raw. Inhuman.

"I couldn't have stopped him."

How could she believe him? He'd done nothing to help her mother. But what *could* a thirteen year old do against a rapist? Deep within her rational mind, she wanted to believe him. She needed to believe him. But the instinct to blame him overwhelmed her.

Overwhelmed, she didn't want to think about his culpability. One word twisted in her gut – revenge. It surged through every cell in her body taking over like a malignancy.

She watched her reflection in the mirror as she rose to her feet. The pain in her eyes had been replaced with merciless intent. She flung open the door. A razor sharp need for revenge fueled her. And, she had the perfect person, the perfect weapon, to help her.

"If you want to prove remorse, you have to help me."

He took a step back as if afraid of her. "What do you need from me?"

"Help me destroy your father." The icy quality of her voice seeped into her rigid muscles.

His eyes seemed to bore into hers as if he was looking for any hint that she wasn't serious. He cleared his throat. "I've wanted revenge against my father from the time I was five years old. One night, after one of their more violent fights, my mother ran off into the woods. She never returned. I've hired countless private investigators but no one has ever been able to find her. No one. Sometimes I wonder if he killed her. The bastard is capable of anything."

She grasped his outstretched hand in hers and met his eyes as he squeezed it.

He took a step toward her, his smoky brown eyes sparkling with intensity. "I'll never know what happened to my mother. But you do, and I'll do whatever it takes to make sure my father never destroys another woman. It's time he paid for his sins."

The passion in his voice moved her, yet she still regarded him with suspicion. Eventually, she had to trust him to help her bring down his father. It was her best chance of destroying him. Even gazelles have to trust each other to outrun a lion.

"How bad do you want this?" she asked.

His expression didn't waver. "I want this more than I could ever explain. I didn't know exactly how I'd avenge my mother's... Death? Disappearance? I don't even know what to call it because I'll never know what happened to her."

"Your father essentially made us both orphans. Let's do this together."

"Together," he agreed.

"We need a plan. What can we go after that he treasures the most?"

"His reputation."

"He wouldn't be able to orchestrate another merger and acquisition without it."

He smiled. "Absolutely. With a damaged reputation he won't be able to make a business deal. Eventually, his money will dry up."

"What's he working on right now?"

"The Denning Corp-Bareli Enterprises merger."

A Cheshire cat-like smile spread across her face. "What a coincidence, Senator Garvin was just made aware of the merger. Were he to discover that Anton has a criminal history, he might not be so quick to push the merger through the Acquisitions Committee."

"We need to trick Anton into admitting what he did to your mother."

"And yours."

Silence stretched into minutes. A range of emotions passed through his eyes and settled on sadness. "I miss her. I'd give anything in the world to see her again. Just once," he said.

Caroline went to him and pulled him into her arms. "I know."

The simple admission changed the energy between

them. His lips brushed across hers. She took comfort in the gentle kisses and silenced the negative voice warning her to stop.

The softness of his lips soothed her. She didn't need to struggle through lengthy rationalizations; she simply needed to wash the pain away. Her fingers interlaced with his. As the kiss deepened, his moist tongue pressed between her lips. She welcomed the caress and relaxed against his mouth.

He stroked her cheeks with his thumbs. Her breath caught in her throat as he continued the compassionate gesture. He tasted like Thanksgiving. Warm. Spiced. Comforting.

He encircled her with his arms drawing her closer. She inhaled, drawing in the earthy scent of his skin. She marveled at how different this felt compared to their first frantic lust-filled encounter. Waves of vulnerability billowed off of her, but he seemed to sense it. He touched her with reverence as he brushed his hands down her tingling back.

"I need this," Edward murmured.

She tangled her fingers in his hair. "We need this."

He cupped her butt and pulled her closer. Pressing against his rigid cock, she moaned into his lips. The unspoken invitation had them swaying across the room.

As they moved toward the sofa, he peeled her shirt off then tossed it across the room. Her hands tugged at the edge of his shirt releasing it. He caught her hands and lavished her with a disarming smile.

"Wait, I like this shirt. Let me." His eyes glistened as he unbuttoned the shirt then tossed it into the growing pile of clothes.

On her knees, she unzipped his pants. Her eyes didn't leave his face when she took him into her mouth. The pleasure of tasting him transformed into a searing heat between her thighs. She wanted him. To comfort him. To pleasure him. To drive him wild with desire.

Her lips traveled across his cock. His rumbling groan rose above the pounding waves. Intoxicated by the pure masculine scent of him, she had to taste every inch. A dash of salt mingled with a hint of lavender soap, it reminded her of ice cream. She nibbled at the hard shaft then caressed the head with her tongue.

He responded in a low punctuated growl. "You. Are. A. Vixen."

"We'll see about that." She smiled.

He gripped her hips and rose from the sofa taking her with him. She yelped and wrapped her legs around his waist. What the hell was he doing?

"Put me down." She held him in a death grip while he flipped her onto the sofa. He propped himself on one arm and gazed at her. She'd never forget the look of wonder in his eyes.

"My turn." His lips drifted across hers before burning a trail along the hollow of her throat. A lock of coconut scented hair tickled her lips overwhelming her senses.

Still dizzy from the sudden motion and his sensual assault, she wasn't prepared when he slid down her body. Her heart raced. He tugged her pants off, the fabric scraping along her legs. He pushed her thighs apart and buried his head between her legs.

The moment his masterful lips caressed her, she cried out. Her heart threatened to explode as he carried out his impossibly gentle exploration.

"Wait," she gasped. The unending pleasure would kill her. A hint of a coherent thought had been blasted from her mind.

With lips and tongue and teeth, he nipped at her taking away any hope of reprieve. The roaring in her ears grew louder when he brushed her clit with his tongue.

"Please," she begged.

His responded by pushing her legs further apart. The way he leisurely tugged the most sensitive part of her into his mouth rendered her inconceivably hot. No man had ever made her feel so consumed. So eager. So greedy.

He sucked and licked her, drawing her closer to delirium. A clenching sensation broke through the haze of pleasure signaling her approaching orgasm. If she could live in this one moment forever, she would.

Then, he abruptly stopped.

She propped herself onto her elbows. "Why the hell did you stop?"

A naughty glint flashed in his eyes. "I didn't think you were that into it."

"What? No. I mean yes. More."

He grinned.

"Now!" she yelled.

He chuckled then captured her once again with his mouth. Frantic lust coiled inside her. Her head rolled back against the pillows. A storm built between her thighs. Nothing but the contours of his tongue mattered as he wrapped it around her clit.

The slow tingling built like an avalanche until she was sliding underneath his lips. The sucking, licking, nipping of his tongue, lips and teeth forced her over the edge. She screamed. The room dissolved into a haze. He pinned her to the sofa with his hands and continued to wring every last ounce of pleasure from her.

She didn't realize her hands were tangled in his hair until he tried to pull away from her.

"Oh." She released him.

He leaned over her and eased his cock between her thighs. A primal groan escaped his lips. He trembled against her. A light sheen of moisture gathered on his upper lip. She licked the saltiness then kissed him. He filled her so completely; it was as if they were made to fit together.

Every undulation pushed her closer to complete surrender. The scratchy shadow on his jaw thrilled her. Cheek to cheek, she moved with him.

"You're an enchantress," he murmured. His lips brushed against her earlobe sending a flutter through her belly.

"And you're a playboy." Her throaty laughter echoed through the room until he grabbed her butt and stood. With a surprised yelp, she threw her arms around his neck and gripped his waist with her legs.

"Put me down before you drop me."

"Not a chance."

In three steps, he'd crossed the room and pinned her to the wall. He thrust deep into her. The angle of his body against hers drove her closer to the edge.

"I'll fall if I come," she gasped.

"I'll never let you fall."

His eyes locked with hers and the tendrils of trust between then strengthened. She realized he wouldn't hurt her, wouldn't let her fall. She molded herself to him matching the erotic rhythm.

Tension built with every passing movement. Her fingers clawed at his back, slipping in the sweat collecting on his skin. The breeze from his deepening breaths caressed her neck. His arms began to tremble and yet he didn't pause.

So close, her pussy tightened around his thick cock.

"Come with me," he growled.

The suggestive command sent her cascading over the

edge. He moaned into the hollow of her throat as he found his own release.

She slid down his body until her feet touched the cool floor, bringing her back to reality. He drew her against him.

Locked in his tender embrace, her mind wandered back to their conversation about his father. So many questions pounded in her head. Could she trust him? Was he telling her the truth about her mother? His mother? His father? How could she feel so good pressed against a man whose father was a monster?

TRAINING TEMPTATION
CHAPTER 7

"I need to go."

Stunned, Edward watched her gather her clothes. The sex started out as a way to relieve his pain, but it turned into so much more. She'd reached him in a way no other woman had and he just wanted to hold her for a little longer. But, maybe she didn't feel the same way. Maybe she'd convinced herself she'd made a mistake?

"Stay... Please?"

She yanked her shirt over her head. "I need to tell Senator Garvin about your father."

"Garvin? Why him?"

"He's on the board at the bank with your father. If he knew the type of man he was working with, maybe he'd fire him."

His brow furrowed. "You can't just walk up and tell him."

"I can try. Do you want to try talking to him?" Her brown eyes simmered with anger.

Following her lead, he pulled his pants on. "I don't know if he'll listen, but I can try. He's known my family for as long as I can remember."

"He's staying at the house." She glanced out the window. "Tomorrow night is the mid-week dinner. You could join us and talk to him after."

He nodded. It could work, he tried convincing himself. "We should come up with a plan."

"Have him meet you in the library. Tell him what you told me. He has no reason not to believe you."

"He has no reason to believe me. No. He's the type of man who's going to want proof."

"We don't have any."

He tapped his finger against his lower lip. "The only other option we have is somehow tricking my father into confessing."

"That'll never happen."

"I know." He shook his head.

"You have an excellent reputation...well, outside of the bedroom." She chuckled for a second before continuing in a more serious tone. "Reputation counts for a lot in this community. The senator will listen to you."

He wasn't convinced the plan would work, but he had to try. "I'll talk to him tomorrow night. Meet me in the garden around midnight and I'll tell you what he said."

"You can do this."

"I sure hope so."

She glanced at him as she slipped into her coat. "Good luck."

"Thanks," he said as he watched her walk through the door.

She peaked back in. "Let's skip training tomorrow. I can run on my own and I need a break."

From you. His shoulders fell as he completed the rest of her statement. He held up his hand. "Wait."

"Look, today was... We got carried away."

"I didn't exactly drag you into an afternoon of mind-blowing sex." No way was she getting away with pretending there wasn't more to what happened between them.

"True. I got swept up in the sex because I needed comforting." Her gaze rested on him.

Using a softer tone, he said, "You're wound too tight. You needed it. Hell, I needed it."

"I don't want our relationship any more complicated than it already is. This week is already the most complicated week of my life."

Wanting to lighten the mood he shot her a mischievous smile. "All right, let's uncomplicate things. I'll let you have me all week... if you're a good pony."

Her eyebrows arched and a playful sarcasm dripped from her voice. "You'll let me have you all week? Really?"

"Really." He lowered his mouth to hers. As he coaxed a kiss from her, the feathery softness of her lips made his heart beat faster.

His tongue slid between his lips, opening her to him. He groaned. Heat simmered through his core, he would never get sick of kissing her. Of tasting the sweetness of her lips.

She pulled away and backed toward the door. "I'll see you tomorrow, *after* you talk to the senator."

The second the door closed, he sighed. He'd wanted her for years, finally had her, and now he was losing her. The look in her eyes as she left told him everything he needed to know. All he could do for her at this point was hope that Senator Gavin would believe him.

"Thanks for meeting me, Senator." Edward shook the older man's hand as they strolled into the second floor library.

"Seems that you've grown up into a fine young man, the

kind of man who can catch any woman's eye." He shot a knowing wink.

Edward glanced at the second floor balcony, was Caroline listening in the shadows? "Cognac?"

"Not just any cognac, young man, Courvoisier L'Esprit de Cognac. One of the finest in the world." He poured with a flourish and handed him the brandy snifter.

Swirling his glass, he inhaled the thick aroma and allowed it to calm his nerves. "It's good to have access to the finer things in life."

The senator laughed, his belly jiggling. He sipped the amber liquid and his hawk-like eyes settled on Edward. "So, I take it this is not a social visit?"

The heat from the fire did nothing to help the dampness under his arms. Edward shifted in his chair. "How well do you know my father?"

"I've known him twenty-five years. We met at a Harvard gathering for distinguished gentlemen in business a few years after we graduated. He's a shark of a businessman, some might say ruthless. But he's extremely loyal to those who don't cross him."

The praise heaped on his father made his stomach churn. How could he possibly convince this man that the business partner and friend that he'd known for twenty-five years was a murderer? Maybe not directly, but he may has well have tied the noose that killed Caroline's mother.

He stood and paced in front of the fireplace. A shift in the shadows brought his gaze up to the second floor. Caroline's illuminated face flashed for a moment before she retreated wraith-like into the darkness. Even if this was a hopeless mission, he had to try. For her.

"My father isn't the man you think he is," he began.

"How so?"

"Do you remember the masquerade ball?"

The senator smirked. "Doesn't everyone? It was a legendary party. I never understood why he refused to throw another masquerade themed ball."

A chill slithered down his spine but he continued. "Caroline's mother was there that night."

"Making a scene, if I remember correctly. The poor thing was a mess, yelling from the front door."

"My father let her in and took her upstairs."

"As would any hot-blooded man."

His fists clenched. "But not every man would rape her."

The older man lowered the glass from his lips. "What did you say?"

"He. Raped. Her."

With his full attention on the younger man, he asked, "Who told you this?"

Bile rose in his throat as the scene replayed in his head. It was as if he was thirteen years old again, hiding in that closet, witnessing the horrible event. "I was there."

"There? In the room?" Skepticism carved deeper lines in the grooves of his face.

"Yes."

"If you were there, why didn't you stop him? *If*, he did what you say."

"I was thirteen and he was my father. What could I do?" The excuse sounded feeble when he voiced it. Guilt coiled in his gut. He heard her cries for help as if she was in the room with them and he did nothing.

The older man's face turned red. "That is a serious accusation. If that is what actually happened, he wouldn't be fit to serve on the executive board. I would need to have overwhelming proof to take to the other board members."

He rushed his words together. "We can get proof."

"We?"

His eyes flicked toward the second floor. "Caroline and I."

"You told her?" The senator's eyes bugged out. "Are you insane?"

"I know what I saw."

"Are you sure you want to do this? He's your father and your reputation is on the line if you can't come up with undeniable proof."

Edward knew in the depths of his heart he couldn't live with himself if he couldn't expose his father. What kind of man could rape a woman, then return to a party and act like nothing happened?

A gentle but firm voice floated down from the second floor. "We can get you proof."

"Caroline?" The senator's eyes darted from her to him and back.

She descended the staircase. "I know that it's hard to believe, but we will find a way to get the proof. And once you have proof, you have to stop the merger."

"Anton would have to commit murder before the other senators would stop the merger. What information do you have on him?" Senator Garvin asked.

A glint of fire lit up her eyes. "Midnight Saturday night after the race, if you can get a few of the other board members to sneak out of the party and hide up there," she pointed at the second floor. "You will have your proof."

Senator Garvin took the last swig of his drink, and then tossed the glass into the fire where it shattered. "Saturday night. Midnight."

The door clicked shut. With the senator gone, Edward could breathe again.

"Pretty ballsy coming out of hiding."

"I want the world to know what he did." Her hands flew to her hips.

"They will," he said. The sheer determination in her eyes nearly convinced him that they could actually pull this off.

TRAINING TEMPTATION
CHAPTER 8

Caroline paced back and forth in the living room at the beach house replaying the scene from the previous night over and over in her head. Two days until the confrontation with Anton. Two days until the race, the outcome of which would change her life drastically. Her mind churned out every worst case scenario imaginable.

What if Anton didn't confess? Senator Garvin intended to bring as many people from the board as possible to witness his confession. They would scorn her if she didn't manage to trick him into divulging his criminal actions.

What if she didn't win the race? Now that she knew what caused her mother to kill herself, she was even more determined to remain mistress of Sheridan Estate. Her only hope lay in the race so training was of the utmost importance.

Through the window, she watched Edward sauntering down the path to the beach house. The rising sun peaked through the clouds and hit his bare chest at just the right angle making him glow like a sun god. Caroline caught her lip between her teeth.

Every whisper and touch replayed in her mind. Every

lick and nip of his teeth. Every heated glance. And his roving tongue? Distractions. Part of her enjoyed him, wanted more and would only be satisfied by him. But she knew a relationship with him would be impossible.

She couldn't deny something had changed between them since their afternoon beach house romp. He'd been brave, talking to the senator, putting his own reputation on the line. He'd stayed true to his word and she knew he was committed to helping her bring his father down. The softer, gentler side of him had emerged.

Still, she couldn't shake the nagging doubts cluttering her mind. Her mother's death served as a constant reminder that men can't be trusted. Every one of them has an ulterior motive. She wanted so badly to trust him but she couldn't. How could she when his father had caused her mother's death?

The pain in her chest expanded, shutting off her heart to him. Anyone could pretend to help for a few days. He was probably only after her for the sex anyway. It didn't mean he cared about her. She knew what kind of man he was and at the end of the week, he'd probably run off with another conquest. Pushing him away was her only option. She had to protect her heart. She backed away from the door as he entered.

"Hello sexy." His bedroom eyes roamed over her body.

The fluttering in her belly intensified as she launched into him. "Look, what happened the other day was a fluke, we were caught up in the moment and it happened."

"Didn't you like it? I did."

Sarcasm coated her words. "Of course, I liked it. Who wouldn't like being bedded by the reincarnation of Casanova?"

His eyes narrowed. "You keep calling me that but I'm no

Casanova. I haven't been with another woman since I got here this week."

"A week," she snickered.

A deep red flush rose from his neck into his face. Through his teeth, he said, "Why are you doing this? I thought…"

"What did you think? We'd fuck a couple of times? Get married? Have 2.5 kids and a white picket fence? Grow old together?" She hated baiting him, but she needed to protect her heart.

Pain flashed in his eyes. He opened his mouth to speak but then pressed his lips into a thin line.

The room fell into a grey haze as storm clouds gathered over the ocean. With her eyes riveted on the crashing waves, she went in for the kill. "The only reason we have to speak to each other is to prove your father's guilt. I don't need you to train me. It was a terrible idea and a mistake on my part."

"You're making a huge mistake."

"How so?"

"I don't understand why you're so angry all of a sudden, but I'm not letting you push me away. You need me and I need you."

Edward stepped toward her but she stepped back. "Please leave. I don't want to see you again until Saturday night."

The slump in his shoulders tore at her heart making her want to take back her angry words. She hated what she was doing to him but she had no choice.

Sudden storm clouds gathered over the churning ocean blocking the sun and casting grey shadows throughout the room.

"Midnight." His dejected voice became a whisper.

"Midnight."

As he turned and left the house, Caroline's hands trembled. She tried to convince herself that she made the right choice, but tears trickled down her cheeks as the first clap of thunder sounded in the distance.

On Friday morning, a storm raged in his heart. In his room on the third floor of the mansion, he leaned his forehead on his arm. Slouching against the window, he watched as gale force winds tore tree limbs from their trunks.

A crack of thunder rattled the windows. Out of habit he counted to himself. One, one thousand. Two, one thousand. Three, one thousand. Lightning streaked through the sky. Three miles away. He sighed, envious of the storm. It could fully express its strength and passionate nature but he couldn't. He tried using the watching, waiting and counting as a way to take his mind off of her but it was useless.

He padded into the bathroom and turned the water for the bathtub to scalding. As the bathtub filled, he stripped. He tossed his discarded clothes into a pile on the floor.

A soft knock at the door had him wrapping a towel around his waist. He opened the door and let out an audible sigh. Amanda leaned a curvy hip against the door and flashed a seductive smile.

"Busy?" She pushed past him into the room.

"Yes."

Her gaze turned calculating as it traveled to the towel around his hips. Wishing he'd put his robe on, he took a step back away from her. Whatever she was up to, he wasn't interested. No one but Caroline could satisfy the hunger within him.

"You haven't come to see me since you got here."

"I've been busy."

"I'm sure. Find a new flavor of the month?"

"Not looking for one."

"Don't kid yourself," she laughed. "You're always looking for a new tasty bite. But sometimes knowing what you're getting is better than chasing after someone who doesn't want you."

Was she talking about Caroline? Had she confided in her?

"I don't know what you mean."

She took a step forward and tossed her chestnut hair over her shoulder. "She's not interested."

"Who?"

"Caroline."

"She told you?"

"She tells me everything."

Somehow he doubted that the maid was her confidante. Was she setting some kind of trap?

"Well, the next time I see her, I'll let her know we talked."

The maid turned the color of bleached coral. "You don't have to do that."

"You can leave now." He waved his arm toward the door.

She scurried into the hallway. "You're an asshole."

He silently agreed. His reputation as a womanizing playboy was destroying any chance he had with Caroline.

Closing the door, a wave of longing crashed into his heart. He didn't just want Caroline for sex. He could entice any willing woman into a myriad of positions and role-playing games. But she meant so much more.

He'd watched her grow over the years into the formidable mistress of Sheridan Estate. Without anyone's help, she'd created an impressive empire. She was tough.

Smart as a whip. She embodied everything he never knew he needed until this week. Really getting to know her changed him and he knew, he'd finally met his match.

He yearned to find out everything about her life. Her ability to rule over the International Ponygirl competition amazed him. The vibrant energy surrounding her drew him in and captivated him. And her body? The sexiest woman alive, by far.

Visions of her smooth lithe body swirling through his head, he returned to the bathroom. He peeled his towel from his hips. It caught on his growing erection. Fantasizing about her always made him rock hard.

He hung up his towel and dipped a toe into the water. It had cooled from scalding hot to the warmth of Caribbean water.

Tropical water didn't have bubbles in it, but he poured a cap of bubble bath in anyway. Soaking in the cinnamon scented warmth relaxed him. He leaned his head against a fluffy bath pillow.

Images of her made him restless. The way her mouth parted ever so slightly when he kissed her. The way she nipped at his bottom lip had him squirming. His hand slid under the water. Running it across his thigh, he remembered her scent. Some illusive French cologne, no doubt expensive as hell.

Edward's cock grew firm and peeked through the bubbles. It grew as he lightly stroked. An image—no, it was more than an image, an entire fantasy played out in his mind like a movie. In the daydream, he envisioned her head thrown back. If felt so real that his lips tingled as if they were on her neck. As if she lay naked, her legs parted under him. Her thighs wide and trembling, waiting for him to sink his cock into her warm, hot pussy.

Water lapped over the edge of the tub as he stroked faster. Breathing hard, he could almost smell the wild berry scent that lingered when she left a room. He imagined her luxurious hair, damp with sweat, clinging to her shoulders. He wanted to plunge into her, feel her beneath him crying out for more.

His hips jerked up. On top of him now, he'd bury his face in her swinging breasts. Dig his fingers into her taut ass. Thrust into her over and over. His balls, so full and heavy ached for release, but he wanted it to last longer.

Her head would be thrown back, pussy clamping onto him, spasms wracking her body over and over, coupled with her passionate cries. The fabrication sent him into a frenzy. Water sloshed over the edge of the tub but he didn't stop, couldn't stop.

In his chest, his heart threatened to explode. A finale image transformed her into a portrait of innocence. She called his name and clung to him until they were joined as one. Half of the tub had spilled into the bathroom before a final thrust threw him over the edge. Arching, twitching, he moaned her name as he came. He swore through clenched teeth then collapsed into the tub.

As his sense of time and place returned, Edward looked around the bathroom. Good god, he'd never made such a mess over a woman before. An inch of water coated the floor and bubbles floated in the air. He reached out to grab one and it popped on impact. A smile moved across his face.

He wanted to share more playful moments like this with her. She'd laugh with him, be silly and playful. Maybe she'd even look at him with love in her eyes.

Halfway out of the bath he froze. *Love? I don't fall in love. Ever.*

With his foot still poised over the bathtub, he looked in

the mirror. The expression on his face scared him. Loving her could bring pain, a broken heart, and shattered dreams. After he'd lost his mother he promised himself never to care about a woman because eventually, she's leave him.

But he couldn't deny the truth in his reflection. Caroline was worth the risk. He'd fallen for her. Hard.

In that moment, he shoved the fear down and vowed to do whatever it took to win her heart.

TRAINING TEMPTATION
CHAPTER 9

Saturday morning Caroline rose as dawn streaked the sky with trails of fire. Propelled by nervous energy, she padded to the window and gazed at the track in the distance. After the storm, the track was going to be a muddy mess. She'd be lucky if she didn't slip.

Stop psyching yourself out. You can't lose this race. She rubbed the back of her neck and sighed. Today would determine the course of the rest of her life.

Throughout the night, she'd lost the race a thousand times. Each nightmare putting her closer to the finish line, only to be captured by quicksand, or held back by an invisible force.

Guilt infused her dreams. In one failed race, ten feet from the finish line, she looked up to see Edward shaking his head and turning away from her. She hesitated. That was all it took for another ponygirl to pass her. She lost. Again.

Nauseous, she was about to turn away from the window when she spotted Edward strolling out of the rose garden toward the house. He was her only ally and she'd pushed him away.

The admission pricked like thorns, piercing her heart. She could only blame herself. Ruled by fear, she'd lost him.

Caroline turned away from the window. The bridle lay on the bed. The long tail and exquisite leather harness should have made her feel powerful, but it only reminded her of him.

One hour until post time. She fingered the soft leather boots and sighed. Maybe once she had the outfit on, she'd feel the usual pre-race excitement and energy.

She let her robe slipped to the floor and was about to step into the ensemble when someone knocked on the door.

"Who is it?"

"It's me," Edward responded.

Her heart thumped in her chest as she opened the door a few inches. "I'm getting ready for the race."

"I wanted to see you. Wish you luck. May I come in?"

She hesitated.

"You may not want me here, but I'm not leaving. Just for a minute?" He flashed a smile bright enough to burn through her resistance.

"One minute." Caroline scooped her robe up and slipped in on. She released the breath she'd been holding then opened the door.

Edward stepped into the room and glanced at her race gear. "Shouldn't you be dressed and warming up by now?"

She offered a weak smile and waved her hand toward the pile. "Too many buckles and straps."

"Good timing then." His appraising glance swept over her.

She averted her eyes, attempting to hide from his scrutiny.

"Are you okay?"

With the back of his hand, he brushed her cheek. The simple gesture had her eyes brimming with tears. He pulled her against him and she buried her face in his shoulder.

"Shh…" he whispered. "I know you're nervous but you have a race to win." He tipped her face back and looked into her eyes. "You can do this."

Grateful for his comforting warmth, she closed the remaining distance between them. Her mouth molded to his. The sweet taste of him invaded her senses. He was everything she needed, at least for right now.

His fingers trailed down the nape of her neck sending shivers of delight through her. Her lips parted under his tongue and she inhaled the sweetness of his breath. As he gently biting her bottom lip, he groaned. The sound of his desire made her want more, but she stopped when a trumpet sounded in the distance.

"We need to hurry," he murmured.

"All right."

His hands slipped under the robe's collar. While he eased it from her shoulders, he ran his hands over her arms.

"You're shivering."

Because of you. "Just the jitters, it will go away once I get to the start line."

He didn't look convinced by didn't comment as he gathered up the leather straps. She stepped into the outfit and tried to relax as his fingers grazed her skin. Acutely aware of every movement, she tried not to shutter. The warm breath on her neck, the light touches, and the familiar way his hands traveled over her left her breathless.

The softness in his gaze almost tore apart her shaky calm.

"Caroline, I…"

"No." She held her finger over his lips. Not wanting anything to complicate the moment, she silenced him.

His lips pressed into a thin line as he pulled the last strap taut. The way his palm splayed across her hip soothed her. "There is something I want you to do for me."

"What?"

"Close your eyes."

"We don't have a lot of time."

"It will only take a minute. This is an old racing trick I do with my other ponies."

Caroline closed her eyes.

"Imagine you're on the track. Ready to race. You hear the crowd cheering. Smell the dirt, the sweat, the desire. They're all cheering for you. Not the other ponies. Only you…"

As she listened, the entirety of her existence became his voice. The images became vivid in her mind as he continued.

"Your muscles are poised, ready. You've trained for this and know in your soul you will win this race. When you fly out of the gate you know one singular truth. Winning is your destiny."

Her heart soared as he described the race and the sensations she would experience. The confidence in his tone was contagious.

"You run faster than you ever imagined. Women and men alike will scream and cheer you on. They know you'll win. They know what I know…"

Her eyes fluttered open when he paused. A palpable intensity emanated from him like an all-consuming force of nature. His strength radiated like the sun and moon, aligned to create the perfect tidal wave of hope. She drew it into herself.

"This race, this moment in time, is yours."

And she believed him in her soul. She stood taller, jutted out her chest, and shook her hair behind her. For the first time this week, she felt calm, grounded. Determination coursed through her veins.

"I'm ready," she declared.

∼

Filled with raw energy, Caroline trotted across the thick grass and approached the starting gates. Every muscle tense, ready.

She ignored the pointing and murmuring. The gossip-mongers would have a field day at her expense, but she didn't care. She had so much more riding on this race.

The shocked faces in the crowd blended into a kaleidoscope of color until they no longer represented individuals. Their collective energy fed her. Adrenaline surged.

The other ponies gathered around the gates. Ribbons of gold, scarlet and emerald green glistened in their intricately woven braids. Each color represented a different owner. She wore her own shades of purple and gold with pride.

Even in their finest racing gear, she remained a jaguar amongst house cats. In her mind, no one could beat her because she had something they didn't, Edward.

She scanned the crowd until she spotted him. With a slight inclination of his head, he acknowledged her. The edge of his lips inched upward into a smile. He would be watching her, supporting her.

As Caroline reflected on the week, she realized he'd supported her from the minute he ran into her after Tiffany Rose's accident to the minute she stepped onto the racetrack. Even though she'd tried to push him away, he'd come back when she needed him the most. She could hardly remember the last time she'd felt so supported.

The announcer took to the field. His voice boomed through the speakers, "Ladies and gentlemen, welcome to the final race in the 13th Annual Ponygirl Competition. The purse for this race is $250,000."

The crowd cheered and clapped. Men whistled while women waved their Kentucky Derby hats in the air. Palpable excitement simmered through the stands.

The starting gate clicked shut behind her and a groom whispered, "Good luck Lady Caroline."

"Thank you," she replied.

Tiffany Rose hobbled toward her on crutches. "I'd say break a leg but..."

Caroline flashed a lopsided smile. "I'm glad to see you up and walking."

"There's a little less pain every day. I'll be running again in no time. The race is about to start. I'll see you in the winner's circle."

"I hope so."

As her friend hobbled away, Caroline turned her attention back to the track. Poised to sprint, the red ribbon at the finish line beckoned to her. The knot shimmied as wind whipped over the ribbon.

The announcer concluded his speech then raised a pistol into the air. Her calves tensed. An entire week of pent-up stress coiled in the muscles in her legs. The ponies on either side of her bent forward, ready to spring out of the gate.

When the shot rang out, she exploded of the gate. Her boots pounded the earth as she rounded the first corner. In her peripheral vision, she monitored the pace of the other ponies. She was ahead of the pack.

Concentrate. Don't lose momentum.

The sun caused heat to shimmy off the track so the lines blurred in the distance. She couldn't hear the crowd over the blood thumping through her ears.

You're almost there. A few hundred yards to go, then victory.

Rounding the final curve, she sensed another pony gaining on her. She reached into the very core of her being and summoned a last burst of energy. For her mother, for her legacy, for herself. *Ten feet to go. Five.*

Then the unthinkable happened, one of the ponygirls passed her. Caroline stretched each step as far as possible, the muscles in her legs burned. Her breath exploded from her chest. Every ounce of energy in her body helped her surge forward. But it wasn't enough. The other pony passed through the finish line, the ribbon tore.

And so did her heart.

Caroline kept running. Past the cheering spectators. Past people's looks of pity. Past the racing area. She almost believed that if she ran fast enough, she could outrun the week's nightmarish events. Everything would return to normal. The estate wouldn't be bankrupt. She wouldn't be tangled up with Edward, or his father. Even the small amount of closure she'd managed to have since her mother's death, gone.

She raced to the beach and across the burning sand. Sweat dripped into her eyes mixing with the tears she held back. Through the blood pounding in her ears, she heard Edward calling her name. She ignored him.

The burning in her lungs slowed her pace. The stitch in her side burned. But she didn't stop until she reached the beach house.

Safely inside, she collapsed on the sofa. Hunched over, her head between her legs, she couldn't faint, wouldn't.

Deep breaths... Count to ten...
It's not working.
Dammit!

She sat up slowly and stared at the ocean. A sudden urge to swim to Hawaii, to Fiji, or Japan washed over her. Somewhere far away so she could escape as her world crashed down around her.

She glanced at the painting of her mother, her lips pressed together. Everything her mother had given her would be lost. A bank would own her legacy.

Caroline jumped as Edward burst through the front door.

"Jesus, you took off right after the race."

"Maybe if I'd run faster during the race, I would have won."

"I didn't mean..." His voice trailed off.

"Go away."

"I'm not walking away from you, especially now."

He sat by her side and she allowed him to draw her into his arms. She pressed her cheek against his chest. Tears began to fall. The tidal wave of emotion locked in her heart unleashed on his pressed slacks.

She sniffed. "She'd be so disappointed."

"No. She loved you. She'd understand. The barn fire caused this, not you."

"Sheridan Estate is all I have of her."

"No. You still have your memories. All the good times."

"And the bad."

"And the bad. Life's a twisted mess sometimes. But you can choose not to focus on the bad and focus on the good instead."

She sat up and wiped her palms across her tear stained

cheeks. "What possible good could come from losing my home?"

"I don't know." He shook his head.

"I'm so tired."

"You need to rest. Even if you aren't able to keep the estate, you can still defend her legacy. Tonight when you trick Anton into confessing, people will know she didn't kill herself over something frivolous."

"*If* I can trick him."

"You can do it. Use his ego against him."

"How?"

"Get him talking about your mother. Interrupt him, he hates that, and casually mention that she called him impotent."

"Impotent? He'll lose it. What if he attacks me?" She wrapped her arms around herself.

"I'll be upstairs with the others. You'll be perfectly safe."

"Promise?"

He scooted closer to her and took her hands in his. "I would die before I let him hurt you."

The fierce look in his eyes calmed her. Nothing would happen as long as he was with her.

"I want this to be over," she said.

"Me too," he paused. "There's something else I wanted to say."

She shifted and pulled her hands from his as warning bells went off in her head. "I'm really tired."

"I know. But, this week has been one of the most frustrating weeks of my life…"

"Mine too."

"I know. But something else happened this week." His molten brown eyes locked with hers. "Something changed between us."

"Whatever you think you're feeling, it's nothing."

"You can't deny there's something between us."

"Hormones. Stress." All week she'd been trying to convince herself that stress was the only thing pushing her into his arms.

He seemed to struggle for the right words. "It's more than hormones. I wake up in the morning and can't wait to see you. I never know what you're going to do or say next and I find that intriguing. The insanity of this week was worth living through because I got to know you so much better."

"Every time I look at you, I see your father." She turned slightly away from him.

"I'm not my father."

"I know. But whatever connection we have, it's tainted. We have too much family history now for anything to work. I appreciate everything you did for me this week. I know how hard it must be to help set up your father."

"It's the right thing to do."

She nodded. "He's still family. The only family you have left."

"He's not my family. Family is about respect and love. He's about fear and pain."

"We'll expose him. Everyone will know about the evil lurking inside of him."

The tension melted from his face. "No more secrets."

"No more lies."

"We won't have to live in our parent's wake anymore. We can be together."

She shook her head. "I'm sorry, but nothing more will ever happen between us."

TRAINING TEMPTATION
CHAPTER 10

Caroline pulled her faux fur wrap tight across her bare shoulders. The balcony's shadows gathered around her. She cringed each time the ballroom doors opened to expel another drunken couple. High-pitched laughter from the post-race party intensified the headache throbbing at the base of her skull.

She glanced at her watch. Thirty minutes to midnight.

Still reeling from losing the race, she tried to ignore the nagging fear coiling in her stomach. Tricking Anton into admitting his perverse past seemed possible before the loss. But now, her confidence was shaken. Doubt's cancerous tendrils ripped holes in every scenario she'd concocted.

A voice behind her snapped her out of her brooding. "Lovely night."

Every muscle in her body went rigid. Anton stood behind her, so close she could feel his breath on her neck.

"It is." She forced her voice to remain even, calm.

He brushed against her as he moved to stand on her left. "You're the talk of the party. Naughty girl, not telling anyone you were going to race."

The sing-song quality of his voice slid down her spine like a hot poker.

"I'm good at keeping secrets."

"As am I."

I bet, you disgusting pig. She glanced at her watch. Twenty minutes until midnight. The senator had agreed to gather witnesses in the library by quarter to midnight. She needed to keep him talking and lure him into the library.

"I hear you're working on a new merger."

His head tipped to the side. "You're well connected with gossip."

"I like the stay aware of what's happening in the community."

"A woman as beautiful as you shouldn't be worried with business matters." His lecherous eyes raked across her neckline. His simmering gaze made her feel like he'd actually touched her.

She bit the inside of her lip to keep from snapping a retort. "Some women weren't meant to be bedded and wedded."

"And some were born for it."

She glanced at the time. Ten minutes to midnight. She needed to get him to the library.

He tapped a finger on his wrist. "In a hurry to be somewhere?"

She tilted her head to the side and flashed her most winning smile. "It's rather chilly out here. Would you accompany me to the library? A midnight brandy tends to take the chill away."

He arched an eyebrow as if surprised by her invitation. "That is does my dear."

She shivered as he placed his palm uncomfortably low on her back and guided her toward the door.

Inside the library, she broke away from him and rushed toward the brandy. The heavy crystal decanter cast an unworldly glow in the firelight. The crystal tinged against the glass as her trembling hands poured. She hoped he couldn't read her nervousness in the dimly lit room.

She took a breath. *Calm down, you can do this.*

"Are you married?" she asked.

A dark shadow flickered across his face. "I was. Not anymore."

"What happened?"

"She disappeared."

She took a sip of brandy. "How long ago?"

He ignored her question. "How did a woman like you never marry?"

"Never found the right man, I guess."

"Maybe you didn't look hard enough. Sit with me." He patted the sofa. She sat as far away from him as possible, but he slid closer.

At a loss for how to begin questioning him, she said the first thing that popped into her mind. "My mother used to talk about you."

He stiffened and took a swig of his brandy. "Is that right?"

"Do you remember her?"

"Vaguely."

"I would think you would remember her."

A menacing undertone crept into his voice. "Why would I remember her?"

"She went to the masquerade party. Ten years ago this Christmas."

His eyes narrowed. "What did she tell you about the party?"

She leaned forward. "She told me what happened."

"What do you mean?"

"I know all about what happened that night."

He stood and walked to decanter on the desk. Flames licked the sharp edges of his face. "What is it that you think you know?"

Unsure of how to continue, she decided to go on instinct. "I'd like to hear your side of the story."

"After ten years—why would you want to know now?"

"I never believed you could be the monster she said you were," she lied.

"A monster?" His rough laugh echoed across the room. "Hardly."

"After what she told me, it's hard not to believe her."

"What did she tell you?"

"You're a rapist."

He crossed the room in three swift paces and stood so close she smelled the alcohol on his breath. She cringed into the cushions.

"Your mother was a liar. A compulsive liar. Always trying to blackmail me."

"What would she think she could blackmail you?"

"A money hungry bitch doesn't need a reason." He spat. Flames danced in his eyes.

She jumped to her feet and poked him with her index finger. "Admit it."

He smacked her hand away. "You're just like your mother. Spoiled fruit. You should be left to rot."

"Are you threatening me?"

A cruel smile spread across his features. "Of course not. You may as well ask the senator and his friends to come out now."

Shocked, her eyes darted toward the second floor

balcony. How could he know about her plan? Had Edward betrayed her?

Several men—including Edward—stepped out of the shadows. She took one look at the stricken expression on his face and knew he couldn't have betrayed her. If not him, then who?

The noise created by the men descending the stairs prevented anyone from hearing Anton whisper to her, "She was sweet, like fresh peach pie."

"Lying bastard." She lunged at him.

Edward jumped in front of her and grabbed her. "Stop. It's not worth it."

His father's lips curled into a smirk. "Good evening, son."

"I know what you did. I was hiding in the closet. I saw you."

A flicker of rage crossed the older man's face before his squelched it. "Gentlemen, I trust you won't mind if I leave this little farce."

Senator Garvin stepped forward. "Of course no one believed them, Anton." He turned and looked at her. "Young lady, you need to consider your accusations carefully before you make them. I highly recommend you get the counseling you need to get past your mother's death."

The men filed out of the room behind Anton and Senator Garvin. As they passed her, they skewered her with disapproving looks.

Alone, she frowned at Edward. "Only three people knew about this. Me, you and Senator Garvin."

"Maybe he warned my father."

"Possibly." Her shoulders slumped. "I guess this is it."

"I'm so sorry." He hugged her against the broad expanse

of his chest. The rhythmic thump of his heartbeat soothed her.

All of the failures of the day caught up to her. The pain in her chest radiated outward through her body. She wanted more than anything for the pain to end.

"Kiss me," she murmured as she glanced up at him.

Concern and desire swirled in his gaze. "Are you sure?"

She stood on the balls of her toes and pressed her lips to his.

"Not here." He expelled a breath and grabbed her hand.

Edward kicked the door to Caroline's bedroom closed behind them. Her frantic lips on his throat made him forget about the disaster in the library. All he could think about was the feel of her in his arms. The scent of desire on her skin. The warmth of her breath on his neck.

He groaned. "Wait. You said earlier."

"Forget what I said."

"But you were so adamant," he whispered between kisses.

"I lied."

"We should talk about—"

She slid the zipper of her dress down. "You really want to talk? Right now?"

The thin silk pooled at her feet. His mouth went dry. How could he resist the most seductive, dangerous, sensual woman in the world?

She'll tear my heart out later if I don't stop. He snapped out of a lust-fueled haze. He walked into her bathroom and grabbed a fluffy white robe.

He returned to her bedroom. "You should put this on. I'll run a bath for you."

Her breasts swayed as she stalked toward him. "Adventurous. If you want to do it in the bath, we can."

His face grew hot. If she only knew what he did in the bath. "You should take a bath. Get some sleep. We can talk when you're thinking clearly."

"I am thinking clearly." Caroline grabbed a pillow and tossed it at him.

He caught it. Through clenched teeth, he said, "I care about you too much to take advantage of you. We can talk when you're calm."

"I. Am. Calm."

He retreated to the door. "We'll talk tomorrow."

A fraction of a second of hesitation passed before he slipped out of her door and into the hallway. He leaned against the wall. The sound of her sobbing leaked through the door and tugged at his heart. But engaging in grief ridden sex would only make things worse.

A spark of pride perked him up as he walked down the hallway. A week ago, he would have gladly taken advantage of her. Used her for sex and then left her. Not giving in to her seduction took immense self-control.

It was the right thing to do, he reasoned. She needed time to calm down. Besides, she'd been clear at the beach house. He doubted she'd want him once her raw emotions subsided.

Sleep eluded Caroline. Stars twinkling in the night sky seemed like teardrops from the heavens. Maybe her mother wept for her. She rolled away from the window and curled up into her pillows. At least Edward had the sense to stop her before she ended up further complicating their relationship. The events of the day replayed in her mind like a silent film. Beating herself up over her mistakes was exhausting, but still, no sleep.

She slipped out of bed, pulled the edges of her robe closed and tightened the sash. Moonlight cast an eerie glow through the garden. The clock on her nightstand read 3:15a.m.

On other sleepless nights, she'd strolled through the garden. Deciding it might help, she slipped into her favorite jeans, a comfortable sweater and one of her warmer jackets.

The clicking of her boots echoed down the otherwise silent hallway. She slipped out the rear hallway door and crossed the dew-dampened lawn to the garden. The sweet scent of honeysuckle blended with roses filled the air. She strolled along the spiral cobblestone path nestled within the rose garden. Crickets chirped filling the night with their eerie songs.

At the center of the garden, she sat on the cold wrought iron bench. The distant sound of waves crashing along the shore did nothing to sooth her.

The manor loomed over the roses. The strange sensation of being watched drew her eyes toward the third floor. The outline of a man passed in front of a window. Backlit, she couldn't see the person's face. Maybe Edward couldn't sleep either.

Tormented by the events of the day, she cringed. The confrontation with Anton in the library ended in disaster. After that scene, no one would believe a word she said. They might even decide she's a paranoid lunatic. Her reputation, ruined.

And on top of that failure, flinging herself at Edward in a desperate attempt to relieve her pain away was embarrassing. Normally she had more self-control. Why would he ever want to be around her after a scene like that?

A tear spilled down her cheek. She brushed it away, refusing to continue to feel sorry for herself. She'd figure out some way to hold onto the estate. Even if no one found out the truth about her mother, she knew. It gave her some comfort.

As fog rolled in from the coast, the temperature dropped another ten degrees. Chilly air seeped into her jacket. She shivered. Time to go back to bed and try to sleep.

As Caroline stood, she heard the scuff of footsteps on the cobblestones. She paused and listened. The sound stopped. The crickets were silent too but the ocean waves continued to crash on the shore. Maybe she'd imagined the footsteps.

She started around the first turn of the spiral path and froze as she heard the familiar sound. The footsteps stopped too. Fear swirled around her like the fog. Who else would be in the garden at this time of night?

TRAINING TEMPTATION
CHAPTER 11

Footsteps crunched in the gravel behind her. A sinister voice forced adrenaline through every inch of her flesh. "You little bitch!"

Caroline spun to face Anton.

He slapped her so hard she stumbled backward and landed with a thud on the edge of a stone.

His bulky frame towered over her. "You think you're so smart. Trying to trick me as if I was a pathetic drooling retard."

Trapped by the thorny roses, she had nowhere to run. His massive frame blocked the only exit.

"Get away from me."

He knelt, straddling her thighs. She opened her mouth to scream but his hands clamped around her throat. "Don't worry darling, no one will hear you scream."

Caroline thrashed against the earth and kicked at him, struggling to free herself from his grasp. Unable to reach him with her kicks, rage coursed through her. He slammed her head against the ground. His face blurred and everything went black for a moment.

Dazed, she clawed at his face but the strength was draining from her arms. Her lungs burned. She needed air.

Venomous rage spilled from his lips. "I should have known she wouldn't keep her mouth shut."

She knew instantly he was referring to her mother.

"I should have gotten rid of her that night. Taken her on the boat and tossed her overboard."

He released her throat. The sudden burst of air tasted metallic. Her hands flew up to protect her neck. She wanted to scream but she couldn't catch her breath.

"I won't make the same mistake with you." Anton climbed off of her.

She scrambled to sit up. A sharp rock scraped against her palm as she pushed herself away from him.

He rattled on as she closed her fingers around the rock. "When I'm done with you, no one will find you. It will be like you never existed."

She lunged to her feet and swung her arm in a wide arch. The rock smashed against his temple. He staggered backward.

"Help!" She screamed with every ounce of energy in her body.

A light flicked on in the third floor of the house edging the roses in silvery light.

"You sick bastard," she screamed.

He ran towards her but she dodged him. She shoved his back, trying to use his momentum against him. He landed in the roses. Thorns tore his sleeves leaving rivulets of blood to stain the fabric.

Acutely aware of his every move, she backed away. Footsteps pounded down the pathway. *It's about time.*

"Caroline!" Edward called. "Where are you?"

"Over here!" she called back.

He rushed into the center of the garden. "What's—"

In less than a second, he assessed the scene. He stepped between her and his father. "What the hell is going on?"

"I was just about to turn that bitch into fish bait."

She held up the rock. "Not exactly."

"Weak, pathetic women like her don't stand a chance against me." He sneered.

"Women tend to disappear around you," snapped Edward. "Women like my mother."

"Your mother," Anton laughed. "That little whore deserved what she got. No one runs out on me."

He advanced on his father. "What did you do to her?"

"Turned the bitch into shark bait."

"Bastard." Edward lunged at his father. His fist cracked against the old man's jaw causing his head to snap back.

Blood oozed from his busted lip. He pulled a gun from his jacket. She backed up a step, but Edward rushed him.

"Murderer!"

He knocked the gun into the air. As if in slow motion, she followed its arc into the bushes. Ignoring the thorns clawing at her face, she dove for it.

"Stop!"

She froze at the command. Turning her head, she spotted Senator Garvin standing with two other bank board members. The brawling men lay sprawled in the dirt. A could of dust settled to the ground.

Edward spoke first, pointing at his father. "He tried to kill her."

"I heard a scream and went to the window." The senator fixed his gaze on her attacker. "What the hell were you thinking?"

"She tried to ruin my good name."

"You've succeeded in accomplishing that yourself."

A wild desperation flickered in Anton's eyes. "She's a liar!"

"And you're done. I called the cops. There are enough witnesses to take this to the board. You're finished."

Several police officers entered the garden. The lead officer pointed at the two men on the ground. "Which one pulled the gun?"

She pointed him out. Relief spread through her as the officers cuffed him. Edward got to his feet and put his arm around her waist.

"Are you okay?" he asked.

She nodded.

The senator approached shaking his head. "I'm sorry I didn't believe you."

"You needed proof. I understand."

"If you need anything, let me know. I want to find a way to make this up to you."

An idea occurred to her. "There is something I need help with. Can we talk later?"

"Feel free to call me anytime," he said.

Crime scene investigators and police crowded the garden. The lead officer said, "We need to interview you individually."

"We can go to the library," she offered.

The officers interviewed him first, and then called her into the room as he left. After she told them what happened, they left and Edward entered.

He closed the distance between them and gathered her into his arms. His warm embrace warded of the remaining chill in her body.

"I'm sorry I wasn't there sooner," his voice cracked.

"You couldn't have known."

"I'm sorry about your mother."

"We both lost our mothers to his rage."

A grim look crossed his face. "I always suspected, but now I know."

Silence stretched between them.

"If I had lost you—" His voice cracked.

"You didn't."

"I can't ever lose you," he whispered into her hair.

She tipped her head up to look at him. The look in his eyes left no doubt in her mind. She couldn't lose him either.

"This week, at least something good came of it."

He shot her a surprised look. "Good?"

"Amidst all the chaos, we found each other."

He knelt down in front of her. "I know it's only been a week and a crazy one at that. But, I can't imagine another moment without you. I want to be with you forever."

"Forever's a long time." She smiled.

"I want to start forever today, right now. Can we? I mean, do you think?"

"Yes." She flung herself into his arms toppling him over.

He laughed and brushed the hair from her face. "I love you."

"Forever." She sealed their promise with a gentle kiss.

Three weeks later, Caroline sat at the long conference room table at Garvin, Lexington and Associates, LLC. She threaded her hand through Edward's as Senator Garvin read the end of the non-disclosure agreement.

"...If the recipient loses or makes unauthorized disclosure of any of the confidential information, the recipient will immediately notify the provider and take all reasonable steps necessary to retrieve the lost or improperly disclosed confidential information."

She winked at the senator. "There better not be any accidental disclosure."

"You have my word."

"I can't thank you enough for loaning me the money to keep the estate running."

"It's the least I could do. Your secret's safe with me."

She stood and shook his hand. "You're welcome to come by the estate anytime."

"You know I'll take you up on your offer." He chuckled.

He walked them to the lobby then turned to Edward. "Take care of her."

"After seeing her wield that rock, I think she's got that covered."

"A rock and some rage are a heady combination." She arched an eyebrow and the men laughed in unison.

Edward reached for her hand. "Shall we?"

Sign up for Lacey's email newsletter

ABOUT THE AUTHOR

Lacey Harper writes edgy romance for readers who like it a little rough, dark, and dirty. To find out more about her books, please check out her Amazon Page.

Twitter: @LickLaceyHarper
Facebook: www.facebook.com/lacey.harper.1232

Sign up for Lacey's email newsletter

Printed in Dunstable, United Kingdom